PRAISE FOR MINA AND THE UNDEAD:

'A dark and thrilling tale of the paranormal set in the nineties in New Orleans. With haunted houses, family secrets and murder galore, this delicious and gruesome tale of the macabre will ignite a whole new generation of vampire fans.'

LAUREN JAMES

'Brimming full of nostalgia and cinematic atmosphere. I loved this heart-pounding mystery so much, I couldn't put it down. A thrilling read and a clever new twist on the vampire stories you love.'

LAURA WOOD

'A book of blood-thirsty fun, from the New Orleans setting to the strong *Buffy* vibes. Amy McCaw brings vampires back from the dead in style. I loved it!'

KATHRYN FOXFIELD

'I could not put this down! Strong *Buffy* meets *Charmed* in New Orleans vibes . . . so much nineties nostalgia. I want to go for drinks at the Empire of the Dead with Mina and the gang. Vampires are officially cool again!'

CYNTHIA MU

'A fun romp through nineties pop culture – vampires, *Buffy*, *The Crow* . . . need I say more?'
DAWN KURTAGICH

'Bloody, brooding and brilliant! This brought my love of decadent '90s vampires screaming back to life.'
KAT ELLIS

'I very much enjoyed this debut by Amy McCaw. Smouldering vampires, a New Orleans setting and a generous dash of bloodshed. A fun YA horror read!'
ALEX BELL

'I absolutely raced through this book! As soon as I started it, I was hooked. It has a very distinct flavour, with lots of horror, 90s references and relationship drama. I loved it and I hope there will be a sequel!'
HARRIET MUNCASTER

'I devoured this dark and delicious tale of vampires in nineties New Orleans. Fresh and original and packed with pop culture references, this is *Buffy* for YA readers.'
MARIA KUZNIAR

PRAISE FOR MINA AND THE SLAYERS:

'Mina is back with bite in this action-packed romp of a sequel. It was absolute, murderous fun to travel with her through the gothic atmosphere of vampire-loving 90s New Orleans.'

KENDARE BLAKE

'*Buffy* meets *Scream* in this high-stakes rush through a darkly atmospheric 90s New Orleans.'

M.A. KUZNIAR

'I couldn't wait to sink my fangs into this book and I wasn't disappointed. It leaves you gasping for more and never knowing who to trust.'

CYNTHIA MURPHY

'A fiendishly good sequel, brimming with 90s pop culture, smooth Southern vampires and a body count to rival *Buffy*.'

KAT ELLIS

'Amy McCaw's much-anticipated sequel is everything a discerning horror fan could wish for. With added 90s US police shenanigans!'

SUE WALLMAN

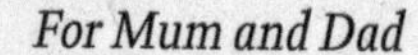

For Mum and Dad

Mina and the Cult is a uclanpublishing book

First published in Great Britain in 2024 by
uclanpublishing
University of Central Lancashire
Preston, PR1 2HE, UK

978-1-915235-91-6

1 3 5 7 9 10 8 6 4 2

Set in 10/16pt Kingfisher by Becky Chilcott.

A CIP catalogue record for this book is available from the British Library.

Printed and bound in Great Britain by Clays Ltd, Elcograf S.p.A.

Amy McCaw

MINA and the Cult

uclanpublishing

Chapter 1

If you'd told me a few months ago that I'd soon be on the way to visit my parents with a slayer and my vampire boyfriend, I would've smiled politely and backed away. Now, the weirdest part was that I'd be seeing my dad for the first time in ten years. The existence of vampires was old news to me and even I'd jumped on the slayer bandwagon.

"Can't I crack one window? I'm missing the view! And I'm pretty sure the air conditioning is on its last legs." Libby twisted round to glare at Jared. After a day in the car, her dark, curly hair was especially wild, and even though mine was shorter it wasn't faring much better.

"They're tinted for a reason. Unless you want a dead vampire stinking up the back seat, then sure," Jared said good-naturedly, his accent tinged with Hawaiian. He was used to Libby's moods, but there was a slight strain to his smile from travelling in daylight hours. He slouched down low, readjusting his long legs and jamming his cap down over his thick, wavy hair.

Libby was crabby because we'd left the Mansion of the Macabre closed so contractors could renovate one of the older rooms. Running the horror movie experience where we lived and worked was expensive, because we had to move with the times.

Cabin fever also seemed to be creeping in. After the distant cities, small towns and endless crop fields of Texas, we'd been looking at the same sprawling, dusty New Mexico desert and blue sky for hours, with only a sleepy town for occasional variation. Small patches of scrub and spindly trees broke up the endless light brown earth and grasses. The Jeep had also developed a greasy fries-and-burger odour after too many takeaway meals, the wrappers of which were clogging up the footwells. Listening to music was keeping me going, and I sang along quietly to The Muffs' cover of 'Kids in America'.

"Spoil my fun," Libby grumbled. "How about using that healing action on my sunburn?"

Her girlfriend, Della, grinned in the rear-view mirror, making dimples in her dark brown skin. In her sunglasses and neat braids down her back, she was faring a lot better with the heat. "I did tell you the windscreen isn't tinted."

"And as always, I should've listened to you. How about it, Jared?"

"You want to wipe me out for hours because you forgot to wear sunscreen?" Jared finally showed his annoyance.

"Yes?" Libby replied, having the decency to let her voice rise in a question.

Jared's healing power was a sore subject. He'd tested it on all of us, most notably when saving Libby's life after Sam stabbed her – the moment he'd discovered his power. His ability saved lives, but it left him exhausted.

"How long until we arrive?" I asked, opting for a conversation change before Libby and Jared started bickering like they meant it.

"We got less than an hour to go," Della said, checking the Jeep's clock. "Perfect timing – we should arrive right after sunset."

"Awesome," Jared said. "You don't talk about your dad much. Anything we should know before we meet him?"

"There's not a lot to say." I pushed through the urge to close down – our friends needed to know this stuff. "He's originally from New Mexico, and he met Mum on a plane to the UK. They were together until I was eight, when he went back to the States. He's always had strange interests. Never had a job but always had a lot of cash. That kind of thing."

Jared's heavy eyebrows knitted together, and I tried to lift the mood. "You'll like him though. He's definitely charming, and he sees himself as a bit of a philosopher."

"He sounds like a real character," Della said.

"Don't listen to Mina," Libby said, not quite coming across playful. "She's always down on him. He's great."

In the Shepherd family way, Libby would've run straight to New Mexico when we got Mum's postcard about being with Dad. Della and I convinced her we needed to let the dust settle after everything that had happened at Halloween. After I'd killed Sam.

It hadn't taken long for the police to determine I'd acted in self-defence, but I'd still taken a life. The start of panic tightened my chest when I thought about Sam, coming after me when he'd already left Libby bleeding out behind him. I'd done what was necessary to keep me and Libby alive, but it'd weigh on my conscience forever. One small mercy was that our friend Will had forgiven me for killing his half-brother. As far as he was concerned, Sam had deserved it. I felt bad for leaving Will to go and see my parents, but he was doing well. He was spending a lot of time with Fiona, a colleague of Della's who seemed to be one of the good vampires. If they stayed together, she'd have to tell him what she was.

I'd agreed to miss a few days of school so we'd be back in New Orleans in time for Thanksgiving. Both of our parents had made a habit of ditching us, so they didn't get to have the big family celebration without making serious changes first.

"So you haven't seen him since you were a kid?" Jared asked quietly.

"Nope. He sent the occasional letter and phoned, but it always felt half-hearted. I don't know if he and Mum reconnected when she first moved over here, but they obviously have now." Our parents had never been the sharing types.

Libby made a scoffing sound from the front seat but kept her opinions to herself. I wasn't sure how she'd kept worshipping Dad for all these years.

While we'd been talking, the western sky had taken on a burnt orange shade, bathing the desert in a golden glow.

Jared sat up straighter, sliding off his sunglasses. "About time." Usually, Jared slept during the day, but driving for fifteen hours had thrown everything off. Jared had taken part of the night shift, but he hadn't managed to sleep much during the day with the sun blazing through the windscreen.

Libby grabbed the directions from the glove box. The road was rougher here, but Taz's black Jeep Cherokee was built for the landscape. I still thought of it as hers, even though her family sold it to Della after Taz died. My stomach twisted at the memory of Taz – killed during the battle against Veronica and her rogue vampires at Halloween. Veronica had slammed Taz to the ground, and I'd seen the light go out of her eyes. We'd taken Veronica down, but the hurt remained.

Soon, we were driving along the metal fence that lined Dad's property. It snaked off in both directions, barbed wire glinting along the top. Abandoned vehicles littered the weeds beyond the fence. Some cars were completely smashed up or burned out, but a few were in decent shape apart from flat tyres and rust.

"Anyone else getting *Texas Chainsaw Massacre* vibes?" Jared asked. "Either your dad collects wrecked cars or we're about to drive into our very own horror movie."

"We left Texas hours ago," Libby said. "And I think you should start being nicer. That's our dad you're talking about."

Jared shrugged. "They sell chainsaws in every state."

"I'm with you," Della said. "It seems kinda weird to me."

I took a moment to appreciate how Jared and Della were getting on. The vampire/vampire slayer dynamic hadn't always been easy, but they'd worked it out. Jared saving Libby from dying had sealed the deal.

"Let's keep an open mind," I said. "Dad isn't the most reliable guy, but I don't think he's serial killer material." It wasn't the best feeling to say that with a touch of doubt.

"Thanks for ganging up on me," Libby said, without much real hurt. She'd always been the first to defend Dad, but we'd been through enough together that I hoped it wouldn't get between us.

Finally, an opening in the fence interrupted the endless streak of metal. Two red recording lights glared down from a camera on either side of the gate.

"Looks like we're about to see for ourselves," Della said. She let the car roll up to a sign. 'TRESPASSERS WILL BE SHOT' was painted in red slashes across its grubby white surface.

"That doesn't mean us though," Libby said, her confrontational tone daring us to correct her.

"Let's do this then," Della said. The gates opened as we approached, adding to the creep factor.

'Goo Goo Muck' by the Cramps started playing as Della turned the Jeep onto a long, gravelled drive that wound through a wild growth of weeds and stunted trees. The car bumped over a line of crocodile teeth – no going back this way.

"If it's any consolation, I have weapons."

"Not funny," Libby said, grinning too widely at Della to come across severe. The expression withered on her face.

Through the driver's window, I saw what had her so rattled. A rusted pickup truck was racing towards us through the weeds.

Chapter 2

The truck was advancing fast, but the windscreen was too crusted in dirt to make out who was driving.

"This doesn't feel right," Della said, whipping her head around and jamming the Jeep into reverse. "Right . . . We're not going over those crocodile teeth unless we want to blow out our tyres." She put the car into park, hands tight on the steering wheel as we eyed the approaching truck.

"What do we do?" Libby asked, already crossed over into panic.

"Talk to them," Jared said, his voice like steel. "We have advantages they can't know about. We're not the stupid kids in a horror movie. We're the monster and the people who fight them."

Pride cut away some of my fear. "Where are your weapons?"

"Most are in the trunk and one stake in the glove box. Not exactly meant for humans . . ." Della trailed off.

But it'd do if we needed it. The four of us had what it took to survive.

The crusty old truck slammed on the brakes in front of us, cutting us off in case we'd decided to plunge on ahead.

A young guy got out, and the four of us followed suit. With the sun below the horizon, the temperature had dropped.

The guy's hair was brown and wavy, falling to an uneven line around his shoulders. He was wearing a threadbare blue shirt open over a white vest that displayed the butt of a gun in a leather holster. His brow was scrunched low over narrow blue eyes, and even though he appeared to be in his early 20s, his skin had the weathered look of someone who spends their days in the sun. "You The Shepherd's kids?" he barked in a thick Southern accent that I couldn't quite pin down.

"Yeah, Mina and Libby Shepherd," I said, gesturing to my sister. He obviously had some idea, so there was no point playing games. "This is Jared and Della."

"Right on," he said, an unpleasant edge behind his easy manner.

"And you are?" Jared asked, almost equalling the guy's hostility.

"Chase," he said, squinting at us. "Hold on." He removed a remote control from his pocket and aimed at the open gate. Even though he clicked a few times, nothing happened. "Piece of junk." He smacked the remote against his palm until the gate finally started to close.

"Follow me." He got into his truck and set off at a crawl, so we clambered back into the Jeep.

"The Shepherd?" Jared said. "I've upgraded my assessment from Leatherface to Charles Manson."

"I know you're going to tell us who that is even if we don't want to know," Libby said.

I'd heard pieces of the story, but Jared always told them better. "I do."

"Just tell us before we get wherever we're going," Della said. We were inching past the wild land on either side, the truck ahead occasionally coughing out black clouds of exhaust. Libby closed our vents. The encroaching darkness made the land shadowy and even less hospitable.

Jared's eyebrows scrunched low. "Charles Manson was the leader of this cult called the Manson Family. Of course, *they* didn't call it a cult. That's the name people used after all the shit went down.

"In the late 60s, around one hundred members of the Family lived on a commune, taking a whole lot of drugs and listening to this guy Charles Manson's teachings. Manson made prophecies about an apocalyptic war over race, which he said was due to happen real soon. So, basically your average terrible human being. But his members ate it up.

"In 1969 I think it was, three members of the Manson Family broke into the home of a Hollywood actress called Sharon Tate. They brutally murdered her and four friends. The Family were eventually convicted of other murders and a bunch of different crimes. Charles Manson has been in prison for decades."

"Good," Libby said.

"That's horrible," I added. "I don't understand why people follow someone making such ridiculous claims."

"Come on! Our dad isn't a cult leader," Libby said. "And I wish you wouldn't encourage him," she added, glaring at Jared. "Sometimes I swear we're not related."

"You're the odd one out – the rest of our family are all about the weird," I teased, though it turned sour. I was into a lot of the same things as my parents, but I hoped I wasn't going to turn out like them. My mum's obsession with vampires had led her to becoming one, and my dad had always left research around the house about every bizarre subject imaginable. They were more interested in their strange hobbies than their children.

The narrow road opened out ahead, and I wasn't prepared for the sight. There was a Western town on my dad's property: a string of wooden buildings on either side of a dusty street. Each had a glowing electric lantern attached to it, creating little puddles of light in the darkness.

Chase parked the beaten-up truck at the end of the street. Della pulled up behind him, and the five of us got out. Chase's blue shirt was buttoned up, the point about his gun already made.

Giving a shifty, lopsided grin, Chase spat on the ground between us. "Y'all can drop off your bags in here, then I'll take you on a tour of the Community. I'll be waitin'." He scratched the back of his head, exposing the black smudge of a tattoo inside his wrist. I couldn't see what it was, and I wasn't about to ask for a closer look.

"Awesome," Libby said flatly. "Where's our dad?"

"Not here right now," Chase said, his eye contact straying in textbook avoidance.

We grabbed our bags from the boot, all four of us pointedly not looking at Chase. The building was labelled 'Molly Haggerly's Saloon', and we piled inside. Della grabbed the key sticking out of the front door and locked us in.

"The Shepherd . . . Community . . . We haven't even seen the rest of this place and I'm still going with cult," Jared said.

"I mean . . . Shepherd is our surname, so it's not that weird." Libby dropped down onto the nearest bed. "I call dibs."

Jared and Libby's squabbling faded away. Even the name of our room hadn't clued me in that we were staying in an actual saloon. The beds were covered with fake cow print bedding that looked clean, thank goodness. The walls and floor were made of a pale wood, and a polished dark wooden bar ran along one side of the room with glasses and rows of bottles behind it. A green-felt poker table with a set of chips and cards took up one corner, and there was a small piano in another. The overhead light had stag antlers wrapped around it, stirring up horrible memories. The bear trap light at the mansion . . . Veronica's mallet in my hands, smashing the chain when Sam walked under it. I scrunched my eyes shut, opening them to refocus on the room.

"So, the two of us in this bed and you two in that one," Della said carefully. "Will you be OK with that?" She directed the last part at Jared.

A muscle in his jaw twitched. "I'll be fine. I need to feed tonight, and then I'll be all good."

"I can do it," I said. Jared only needed to feed every couple of days now. He'd been taking some blood from me, but one of the new blood bars covered most of it. Anaemia would be no fun.

"I think we're in agreement that we're getting some strange vibes from that Chase guy. Let's be on our guard and see how it goes," Della said.

"Agreed," I said. "And when it comes to Dad, that was already my plan."

"This was supposed to be a nice trip!" Libby said. "Our parents are finally together, and we know where they are. Can't we take that as a win and try to enjoy ourselves?"

"Sure," I said. "But we can be careful too. Shall we go back out on Chase's tour?" I was nervous but intrigued. Jared's story about the Manson Family cult was mingling with what we'd seen, and I had to know what our dad had been up to all these years.

We headed outside to find Chase smoking something that smelled terrible. "Hey," he said, crushing the butt under the heel of one battered cowboy boot. "Y'all ready?"

"What is this place?" I asked, gesturing at the Western town.

"Used to be a motel," Chase said, setting off at an amble down the street. "We don't do that no more – not since your grandpappy passed."

The granddad we'd never met. "What do you all do for an income now?"

Chase squinted at me. "This and that – mostly fixin' up vehicles." When I was a kid, Dad had given similarly sketchy explanations about money. In the distance, there was another cluster of vehicles that had seen better days: a car with a smashed-up bonnet, a rusty yellow school bus and a TV news van with a satellite dish on top that looked in better shape.

When we passed through the fake-Western town, we hit the real ranch. Lanterns on crooked poles lit our path. I wouldn't say it was a hive of activity, but there were signs of life. There was a stable on one side of the path. To the other side was a massive greenhouse, and beyond that, a cornfield rippled.

Chase gestured in the direction I was looking. "We're pretty self-sufficient – ready for when the zombies come." At the shock on our faces, Chase cracked up. "I'm just messin' with ya. It ain't the zombies you gotta worry about."

"Right . . ." Libby said with a fake chuckle. "So, where is everyone?" she asked, likely assuming as I had that Dad would have people around him like always, and that the ominous term 'Community' meant something.

"They're around," Chase said. "Mostly in the house at this time of day. This here's the stable," he said, bringing us closer to the expected animal smell than I would've liked. A few horses were in residence, and they looked clean and well taken care of.

A girl appeared in the open doorway, making us jump. "Y'all The Shepherd's girls?"

"They are," Jared said, saving us from explaining again.

"This here's Rebecca," Chase said, his tone surly even when introducing someone he knew. Maybe it wasn't us making him grumpy.

Rebecca looked about Libby's age. She was wearing a white summer dress despite the cold night. "You're lucky to have grown up with him," she said in a dreamy voice, twirling a long strand of straight brown hair.

"That's one way of describing it," I said.

Libby sidled up to dig an elbow into my ribs. "We do feel lucky," she said.

"I'm sure y'all will like this place," Rebecca said. She gave a broad, provocative grin. Jared seemed about ready to burst, spilling out questions. Libby and Della were making the same kind of warning look I could feel on my face. We weren't here to make conversation. I wanted to see my parents and figure out what we were walking into.

Rebecca rounded on me and Libby. "You're from England, right? I've never left New Mexico, but I'd love to go on one of our missions some day."

I nearly forgot my resolve to get to our parents, because I had to find out what Rebecca was talking about. Chase had other ideas. "Come on – I need to get y'all to the house."

We carried on past a ramshackle hut with a huge padlock on

the door – a 'contemplation space', whatever that meant. I was contemplating getting back in the Jeep and going home. We'd suffered through some horrendous things this past year, which had trained me to detect when something shady was going on.

Finally, the house materialised in the distance. If it wasn't for the lights, I'd say the building had been abandoned. Advancing closer revealed uneven white boards across its front that were shedding paint. The grey roof was short a few slates, and some windows were boarded up. Two peaked roofs at the front were sloping as if the whole place was about to collapse.

"It's . . . got character," Libby said. This was Dad's home we were talking about. The rose-tinted glasses were working hard.

"If that character's from a slasher movie," Jared muttered.

Chase coughed out a laugh. "It's not what the place looks like on the outside. Y'all know what we do here?"

I had some ideas – none of them good. "Not a clue."

"Y'all had better come on in then."

Chapter 3

I'd been trying not to leap to conclusions, since I tended to err on the harsh side when it came to Dad. But first he was some 'Shepherd' in charge of a 'Community', and then we'd walked past a shed where people were left to think. If I didn't get answers soon, I'd be left painting a bleak picture. One relief was that Chase had invited Jared in without us having to push for it. Requiring an invitation was one of those pesky vampire rules that was actually true.

"You said Dad is out. Is our mum here?" Libby asked.

"Sure is," Chase said. "I'll take you to her. But first, come meet some of our people."

Chase pushed open the battered, swollen front door. He must have noticed my shocked face – locked doors were a must in my experience. "No need for locks here. No secrets either."

Mum and Dad had never kept a tidy house. There were always piles of papers and books everywhere, about vampires for Mum and whatever fleeting obsession had grabbed Dad's interest. This place not only had surfaces heaped with papers, newspapers, magazines and books. The floor was also obscured by piles that came past our knees.

Paths through it all led to three doors and up the stairs, though they had a stack to one side of each step. The air was stuffy and tinged with cigarette smoke. A girl drifted across the hallway and up the stairs, also sporting a white dress and waist-length hair. Della followed her path with narrowed eyes.

We followed Chase into the living room, which had no TV and a lot of people crammed into it. Their ages ranged from a baby in its mother's lap to an elderly man and woman talking animatedly on a battered sofa. They were all wearing clothes that looked handmade. Several of the people were smoking with books on their laps – a recipe for disaster if ever I'd seen one.

The conversation stopped when we entered, so I was still none the wiser about what was going on. There was a chorus of welcomes when Chase introduced us, so at least they seemed friendly.

I was glad to leave the smoky room, and Chase took us into a cramped office next. 'Man on the Moon' by R.E.M. was playing quietly on an old radio. I'd have preferred not to have been squashed into a room with Chase, but the four of us clustered together in a space not taken over by stacks of paperwork.

"This here's our resident electrical whiz," Chase said.

An older man was sitting behind a massive computer, the desk around him strewn with electrical components and wires. He moved to one side so we could see him, his dark brown skin crinkling into a friendly smile. His hair came down to his collarbone in neat locs, thin strands of grey threading through the black. He was tall and solidly built, like an ex-American football player maybe.

"The Shepherd kids," he said. "Welcome to our Community." When he spread his hands, it revealed the dark shadow of a tattoo like the one on Chase's wrist.

Finally, a person who didn't creep me the hell out, despite the matching ink. "I'm Mina, and this is Libby, Jared and Della."

"I'm Hayes. I'm sure y'all are wonderin' why your parents are holed up with a bunch of people. It prob'ly looks pretty strange to those on the outside. I'd love to talk more when you've seen The Shepherd. I'm sure he'll be excited to share with his kids."

"Thank you," Della said. "Is it possible to see Mina and Libby's mom?"

She addressed that part to Chase. I'd almost forgotten him, listening in the corner. "She's right upstairs," he said.

We followed Chase up the creaking wooden stairs, trying not to dislodge the stacks of papers. I walked up with Jared, even though it was a tight fit. He grabbed my hand, giving it a few comforting pulses. He knew I was nervous about seeing my mum, but he'd also have been able to hear my quickening heart.

Upstairs, the house smelled of unwashed clothing and the unpleasant tinge of mould. There were no piles of clutter, but I caught sight of groups of people as we passed several open doors. They were talking quietly, reading or making notes.

Chase pointed to a door at the end of the hallway. Even in the faint light, I finally made out that tattoo on his inner wrist. It was a raven coloured in solid black.

"She's in there. Like I said, we don't lock our doors, but y'all will wanna knock first." At that, he strode off down the hallway and back downstairs.

"Friendly folk round here," Jared said quietly.

Libby either didn't hear him or chose not to. She rapped her knuckles gently on the door.

"Come in!" The voice was weak, but it was definitely Mum.

Libby pushed the door open, and the four of us piled in. The curtains were shut, casting us in near darkness. From the musty smell, I guessed they hadn't been opened in quite some time.

Not feeling especially patient, I turned on the light. It was a bare bulb that gave off a weak orange glow, but Mum still groaned and flung a pillow over her head. "What time is it?"

I hadn't expected a warm welcome, but she could've removed the pillow. "It's nighttime – you're safe."

Mum shot up in bed, the pillow falling aside. "You're here! My two girls . . . Our family's together again."

She scrambled off the bed and opened both arms as if she was going to catch me and Libby in them. I stepped aside and let my sister accept the hug. Mum had made similar declarations at Halloween before running off here, so I couldn't take her too seriously. Libby, on the other hand, was squeezing so hard it was lucky Mum no longer needed oxygen.

"Have you seen your dad yet?" Mum asked, disentangling herself from Libby.

"He's out," I said. Also nothing new there.

"Oh, right . . . He'll be back soon with dinner. They grow most of their own food here, but this is a special occasion," Mum said, practically glowing with excitement. On the face of it, living with Dad again was agreeing with her. Mum wasn't usually a big smiler or known for showing much emotion at all. Her wavy hair was clean and smooth, and she was wearing a flowing black dress that looked very Morticia Addams.

"Can't wait!" Libby said, adding to Della and Jared, "You two are going to love him." If she said it often enough, maybe it would convince somebody.

"I'm sure we will," Jared said dryly.

Mum seemed to notice them for the first time. "Nice to see you both. I hope you're being good to my girls."

"Of course," Della said, her usual patience fraying. "Does Mr Shepherd know about what you are?"

"He does," Mum said. "Your dad and I have nothing to hide from each other. You'll soon find out what it's like here – we don't keep secrets." Didn't we just hear the same words coming out of Chase's mouth? And then there was Mum's willingness to open up – not a quality that had ever been her strong suit.

"What about other people's secrets?" I asked, wondering if she'd already spilled about my slayer status or my vampire boyfriend. Nothing I'd seen here had made me want to offer up our secrets. Even as a child, Dad had been unpredictable. There was no telling how he'd react.

There was the cloud of secrecy that usually hovered around Mum. "You don't have to worry about that . . . But I should warn you – some of your dad's views are a bit . . . extreme. He'll want to tell you himself, but know that he's trying to keep people safe."

"What kind of . . .?" I was interrupted by a bell jangling somewhere beneath us. Mum rushed for the door with Libby close behind. I followed much more warily with Della and Jared.

The house was suddenly full of excited voices, but one stood out over all the rest: loud, deep and positively oozing with charm. Dad was home.

Chapter 4

Libby and Mum reached the top of the stairs first, blocking my view. They were halfway down when I saw him.

The sight almost took my legs out from under me. Ten years had passed since we'd been in the same room, and he'd hardly changed. His black hair and stubble were touched with grey and the lines around his eyes and mouth were deeper, but he was as tall and leanly muscled as ever. He was wearing a black leather jacket over a grey Pearl Jam T-shirt. He'd always been this interesting kind of handsome that was hard to ignore, with exaggerated lips and eyes. Coupled with an abundance of confidence, it was easy to see why most people were drawn to him.

"My three girls!" His voice boomed, quieting the crowd that had gathered.

Libby flung herself against him. He embraced her, laughing, while his eyes were on me. I was always going to be the most difficult to sway.

"Hi, Dad," I said, the name sounding weird coming out of my mouth. It'd been too long since I'd had a face to direct it at.

"I brought take-out," he said, holding up several bags in each hand. "Everyone come eat while the food's still hot."

We followed Dad and the others into a plain white dining room with a brown tiled floor. The beginning of the meal was carnage. I wasn't sure how many people lived in this so-called Community, but at least twenty descended on the food and filled their plates with buttery corn on the cob, fried chicken, French fries and coleslaw. As they reached for the food, I clocked a matching tattoo on every wrist except my parents'.

Most of the group took their plates with a curious glance for us before going off to other rooms. That left me, Jared, Della and Libby with Mum, Dad, Hayes and Chase.

"Sorry, y'all." A girl rushed in, pulling out the empty chair next to Chase. She had sun-bleached reddish blonde hair and a sprinkling of freckles over tanned skin.

Chase stood up, and his surly persona fell away. They gave each other the kind of smiles reserved for that one special person as they sat down. "I'm Ellie," she said with a bright, genuine smile. "It's good to meet y'all, finally."

"You too," I said, surprised that I meant it. "I'm Mina, and this is Libby, Della and Jared." I pointed them out in turn.

Conversation was scarce while everyone filled their plates, and I took the time to adjust. My dad was here, in the same room as me. I couldn't stop looking at him. He'd always had this magnetism. Most of it came from his eyes. They were a clear, cool green that was quite unusual, but it was the way he used them that counted: like you mattered and only he really saw you. Paired with his wide, dimpled smile, it was hard to resist letting Dad sway your mood.

"So," Dad began once everyone's plates were full, "you're the Jared and Della I've heard so much about."

"That's right," Della said, her voice polite and even. Jared nodded, very intent on moving food around his plate and subtly depositing it in napkins or back in the bags. So Jared was presumably with me when it came to keeping our secrets from Dad. Even if Dad was seemingly fine with Mum's undead status, he needed to earn our trust.

"I've heard great things about you both from Emma," Dad said, smiling at Mum. She was making no pretence at eating, toying with a fork and showing very little interest in the proceedings. She brightened at the mention from Dad though.

"Thank you, sir," Jared said quietly. Both he and Della had an undercurrent of defensiveness, likely because of what I'd told them about my parents.

"So, has someone explained to y'all what we do here?" Dad asked.

"Nope," I said.

Dad rocked back in his chair, pleased. He always loved a performance. "It's exciting to finally share this with all of my girls. We're a research team with a very important goal. We don't have the impressive facilities y'all might expect, but our work is impeccable. Some of our members do fieldwork, but most concentrate on our mission here. You might say our focus is fringe science and its impact on humanity."

"What fringe science?" Jared asked, probably coming across pleasant to those who didn't know him. I could read the twitch along his jaw muscles that showed he wasn't at ease.

"All in good time," Dad said genially. "For now, let's eat and talk some more later. What do you think so far, honey?"

He directed the question at me. Everyone looked my way, and I squirmed. Audiences at the mansion weren't a problem, but here

I had no character to hide behind.

Dad had told us next to nothing, so I tried to be polite. "It sounds very . . . interesting." I skewered a fry with my fork, even though I wasn't hungry. It somehow stung more that the reason he'd left us was to study . . . something. He could've done that from home. He'd missed everything from school days to family nights around a horror movie for what – the chance to be a student again?

"You're not convinced," he said, not seeming too phased. He was the only one. Ellie, Chase and Hayes all looked disgruntled. Surely he'd not told us enough for them to be mad at me for not being immediately won over.

"I'll take you and Libby to see my collection after dinner. You'll see." Confident that he was right, he picked up a chicken leg and tore off a long strip of meat with his teeth.

We carried on eating, and I was glad to be sandwiched between Della and Jared. I wanted to get away from this table, not only to escape the atmosphere but to finally see what Dad had been doing.

The conversation ran out while people tucked in, but I still felt their scrutiny.

After a few minutes, Dad broke the silence. "I think that'll do it. Come with me," he said, not checking to see if Libby and I were ready.

The command was only meant for us, but it had an immediate effect on Ellie, Hayes and Chase. It didn't matter if they were still eating. The food went down and the plates were scraped and stacked with quick, practised hands.

Jared and Della stood up with me, and Dad levelled them with a hard gaze. He was still grinning, but it wasn't especially friendly.

"Just Mina and Libby. It's been a long while since I spent time with my girls."

He did it again, marking us as his property when he'd made it clear since we were children that he wasn't interested in us.

"Shall we make this a family occasion?" he asked, turning to Mum.

She shook her head, the smile not quite reaching her eyes. "You take the opportunity to spend time with our daughters."

Libby stood eagerly, eating it all up. Coming here would be worse for her in the end. They'd end up disappointing us, and Libby had further to fall.

Dad led us to a door under the stairs. He pulled out a key ring that held a lot of keys for a place that didn't lock their doors. Was he the gentle shepherd or jailer?

He unlocked the door, leading us down a chilly concrete stairwell. Photographs on the wall gave hints about what Dad was studying. The first featured a grinning family in black and white: two young children on women's knees. It was the figure to the left that set off a gnawing sense of unease in my stomach. The apparition was upside down, with only its torso, head and arms showing. It had a black void for a face. The next photograph was less frightening: a mountain range beneath the blip of a black oval in a clear sky. I'd seen the last photograph before, which featured a huge furred creature strolling in the woods, its shape roughly human and head turned towards the camera.

This was one of the few ways where I was undeniably my dad's daughter. The whiff of a mystery wrapped up in learning made me come over all curious. It was less Libby's thing, but she would've followed Dad anywhere.

The king of paranoia, among other things, Dad unlocked a second door, pausing with his hand on it. "I'm sure I don't have to tell y'all that what you see in here won't leave this room. It can be our secret."

His tone was gentle, but I read a threat into it. "We don't keep anything from Della and Jared." Libby raised her eyebrows but didn't argue with me. We were on the same side, for now at least.

Dad looked taken aback, and the silence dragged on. Was he really so used to getting his own way? "I suppose I can't argue with that kind of loyalty. Keep it between the four of you then."

With that, he opened the door.

Chapter 5

If I'd thought the rest of the house was cluttered, this room was on another level. Shelves on every wall were spilling over with objects. There were plaster casts of large footprints and strange teeth, along with skulls from no creature I'd seen on Earth. All of the available wall space was covered with a collage of imagery: a creature somewhere between a dog and a reptile, a rabbit with deer antlers, a humanoid figure with glowing red eyes and a pointed hat . . . Dad also had books about hypnosis and behavioural psychology that cast him in an unsavoury light. Were those the techniques he'd been using on everyone here?

"This place is . . . great," Libby said, fixing a smile on her face that mostly made her look confused. This was more my thing than Libby's, and I hated how into it I was. One thing I'd always had in common with my parents was a love of creepy things, and I had a sneaking suspicion that Dad was using it against me.

Whatever the reason, I wasn't about to pass up this opportunity. "What is all of this?"

"The secure location for the products of my research. No one outside the group has come down here, and even they only come on occasion. It's a very special place." Dad radiated warmth and sincerity, and I couldn't help but feel pleased that he trusted us with something so important.

I wanted a poke around, but there were too many things I had to understand. "So . . . what is it that you do here?"

"It's a long story," Dad said, gesturing to a worn velvet sofa.

I sat down next to Libby, examining more objects. A shiny silver disc, a shelf packed with claws of many sizes, all tagged and labelled . . .

Dad pulled up a chair, sitting on it backwards like he was the coolest guy in the world. From the look on Libby's face, she believed that. "I never talked to you much about your grandfather."

"No, you didn't," Libby said with a touch of accusation. Good girl.

"We had a disagreement before the two of you were born. It's why I moved to the UK, in fact. I wanted to branch out on my own. Anyway, he was the one who got me into all of this. My dad was about your age the year of the Roswell incident, and he lived in this house when it happened." He paused expectantly, but even I wasn't clued in. "You girls haven't heard of the Roswell incident? I've been away too long."

"It's something to do with aliens, isn't it?" I asked.

Libby made a contemptuous sound, but the noise cut off at Dad's cold expression. "That's right, *honey*," he said to me, laying the endearment on thick. "In the summer of '47, the US Army Air Forces put out a press release that they'd collected the wreckage from a fallen disc that had been flying over a ranch on the outskirts of Roswell. A rancher named Mac Brazel found it on his property not far from here, out on the grassy lands where his herds roamed. He called my daddy and my grandpa over to take a look. They were the Brazels' closest neighbours."

I could see how my dad had collected a houseful of followers. He spoke with a passion that was hard to withstand, conjuring the image of a rancher on his dusty land, two ancestors I'd never met trudging over to take a look at . . . what? That was where my imagination failed. "What did he find?"

"All kinds of stuff: rubber strips, thick paper and a kind of foil never seen before on Earth." Dad stood up, retrieving a small cardboard box from a crowded shelf behind him. Carefully, he raised the lid for us to see. A shimmering piece of foil was enclosed in a glass slide.

"It's pretty," Libby said, leaning in with the most interest she'd shown up to this point.

"That's from the crash site," I said, feeling the mirror of the excitement I saw on my dad's face.

"You got it. There'd been sightings of flying discs reported in the national press, and my dad and Mac concluded this might be related. The commanding officer of the Roswell Army Air Field then released a statement confirming it."

Dad paused to grab a photo frame containing a newspaper article. "This piece right here has all the details. After that, it got even more interesting. The next day, the RAAF put out another statement that the debris was actually from a weather balloon, even including a photograph."

"They changed their minds pretty fast, didn't they?" I said as he set the frame down carefully.

"Sure did. My dad didn't even get to hear about their next about-face before he died. Just last year, the US Air Force admitted the weather balloon story was untrue. They said the materials were from a classified spy device."

Dad leaned back in his chair, grinning. "Now why would they keep changing their story? Isn't it better to let it slide forgotten into history? My father wondered the same thing back in the day, and he became fascinated. He read every article he could lay his hands on and talked to everyone involved. Some witnesses even claimed they saw alien bodies taken away from the site. Whatever people saw, they agreed the wreckage and deceased extra-terrestrials were taken to Area 51 in Nevada. If it was some weather balloon, why'd the government hide it in the most secure Air Force facility in the area? My dad dedicated the rest of his life to proving the Roswell incident wasn't what the government claimed and that aliens were real."

"And you carried on his work?" I asked, the unease from earlier in the day returning. The grandfather I'd never known had given his life to this research at the expense of everything else, and my dad was following in his footsteps.

"Of course." Dad inched his chair closer, leaning in. "The pursuit of knowledge is one of the few worthy endeavours we have at our disposal. If we're not learning, then we might as well be dead."

His green eyes burned with fervour. There had to be more to life than chasing knowledge if it meant abandoning the people you loved.

Libby nodded so ferociously that I felt the vibration through the chair. I was about to pull Libby up on her personality transplant when Dad's expression turned bleak. "I'm afraid there's more. This part of the story is much more troublin' – I don't wanna worry you girls."

Libby sighed next to me. She preferred to bow out when things got serious. "We can handle it," I said.

"All right. Near the end of Dad's life, he noticed a worrying pattern. I didn't find out until after he died, but when I went through his things, I saw it too. I've talked to countless people who have encountered supernatural beings. Some themes came through that can't be ignored. There's plenty of evidence aliens have had an impact on Earth. They appear in prehistoric cave paintings, and some people even believe they built the pyramids. Much of my research concluded that cryptids, vampires, witches . . . They all came to be on this Earth because of aliens imbuing beings with power. They come back over time to abduct ordinary humans and animals, carrying out experiments to make them extraordinary and creating new cryptids. You with me so far, girls?"

I was a bit stunned that he believed it, but tried to see things from his point of view. "I follow so far, except for one thing. What's a cryptid?"

"Sorry, honey – I should've been clearer. It's an animal whose existence hasn't been confirmed by the wider scientific community. So, what do y'all think? I mean – y'all already know your mom is a vampire. Is this really so different?"

Of course Mum had told him we knew about her – the no secrets thing. Let's hope that was the only confidence she'd broken.

Libby jabbed her elbow into my side, which I took as my cue to try digging us out of this. "I wasn't expecting other things to be real . . . Maybe I should have done. I'll need time to process."

A wounded look came over Dad's face. "I understand," he said, though I wasn't sure he did.

"Have you ever seen a cryptid?" I asked.

Some of Dad's swagger evaporated, though he disguised it well. "Sure have," he said boldly, though I wasn't sure I bought it. "And your mother, of course. But my role in this is as an active player rather than a witness. I have some difficult acts ahead of me, but it will all be worth it."

"So how did everyone else end up here?" I asked, taking advantage while he was being candid.

Dad smiled easily, but his hands flexed into tight fists and then relaxed. Touchy subject? "Everyone has earned their place through the focused pursuit of knowledge. After their encounters, a lot of folks here suffered scepticism and sometimes worse in their communities, so we made our own. People didn't believe what they'd seen with their own eyes, but I do. The beauty is that all of their interests have come together in one place, where judgement and disbelief are left at the door." Dad gestured at the artefacts around him. "We've had people come here to study the Loch Ness Monster, the Yeti, Mothman and countless others. Those who reach a point of true understanding in their research are authorised to go on research trips. It's been a wonderful journey, and you've arrived at an exciting time."

"How come?" I asked.

Dad's smile became guarded, like he hadn't decided to trust us yet. That went both ways. "We'll get to that. Come on, let me show you everything."

Chapter 6

We lost Libby pretty quickly. She ended up drifting around the room with alternating looks of confusion and disgust. Apparently she hadn't fully bought what Dad was selling.

It was the opposite for me. This was the part of Dad that I could get behind. I set aside Jared's talk of cults and Dad's alien theories, and let myself enjoy this place. "What's Mothman?" I asked, zeroing in on a newspaper article.

"Good eye," Dad said. "One of our people, Hayes, hails from Point Pleasant, West Virginia. He brought this story to us. Mothman is a humanoid creature with red, glowing eyes and bat-like wings. Hayes grew up in the 60s when a bunch of locals reported seeing Mothman. Young Hayes was fascinated, so he and his uncle went camping in the hotspot for sightings. They stayed two nights when a red-eyed shadow appeared at the other side of the campfire, stalking back and forth. The creature fled, leaving Hayes and his uncle thrilled that they'd finally done it. But when they got back to town, they were met with ridicule.

"That was until a bridge over the Ohio River collapsed on December 15th 1967, killing almost fifty people. Some locals believed Mothman was responsible. Since then, a statue, a festival and a museum have sprung up to commemorate Mothman sightings. Pretty impressive for a creature most people will tell you doesn't exist. It was all the proof Hayes needed. By the time he was an adult, he was desperate to meet people like him. He found a notice I'd posted on an online bulletin board and came here."

We spent over an hour scrutinising photographs of the Loch Ness Monster, discussing Yeti sightings and becoming deliciously squeamish about the Mongolian Death Worm. I loved getting lost in these stories. It was nice to enjoy something with Dad and to have him right there, breathing in the comforting cinnamon smell of him and feeling his solid heat. I hoped we'd get to the bottom of what was going on here, concluding it was all innocent. Even if I might never believe Dad's theories, I didn't want my relationship with him to shrivel and die for good this time.

"Who's this?" I asked, spotting a picture frame in the disarray that didn't belong amidst the macabre and uncanny items. It was a picture of Dad and a skinny white guy about his age. Dad had his arm around the man's shoulder, and they were standing in front of this house.

Dad took the photo from me, frowning at it. "I haven't seen this in a long time. Clem was one of our members – one of my best friends, in fact. He arrived here not long after I came back. Almost lost his life to a hidebehind – a fearsome woodland creature that stalks human prey. But gradually, Clem's opinions and goals moved away from ours, becoming more violent. The time came when I had to ask him and his buddies to go, which was a true shame. People don't often leave the Community."

I had so many questions, but Dad put the photograph back and Libby took her opportunity. "This has been so great, but it's been a long couple of days. I think we should go to bed."

Dad seemed to have recovered from traipsing down memory lane, throwing a wicked grin my way. "You can come down here any time you want, honey. You have a few more days here. Tomorrow, I'll take you two to Roswell."

"She's right. We should go and find Jared and Della," I said. I felt guilty for not considering them while I got sucked into Dad's stories. I was sure they'd have opinions when I told them about Dad's work. "Thank you for showing us."

"You're welcome," Dad said. "It's been a pleasure. You remind me a lot of myself as a child. And Libby reminds me of your mom." We shared a knowing grin, and for the first time in a decade, I felt a connection between us.

Della and Jared were waiting in our room. The space smelled faintly of sawdust, but I was glad to be back among the four of us.

"Well, that was a trip," Jared said, sinking down onto our bed. I sat next to him, leaning against his cool body. He wrapped an arm around me, instantly blanketing me in comfort. "We talked to some of your dad's friends while you were gone. They really believe in their wild pseudo-science. Most of them claim they've encountered some kind of supernatural creature face to face."

"Says the vampire," I teased, bumping my shoulder against him. "Did they tell you Dad's alien theory?"

"I don't think they covered that," Della said as she and Libby settled on their bed, her head leaning against my sister's shoulder.

"You know I'm team Dad, and even I think he's gone too far with this one," Libby chirped up.

"Dad has this theory that aliens made all of the supernatural creatures. He reckons they come down every once in a while to do experiments, giving powers to humans and animals and creating the first vampires, cryptids and stuff. So surprise, Jared – you're part alien."

Jared's chuckle quickly died away. "You're not joking."

"I wish. It's weird, because I can see why they're invested. They have cool artefacts supposedly proving the existence of these creatures. I'm not sure how much of it I buy, but who am I to assume we know everything? It's just . . . they've taken it all to extremes."

"You're right," Della said. "They're obsessed – they won't talk about anything else. And they seem real fixated on your dad."

Libby sat up straighter. "Dad hasn't done anything! All I heard was that he takes in people whose families won't believe them. He can't help it if they want to follow him round and stuff."

"We're not saying he can," Jared said, adjusting his arms around me. "But I think we should be on our guard. The people here are definitely exhibiting cult-like behaviour."

Being enamoured with parts of Dad's work had been fun while it lasted. First his alien theory, and now we were back to cults. "Like what?" I asked, wriggling free so I could see Jared.

He checked off the answers on his fingers. "Obsession with the leader or the group as a whole, excessively defensive when challenged about the group, working towards a cause that becomes their identity, lack of independent thought, pouring their own funds into their work . . . Plus, did you notice the tattoos?"

"I did," Della said. "A raven, right? As far as I could see, they all have one."

"Except my parents," I said. "But why a raven?"

"Maybe because of that Edgar Allan Poe poem," Jared said thoughtfully. "*Quoth the Raven, 'Nevermore'.* I know animals have different meanings for various cultures, but I'm coming up empty on this one."

Libby's smile came across forced. "OK, so this place is a bit . . . off. But a cult – really? Anyway, I've had enough of today. I need to wash off the dust and then I'm going to bed."

There was no way I could sleep with all of this looping around my head. "Do you want to go for a walk?" I asked Jared.

"Don't go too far," Della said. "We still don't know what we're dealin' with."

"Agreed," Jared said, offering me a hand.

I grabbed an old *Fraggle Rock* sweatshirt on the way out, and it was a good move. Nights in the desert were the kind of cold that sinks in deep.

"Can we walk around a bit?" I asked, gripping Jared's hand. "I need to clear my head."

"Sure thing," he said. We set off through the abandoned Western town, crossing pockets of light and swathes of darkness. It wasn't much of a stretch to imagine one of my dad's people watching us from the dark and reporting back.

"Wanna talk about it?" Jared asked.

"Yeah, but let's do it quietly – just in case," I said, looking up at a building labelled 'Lily Anne's Bordello'. The shadows around it were too dense, and I couldn't trust that we were alone. "You know a lot about . . . *cults.*" The last word came out not much louder than a breath, but Jared had vampire hearing.

"You wouldn't think it to look at them, but my family are true-crime nuts. There are shelves of books on a lot of topics around my house back in Honolulu. My older sister, Jessica, is the cult fan."

Jared didn't talk about his family much anymore. We discussed most things, but he'd not said when he was planning to tell them what he was.

I circled back to what we were talking about. "Tell me the bite-size version about some more cults," I said. It was time to arm myself with knowledge, before I decided how deep into this relationship with Dad I wanted to get.

"OK, I'll start with one of the worst. You ready?"

Usually I loved Jared's creepy stories, but this one felt too personal. "Ready as I'll ever be."

Chapter 7

Jared treated this story differently, starting with a serious tone. "Have you heard the expression about not drinking the Kool-Aid?" I shook my head and he continued. "This one group had a powerful, controlling leader called Jim Jones who moved them into the South American jungle after some seriously bad press. Someone from the government went to investigate and was murdered. In the end, Jones ordered his followers to drink poisoned Kool-Aid punch, which they did. 900 of them died. He didn't drink it himself, but was later found dead from a gunshot wound."

"Oh my God. Let's hope we're not dealing with anything approaching that." The worst traits Dad had displayed were strange habits and inattention to his children. "Tell me another one."

"All right . . ." Jared began, putting an arm around me as we walked. "A couple years ago, in Waco, Texas, this cult called the Branch Davidians had a two-month stand-off with law enforcement that ended in a massive fire. Loads of people were killed on both sides. The leader, David Koresh, had set up his own community based on some seriously messed-up values." Jared's expression went sombre. "The cult were suspected of having weapons stockpiled to prepare for an apocalypse predicted by Koresh. Sure enough, they opened fire when the feds arrived. A load of different agencies descended on them, and that's when the siege started."

"Another apocalypse prediction . . . So cults are seriously extreme and usually end with mass casualties?"

"Yeah, that sounds about right," Jared said. "I'm sure this place is nothing like that. I know you wanna reconnect with your dad – sorry to be a downer."

"I'm glad you told me. I don't plan to bury my head in the sand, even if he is my dad."

"Whatever happens, we're in this together." Jared hugged me against his body. Being close to him quieted a lot of the horrors my imagination was churning up, so I tilted my face upwards.

He rested a thumb on my chin, curving his fingers underneath it. "What is it? Do you need a distraction?"

"I really do, so this had better be good," I teased.

He leaned in slowly, that full-lipped grin bringing me out in all kinds of delicious shivers. When his lips were hovering over mine, he murmured, "I aim to please." Then, he finally kissed me.

We'd got really, really good at this. He knew exactly how to tease my lips with the lightest pressure, holding off until I couldn't bear it any longer. I crushed my mouth against his, our bodies locked together, and my mind went quiet. The only thought I could hold on to was that Jared and I would be sleeping in the same bed, and we could spend the whole night close like this.

Jared pulled back, his hands still on my cheeks. "Do you hear that?"

"You might have to be more specific. Vampire hearing, remember?"

Jared took my hand and pulled me towards the house. The shadowy outline of it came into view, and the darkness wasn't kinder than the daylight. If anything, the sloping shape looked more menacing.

I heard it then – unaccompanied singing in the still night. "Is it coming from the house?"

"Behind it, I think." We followed the porch around the back. A campfire was set up, the flames a vibrant orange in the darkness. From our shadowy spot I couldn't tell who was there, but I picked out some details. The light shone off a sheet of long, reddish blonde hair, so that was likely Ellie. The figure with an arm around her would be Chase.

Then I heard my dad's voice, carrying like always. "Tonight, I'm thankful my daughters are visiting our Community. I'm thankful for the work we do."

"We're thankful for the work we do." The chant came back in unison, a host of voices repeating after my dad.

"We're getting close to something incredible, and I couldn't be more grateful to y'all."

"We are all grateful."

"Shall we go over there?" Jared whispered.

I shook my head and pulled him back the way we'd come. I wasn't keen on making an appearance after what we'd heard.

"Well, that was creepy," Jared said. "Did you hear them repeating everything back to him?"

"Yeah," I said, equally occupied with how Dad was so thankful for us that we weren't invited to whatever that was.

Libby and Della were asleep when we got inside. One of them, probably Della, had left a small lamp on so we could navigate the unfamiliar space.

"Do you mind?" Jared whispered, baring his still-human teeth. The fangs wouldn't make an appearance until he needed them.

The curtains were closed, and with my sister and Della asleep, it felt like our own world as we sat on the bed and I offered the crook of my elbow to Jared. Old scars marred the skin where he'd fed before, but it didn't bother me. He needed blood to survive, and I was willing to give it.

Jared pressed his lips to the sensitive skin of my inner elbow. I shivered, watching as his mouth latched on. There was a sting when the skin broke, then a rhythmic pulling. When Jared took his time, the feeling was pleasant, with his body curved over mine and his soft mouth on my skin. He pulled away, and I caught a flash of fangs as he wiped the back of his hand against his mouth.

"Thanks," he said, placing a hand over the stinging wound. Heat coursed through my arm, the skin tightening and pulling as it healed. He kissed me, the sweet touch of his mouth balancing out the itchy sensation in my arm. When the healing was done, we parted.

I took the first turn in the bathroom, getting ready and taking my iron supplements. By the time Jared was ready, I was comfortably sleepy. All the crap with Dad could wait.

Jared tucked into bed behind me, shuffling forwards until his chest was against my back. I pulled my hair under me, and Jared nuzzled his face into the crook of my neck. Sleeping in the same bed was a rare pleasure, since we had our own rooms at the mansion. Jared's blood lust was a lot less intense than when he first turned, but we were in no rush to push it too far. I stayed awake as long as I could, enjoying the closeness, but soon succumbed.

I woke up feeling optimistic. Dad had promised us a trip into Roswell, and we wouldn't be here much longer. Whatever potentially shady stuff he was up to, we'd be back in New Orleans before we knew it. As always, Mum was an unknown entity. She'd come to be with Dad but didn't seem to be a member of this Community my grandfather had created.

Libby, Della and I got ready and left Jared in bed. We decided on a story for him before heading out into the sunshine. If this whole place was obsessed with the paranormal, we didn't want Jared in their crosshairs, whether everyone knew about Mum or not.

In the daytime, the earth was golden brown and the sky was a pale, shimmering blue. The ranch was too beautiful to feel as eerie as it had last night. In the distance, I spotted the TV news van with a satellite attachment that we saw yesterday. It bumped down the footpath ahead of us and disappeared around the house. They must have got it working, ready to sell.

Our growling stomachs led us to the kitchen in the main house. Della still wore a slight look of wariness, and I was glad she was there for backup.

Mum and Dad were alone at the kitchen table, a pan sizzling behind them. They didn't notice us at first, because they were too busy staring into each other's eyes. When we were kids, Libby would've made pretend puking noises, but we let them have this moment.

"Mornin' girls," Dad said, turning his dazzling smile on us. "Y'all sleep well?"

"Like a log," Libby said, sinking down at the table like she belonged there. Della and I sat on either side of her.

Dad stood up to mix whatever smelled so spicy and delicious. "Breakfast burrito? There are tortillas and green chilli sauce on the table."

"Awesome!" Libby said, jumping up. "I'll get plates!"

I put a tortilla on each plate as Dad came and heaped a mixture of meat, eggs, potatoes and cheese onto each tortilla. We watched him wrap his into a neat bundle, going heavy on the chilli sauce. We made our own efforts and bit in. His cooking was as good as I remembered. It was spicy and packed with flavour against the creamy fluffiness of the eggs. Until I was eight, he'd been the main cook. Mum had tried when he left, but she tended towards burned disasters, the same as Libby.

Mum sipped black coffee while we ate, her eyes sleepy. "You have much planned for Roswell?"

"The museum and a few other spots," Dad said, like we were a family who had these kinds of conversations. I had to admit I liked it.

"Wish I could join you," Mum said, shame in her eyes. She'd made the choice to run away and become a vampire. I wondered if she regretted it as much as I did.

"Will your handsome boy be coming?" Dad asked me.

"No," I lied way too easily. "He's wiped out from doing most of the driving, and he has studying to do. He's training to be a nurse." That wasn't too far from the truth. Jared was hoping to pick up his training at night school one day.

"Very admirable," Dad said, skewering the last bite of his burrito and chewing slowly as if he was pondering something.

“I’ll stay back here too,” Della said. “Y’all should spend some time together.”

Libby looked wounded, even though we’d discussed this. I was torn about whether I actually wanted quality Dad time, but that was the idea in principle.

“It’s quiet this morning. Where is everyone?” I asked, cutting up the last of my burrito.

“Some of us are on the way to a basketball game,” Dad said. “I thought y’all might prefer Roswell.”

The look on Libby’s face suggested she’d prefer neither, but she found some enthusiasm for Dad. “Shall we go?”

Chapter 8

I ended up sitting between Libby and Dad on the cracked leather bench seat in the front of his truck, closer than I'd been to Dad for ten years. We'd had good times when I was younger. He'd encouraged my love of reading and writing, buying as many notepads and books as I wanted. But there'd been so much absence since then, and at the time it'd never quite felt like he was there.

The desert stretched out on either side of us as Dad drove. It was wild and oddly dazzling during the day with the late fall sun blazing down.

"Listen . . . I know this is awkward as hell, but I'm gonna come out and say it." He kept his eyes on the road, his hands sliding up and down the steering wheel. "You always gave me a lot of slack, Libby, but I reckon you were right to hold a grudge, Mina." He glanced sideways at me. "I shouldn't have left you girls. My dad got sick, and I felt like it was more important for me to be here. Then when he passed, I got pulled into headin' up the Community . . . I should've come back to you girls, but I did what your mom and I always do, putting our needs and interests first. I'm real sorry for that. I know y'all won't always agree with what I do, but I hope you understand. I really believe humans have a right to know the things I'm researching – for the greater good."

The apology washed over me, but I latched on to the last thing he'd said. I was sure he'd not mentioned it before – that he wanted to tell the world about his research. Why did he get to decide what was best for everyone?

For now, I held back my misgivings and focused on his apology. "I appreciate that, and I'll try to keep an open mind. So, where are you taking us again?"

"Why, the UFO museum of course." He gave me one of his dimpled grins, and I felt an irresistible pull to smile back.

The museum was a blocky white building with bright signs promising what we'd get inside, and we weren't disappointed. It was one of those entertaining, cheesy places that Libby and I both enjoyed. We walked through the darkness of an alien crash site, dry ice billowing around us. Libby moved closer to me as an alien wailed inside a shiny disc. Red lights flickered to represent a fire. The flames reflected in Dad's eyes, highlighting the odd expression on his face. He was much too into it for the circumstances, like we were in a place that deserved reverence. He flinched in annoyance every time Libby squealed or giggled, showing the side of him she never noticed.

The next room was a bright, bland laboratory, and the scene made me queasy. An alien with greyish skin and an elongated skull was strapped down on a gurney, a wax model of a doctor hovering over him. The doctor's face was lifelike but the angles were off, creating a distorted, sly quality. There was only one monster in the scene, and it wasn't wearing restraints.

"To think of all this playing out in Area 51, and the world has determined it a hoax. Disproving that is what your grandpa was working towards, what I'm hoping to do. As far as the public is concerned, alien stories are dead in the water, but with something else..."

Dad's green eyes were bright, and his tone was almost feverish with excitement. I wasn't sure he remembered we were there until his gaze pinned me in place. "Imagine if I broke a story like that."

"You said in the car that people have a right to know. Is that your plan – to go public?"

Dad froze, giving me nervous side-eyes. I wasn't sure he'd meant to tell us that. "Yes... I don't like to throw around the term lightly, but it's truly a matter of life and death. I trust you girls, of course I do. But this one might be a tough pill to swallow."

"Try us," I said, though I doubted Libby was as invested in the conversation. She'd drifted towards the exit and seemed to be trying not to look at the disturbing experiment scene.

"Some witnesses of the Roswell crash that my dad consulted had seen visions in dreams or even claimed to have been abducted and overheard aliens talkin' in their own language. I gotta admit, some of that sounded far-fetched to me at first. But how did countless people independently come up with the same stories? And they kept showing up here or more recently reaching out online – it became impossible to ignore." Desperation coloured Dad's words, and it was obvious how much he wanted me to be on board.

"What did they say?" I asked, doing my best to put aside all judgement. It mattered more that Dad believed in this than what I thought.

"Some of these accounts were years apart, but they all came down to one point in time. They said that some time around the summer of 1997 – fifty years after the Roswell crash – the paranormal beings created on Earth by aliens would use their abilities to rise up against humans. They didn't say what it'd look like or exactly when it would take place, but the terms 'end of days' and 'Armageddon' generally came up. Could be one creature in particular or the whole lot of them, but that's not the point. I believe humans deserve to know first that these creatures exist and second that this may be coming, so they can be prepared. These beings need to be registered and laws put in place to hold them to account. And as for the general public . . . People generally don't find information like this easy to grasp, so it needs to be communicated right."

"That's . . . a lot." It sounded like a *Terminator* movie plot, or one of Jared's cult stories. Werewolves, vampires and other creatures blending in and living their lives was easier to digest than aliens coming to Earth to make new cryptids . . . creatures Dad thought were going to end the world within the next two years. "How would that even happen?"

"I don't know, but I believe the aliens that crash-landed at Roswell were trying to warn us that the creatures they created could turn on us. And humans deserve to know."

"I'm not sure that's for us to decide," I said slowly, working out my stance. "Do you get to tell everyone what Mum is and people like her who are trying to live their lives?"

"I'd never do *anything* to hurt your mom. Whatever else comes to pass, I swear I'll keep her safe."

I could tell from the fervour in his eyes that he meant it. "But have you asked her if she wants this?"

"That's a bigger conversation than the time we have, honey,"

Dad said. I took that as a no. "I'd never let your mom get hurt, but this is the end of days we're talkin' about. Sometimes . . ." He grasped around for words – a rarity. "Sometimes sacrifices have to be made, ones we might not accept at the time. Anyway, we should get goin' – other people might be comin' through the museum."

"Seconded," Libby said, pushing open the door. "Ooh – the shop."

I stewed on what Dad had told us while we examined mugs with silly slogans, stretchy toy aliens in slime and even pool inflatables. The living conditions on Dad's ranch were troubling enough, but if Dad was planning to take his research public one day, that would affect everyone in communities that weren't quite human – including some of the people nearest and dearest to me.

"Are you done, girls?" Dad was smiling and at ease again. "Anyone want an alien magnet?"

"I think we'll live without one," Libby said. "So, what next?"

We grabbed really good food at a cheap diner. Everything had names like 'Out-of-this-world burger' and 'We-come-in-peace fries'. The ceiling was black with silver stars, and neon images of aliens were painted on the walls.

Afterwards, we wandered round town. Even though it was November, the sun was bearing down as we window-shopped in lots of places with an alien theme.

Libby and I both lingered outside a creamery selling a range of brightly coloured flavours. "I could eat a scoop or three," Libby said.

"Sorry girls, but we need to get back. I've arranged horseback riding for this afternoon." The three of us had always loved it, so I wasn't sure why Dad looked so on edge. Had the time with us been such an inconvenience?

"Awesome!" Libby said. "I haven't been since we were kids."

"You should bring your lovely partners," Dad said, recovering his charm.

"Jared's not a fan, but we can ask Della," I said quickly. If this visit had been any longer, I wouldn't have been able to handle the constant excuses. "I'm looking forward to it."

The last part was true, though hopefully for a different reason than Dad would suspect. It was becoming clear that I wanted Dad in my life. But one afternoon together didn't make us square for the missing years. I still had plenty of questions for him, and it was time to get some answers.

Chapter 9

Dad was quiet on the journey, fending off Libby's attempts to make conversation. I'd thought the outing went pretty well, Dad's wild ideas notwithstanding.

We extended his invitation to go horse riding to Della, but she assured us the last place she wanted to be was on the back of a horse. Then she slipped back into the room so we didn't accidentally catch Jared with the sunlight.

Libby and I headed over to the stables and discovered that even though Dad had invited us to go horse riding, he wasn't there. Some things never changed.

Chase was waiting with Ellie, his arm slung around her shoulders. Her wavy reddish blonde hair was pulled back in a ponytail under a cowboy hat, and the two of them were wearing checked shirts, jeans and battered cowboy boots. She was smiling and cheerful against Chase's grumpiness. I was intrigued what had brought them together and how they'd come to be here.

"My girl tells me I owe y'all an apology," Chase said. "I wasn't too friendly when you arrived."

"You gotta understand, we don't get many outsiders round here who've seen the things we have," Ellie said. "We're used to people bein' suspicious of us or making fun, but we should've known y'all would be diff'rent. You're *his* kids, after all."

I nodded, my smile too tight for my face. "It's fine. We get it."

"All righty then," Chase said, visibly relaxing. "Y'all been around horses much?"

"When we were younger," Libby said. Dad had always liked horses, and for a while he'd taken us to riding school every Sunday morning, back when Whitby was home for all of us. That gave his absence today a special sting, but I'd get over it. Like Libby had said, it'd been a while since we'd ridden. I wouldn't let Dad spoil it. If I was going to wrap my head around what Dad was doing and quiz some of his people, I may as well do it while we were riding.

Five horses were tied up outside the stable in the shade. Three were bays with a reddish brown colour and black manes and tails. The others were more distinctive, a white horse splashed with small black spots and the other a pure, shiny black.

"We missin' someone?" Chase asked.

"Della wanted to stay back at the room," Libby said.

"Not a problem," Ellie chirped up, leading the extra bay back to the stable.

"These two are ours," Chase said as he untied the reins of the remaining bays for him and Ellie. "You got Inky and Midnight here. Both good girls."

He and Ellie mounted their horses while Libby and I got to know ours. She went straight for Inky, which suited me. Midnight's wise, glossy eyes greeted me as I stroked the side of her face. "You do look like a good girl," I said, letting her sniff my hand and moving on to pat her side.

"Midnight here's a bit of a celebrity," Chase said, adjusting the reins on his bay. "You a Brad Pitt fan?"

"Most definitely," I said.

"Midnight was in *Legends of the Fall* last year. The studio let her go, and we adopted her."

"Can't believe you got the celebrity horse," Libby grumbled, clumsily climbing onto Inky's back.

I couldn't wait to tell Will – he was an even bigger Brad Pitt fan than I was. Last time I saw him, he was deciding on the best movies to start Fiona's Brad Pitt education.

When Midnight and I were comfortable with each other, I pulled myself into the saddle.

Chase checked his watch, frowning. His horse circled a couple of times in front of ours. "We should get goin'."

Riding is one of those things you don't forget, and I felt at ease following Chase, with Ellie bringing her horse around behind mine and Libby's.

They took us to a well-used dirt trail with occasional small trees alongside it. Soon, the rhythm of the horse and its warm bulk lulled me into relaxation. The sun felt good on my head, something I'd never been able to enjoy at this time of year before.

Libby pulled ahead, and Ellie brought her horse up alongside mine. "How'd it go in Roswell?"

"It was very . . . illuminating," I said.

"I'm sure your dad told you our thoughts about aliens and other things? It must seem very out there." Ellie's brown eyes were all too astute. "Your dad's take is that you don't have to believe everything he does, but you need to be open-minded."

"I'm trying. And in that spirit, can I ask you something?"

I asked, and Ellie nodded. "What's the significance of the tattoos?"

A cloud passed over Ellie's face, and she rubbed her wrist. "We all get them to show our commitment. Ravens are a symbol of knowledge and insight in many cultures. They're sometimes seen as a bad omen, but not by us. It's not always easy bearing what people think of our group, and we appreciate the duality."

"My dad doesn't have one though," I said. Midnight shifted under me, whinnying. I patted her side, trying not to spread my unease to her.

"That's true," Ellie said. "Everyone in the group is free to choose their own path." Her smile never wavered, but I was struggling with mine. "Is there anythin' else you want to know?"

Since she asked, I plunged into a difficult subject. "How did you end up here?"

"I assume you don't mean on the back of a horse." Her smile was so inviting that I returned it. I'd expected her to slither around the truth like Dad or brush me off like Chase. "Mine is probably one of the wildest stories, so if you've had a hard time so far, you might need to buckle up."

"I'm ready," I said, pulling my reins into one hand to pat Midnight's neck.

"One night, I was doing a college assignment on my bed when a bright light shone through my window. And I mean *bright* – so strong I had to cover my eyes. The next thing I knew I landed in my yard, hard enough to knock the wind out of me." Ellie's eyes were trained on the dusty trail, and she was talking so matter-of-factly that I wasn't sure what to make of the story. "I had no recollection of the time that had passed – it was a big old black hole in my memory. Mom and Dad chalked it up to exam stress, but then the dreams started. That night, I saw myself in a metal room, every surface smooth with no way in or out. In the dream, I screamed and screamed, but no one came. Turned out I was screaming out loud, and I woke my parents. A few weeks passed in the same way, and each time I got glimpses of the ship . . . and other things." Ellie eyed me, looking embarrassed. "A leathery grey hand reaching for me . . . A thick needle sliding into my arm. Some chemical drink that tasted nasty. It soon became clear to me that I'd been abducted."

I was so caught up in Ellie's story that I hadn't noticed Chase letting his horse drop back until it was just in front of mine and Ellie's. "Is this the point where you tell her she's full of it?" he crowed over one shoulder. "I see the look on her face. She's not like us, Ellie. Your parents were the same damn way. They would've had you locked up and done worse things than them aliens did to you."

"And I'm eternally grateful to you for bringing me here, but Mina's not like them," Ellie said.

"So you brought Ellie here?" I called ahead. Chase had turned back to the trail, but he sat up straight in his saddle. "Why did you come?"

"Ain't none of your business," Chase said without looking back. He tapped the sides of his horse with both heels and pulled ahead of Libby.

"Chase was already living here when you met?" I asked.

"Sort of," Ellie said. "It's his story to tell, when he's ready. Back then, people came and went a little more."

"I'm sorry that happened to you," I said. She believed the story, whether or not I did.

Ellie shrugged. "One good thing to come out of it was that I found this place. I still get nightmares, but being on the ranch helps. I go for a walk or visit the horses, and usually get back to sleep."

"I'm glad," I said, seeing Dad's Community from Ellie's perspective. To her, it was a sanctuary rather than a cage. "Can I ask you one more thing?"

"Go ahead," Ellie said.

She'd gone quiet and introspective, so I resolved to leave her alone after this. It was supposed to be a ride – not an interrogation. "Chase mentioned your family. What do they think of you living here?"

"I don't speak to them," Ellie said. "That's a familiar story round here. We made a new family out of people who lift each other up."

For the first time, her smile didn't convince me, but I let it go. "Thank you for being so open."

"Any time."

We continued to ride next to each other, but neither of us spoke. The trail followed a loop around Dad's property. Apart from enjoying the sensation of riding again, I was too busy thinking to pay the surroundings much attention.

After about an hour, Chase and Ellie led us back to the stables. My thighs were aching when I got off the horse. I was out of practice with the riding position. "Thank you so much," I said. I'd missed riding, and the conversation had given me plenty of food for thought.

"You're here a couple more days, right? You can ride with us any time," Ellie said.

Chase's eyes narrowed, and I wasn't sure what it meant. We weren't likely to win him over in the short time we had left.

"Thanks," Libby said sadly, probably reflecting on our time here running out.

We offered to help with the horses, but Ellie shook her head. "You're fine. You go on about your day." She led two of the horses into the stable while the other two grazed on the tangle of weeds.

"See you later," I said.

"The Shepherd asked me to bring you somewhere," Chase said, not quite meeting our eyes.

Ellie came out of the stables for the other two horses. "Where?" She grabbed a set of reins in each hand, but made no move to return the horses.

"Private business for The Shepherd," Chase said coldly.

Ellie ran her tongue over her teeth. Her displeasure was plain, but she didn't voice it. "Fine," she said, her tone crisp as she led the horses into the stable.

"We don't have to go anywhere with you." Libby stood by me with fear etched into her face.

"I think you'll wanna hear what he has to say," Chase replied through a sneer. "It concerns your boyfriend."

That was all the warning I needed. I took off at a run towards our room, skidding on the dry earth. His heavy steps thudded behind me, but I'd trained to run from scarier things than him.

Still running, I grabbed our key from my pocket and jabbed it in the door with the sound of Chase's feet still pounding.

With a sickened feeling, I flung the door open. The room was empty.

Chapter 10

"Where are they?" I asked, my voice so high and frantic that it didn't sound like me.

"Come see your dad. He'll explain everything," Chase said as he caught up to me.

Libby was close behind us, gasping for breath. "What's going on?"

"Jared and Della are gone," I said, locking the door with shaky hands. Jared wouldn't have left the room by choice in broad daylight. If they hadn't taken him under a thick cover, he could be dead already.

"Where are they?" Libby asked.

Ignoring her, Chase checked his watch again. "Come on! We have to get goin'." What timeline were we on?

He strode off and we rushed behind him. Sweat trickled down my back in the heat of the day, but dread had chilled me right through. We peppered him with questions about what had happened to our friends, but he ignored them. He just kept walking, kicking up puffs of dust under his cowboy boots.

At first, Chase led us towards the house. It was too quiet, with no sign of Dad's herds of followers. Some had gone to the basketball game earlier, but where were the rest?

We veered around the building, heading towards a barn behind it. The building looked new – all strong, pale wood and a metal door that Chase rapped his knuckles on three times.

Hayes opened it, guilt passing over his features. "I hope you two will realise this is for the greater good."

There were Dad's words from earlier again. Before I could ask what that was supposed to mean, I heard his voice from inside the barn. "That's enough, Hayes. Come on in, girls."

The door clanged shut behind us and I heard a key turn in the lock. There were no sources of natural light, and the exposed bulbs cast a weak glow over my dad. They made him look shadowy and menacing, the perfect movie villain he always had the potential to be. Doing what Della had taught me, I checked for exits and things I could use. The only way out was the locked door behind me, and there was nothing especially useful: just some old household appliances and furniture. I couldn't threaten my way out with a broken fridge or a saggy sofa.

"Where are Della and Jared?" Libby asked. I was glad she was showing her strength. Being around Dad often made her come over all compliant.

"Della is in a secure location," Dad said. "But she's fine, I can promise you that."

How generous of him. "And Jared?" I asked.

"He's helping us fulfil a very important purpose."

Hayes walked over to the pile of junk behind Dad and wheeled over a TV. He pushed the button on the front and a basketball game came on television.

"I want to see Della," Libby said, "and Mina needs to see Jared. You can't keep us here. Even if . . . It's not right."

"It won't take long, honey," Dad said. "Let me explain. This basketball game is going to be on television screens all over America. That's why we chose it. My people are there to hijack the channel so we can film our own broadcast right here during the commercial break. Hayes, switch to our feed."

Hayes turned over the channel. "From the moment you walk onto the field, we'll start broadcasting live from the repaired TV news van, thanks to our friends at the game tapping in to the signal. You got one minute because by then the Feds will be scrambling to triangulate our location."

The pieces started coming together with horrible clarity. Onscreen, a figure was sitting in one of Dad's sun-scorched fields, a blanket covering their identity . . . or protecting them from the sun's deadly rays. I knew those jeans and scruffy Converse, and the shape of Jared's outline. "You can't do this!" I said to Dad, the plea tearing out of me. My eyes burned, and I was startled by the power of my hatred for him.

"Look, you obviously know what Jared is," Libby said with tears filling up her eyes. "He'll die if you expose him to the sun."

"Your mom let it slip, and I saw an opportunity. I really did want to see you when I asked her to send the invitation to come here, but this is my one shot to set everything in motion. If people know vampires are real, they'll become more open to the rest. Then humanity can prepare. We have two years before hell is meant to break loose on Earth. I'm not going to let that happen."

He pulled a rubber mask over his face, the brown plastic hair settling over his own. He was Fox Mulder, the guy on *The X-Files* who believed the truth was out there.

"You don't get to decide that!" I said, hanging onto his arm in desperation. "Please . . . You can convince people vampires are real without killing him."

Dad's green eyes gave nothing away through the rubber mask as he shook me off and then marched to the door of the barn. I raced after him but he slipped out, letting Chase in as he left.

I bolted for the gap in the door, but Chase stepped in front of me. "Guess what," he said, his grin crooked and unpleasant. "Your dad said to do whatever it takes to keep you in here."

Ignoring him and the sorry figure of Hayes, watching us but not doing anything to help, I raced around the interior of the barn looking for ways out – a gap in the boards or a hole in the dirt floor, a weapon to threaten Chase . . . The wood was solid and the floor was hard-packed dirt – no way out. Jared was out on one of Dad's fields, and I couldn't get to him. My pulse and breathing were coming way too fast, every inhale and exhale counting down the seconds of Jared's life. Everything seemed unreal through my panic. Dad couldn't be doing this.

I went for the door again, and Chase came up in front of me. "Your dad wants you to watch. He thinks when you hear him speak that you'll understand the sacrifice he's making. You'd better get in front of that screen. I don't wanna hurt you, but I will."

We were out of time. Hayes had turned the television back to the basketball game, and the cheerful announcer said they were going to an ad break.

Ronald McDonald's unintentionally creepy face grinned at us. He rippled and distorted, white snow covering the screen. Then it was replaced by a scene from my worst nightmares. We were back to the shrouded figure in the field, but Jared wasn't alone. And this time, it was being beamed out to viewers all over America who were watching the basketball game.

Dad was there, disguised by his mask and clutching a portable microphone. "Apologies for the interruption to your scheduled programming," he said smoothly, so charming even as he was preparing to rip my life apart. "It shouldn't come as any surprise that we've been lied to – by the government, the press and even our loving families. Humans aren't alone on this Earth. The powers that be don't want us to have this information, but I have the proof right here."

He paused to rest a hand on Jared's shoulder. I'd thought Dad's interest in the supernatural was academic – that he was going to lobby for legal changes and present his research to the media. I'd underestimated his fanaticism, and I was about to lose Jared because of my mistake. I'd never felt such depths of despair, like it might kill me too if Jared died.

Dad continued calmly. "This young man is, in reality, a vampire, and you're about to see him burn up and die before your very eyes in the daylight. And if this vampire is real, then I ask you to ponder what else is out there. Are we truly safe? Should we rise up now before we're attacked by these creatures? I'd say more, but I'm sure the network is trying to regain control of its broadcast as we speak."

He laid a hand on the blanket, grabbing a bunch of fabric from behind Jared's head. "Here he is, folks. Your first look at a vampire. I'm sure more will follow."

He yanked at the blanket, and I screamed so hard it seared my throat. Jared's eye was swollen shut and he looked out of it, like he'd taken a beating. This couldn't be the last time I was going to see him.

Pure terror ravaged his features as he stared up at the last sky he'd ever see.

Chapter 11

Jared's eyes were squeezed shut and his teeth were clenched, pain ripping through his body. Grief burned in my chest, my mind creating images of his skin blistering before my eyes. I couldn't lose Jared, especially not like this.

Dad stalked around Jared, his pace becoming more frantic as time stretched on. Nothing was happening. Jared's skin should've been smoking and charring in the sun, but it remained smooth and bronze.

Dad's arm went slack, the microphone still in his hand. "That's impossible," he said, his voice barely audible. Something must have hit the camera because it lurched forwards, filming an expanse of brown earth and dry grass before a shadow passed over it.

Then interference rippled over the field, before it disappeared completely in a white haze of static. The feed cut to two puzzled commentators. "Well, I don't know what to say about that," a chirpy blonde woman said, her teeth bright as she forced a smile.

Her co-presenter was a tall, handsome man with warm brown skin. "I'm assuming it was some kind of commercial, but I can't for the life of me tell you what the product was – sunscreen maybe? Let's get back to the game . . ."

Tears coursed down my face, and Chase kicked the bottom of the TV stand as the presenters chattered on. "Dammit! We were so sure he was a vampire." A sneer twisted his mouth, and he got right up to my face. "Did y'all set us up?"

"Step back from the girl," Hayes said, ambling towards us with a dangerous look of calm. He towered over Chase, finally on our side. Chase glowered as Hayes continued. "The boy is certainly a vampire, but for some reason we failed anyway. And we undermined any credibility we might have had."

To add to their problems, Taz's black Jeep crashed through the barn wall. Hayes and Chase both leaped back, but the vehicle was nowhere near us. Cafferty, my friend and mentor, was driving. He knew what he was doing, even though being in the police probably hadn't prepared him for this exact situation. He was pointing a gun through his open window, his blonde hair mussed and angular jaw set in a stern expression. "Get in," he yelled, though Libby and I were already piling into the back. As we settled, he pointed the gun back and forth between Hayes and Chase. "Whoever's got a gate clicker needs to hand it over."

Della was in the front, and Jared was in the back with Armand, Della's vampire boss, the tinted windows providing protection from the daylight. It was a tight squeeze with me, Libby and the two of them. Being careful not to hurt Jared more, I checked him over with frantic hands. He was unconscious, with a pale cast to his bronze skin. The bruises around his eyes and cheekbones weren't healing as vampires normally did, but he was still with us.

"He'll live," Armand said. Still worried for Jared, I tore my attention away. Armand gave me a weak smile, his light brown skin not looking its healthiest with the sunlight glaring outside and his normally bright blue eyes missing their sparkle.

Cafferty slammed the Jeep into four-wheel drive and floored the accelerator, the wheels spinning before we reversed out of the barn.

Dad was jogging over as the Jeep shot onto the gravelled road that cut through the ranch. Too angry, I didn't watch him disappear from view.

Jared's eyelids flickered before opening to narrow cracks. "Hey," I said, running a hand through his hair. His lips curved in a faint smile, and tears blurred my vision. "Are you OK?"

"I'll be fine . . . I think." I had no idea how, but I was endlessly grateful.

We were barrelling down the ranch's gravel drive when another problem dawned on me. "The crocodile teeth! How are we going to get past them?"

Cafferty pulled to a sharp halt in front of the gate and leaped out of the Jeep, slamming the door shut before he ran over to the weeds by the gate. "We threw it over," Armand explained as Cafferty dragged a long wooden plank over the teeth. "We cased the place beforehand and climbed over at the lowest point."

"How did you know about it?" Della asked.

"Story time later. Let's get out of here first," Armand said.

"Wait – what about Mum?" Libby said. "We can't leave her with Dad."

"I tried," Della said. "She wouldn't come. Your dad didn't let her in on his plan, but she's sure he won't hurt her. What else can we do?"

"Not much. She made her choice," I said, hanging on to Jared's hand to reassure myself that he was there. "I don't think Dad would hurt her – that's why he needed Jared."

Anger towards Dad flared up again, burning hot as Cafferty clicked the remote control and the gate eased open. He tossed the remote and jumped back in the car. Checking the rear window confirmed there was still no one chasing us. That had to be on Dad's orders, though I couldn't imagine why he'd let us go. I was too furious at him to think straight.

Cafferty's black Chevy Impala was parked by the road, looking filthy and lived in compared to the pristine condition I'd last seen it in. "We need to put some distance between us and this place," Cafferty said. "You wanna follow me and we'll regroup at a motel after nightfall?"

"Sure," Della said, sliding over to the driver's seat when he got out.

"I'll take the next shift at the wheel," Libby said, climbing between the front seats to sit beside Della.

Cafferty jogged over to his car as Jared, Armand and I spread out across the back, fastening our seatbelts. Jared sat in the middle, with one long leg in each of the two rear footwells. He leaned against me, and I was happy to prop him up.

Della pulled the Jeep out behind Cafferty's car. Armand pinched the bridge of his nose. "I suppose you want to know how we found you. As soon as you arrived at the ranch, I started getting flashes of it." Armand often had visions of different points in time. He couldn't control when they came or tell if he was seeing the past, present or future, but the visions tended to be clearer when involving someone he knew. "It all seemed innocent at first, until I saw your father setting his plan into motion. I'm relieved we were close enough to reach Jared in time." We were lucky that he and Cafferty were in the area on a reluctant mission for Saint Germain, self-proclaimed vampire king of New Orleans.

"Me too." Jared rubbed his face, looking utterly drained. "Shouldn't I be dead? Or, you know, burned to a crisp?"

"It appears Mr Shepherd selected the wrong vampire to prove his point," Armand said. "In your position, I'd be dying from extensive burns at best and most likely dead. I'm curious how you feel."

"Exhausted . . . like when I heal people. Wait – did I heal myself? Is that why I didn't die when Libby staked me over summer?"

Libby let out a loud sigh. "I thought you'd let that go – John Carter was mind controlling me!"

"Yes, he should be more understanding about *almost dying*," Armand said drily. "It appears that as well as healing others, you can heal yourself at an incredible rate, including after sun damage. Like the arrival of your healing power when you were saving Libby's life, the stress of your dilemma may have brought out this new dimension. But no, you couldn't heal a heart destroyed by a stake. Libby simply has a bad aim."

"Hey," she grumbled. "You should be thanking me."

Ignoring her, Jared said, "That's . . . wild." He eyed the back of his hand as if expecting to see the burned skin Armand had described.

I took the hand in mine, reeling at what this might mean. There were more important short-term matters. "Do you need blood?"

Jared nodded, pulling the blanket tighter around his shoulders. "Yeah, my injuries aren't healing . . . but you only fed me last night. Are you sure?"

"It won't hurt for this once."

That ended up being very badly wrong.

Chapter 12

Jared's lips flared back, exposing fangs as they slid down over his teeth. I'd only seen the skin around his eyes inflamed that badly right before he'd first bitten me, overcome by blood lust on the day he was turned. This time he was more in control, but barely. His teeth and fangs tore into my arm, his mouth latching on and dragging out my blood in an incessant pull and release. Cold rolled through my body, and the pain was almost too intense. I was about to step in when Armand did. "Jared. That's *enough*."

I wasn't used to him showing authority over us, but it worked. Jared carefully released my arm, the feeling of his teeth pulling through my flesh making me shudder. "God, I'm so sorry. I got carried away there." He leaned his forehead against mine.

"Don't worry. You had a good reason." His eyes were warm, and his colour already looked much better. He placed a hand over my wound, and I felt heat and the itching sensation of flesh knitting together. It sent my skin crawling, but I stayed still until he was done. Then I was left with more puckered scar tissue.

Libby passed a bottle of water back to me and I took a long drink. It was warm from being left in the car, but it helped. Feeling clearer headed, I checked the road behind us. Still empty. If this was Dad's attempt at an olive branch, it wasn't nearly enough. He'd almost killed Jared. While I sipped the water, Libby flicked between radio stations. Country music and people talking about religion blurred together, until Libby settled on a rock station playing 'Life is a Highway'.

Soon, Armand closed his eyes. He'd usually be asleep during the day instead of trapped in a car. Jared drifted off too, leaning his head against mine. I looked out of the window at the wild landscape, thinking about the monsters we were leaving behind and the ones we were heading towards back in New Orleans.

We followed Cafferty's car for hours, occasionally encountering other traffic but none that seemed to be following us. My anger towards Dad stayed as fierce as ever, but the fear of pursuit started to fade. Still, we only stopped once for petrol, then later for decent burgers and fantastic milkshakes from a Sonic drive-in. None of us spoke much. If the others were anything like me, we were all weighed down by what Dad had done. He was willing to sacrifice someone I loved to reveal vampires, a secret that wasn't his own to share. One point in Mum's favour was that she hadn't known, but that probably came down to her not being truly interested in anyone else's life, including Dad's.

A couple of hours after night fell, Cafferty pulled off at a rundown motel that looked very Norman Bates, but I wasn't too worried, knowing we had vampires, slayers and a vampire-slaying cop in our party.

"Well, I've slept for hours and still feel like I've been run over," Jared said after we got out, stretching his neck from side to side.

"Sorry to hear that," Cafferty said. "But we've put enough distance between us and the ranch now. I doubt anyone is comin' after us. Shall we crash for a few hours, then drive the next six hours or so at night?"

"You're spending too much time with vampires," Armand said. "If you're not careful, your days and nights will flip."

"No way," Cafferty said. "I couldn't give up the sun. Night, y'all."

We all went our separate ways, taking two rooms that each had two double beds.

After a few hours of fitful sleep, we were ready to go. The vampires took the night shift at driving. Armand drove Cafferty's car and Jared drove the Jeep. I took the front seat next to him, turning around regularly to chat.

"I always get that feeling after a holiday of wanting to be home," Libby said, "but this time I really, really want to be home. I still can't believe what Dad did. I want to think there's a good explanation, but . . ."

Libby usually kept her problems locked down tight. Dad must have hurt her badly to crack them wide open. "He and Mum have set my expectations low, but he's hit rock bottom this time," I said.

"I'm sorry you never had anybody growing up," Della said. "My mom died too young, but at least she was there for me when she was alive."

"It wasn't too bad," Libby said. "We had each other."

Lately, Jared always stayed quiet when the conversation turned to family. He'd barely mentioned his parents and sisters since John Carter forced him to become a vampire this summer. He'd kidnapped Jared to turn him as part of a cruel plan to replicate New Orleans myths.

We swapped drivers a few times and took plenty of breaks over the night and the following morning, so Libby was driving the Jeep with Della in the passenger seat as we approached New Orleans.

Cafferty was back behind his own wheel, with me in the front and the vampires in the back. He was tapping his hands irritably on the steering wheel. "Don't get me wrong, I'm happy to be home, but I'm not looking forward to reporting back to Saint Germain. He sent us to New Mexico to track down a group that matches the description of your dad's."

That had crossed my mind since we left the ranch, but it hit home now. "He's looking for our dad?" I asked. Dad had done something unforgiveable to Jared, but he and all of his dubious Community didn't deserve to be slaughtered by one of the most powerful and ruthless vampires we knew. The last time we crossed Saint Germain, he killed Rosario, the leader of the slayers, before forcing Armand and Cafferty to work for him under threat of death to the rest of us.

"He's heard whisperings of a group fixated on revealing supernatural entities, but he doesn't know your dad is the one he seeks," Armand said. "We'll tell him we didn't find them. If he found the location of the ranch . . . It doesn't bear thinking about what he'd do to the people there. He'll be displeased with us, but that's nothing new."

"Is anyone else concerned that Saint Germain might be a basketball fan?" Cafferty asked.

"I don't really care what he . . ." Jared began. "Oh, shit."

Saint Germain was also known for having vampires with

powers in his group of minions, in the absence of his own ability. "I think it's safe to say he'll find out," I said glumly.

"No way I'm following him around like his new puppy," Jared said. I reached a hand back between the seats to touch his knee. After nearly losing Jared, I needed to keep hold of him.

"You may not have a choice," Armand said. "The alternative would be far more unpleasant."

Jared scowled. "Just when I thought I might get my life back. Do you think . . . Does this mean I can go out in the day?"

"I wouldn't go rushing out into the daylight," Armand said. "You'll likely need to build up your tolerance, if you can withstand prolonged exposure at all. In my experience, vampire's abilities take time to mature. Look at yours – they started as healing others and developed in this new and potentially very useful direction."

"I'll take that," Jared said. "Just not the Saint Germain part."

"We'll figure it out," Cafferty said. "Shame y'all can't set the slayers on him. They're still in his pocket."

"He's a vampire – I wish he'd leave the slayers alone," I said. "No offence to present company. You're nice vampires."

"None taken. He wants control of the whole city, not just the slayers," Armand said. "Cafferty and I are already doing his bidding. He's controlling the slayers so they'll leave his friends alone to do what they will. One saving grace is that they're old and extremely careful, so they pose little danger of exposing us. That means if they go too far, their victims simply disappear."

"Thanks for that image," I said, turning to look out of the window. While we'd been angsting over Saint Germain, we'd arrived in New Orleans.

I loved where we'd grown up in Whitby, with the crisp coastal air and skeletal abbey perched on the cliff top, but there was something about this place. The French Quarter always felt so alive, packed with tourists and locals having a good time. With November well underway, Halloween decorations had given way to fall. Piles of squashes and sheaves of dried corn decorated shop windows, with autumn-leaf garlands threaded along balconies. One apartment had a huge vase of sunflowers in the window. We passed Crescent Screens, the cinema where we saw *Mallrats* not long ago. *GoldenEye, Ace Ventura: When Nature Calls* and *Toy Story* were playing now. We'd probably see all of them soon.

Slowly, I started coming out of the hole I'd sunk into over the journey. We were home.

Chapter 13

Even though Armand looked exhausted, he insisted that we drop him at his bar, Empire of the Dead. Cafferty pulled up close to the door and Armand scurried inside with a heavy blanket over him.

Cafferty parked behind Della outside the mansion, but I'd already guessed he wouldn't stay. "I'm going into the station to smooth some ruffled feathers. Assuming I still have a job, that is. I said I had a family emergency, but I don't know if they bought it. Call me if you need anything."

"We will," I said. I felt bad for Cafferty. The police wouldn't be happy with him for leaving, and he'd also have to convince Saint Germain he'd not found anything.

The mansion would be closed for a few more days while contractors worked in the new *Lost Boys* room, and Della had booked time off work to visit our parents. No one expected us back in New Orleans yet, so the rest of the afternoon and evening were ours.

We piled into the living room upstairs that I still thought of as Thandie's, our former boss who'd left the house to Libby when she died. The neutral colours and many curios Thandie had collected over the years were instantly reassuring. "What can we watch that has zero violence and horror? Oh, and definitely no cults." Libby crawled over to the stack of videos, running her finger down it.

"*Back to the Future*?" Jared suggested, slouching down on the sofa. He'd got a lot of sleep over the journey, but he still looked drained. Using his power to heal others had always taken it out of him, and uncovering this new branch to his ability seemed to have hit him harder.

"Perfect!" Libby said, yanking it out of the stack. The other videos wobbled but stayed put.

"I'll get snacks," Della said.

"I'll come with." Jared stood up to help with the food, even though he wouldn't be able to eat it.

The answerphone was blinking red. It was so convenient having an extra phone up here, and not just because I'd almost been murdered when I went downstairs to answer it over Halloween.

Dad's voice was a punch to the stomach, knocking the air out of me. "Hi, girls. I'm so sorry. I don't know who might hear this so I'll speak carefully. I made a mistake – I misread the signs. I hope with how things turned out that you can forgive me." His pause allowed my rage to gather steam again. How could he expect forgiveness?

He went on, laying the regret on thick. "My thinking is that revealing a thing lessens its power – everyone has a right to know and be on their guard. It was too important an opportunity . . . We could've told the whole world the truth. One good thing to come from this is that I have a new plan, and I'm coming to you – to New Orleans, I mean. We're planning to drive without stopping, so we might even beat you there. I'm gonna stay with that friend I didn't always see eye to eye with from the picture I showed you.

"Listen . . . I only just got you back in my life. I'm sure y'all will need time after what I did, so I won't reach out right away. I really . . . I hope that when I do, we can move past this."

I'd been so caught up in Dad's speech that I wasn't aware of Libby appearing beside me. Did he really think one voicemail message could erase everything he'd done?

"He's really done it this time, hasn't he?" she said quietly.

"Yeah, he's put the last nail in the coffin and buried it six feet under." I'd had some good moments with Dad, even contemplating what a life with him in it would look like. And his actions had made that impossible.

Panic wormed in around the hurt as what he'd said sank in. "He's coming here . . . right into Saint Germain's clutches, and he has no idea."

Libby hugged herself. "Knowing Dad, he might be thrilled about that."

"Sure, until he gets himself and all of his cult killed."

"What's this about cults?" Jared appeared in the living room doorway with a bowl of crisps.

"Dad left a voicemail – he's coming to the city, but he's going to steer clear of us." Libby had the slightest sulk to her tone, like she wanted to see him.

"Good," Jared said, his voice hard as he set the crisps down. He sank onto the sofa, slouching right down.

I wasn't usually one for avoiding difficult subjects, but I was so tired of stressing about Dad. If he wanted to come into the lions' den and not bother to see us, then we could hardly warn him. "I just need to call Will, then we can put the movie on."

"I'll see how Della's getting on," Libby said, bouncing out of the room like the latest Dad revelation hadn't affected her too much. Denial had its perks.

While the phone rang, I spared a thought for Mum. Was she coming to New Orleans with Dad? How did she feel about his latest escapades?

Will answered before I could obsess any longer. "Hello?" He sounded terrible, which was hardly surprising after what he'd been through.

"Hey, I wanted to let you know we're back."

There was a crackling sound like he was swapping the receiver to the other side. "Did I mix up the dates?"

"We came back early – long story. Do you want to come round? We're watching a movie."

"Sure . . . I have somewhere to be right now, but I'll catch up with you later."

I felt better once I put the phone down. By the end of the call, Will had seemed like himself.

Della and Libby surfaced with an impressive selection of cookies, Twinkies and Dunkaroos to go with the crisps. Jared eyed the spread, but he'd assured me he was getting used to not being able to sample it.

Libby pressed play, and we settled down on the huge sofa to watch the camera panning across Doc Brown's clocks and inventions. Cue Marty pushing Doc's sound system to the max with his electric guitar, a mysterious phone call and one of the best opening songs of any movie: 'The Power of Love' by Huey Lewis.

"Jennifer Parker," Libby said dreamily. "Played by two different actresses – both amazing."

"I don't think you can beat Elizabeth Shue: *Cocktail*, *Karate Kid*,

Adventures in Babysitting..." Jared served up the trivia without his usual enthusiasm, one hand pressed against his temple.

Della got in there first to check on him. "You need more blood?"

"I'm good for now . . . thanks," he said. I was glad the two of them had got over their animosity. Knowing the four of us were rock solid made it easier to cope with everything else.

As we worked through the snacks and let the movie unfold, I started to relax. Dad wanted to keep his drama away from us, so we should let him get on with it. Jared relaxed against me as the room darkened, the sky slowly turning black behind the curtains.

The movie was wrapping up when there was a knock at the door. I was tempted to leave whoever it was out there until I remembered. "It's probably Will. I'll go."

Libby jumped up and paused the movie. "We'll wait for you."

I'd seen it enough times that I could've filled in the gaps, but I was happy not to miss anything as I jogged downstairs. The new grey carpet showed no trace of what had happened to Will's half-brother, Sam, but I'd never forget what I'd done to him here. I'd had no choice, with Libby dying at the top of the stairs and Sam on his way down for me with the bloody knife in his hand. The bear trap chandelier had taken him down for good, but I was the one with the mallet who broke the chain.

Some of the guilt dissipated when I opened the door to see Will. He grinned at me, his Christian Slater hair flopping over one eye and the collar quirked on his long, black leather jacket. It was unfastened, revealing a *Lost Boys* T-shirt with David's fanged mouth open and snarling. He was excited to see the new room that we were working on with that same theme.

I crushed him in a tight hug, feeling a fresh swell of sorrow for his loss. John Carter had murdered his older sister in the summer, I'd killed his half-brother at Halloween and his remaining sister was in jail for killing one of our friends. He'd suffered so much and was still smiling. "How are you?"

"Don't give me that look," he warned. "I'm fine. Better than fine, in fact. Got room for one more at movie night?"

"Sure, come in," I said, and we hurried up the stairs together. I glanced back at him. His face was relaxed, but he couldn't be coming up here without thinking of his brother who died on this spot. "You'll never guess what I did – I rode a horse that was in *Legends of the Fall*."

"Huh," Will said. "Not the best Brad Pitt movie, but impressive nonetheless."

Will followed me into the apartment and Jared sprang to his feet, suddenly looking wide awake.

"Hey, everyone," Will said, sinking down into the armchair. "How was your trip?"

"That's not important right now," Jared said. "Are you going to tell them, or am I?"

Will gestured for Jared to go on, tipping his head forwards. "You do the honours."

Jared scowled. "Based on Will's missing heartbeat, I'd say he's a vampire."

Chapter 14

The shock hit me like whiplash. How had I not known? Some slayer I was shaping up to be. Della was the first one to speak. "I'm so sorry! How did it happen?"

Will raised one expressive eyebrow. "Wait . . . you're serious? This is the greatest thing that ever happened to me!"

I dropped onto the sofa next to Libby and Della, too shaken to speak.

Jared stood in front of Will, arms folded. "Who did it?"

"Who do you think?" Will asked, frowning slightly as he looked between our faces. "Fine, it was Fiona – but only because I asked her to. She and I are the real deal, and she did this awesome thing for me. Why are you guys looking at me like somebody died?"

"Because *you* did!" I said. "Why did you do it?"

Will was still grinning, but defensiveness had stolen his warmth. "The usual reasons. I get to look like this forever, never get old or sick or . . . you know."

Die like most of the other people around him. We shouldn't have left him alone. I'd tried to convince him to come, but he'd wanted to stay at home with his stepmum. "What about film school and your job at the mall?"

"There's always night school," Will said. "And there'll be other jobs. Don't give me the pity face. I feel better than ever. I'll admit, the pain after she turned me sucked . . . and now I do." He gave us a fanged grin.

"OK, Fiona turned you," Della said calmly. "Did she fill you in on the rules vampires must abide by if they want to experience those long lives?"

"She said a few things," Will said, a defensive sneer quirking his top lip.

Libby tucked her feet under her. "Looks like someone didn't read the small print."

"Do you want to take this one, Jared?" I asked, barely keeping a lid on my frustration. Could Will really be this naïve? "You have first-hand experience."

Jared gestured at me and Della. "I think he needs the slayer perspective first."

"How are you making something so cool sound like such a drag?" Will asked.

"To stop you from gettin' yourself killed," Della shot back. "That a good enough reason? Your pal Mina and I are slayers. Know what that means?"

"I've watched that *Buffy* movie and every version of *Dracula*. Movie student, remember?" Will said sullenly. "What do slayers have to do with anything?"

"Slayers follow a code," I said, wondering if he'd take this more seriously if it came from me. We'd connected from the moment we met, but right now I hardly understood him at all. "If a vampire attacks a human without consent, we put them down."

Will ran his tongue along his teeth. "And you'd do that to me if I broke your little rules?"

"In a heartbeat," Della said, so I wouldn't have to.

"Awesome," Will said flatly. "Good talk."

"We're not done," Jared said, moving towards the door and gesturing for Will to follow. "I need to hit the blood bar anyhow."

Will eased onto his feet with a sigh. "Why do I get the feeling that's going to be less fun than it sounds?"

"We won't be long," Jared said.

"Good luck!" I shot back. Will groaned as he closed the door behind them.

"Will should be grateful to have Jared," Della said.

"He's the responsible vampire dad everyone needs," Libby said, snuggling down lower on the sofa.

"Let's hope he scares Will into conforming," I said. Most of the vampires in our lives toed the line, getting their blood from consenting, carefully screened adults at a blood bar instead of stalking strangers. Saint Germain had set up three new blood bars after Sam burned the last one to the ground. I hated Saint Germain having more power, but it would've been worse if hungry vampires had nowhere to go.

The vampires from the past who hadn't learned how to live alongside humans, namely Armand's brother and Veronica, had found out the hard way not to cross Della and the slayers. "I wonder if Will is ever going to regret his decision."

"I don't know," Della replied, "but he'll have to live with it."

Since she and Libby looked so comfortable, I went to press play and we settled in to watch the rest of *Back to the Future.* My eyes were heavy and I was struggling to stop cycling through the events of the past few days, but slowly the movie quietened my thoughts. I made it to the closing credits before admitting defeat. "If I don't move soon, I'm going to fall asleep."

"Night," Libby said, burrowing down into the sofa. "That doesn't sound like a bad idea."

"Come on – we should move too," Della said, standing and offering Libby a hand. "Night," she said to me. Della technically still had a room at her dad's house, but she stayed over here more often than not.

I got ready slowly, trying to digest the past couple of days. Our dad had failed us on an epic scale, which wasn't exactly breaking news. And Jared had found out that he might get some semblance of his life in the day back . . . right before Will gave his up.

Despite the many things going wrong, it felt good to crawl into clean bedding.

I jolted awake, pyjamas clinging to me along with the knowledge that someone was in the mansion with us. I'd been doing this since Halloween, and I hadn't been right yet. But there was always a first time. I grabbed the stake from by my bed and shoved it down the waistband of my pyjamas. All I needed to do was check the hallway, and then I could sleep.

We always kept a lamp on in the living room, so my eyes were dazzled. I took the chance to listen out while they adjusted. Nothing. So far, so good.

The hallway was darker, descending to eerie blackness downstairs. "Jared?"

A creaking step was the only answer. Jared would call out, so who or whatever I was dealing with wasn't him. They likely had no idea where I was exactly, so I had the upper hand. The terror came with a rush of memories about Sam chasing me through the mansion with a knife in his hand. I stood out of sight at the top of the stairs, listening. Was that another footstep? I left the stake down my waistband. Since a vampire would have to be invited in, this was probably a human. A hard shove down the stairs was my best option.

I wanted so badly to look down the stairs, but I couldn't risk showing myself. I inched up to the corner. The top step was also a creaker, so that would be my cue to move. I held my hand over my mouth, breathing quietly against it like all the girls in horror movies.

The stair creaked and I flung myself around the corner, hands raised to push. Thank goodness training with the slayers had improved my reflexes, because I came face to face with Jared. "Woah!" he said, stepping out of pushing reach. He pulled his headphones down so they rested around his neck.

"God, I'm so sorry!" I whispered.

"Two near-death experiences in two days," he said, smiling tiredly. "Not sure falling down the stairs would've killed me, but I'd rather not test it out."

I wrapped my arms around him, pressing my cheek against his chest. My heart hammered against him, beating for both of us.

Pulling back to look at him, the faint light from the living room illuminated the strong planes of the face I knew so well. "What's up?" He knew me inside out too.

I couldn't explain without falling apart, so I kissed him. We'd always had plenty of heat, but after almost losing him, I couldn't get close enough. Our bodies had no space between them, hands searching as they roamed the soft skin of lower backs and hips under our T-shirts. That was the furthest we'd gone so far, and it wasn't enough. I wanted more of him, kissing deeper and pulling him closer.

Jared's mouth travelled down to my throat, the brush of his lips giving way to the tantalising scratch of fangs. He went no further than that, the point we'd agreed on, but it sent shivers of longing through me. He planted a last kiss on my neck, then cupped my face in both hands to look at me. "As much as I'd like to keep doing this, I'm dead on my feet. Well, more dead than usual."

"Not surprising after the week we've had," I said, the ghost of longing still coiled low in my stomach.

Jared smiled, dropping his hands from my face. "Is it bad that after the whole shit-fest I'm kind of . . . happy? The stuff with your dad, Will turning . . . I know those things are terrible, but if I can go out in the day . . ."

"It's a big deal. You can heal yourself – that's pretty cool in itself. But this would change everything."

"I hope Armand's right that the ability will only get stronger. It's felt like my life has been on hold – ironic considering I might have a long one ahead of me. But this feels like a chance to get back on track. Maybe go back to nursing school, go walking in cemeteries together like when you first came . . . We just need to keep it from Saint Germain."

"There's always a catch. But I don't want to talk about him. One more for the road?"

Jared grinned. "Think I can manage that."

We kissed until I was too sleepy to stand up. "I give in. Now we really have to go to bed."

I watched Jared walk up the stairs to his converted attic bedroom. At first, I hadn't been sure how he could move up to the room where John Carter had dumped Heather's body this summer. I'd never met her when she was alive, but I'd found her afterwards. We'd seen so much death, some of it in this house, but because of the people around me it felt like home.

As I climbed into bed alone, I thought about the night at the ranch and the few hours we'd slept in the same bed in the hotel. Both of those times had been due to necessity, and at the motel we'd been exhausted, but it was a start. When he'd first turned, he couldn't even be close to me without craving my blood, but slowly his tolerance was building. Maybe it wouldn't be too long before we'd be able to share a bed again.

I hadn't set an alarm, since I'd already been authorised not to attend school while I was visiting my parents. It was approaching lunchtime when I woke up, so I must have needed the rest.

Jared was in the kitchen with a black coffee. "I could get used to you being up in the day."

"Almost like a real boy," he replied with a smile. Sitting there in his ratty pyjamas with his hair sleep rumpled, it was like the early days. The only differences were the slight pallor to his bronze skin and the heavy curtains blocking the morning light. I missed seeing his hazel eyes flare green in the sun. "How did you sleep?"

"Not bad," I said, pouring some cereal before joining him. "How are you feeling?"

"Back to my normal self," he said. "Will was unimpressed with the blood bar, but he'll come around. I scared him good about the slayers."

Libby came clomping down the stairs, impressively loud even though she appeared in the doorway with bare feet. "Morning, kids. The mansion is opening in T-minus four days, so I need to keep an eye on the contractors today. How about you two?"

"Nothing specific," Jared said, getting up to put his mug in the sink. He leaned against the counter.

I got a twinge that I wouldn't be using my time off to help out at the police station, since my work experience with Cafferty was on hold. Even though no charges had been filed against me after what happened to Sam, I'd agreed to keep my distance for now. Cafferty didn't think any of this would harm my chances of joining the police cadets, and I hoped he was right.

"Do you want eggs?" Jared got up, already gathering what he needed.

"Absolutely," I said.

"I wouldn't say no either," Libby added.

Jared hummed as he turned up the heat and cracked eggs into the pan with butter and milk. Even though it was daytime, his movements were relaxed. He usually wouldn't have this much energy during the day.

Della walked in as he was serving up, newspaper in hand. "Smells like I came just in time."

"Plenty to go around," Jared said, doling out eggs onto three plates of buttery toast.

Della offered me the newspaper as she sat down. We were quiet while we ate, until I unfolded the paper. The headline read: VAMPIRE RIPPER STRIKES CITY.

Chapter 15

"Look at this," I said, the paper trembling in my hands.

"No . . . We're not doing this again," Libby said, dragging her chair closer to read. Della did the same from the other side, and Jared stood behind us.

VAMPIRE RIPPER
STRIKES CITY

A man's body was found on St Charles Street in the early hours of this morning. The police are yet to release a formal statement regarding his identity, but some details have emerged. The victim suffered extensive trauma to the neck, and early reports point to blood loss as the cause of death.

Moments before this morning's edition went to print, this handwritten letter was delivered to our offices. It confirms what we already know: in a city obsessed with vampires, we have a killer impersonating one.

To the people of New Orleans,

I killed someone last night. By now, the news will have broken. I am not the first of my kind to do so and I certainly will not be the last, though perhaps I am first to declare it publicly. I am a vampire, and I believe it is time for the world to know about us. We walk among you, wolves in your midst with faces like your own.

Many reading this will dismiss my claim, and I understand that. The likes of Bram Stoker and Francis Ford Coppola have made it all but impossible to take my kind seriously. They have reduced us to velvet capes and syrup for blood.

It may take some time to convince you that we are so much more deadly, and I for one am committed to that cause.

Yours,
A vampire of New Orleans

"Oh my God," Libby said a moment before I'd finished reading too.

"That about covers it," Della said. "A vampire murderer . . . The police won't have a chance."

"I don't think that's all we're dealing with," Jared began. "Look at the last line. We got an aspiring serial killer on our hands."

"Why does this keep happening? New Orleans is a nice place!" Libby said, folding her arms.

"It is, mostly," Della said. "But we got monsters like Saint Germain at the helm. Slayers can't do their jobs properly, and his vampires get to do what they like."

I was still processing the news of the murder, but something else was bothering me. "Does anyone else find it suspicious that Dad called us to say he's come to New Orleans?"

Jared followed my thought process, frowning. "And last night an alleged vampire who wants to expose us all made their first kill."

Libby looked blank, before outrage flooded in. "No way! Dad's not a murderer."

I wished I could've been so certain. Luckily, Della spoke up before I did. "But someone in his group might be, or from that new bunch he's hangin' with. Maybe he knows about it or maybe not, but he could have a vampire, or someone tryin' to look like one, carrying out his wishes."

"He's here in the city," I said. "If his group isn't involved somehow, it'd be a serious coincidence. So how are we going to find him and ask to his face?"

"How about we listen to his message again? You were kind of in shock last time – there could be clues," Jared said.

The four of us crowded around to listen to Dad spouting off his vague ideas and apologies. "What was that noise at the end?" Della asked.

She hit rewind, and this time I really focused on it. "Some kind of roaring engine? It doesn't sound like a car."

"Well that was a bust," Libby said, folding her arms. "Is this how your investigations usually go?"

"Sometimes," I said. "If no one has any other ideas, I'll call Cafferty and see if he can tell us anything."

Jared came with me while Libby and Della cleaned up after breakfast. He stood next to me while I listened to Cafferty's phone ringing. "Cafferty," he said.

"It's me."

"You don't have to explain," he said. "Call you back in fifteen."

Libby and Della joined us in the impatient wait. The phone rang exactly fifteen minutes later. "I have to go interview someone, but you got two minutes. This line is clean."

If he was plunging straight into it, I would too. "Is there anything you can tell us about the ripper case?"

"Looks like it could be a real vampire, so Boudreaux put me on it this morning. I'll know more after I speak to the coroner. Time of death was likely around midnight though." His former partner, Boudreaux, was now the supernatural-savvy sergeant that every police force should have. "I'm guessing y'all saw the letter in the paper."

"Yeah, we did."

"So you know we're likely to get more of these killings, if what the letter says is true. I really have to go – is there anythin' else?"

"Just one more thing. Were any facts left out of the article?"

Cafferty made a grumbling sound. "You're way too good at this. The victim had a tarot card from a vampire-themed deck in his hand – the Hanged Man. Armand gave me a consult over the phone. He said that card has a heap of meanings like all of 'em, but he got a sense the correct interpretation was playing the waiting game."

"I don't like the sound of that. Thank you – I'll let you go."

"Be safe."

Then he hung up. I repeated what he'd said, and their expressions all turned serious.

"Definitely in serial killer territory – leaving a calling card on victims," Jared said.

"Just when I thought murderers couldn't get any scarier," Libby said. "So what now? I assume you two are going to investigate."

Jared looked at me, waiting for my decision. "For now, I want to rule out Dad. But we need to find him first."

"I suppose there's only one thing Mulder and Skully would do – deep dive research," Jared said.

"Are there books about what to do when your cult-leader dad might be a murderer?" I asked.

"I don't know, but can I skip this part?" Libby asked. "I'd rather not try to stitch Dad up, and I prefer the movie-montage type of studying to actual studying."

"My shift at Empire starts soon," Della said, "but I can help after."

"I could go with you," Jared said quietly, hands sliding round his mug. "There's a library not far from here that specialises in the supernatural, the occult and all kinds of arcane subjects. They might have books and articles about cults from a local angle – could give us a lead to track any nearby cult-like activity."

"That's not a bad idea," I said. "Except the daylight part."

"Well, we wanted to test my new ability, and it's not too sunny out . . . I want to try being more human – you know, going out in the day and sleeping at night."

"If you're sure, we should do a test run first."

"OK," Jared said with a rueful grin. "Let's get ready before I chicken out."

"I'll take a backpack with a thick blanket just in case."

With the worry about what Dad might be tangled up in and the prospect of taking Jared into the sunlight, I turned the shower onto hot and let the water drum some anxiety out of me. When I'd first met Jared, we'd gone all over New Orleans exploring and investigating together. I'd given up on being like that again, but maybe we could.

When we reached the solid front door of the mansion, I wasn't sure how to feel. Even though Libby and Della had their own things going on, they waited with us. It was a big moment – the first time Jared had ventured out during the day by choice.

"You sure about this?" Della asked. "You can take more time if you need it."

"I can't hide in the darkness forever," Jared said, pulling on a cap and sunglasses. Then he opened the door.

The day was gloomy and overcast, which wouldn't be much consolation to Jared. The sun's rays would still get through.

He shrank back from the doorway and I stepped outside, hand extended to him. "Let's try going out for a minute then come right back in."

Jared tugged the cap down over his eyes and the sleeves over his hands. "OK, let's do this. I'm thinking healing thoughts . . ."

We stood outside the mansion with our hands clasped tightly. Jared squinted at the grey sky, tensing up against me. "How does it feel?" I asked.

"Honestly? Kind of itchy." Jared chuckled, though his face was strained. "Not gonna lie, it's amazing to see the sky during the day."

When he started squeezing harder, I wriggled my hand until he let go. "Vampire strength! Shall we go back in and take a breather?"

"Sorry! Yeah . . . please."

Jared launched himself at the doorway, so Libby and Della had to leap out of the way. Della slammed the door shut as Jared sank down on the stairs. "Well . . .?" Libby asked.

"I'm tired," Jared said quietly, staring down at his hand as he flexed the fingers. "It felt kind of like getting sunburned, but not too bad. Give me a minute, then we can go for real."

"If you're sure." Worry gave way to some excitement as I waited for Jared to recover. If he could go out in the day again, it would be huge.

Within a couple of minutes, he stood up, sliding his sunglasses back on. "I'm ready as I'll ever be."

"Let's move fast and stick to the shadows where we can."

He stepped outside and gripped my hand tight, pulling us down the street at a pace where I had to scurry to keep up. I kept my eyes on the uneven pavement, checking on Jared as often as I dared.

His lips were pressed together and slightly downturned, but his skin wasn't sizzling as Armand had described. Given long enough in the sun, that would be fatal to other vampires. As we walked on, Jared's skin developed a pink tinge like a human who'd spent too long sunbathing.

Soon, the strain was setting in. He fidgeted with his sunglasses and the brim of his cap, pulling me forwards. He started gripping my hand so hard that the bones creaked. I twisted free, and I don't think he noticed.

He broke into a staggering run, the French Quarter shops and bars blurring past as I jogged to keep up. The library was visible at the end of the street: a Gothic replica with dark wooden arches for windows that were decorated with intricate curls and patterns.

Jared looked deep in the throes of pain and panic. Even though it was a short distance, I worried that we weren't going to make it. His steps had taken on a sway, and he stumbled several times.

The building crept closer, the wooden sign reading 'Library of the Arcane' coming into view. Finally, we were through the doors and Jared folded over his knees, head in his hands.

"Is he all right?" A librarian stood up behind his desk by the door. He was wearing tweed with patches on the elbows and concern made deep lines in his warm brown skin.

"Just dehydrated," I whispered, conscious that this was a place for learning rather than drama. I whipped off Jared's cap and sunglasses and popped them into my backpack.

The librarian nodded and vanished through a door behind his desk, so I tended to Jared. I crouched down beside him, and he rested a hand on my back, still doubled over. With difficulty, I took some of his weight.

"How are you doing?" I asked softly.

"Been better," he said in a scratchy voice, plopping down onto the floor. The reddish shade was fading, leaving him grey and drained. "I feel like crap, but not as bad as last time."

By the time the librarian returned with a cold bottle of water, Jared was pushing himself to his feet. "Sorry about that, sir," he said, accepting the water. "I need to take better care of myself."

"I'm glad you appear to be feeling better," the librarian murmured, a little haughtier now we'd established that Jared wasn't about to drop dead on his polished floor. "What may I help you with?"

"We're doing an assigment on cults in our popular culture class," I said, and it came out convincingly enough. "Could you please direct us to any books and articles you might have, sir?"

"We're organised alphabetically in a clockwise direction," the librarian explained. "Books are in the main library, and I can help you with journals and newspaper articles."

"We'll start with books," Jared said. "Thank you, sir."

"No problem," the librarian said, retreating behind his desk.

Confident that Jared was on the mend, I took in the library properly for the first time. Then *I* was the one in danger of collapsing.

Chapter 16

The library was divided into two levels of dark wooden shelves. Beams ran across the ceiling and wooden railings surrounded the second floor. Apart from a few diamond-paned windows, the walls were covered with books and the occasional glass case in between. The room was silent, and no one seemed to have noticed the scene in the entrance. People were working at tables or in cosy nooks. There was an atmosphere of serenity and concentration.

"Can we move in?" I whispered, breathing in the scents of old leather, wood polish and paper.

Jared smiled. "I knew you'd like it. I'm a member – we'll get you signed up too. Wanna take a look around?" He knew me well enough not to wait for an answer. He took my hand and we approached the first shelf. Each section was labelled in swirling script. The titles offered one intrigue after another: Alchemy, Amulets, Astral travel . . . I wanted to know about all of it. The alchemy section was full of leather-bound books in muted shades, the lettering gleaming gold or so faded that it was illegible. A glass cabinet contained alchemical objects like gold scales, slender glass containers and measuring spoons.

"When this mess is over, we're coming back here," I said to Jared. "Until then, where are the Cs?"

We followed the shelves into shadowed corners and tiny alcoves. In one, Jared slowed down, leaning against a shelf. "Can we rest?"

"Take as long as you need." The last thing I wanted was Jared collapsing because I pushed too hard. "How are you feeling?" I asked quietly.

"Tired." He leaned his forehead against mine and closed his eyes. "I'll be all right in a minute."

We were tucked into a nook, dust swirling around us with the whisper and rustle of the library as a quiet accompaniment. "You're doing great," I murmured, our mouths tantalisingly close.

"Thank you," he said, his voice husky and lips drawing ever closer to mine. He lowered his hand to my heart. "I can hear it, you know. It's driving me crazy."

"So do something about it," I said, letting my lips brush against his. We'd spent over three months together, and I wanted him more than ever. Even the proximity had my heart quickening and anticipation unspooling through me.

He gripped my waist and took a step towards me, so I ended up with my back against a shelf. Looping my arms around his neck, I looked into his hazel-green eyes for a lingering moment. The smile in them matched mine as we finally closed the distance.

This kiss was sweet and too brief, setting off a low ache. It wasn't nearly enough, our hands roaming and mouths quick and searching. Reluctantly, I pulled away. "We don't want to get thrown out. We haven't found out anything about my dad yet."

"Your dad – good as any cold shower," Jared murmured wryly,

releasing my waist. "Let's find the cult books."

Holding hands, we wound our way along the shelves until we came to the one we needed. But it was empty.

"This can't be right," Jared whispered, flinching when a woman behind us shushed him.

The shelf was labelled 'Cults', in that same neat handwriting, but instead of books, it was covered by a fine layer of dust.

"Let's ask the librarian."

We explained the situation, and he turned to his computer with a look of confusion. "That's impossible. We have multiple texts about cults, including some that are quite rare and only available for use inside the library. According to our system, one book has been checked out but the rest should be present and accounted for."

"The empty shelf suggests otherwise," Jared said, impatience creeping in.

"Let me check with my manager," the librarian said, disappearing into the back office.

He returned a couple of minutes later with a white woman wheeling out behind him in a self-propelled wheelchair. She was wearing a sleeveless emerald green dress that showed her defined shoulders and arms. "My colleague has explained your situation," she said in an accent close to French. Her shiny brown hair was pulled back into a severe bun, but her smile was kind. "I do apologise for the inconvenience. Our most important patron sent one of his employees to check the books out. He also took our journals and articles, which ordinarily remain in the library. They should be back within a few weeks, if you'd like me to call you then?"

Annoyance drew tight around me as she spoke. "That wouldn't be Claude Sejour, would it?" I asked, remembering to use Saint Germain's assumed name. He wouldn't want to expose his identity as an ancient mythical vampire in polite company.

"I'm afraid we can't share clients' information," the manager said apologetically.

"Sorry, I should've explained. Mr *Sejour* sent me to see if there were any more books," Jared said, emphasising 'Sejour' with a knowing quirk of his eyebrows.

Suspicion passed over the woman's face, but she caved. "As you've already ascertained, he has the entirety of our current collection. I'm still waiting for a few titles from our sister library, so I'll give one of your colleagues a call when those arrive."

"Thanks for your help," I said, already worrying about what we'd learned.

We paused in the entrance to the library. "We really need to find my dad. Saint Germain must know there's cult activity in the area if he's looking into local ones. We can't let him find Dad first." Even if my dad was wrapped up in last night's murder, I wanted to track him down and make sure he paid for it, not leave him to the wolves.

Jared sighed. "There's one more place we could go. It's not far, but I'm really tired of going out in the daylight. After this, we definitely need to crash at home."

"Deal," I said.

Although this was Jared's second foray into the sunlight, his gait was steadier and he gripped my hand evenly instead of crushing it.

It was quite easy to shelter under balconies and trees

still clinging to their leaves on the way. Before long, we were approaching a café called Interwebz, its sign threaded with a silver spider's web.

Jared burst through the door, and I followed. He closed his eyes, the pinkish tinge to his bronze skin slowly draining away. When he looked at me again, his eyes were bloodshot with deep circles underneath them. "It was easier this time . . . But I'd rather not go out again for a while."

"Good thing we have plenty of research to do," I said. Satisfied that Jared seemed OK, I checked out the café. The computers were set up in rows with space for snacks and drinks, and quite a few were occupied. There was a counter at the back of the room with blackboards behind it covered in a sprawl of drinks options. Best of all, the walls were black with shimmering silver spider's webs all over them. They glowed in the bluish light.

'Friday I'm in Love' by The Cure was playing while I queued. I paid for an hour on the computer up front and then tried to decipher the drinks menu. Someone had wiped out the old names and scribbled new ones on top of the smudges.

I ordered a pecan-spiced latte for me and a black coffee for Jared. Vampires could drink liquids, but Jared preferred simpler choices these days. I preferred not to delve into the why on that one.

By the time I got the drinks, Jared had loaded up a search engine called Webcrawler. I wasn't up to speed with internet terms yet, but Jared had a handle on it.

"Are you sure you're OK?" I asked him, putting the huge mug of coffee down.

Steam wisped up in front of his face, and he attempted a smile.

"I'm coping. I'll sleep for hours later, but I can keep it together. Any idea what you want to search for?"

No one seemed interested in what we were up to, but saying it aloud might turn a few heads. Instead, I typed it painfully slowly next to the grey spider logo: 'New Orleans cults'. "Sometimes simple works," I said. I wished I could remember the name of Dad's former friend who'd left on bad terms, in case he showed up in any searches.

"Worth a try," Jared agreed, sipping his coffee. "This is really good, by the way."

It felt like a big moment when I pressed 'enter'. I tasted my drink while we waited for the screen to fill with search results. It was sweet, creamy and nutty with a hint of autumn spices.

A lot of the initial results were about religious groups from the early 1900s that might have strayed into cult-like activity.

"These look too old," Jared said. "Do you mind if I try?"

"Not at all. This is hurting my brain," I replied, and he took over scrolling. I leaned against him while we scanned through the websites. He was a cool, solid presence, out during daylight hours with me like nothing had changed.

None of the searches looked right until Jared found a website called 'Rebel Chat'.

"It's a sort of chat room," Jared said, explaining when I felt my face go blank. "People talk to friends or strangers."

"Sounds like chaos," I said as he clicked in.

"My little sister was on these things all the time when I lived back home, and the crap some of these people say . . ." He let my imagination run with that one. I liked hearing him talk about his family without looking sad. "Just be warned."

A window popped up with a fast-moving conversation.

"OK," Jared said. "There's an open chat and people going off in small groups to the side."

"And someone in here has mentioned a cult?" I asked, slowly getting it.

"Maybe," Jared said, scrolling through the list at the side of the screen. "Usually these things take a while to appear on search histories, so it might be a conversation that's already over. I don't think anyone will admit . . . No way."

He clicked on a thread labelled 'Cult or not?' "It's asking for a username. Hang on . . . We're in."

Chapter 17

"Nice username," I said as Jared jumped into the conversation as *Vamp4life*.

"Thought I'd be honest in an anonymous chat room. Let's see what they have to say."

CultConspir8or: Not funny RebelWithaCause.
Can anyone else help?

RebelWithaCause: Eat me.
Not my fault if you can't take a joke.

Vamp4life: Sorry, just joining. What did I miss?

RebelWithaCause has left the conversation.

CultConspir8or: Sorry bout him. He's such a buzz kill. I was just telling the others about this weird thing that happened. Can I trust you?

Vamp4life: Sure. As much as you can trust anyone on the web.

CultConspir8or: lololol good point. OK, so I went on one of those swamp tours near New Orleans, right? Totally rad if you're ever in the area. They got alligators and everything. Anywho, we went by this scary ass house on stilts, autumn leaves falling down all over it. A guy in my boat says this group has set up there and there are all these stories about them. And I was like holy shit – cult story falling right into my lap on vacation. Excellent!

Vamp4life: What kind of stories?

CultConspir8or: Feel like I got a fellow believer here. Far out, man! He says these guys have been stockpiling weapons, right? But not just the usual guns and shit. Nope, these guys got wooden stakes, crosses, the whole bit. Looks like we got a bunch of vampire hunters in our own backyard! You better watch out Vamp4life!

Vamp4life: I don't know what to say to that.

User87323: I wouldn't talk about them if I were you. The kind of people you're talking about don't like others involved in their business.

CultConspir8or: The group's anonymous, dude. Think I'm safe.

User87323: Are you willing to stake your life on that?

Conspir8or: Stake – good one! Oh wait, you're probably not joking, right? I'm outing. Later Vamp. Later creepy internet guy.

CultConspir8or has left the conversation.

Vamp4life: Are you still there, User87323?

User87323: Unfortunately. Not for long.

Vamp4life: I need to ask a favour.

User87323: I don't know you. Why would I do you a favour?

Vamp4life: Our friend has got mixed up in a group that sounds like this one, and we're worried. We need to know where they are.

User87323: . . .

Vamp4life: Please.

User87323: Fine. Not here. House of Games 4 p.m. I'm guessing you're a local. Wear something vampy and I'll find you. Be there on time or I'm gone.

User87323 has left the conversation.

"That was . . . educational," I said. "Is everyone on the internet terrifying?"

"It's safest to work on that assumption," Jared said. He'd done so well during the chat, typing at a frantic pace and incorporating my suggestions while the conversation raced ahead. He was talking slowly now, propping his head up on one hand. Our daylight adventures had taken their toll.

"Let's get you home," I said, already planning how to meet our new internet friend.

We were lucky it wasn't far because Jared stumbled the whole way, his face set in grim determination. I threaded my arm around him, and he put more weight on me the longer we walked.

When we closed the door of the mansion, he sank down on the bottom steps.

I let him sit and recuperate, his long legs stretched out in front of him. Worry worked into every crevice until I could hardly keep still for fretting about him.

Finally, he looked up. "I think I can function again."

"Do you need blood?" I asked.

His gaze locked on my throat, and he went very still. "No," he said, not looking certain. "I need sleep first." He used the banister to pull himself up, clinging onto it. "I know you're going to the arcade no matter what I say. Just promise me you won't go alone or do anything reckless off the back of it?"

"It's almost like you know me . . . I promise."

"Good." I followed him up the stairs, ready to offer help if needed. Like me, Jared wasn't a fan of the big fuss. He dragged himself on the banister, every step getting slower.

With a clumsy kiss on my forehead, he disappeared up the stairs to the attic.

I headed straight to the phone, and Cafferty picked up on the second ring. "Cafferty."

"Hi, it's me . . . Mina. Are you doing anything at four?"

"Two calls in one day – lucky me. Is this a dangerous plan call or a social one?"

"Not definitely dangerous – just . . . possibly."

"You're lucky I get off at three. Where do you need me?"

"House of Games. I'll explain when we get there. Oh, and don't dress like a detective."

"Got it. I'll meet you outside ten minutes before so you can brief me." He hung up, leaving me with nothing but time to kill.

While I had the phone in my hand, I dialled Empire. Armand picked up, and I could tell he was in a mood. "What?"

"It's me. Is everything OK?"

"I presume you have a question. Do you mind if we skip the niceties? I'm rather busy."

If he wanted to play it like that . . . "Have you had any visions about my dad or the ripper? Or, you know, my dad or someone he knows being the ripper?"

There was a long silence. If it wasn't for the lack of a dialling tone, I would've thought Armand had hung up on me. "Don't you think I would've told you if I had?"

"Sorry . . . I shouldn't assume you're sitting around waiting to get visions. I know you don't control it."

Armand sighed. "I should be the one apologising. My visions haven't been particularly useful lately, and I have rather a lot going on. Saint Germain is not happy with me at the moment, since he expected results from our jaunt to New Mexico. But that's beside the point . . . You do know you don't need to investigate every strange or terrible occurrence that crosses your path."

"I know," I said, "but this ripper one could involve my dad."

"But it may not. And even if it does, that doesn't make you responsible."

"Thanks for the pep talk," I said. "I'll let you go."

"You're welcome, though I'm not sure I did anything." He'd done more than he realised, because I didn't feel quite so hopeless.

I had some time to kill before going to meet Cafferty. The contractors were whirring and hammering away in the new room, so I decided to steer clear. Libby would definitely drag me in to help.

Instead, I made a sandwich, and then my current read, *The Midnight Club*, kept me company for a while. Every so often, the coincidence of my dad's appearance in New Orleans and a vicious murder by a vampire for the purpose of revealing them brought a new surge of panic. Though I didn't want to believe Dad was involved, the timing was too convenient. And Saint Germain seemed to not only know a cult was here, but he was tracking them as well.

Eventually, I gave up on reading and checked my wardrobe for something 'vampy'. I settled on the Mina Harker T-shirt Lucas had made me during summer, experiencing the usual pang that his sweetness had covered so much darkness. I set off early, knowing how easy it was to dawdle in New Orleans before the sun went down.

People were setting up for the fall fair even though it wasn't kicking off until tomorrow. The main event would be along Fulton Street, but businesses all over would be selling fall items from shop fronts or stands outside. Caleb, the owner of the food market near the mansion, was placing squash of all different colours, shapes and sizes onto a wooden stall.

"Can I buy this one?" I asked, picking up a green squash speckled with white that fit into the palm of my hand. The sun had warmed its rough skin. It was too cute to leave on the stall, and I was sure Libby would like it.

"That little guy's on me," Caleb said. "Have a good day!"

Thanking him, I tucked the squash into my bag. New Orleans was such an excellent mixture of creepy places to visit, friendly people and so much history, but with an undercurrent of darkness, like Saint Germain's influence. And now my dad was here too.

Preparations went on around me while I wallowed. I moved through the French Quarter automatically, soon coming upon the narrow side street with House of Games on the corner. It had a yellow sign with black lettering that the sunlight caught in bright flares.

"Hey. You OK?" Cafferty appeared in front of me. He was wearing his leather jacket and jeans again – much better for blending in than his detective suits.

"Define OK," I said.

"That's what I thought. Wanna talk about it? Or tell me what we're doing here?"

"How about option two?" I gave Cafferty a rundown, and he looked more troubled the longer I talked.

"So we're meeting someone you talked to on the internet about a suspected cult." His voice was dangerously calm.

"Yep, that's what you've missed so far."

"Well, I'm glad you brought me along," Cafferty said. "And while we're here, how 'bout we play some games?"

"You really are the perfect person for this mission."

Chapter 18

Cafferty's eyes widened when we headed into the neon lights inside House of Games. 'Young Hearts' by Commuter played over the sound system, clashing with the computer game music and sound effects.

Many customers were around my age or younger, and most were hooked on whatever game they were playing. Some were milling around in search of the next game, or en route to the snack bar at the back of the room. It was the ideal place for a secret meeting: too loud and busy for eavesdropping.

"The internet lead said they'd find you, right?" Cafferty said. He was scanning the room in his usual cop way, but I had a feeling he was choosing the game he wanted to play rather than scoping out our target. "Let's start easy . . . How about *The Simpsons*?"

Cafferty picked Bart and I went for Lisa. The game was a beat-em-up that required taking down a series of henchmen until you got to the big bad at the end of each level. It was relaxing to bash the buttons and watch the two-dimensional villains fall on the way to saving Maggie from kidnappers. If only it was so straightforward in real life.

I got completely absorbed, only breaking my focus to look at

Cafferty every now and again. The tip of his tongue stuck out of the corner of his mouth and his eyes were glazed with concentration. I wasn't sure if it was about escapism or winning for him, but either way he was having a good time. "I've missed having you on ride-alongs," he said. "And just think, when school finishes next year you'll be in training."

Until I'd come to New Orleans, I'd had no idea what I wanted to do with my life. Joining the police cadets felt right, and I liked seeing a path ahead that I'd decided for myself.

"What next?" Cafferty asked, giving the Sega Rally racing game a longing look.

"You drive cars around a track," I said. "I'll see what else there is."

"Stay close," Cafferty warned. I got his meaning. I'd come to meet a stranger, and he didn't want me doing it without backup.

Tekken 2 was on the same row, so there was no need to go far. I picked my favourite character, Ling Xiaoyu, and familiarised myself with the controls. I'd played Tekken 1 at my friend Tina's house in Whitby on her new PlayStation. I'd never been as close to my friends back then as I was here. Still, it was a nice reminder as my character ducked, punched and kicked one opponent after another.

"You're pretty good."

A girl with blonde pigtails was standing next to me, a lollipop making one cheek stick out. She looked about my age. "Thanks," I said, showing off my best move – the one where Ling Xioayu sweeps her arm upwards to knock an opponent off their feet. "Do you want to play?"

"Thanks," she said, putting a coin into the machine.

My game restarted, and we picked our characters. She opted for Nina, a tall blonde like her, and I went for Ling Xiaoyu again.

The girl was seriously good, her fingers flying over the buttons. It took all of my effort to keep up, and she was still winning.

She'd got her first knockout when my brain kicked into gear. "Wait . . . User . . . whatever that string of numbers was?"

"Vamp4life, I presume," she said quietly, already kicking the crap out of me on the next stage. "Love your T-shirt. You're not what I expected."

"Neither are you. You know something about . . . you know? That place?"

"Yeah." The game ended in her favour, and we both contributed an extra coin to keep going. "That's why I came. I can spot people like you a mile off, because I was one. Being part of something is awesome, and the bullshit they're selling sounds exciting at first. But you need to stay away from them. They're bad news, especially their leader – guy called Clem."

The friend Dad was supposed to be staying with, who had stock-piled vampire-killing weapons according to the chat room. "How?"

"I can't say a whole lot," she murmured, flicking her gaze around the amusement arcade. "So, they have this crazy idea that vampires exist. At first, I thought it was a role-playing thing, but they're serious. And since I'm pretty sure vampires aren't real, when they start killing, it's gonna be humans they're taking down. As if that wasn't enough, they started talking about branding members – like actually scorching their skin with red-hot pokers – so when I found out about that, I got the hell out. The swamp hideout should've been a red flag, but I'm a sucker for a bit of danger. If I were you, I wouldn't give them another thought."

"I know you think you're trying to help me, but you have it wrong. I need to get my . . . friend out." I stuck to Jared's story, since I'd learned the hard way not to dole out trust too readily. "Just tell me where they are."

"I guessed you might say something like that," the girl said. "I gotta go, but I brought this." She slid a blank, sealed envelope into my hand. "Don't say I didn't warn you."

I put it in my pocket, and she slipped away. I checked the Sega Rally game, but Cafferty was gone.

"Hey," a voice said quietly and too close to my ear. I jumped as Cafferty slid into view. "Sorry. I was listening behind the machine. I didn't wanna spook her. Let's go."

Night had slipped in while we were inside the arcade. Without daylight, the chill made me wish for gloves. Usually, the late crowd in New Orleans were varying shades of drunk, lively, intimidating or a combination of the above. Tonight, the wholesome fall festivities had started before the fair tomorrow.

Throngs of people were congregating around stalls and buying steaming drinks from vendors with huge vats of mulled wine or spiced apple. The atmosphere could've drawn me in, but the lead needed addressing first.

We stepped to one side of the street and I ripped the envelope open with cold, clumsy fingers. It was a description with co-ordinates instead of an address.

"This is out in the swamps," Cafferty said. "It's a long shot, but I might be able to send a team out there if I can pull together enough evidence for a warrant."

"I don't think we can wait that long. Before this week, I wouldn't have thought my dad would be involved with that vampire ripper, even if they do both want to expose vampires. But after what he did to Jared . . ."

"I'd go myself, but no good comes from hitting the swamps at night. Plus, I'm on the graveyard shift. The powers that be aren't happy that I skipped town for a couple of weeks so I gotta pull some double shifts to make amends." Cafferty hated breaking the rules, and he'd had to do it for Saint Germain. "I'll do some digging while I'm working tonight, then let's talk tomorrow. Can I walk you home?"

"Sure," I said, already knowing I'd be up early and ready to push him on this. "Any progress on the vampire ripper case?"

"None," he said, the line between his eyes deepening. "Forensics have sent off some samples for testing and we have handwriting analysts on the letter, but they're not optimistic that anything useful will come back. Usually, I'd feel more confident that one death is all we'll get, but that letter . . ."

"It seems like they'll kill again."

"Right," Cafferty said, his expression troubled. "Let's hope we're wrong. Most of the police are at a disadvantage because they don't know vampires are real. Ironic, right? That's exactly what the killer is trying to prove."

We rounded the corner and the Mansion of the Macabre came into view. "Yeah . . . I suppose there'd be some advantages to the world knowing. Thanks for walking me. I'll call you tomorrow."

"I don't doubt that," Cafferty said, waiting for me to unlock the door before striding off down the dark street.

Libby was tidying the apartment using her preferred method of moving things around but not putting them away. "Hey," she said. "What did you get up to today?"

"I don't even know where to start," I said, "but I got you this."

I presented her with the tiny squash, and she grinned at it in her palm. “So cute! I’ll call you . . . Sasquash.” I could’ve done without the reminder of dad’s stories, this one referencing Big Foot.

Instead of starting something, I flopped down onto the sofa. If I could stay right in this spot tonight, that would suit me. “Is Jared still asleep?”

“I just went up there. Out like a light.” She hugged the squash. “So did you decide our dad’s not a murderer or is the jury still out on that one?”

So much for not arguing. “I mean, he did try to kill Jared . . .” I amended that in the face of Libby’s outrage. “Or, at the very least, he didn’t care if Jared died as long as he got what he wanted.”

Libby folded her arms, irritation playing across her features. I wasn’t sure if it was directed at me or Dad. “Yeah, he really messed up. But you can’t think he’s this vampire ripper guy.”

“I don’t know. If not him, then maybe one of his Community members is doing it. You have to see that the timing’s weird – he turned up in New Orleans at the same time as a vampire who wants people to know all about them.”

“Whatever you say.” Libby’s tone was flat, shutting me out when we’d made so much progress in the opposite direction. She’d always been inclined to see Dad in the best light, even when he forgot to pick us up from school or brought weird friends to the house who scared us. A smile and some charm from him erased her hurt.

Della arrived, pausing with the key in her hand. “Everything all right?”

“Fine,” Libby said curtly.

“OK . . .” Della said. “Mina and I have to go. Paige has summoned us.”

Chapter 19

"Sure," Libby said sarcastically. "You must go to the almighty leader of the slayers."

My first instinct was to sink deeper into the sofa and let it swallow me up completely. "What does she want?" I pushed myself to my feet instead.

"Emergency meeting," Della said as Libby came over for a kiss.

"I have to check over the contractors' work from today, but I'll catch up with you later." Libby left without looking at me.

"Is somethin' wrong?" Della asked the moment the door closed.

"She's mad that I'm investigating our dad," I said. "But we'll be fine."

"I have faith in y'all to get through anythin'," Della said. "And I'm here if either of you need me."

"I know," I said. "Thank you. I'll check on Jared, then we can go."

I couldn't settle until I saw for myself that he was OK after the big day of going out into the sun. Tiptoeing up the attic stairs, I couldn't hear anything.

A crack in the curtains let in some light from the street. Jared was out cold on the bed, the quilt tangled around his legs and one arm flung back over his pillow. I left pretty fast, because I didn't want to be that person who lingers while someone sleeps. It was a relief to see him relaxed and recovering after what he'd suffered.

Back in the apartment, I grabbed my leather jacket from the coat hook, enjoying how it slipped over my skin. I tucked a stake into the Velcro holster inside it, and we headed downstairs.

The evening was cool and unusually fresh. The later it got in the year, the more I liked the New Orleans climate. I'd never got the hang of summer's humidity, and the fresh air helped me to shake off some of the bad vibes hanging around me.

The Mansion of the Macabre was in the heart of the French Quarter, and soon we were in the Bourbon Street hubbub. We hadn't needed to come this way, but I wondered if Della wanted to immerse herself in the sensory overload of the city like I did. Besides, it was always worth checking down alleys for vampires taking things too far.

Bourbon Street was doing its usual thing – live jazz music pouring from the window of one bar and karaoke from the next. No one but Bon Jovi should be allowed to tackle 'You Give Love a Bad Name', but the girl in the bar was giving it a decent go. People were drinking and laughing, living very much in the now. We passed a gumbo restaurant that set my stomach rumbling at the sweet smell of spices and seafood.

Whatever nastiness we had coming from Paige, being at home gave me comfort.

Even though they were under new leadership, the slayers still trained at a seriously cool location. The Cave was an old nightclub that was meant to have been torn down, but someone had messed up, because we were standing inside it. The wall and ceilings were dripping with thousands of tiny cement stalactites that each looked like they could impale you – appropriate for a room chock full of vampire slayers. The space must have been breathtaking back in the day, but now it was in desperate need of renovation. If one of those spikes came down, it'd be game over for someone.

When I'd first come here, the leader of the slayers had seriously impressed me. Rosario had been strong and fair, sticking rigorously to the code. She'd held on to her convictions right up until two of Saint Germain's minions had killed her. He'd put a slayer in charge who was happy to leave his friends alone to do whatever they wanted.

That's how we'd ended up with Paige. She was standing in the boxing ring in the centre of the room, long red ponytail swishing and glossy red lips forming a smug smile as she lorded it over us. I'd not had the pleasure of seeing Della beat Paige in a boxing match months ago to gain entry to the slayers, but imagining it on repeat kept me sane.

Many slayers had carried on as normal under Paige's leadership – the desire to help unknowing victims stronger than their disdain for Paige. Some had split after the vampire who had Rosario killed became our patron.

The remaining slayers were working out around the room, some pummelling punchbags and others practising their staking technique. The equipment looked past its best, but it got the job done. Della and I shrugged off our coats and sparred with cracked old pads until I felt warm and buzzed from the exercise. Motivational rock music played in the background, and we kicked and punched our way through 'You're the best' and 'Eye of the Tiger'.

"OK, y'all!" Paige called out, clapping her hands.

Beau broke away from a group chatting to the side of the room and climbed into the ring to stand beside her. He was Paige's new lieutenant, which had initially ranked him low in my estimations. He was annoyingly good looking too, with broad shoulders and thick, perfect brown hair that he wore short at the sides. His eyes were dark blue with decisive slashes for eyebrows, and he had a full-lipped mouth. He was also smart and fair, countering Paige's impulsive nature.

"Evenin' everyone," Paige said, her eyes panning round the room. "I'm so pleased to see y'all." Her gaze landed on me and Della. "Well, *some* of you anyway. You're doing an awesome job! Saint Germain tells me we've got the reckless vampires running scared. We're slaying in record numbers, and I'm just *so proud* of you."

Beau jumped in as soon as Paige finished. "We're sure you're continuing to abide by the code. Failure to do so will result in immediate dismissal. We wouldn't want to attract any undue attention."

"You're *so* right," Paige said with a warning in her voice. "Anyway, there are photographs on the noticeboard of the vampires we need to stay clear of." It was a who's who of Saint Germain's friends, the stuffy vampire elders who seemed to steer clear of the streets we patrolled anyway. Armand was the only vampire on there that I knew. Paige went on. "Please study it carefully –

we wouldn't want any mishaps." She gave Della and me a barbed glare that soon shifted to a devious smile.

"Before I send some of y'all off on patrol, I have a surprise. A special guest would like to speak. I'm sure one or two of you will be *especially* glad to see him."

Saint Germain strode through the entrance, flanked by two vampire bodyguards who probably possessed an unpleasant power apiece. Anyone bold enough to attack him would be dead before they got the stake out. "Thank you for that marvellous introduction, darlin'."

Beau ducked out of the ring as Saint Germain stepped onto the edge of it, his minions holding the ropes apart for him to slide inside. A mutter ran through the room at the sight of Saint Germain, but the pockets of discontent quieted as Beau moved through the crowd.

Saint Germain was dressed in a white suit and leaning on a silver cane. He slicked a hand through the side of greying light-brown hair that would never get any greyer, evidently enjoying the moment. "I wanted to come here personally to thank y'all for all of the *fine* work you're doin' keepin' our city safe. I'm sure Paige has impressed upon you the importance of keepin' my connection to y'all a secret. I have an appearance to uphold in this town, and bein' connected to a group of vig-il-an-tes – the police's word, not mine – wouldn't be good for my reputation."

The slayers around us were silent, their tension growing the longer he talked.

Della was normally the master of the controlled expression, but even she was losing the battle with frustration. Her hands kept making and releasing fists at her sides. Paige was the only slayer who looked thrilled to be here, smirking from Saint Germain's side like she had it made. Even Beau was standing in the midst of the crowd with his arms crossed and face serious.

"Despite the good work you're doin', I got a couple problems. And as y'all know, my problems are your problems. Now, I take absolutely no issue with the vampire tourism we got goin' on. If anythin', it only helps us. People encounterin' a real vampire assume it's just another tourist stunt.

"But somethin' different is afoot. There's a trend of tryin' to bring vampires into the spotlight. First an upstart group in another state tried to expose us on national television. But y'all don't gotta worry about that. Two of my people are on it. So far their results are disappointin', but I'm sure they'll get results given some persuasion."

As they'd predicted, Cafferty and Armand hadn't got away with telling Saint Germain nothing – a new worry to add to the list.

Saint Germain hadn't finished yet. "And now a vampire has had the audacity to try a similar stunt in our fair city. I'm sure y'all have read the letter in the paper. We're lucky the press and the public think it's a delusional human for now, but we can't assume that will continue."

Saint Germain had the books about local cults, so he was obviously anticipating a threat closer to home. What would he do if he found out that Dad and his followers were in the same city as him?

Saint Germain continued, unaware of my inner meltdown. "Here's what I propose. Paige here had an ingenious idea about how I could best utilise the slayers. While y'all help me track down this so-called vampire ripper, I'll pour funds into renovating this sorry excuse for a base, weapons, vehicles, surveillance equipment, armour and anything else y'all might need. Oh, and I'll also be providing a basic salary to all of y'all – in cash of course."

Extra funding was exactly what the slayers needed. One thing Paige and I agreed on was that the lack of decent weapons and lightweight protective gear was putting the slayers at risk. She looked pleased as punch that we'd got it at her suggestion. I wasn't keen on the idea of accepting money personally from Saint Germain, but we were already struggling to pay our bills.

"And that's not all." Saint Germain was getting into his stride, his voice booming as the slayers fidgeted. "I'll be offerin' up some of my finest employees to patrol with y'all. I'll also provide any and all information I find out about the little letter-writin' rat. This vampire's days are numbered – y'all don't have to worry your pretty heads about whether your precious code applies. They've murdered a poor, helpless human, and I want you to kill them on sight. I'll provide a handsome reward to whichever slayer deals the killing blow."

That part set the slayers murmuring again, but Paige's victory grin had become strained around the time Saint Germain talked about sending his vampires out on patrol with us. Did I really agree with Paige twice in one night? She was well-known for patrolling alone, something about only being able to trust herself. I always teamed up with Della, and we didn't need one of Saint Germain's vampires reporting our every movement to him.

"One last thing – I've left a case of black ironwood stakes by the door for you to help yourselves. It's the strongest wood in the United States, and I've had them sharpened and heat treated as well. That about covers it, darlin'. I've given your people plenty

to think about. Please – go ahead and finish your meetin'."
He gestured with one hand for Paige to go on, leaning on his stick.

"Thank you," she said coyly, dipping her chin like he deserved a bow. "Beau and I will come round with your assignments . . . and the names of your vampires." Why did she smile at me and Della when she said that? "Let's get this done quickly. A vampire doesn't get to mess around in New Orleans. You're dismissed."
I wasn't so confident about discovering the ripper quickly. In a city full of vampires, how were we supposed to find them?

Saint Germain's smile turned brittle and he gripped his cane more tightly. Was there trouble in paradise?

Beau went to talk to another group of slayers and Paige headed straight towards me and Della. She preferred tormenting us personally.

"So, were you going to tell me about Empire's little vampire problem or were you waiting for me to find out?" Paige asked.

"What vampire problem?" Della asked.

"A bunch of people have been attacked around Empire and Armand's other businesses this past couple weeks," Paige said, looking way too happy about that.

"I've been away for a few days, and the owner hasn't been there for longer than that. If something happened, we don't know about it," Della said.

"I know Armand's been away – I'm not stupid. I was there the night Saint Germain sent him off and promoted me, remember?" Her full, very red lips curled into a grin. "Go to Empire tonight and get your house in order," Paige said, stepping into Della's personal space. Della stood her ground, looking down to meet Paige's eyes. "Because if you don't, I will."

"Is there anything else?" Della asked, perfectly neutral even though Paige was obviously itching to get a rise out of her.

"Yes," Paige said, pulling her ponytail over one shoulder and baring bright white teeth. "Ilian, your assigned vampire, will meet you outside the mansion. 7 p.m. sharp – don't be late."

Della nodded, giving a small smile. "If we got a vampire, I'm assuming you did too. Who's yours?"

"Never you mind," Paige snapped, her cheeks flushing. "Saint Germain knows I can handle it alone, but he can't be seen to treat me any different. You need to watch yourself. I'm the one who kept hassling Saint Germain until he gave us this funding. I can have him take it away from certain people just as easily." She flounced away without giving us time for comebacks.

"She's in a good mood." I said. "Who's Ilian?"

Della's smile was grim. "Sounds like we'll find out."

Chapter 20

Saint Germain watched the slayers filtering out, his gaze drilling into my back. Usually, some stayed behind to meet or work out, but not today. Della stuck to my side as the slayers flowed up the narrow stairway. We often chatted to friends on the way out, but everyone was muttering to their closest allies. I grabbed one of the dark brown stakes, gripping it for a second before I sheathed it in the holster. Saint Germain was right – it had felt good in my hand and that point looked wickedly sharp.

We rushed through the French Quarter, and I was thankful it wasn't far to the mansion. The Quarter was getting pretty wild by this time in the evening. Customers of the nearest bar were belting out the lyrics to 'I'd Do Anything for Love' by Meat Loaf and the streets were full of people with brightly coloured drinks in their hands.

Cafferty was working tonight and our mission to scope out Empire couldn't wait, but tomorrow I had to find Dad. Not only did I need to know if he had anything to do with the ripper, but I had to warn him that he had a seriously bad vampire on his tail. It was the worst time to try to reveal vampires. I'd prefer to stay away from Dad, but I also didn't want Saint Germain to make him disappear.

"Working for Paige is making my blood boil," Della said as the mansion came into view.

Apparently, we'd both had things to stew over during the walk. "Tell me about it. I can't believe she's sent us to snoop around the place you work – but better us than someone else, I guess."

"True," Della said. "I don't know how I feel about some vampire we don't know followin' us around, but how about we bring Jared and Libby along, then make a night of it after we check out Empire?"

"Deal," I said.

The living room was empty when we got back, but I could hear the television from Libby and Della's room (*Xena: Warrior Princess* from the sound of it).

Della went straight for the phone to call Armand, explaining tersely what Paige had asked us to do. He wasn't known for being talkative, so soon Della was talking again. "We'll be there just after 7 p.m. Oh, and there's one more thing. He's sending this vampire Ilian with us. Should we be worried?" She sighed, closing her eyes. "Oh, great. OK, see you soon."

Della put the phone down. "Armand knows about the attacks. He says it's pretty unusual – vamps usually leave his clientele alone."

"I'm not surprised," I said. Armand had always seemed measured in his responses, but his brother, John Carter, had been a serial-killing vampire with the disturbing power of compelling people to do his bidding. Couple that with his associations with Saint Germain and Armand probably had quite the reputation. "So, who's this Ilian?"

"He's the one who froze Cafferty in St. Louis Cathedral without breaking a sweat – one of Saint Germain's favourite and most powerful lackies."

"Awesome. Love being stitched up by Paige."

"Let's tell the others the plan and grab some food," Della said.

She went off to update Libby. I found Jared lying on his bed, focusing intently on his Game Boy. The bed, drawers and an old couch were the only furniture up here, but he'd made it cosy with cushions and blankets on the bed and overlapping rugs of all different patterns on the floor. He'd put up a shelf lately so his books, videos and action figures had pride of place.

Like always, my gaze was drawn to the spot where I'd found Heather's body, chained up on a chair in a pool of blood. Jolting myself out of the memory, I focused on Jared. "Hey. You look better."

"Sleep took care of it this time," he said, switching off the Game Boy. "Libby said you went to a slayer meeting. How did that go?"

"Saint Germain made a cameo, so that was pleasant," I said, making myself comfortable on the bed before giving him a full recap.

Jared frowned. "I don't like the idea of this Ilian guy following you around, but at least I'll be there."

"You should keep a low profile," I said. "We want you to stay off Saint Germain's radar."

He nodded but didn't look happy about it. "OK. Let's get ready."

"Since I've already killed your good mood, I have something else to tell you first. At the arcade, Cafferty and I tracked down a location where we think Dad might be hiding – out in the swamps."

"And you're going to see him," Jared said, his eyebrows knitting together. "I don't know why you'd go anywhere near that guy."

"I don't want to spend time with him," I said, sensing this could cascade into an argument. "I want to ask if he knows anything about the ripper and warn him that Saint Germain is on his tail."

Jared's mouth made a hard line. "I get it. And you don't want me to come."

I hated seeing him so hurt and angry, especially because I'd caused it in part. "I want you far away from him, and the people he's with. They're all about killing vampires, not Dad's slightly less extreme version."

"More people to keep me away from," Jared grumbled, with a spark of humour in his eyes.

"Don't worry – I'll protect you," I teased, leaning in to kiss his cheek. "Now, we should get ready, or Ilian might want to come in."

I changed into jeans and a purple *Beetlejuice* T-shirt – an outfit suitable for patrol and dancing. Then I sat down to eat thick ham and cheese sandwiches with Libby and Della.

The four of us headed down together, and I got a burst of happiness at being part of this tight little unit. Depending how things with my dad and Saint Germain played out, life had the potential to turn pretty grim. But having Libby, Della and Jared went a long way towards making things good.

Ilian was waiting for us outside the mansion, popping my happy bubble. He couldn't have appeared more out of place if he'd tried: his pale grey eyes near-luminescent in the darkness and his crisp black suit a contrast to the Gothic, grunge or chilled-out styles of tourists and locals milling around us. His head was smooth and hairless, and he looked like he'd been around thirty when he'd become a vampire. "Mina and Della?" he asked, though his gaze lingered on Libby and Jared.

"That's right!" Libby chirped, hooking an arm through Jared's. "We have to get going, but we'll see you at Empire." She pulled Jared along the street, and he barely had a chance to say goodbye before they were lost in the crowd.

"I'm here to do whatever you need," Ilian said coldly. He was one of those vampires who'd never pass as human to those in the know, who hardly showed any emotion. "It makes a change from looking into this ripper problem."

"We'll do a pass of the streets on the way to Empire, then start asking around about vampire activity," Della said.

She and I set off, stakes sheathed but slayer senses switched on. I revelled in the thrill of scoping out the streets, passing over innocent interactions and lingering where our help might be needed. Ilian followed behind us. In a way, it was a relief not to be in his immediate presence, but I disliked him being out of sight.

I clocked one or two possible vampires. It was hard to tell in New Orleans, with the abundance of humans trying to look like they were undead. But if they were real vampires out minding their own business, then it didn't fall under our code as slayers. That was an unpleasant reminder of what Dad was trying to do. If he succeeded, vampires like Jared and Armand who never hurt anyone would be put under scrutiny.

That was when I saw a vampire who deserved to be scrutinised. At first, I thought it was a couple having an intimate moment, a girl with her back against the wall by a bar and her boyfriend talking to her, one finger curled under her chin. Then, she batted his hand away and swerved around him, cutting down an alleyway to get away. He followed her.

"Della," I said. I wasn't a hundred percent sure that he was a vampire, but he was a creep in any case. And there was something about the gliding, predatory way he moved into that alleyway . . .

"Let's go," she said, fixing on the guy as he disappeared down the alleyway. We'd been patrolling together long enough that we trusted each other's instincts.

It was lucky for the girl that we did. Della and I got into the narrow alleyway as the guy grabbed her arm. "Hey!" she said, trying to yank it away.

He hung on, letting out an inhuman snarl. We broke into a run, pulling up by the struggling pair right as his fangs appeared. "You really don't want to do that," I said, freeing the stake from my jacket holster.

The vampire let go of the girl. She made a significantly smarter move than her jaunt down the alleyway, bolting in the direction she'd come.

"Have you heard of the slayers?" Della asked. She didn't get to start her speech. In a blur of white skin and black suit, Ilian was between us. He thrust a hand towards the vampire and flicked it upwards. The vampire shot up several feet in the air, his feet kicking at nothing. His face strained and fingers clawed at his throat as if he was being strangled in midair by an invisible hand. "There are vampires far more important than you who prefer to maintain their secrecy. Be more careful next time."

"Let him down," I said, watching the vampire's eyes bulging as Ilian tightened his hands into a fist. "We have a code, and he didn't attack her." If he kept this up much longer, we'd learn firsthand if strangulation could kill a vampire.

"If you insist," Ilian said, his voice flat as he let his hand fall.

The vampire crumpled into a heap on the dirty, smelly floor

of the alleyway. Maybe I should've made my instruction more specific. He scrambled to his feet, his terrified gaze locked on Ilian. He was so shaken up that the ability to run seemed to have left him. "The slayer just saved your life," Ilian said. "If it happens again, she won't be here to protect you."

This vampire wasn't the best example of his kind, but he hadn't broken the code yet. If we'd not been here, Ilian would've murdered him. He finally found his flight instinct and used it. Ilian looked at us with the first expression I'd seen him make – a twinge of impatience. "Well? Shouldn't we get to that Empire of the Dead bar that I've heard so much about?"

"That wasn't OK!" I said, too astonished to think about self-preservation. "You have to follow our lead if you're going to work with us."

He gave me a stare so pointed that I regretted opening my mouth. "I won't make the same mistake again."

"Great," Della said, shooting me a small smile as Ilian went off ahead. "You told him," she added.

"I'm just glad he didn't use his power on me."

We caught up with Ilian outside Empire. "What's the plan?" he asked.

"We need to do some passes of the bar and interview staff. That sound good?" Della asked.

"Good is a strong word, but it will suffice," he said, disappearing inside Empire.

"He's a ray of sunshine, isn't he? Let's get this done," Della said, and we followed Ilian inside.

Chapter 21

The Empire of the Dead bar always had its curtains tightly closed, which I now knew was to protect vampires during daylight hours. I had mixed feelings about the place. The decor was cool, though macabre. Its name also had an intriguing connection to the text in the Paris Catacombs, which translated from French means, 'Stop: you're entering the Empire of the Dead'. But we'd been through a lot here, and I could never shake that off.

At this time of night, the tables had been cleared away and most people were packed into the dance floor or bar area, all under the animal skeletons in bird cages that covered the ceiling.

The place was full, and most people were swaying and singing to 'Everybody Wants to Rule the World'. We moved through the crowd and I wished I was like them – blissfully unaware of the dank cells that had once filled the basement. Armand had dismantled them over the summer. His brother, John Carter, had kidnapped the four of us and dragged us down there to mess with our heads and try to kill us. We'd only survived because Armand got him first. Della still worked at Empire, and we'd had good times here, but they hadn't eclipsed the bad ones.

When we arrived, Libby and Jared were caught in the crush for drinks at the bar. Della and I approached Armand at the opposite end, and Ilian strolled behind us like the undead shadow nobody wanted.

"It feels refreshing that you two are here to help rather than cause trouble tonight," Armand said, conspicuously ignoring Ilian. I was getting to know Armand well enough that I saw the joke behind his flat delivery.

"You're welcome," I said.

"Do you believe the attacks around your bar are connected to the vampire ripper?" Della murmured. 'Just a Girl' by No Doubt was playing loud enough to drown us out anyway. The dance floor had filled at the sound of Gwen Stefani's voice and everyone was bouncing around.

"I highly doubt it," Armand said. "The circumstances are nothing alike."

"Do you think you're being targeted, or is it more a case of the mice playing while the cat's away?" I asked.

Armand's smile was exasperated. "You're altogether too astute about vampire behaviour. I'd assume the latter, so don't trouble yourself with it. Look around if you must, to placate your slayer dictator, but know I'm not the least concerned."

"Thanks, Armand. Any vampires here tonight?" Della asked.

"Present company and hangers on excluded?" Armand asked. "No one unfamiliar. I presume you've noticed Fiona?"

Della nodded, although I hadn't yet. Scanning the room, I saw Will's girlfriend clearing glasses. Her blonde hair was pulled back into a high ponytail and her smile was sweet as she accepted an empty bottle thrust in her direction. Over Halloween, Rosario, Della and I had slayed Fiona's friends when they attacked us, but we'd spared Fiona since she wasn't a threat. I'd got her the job here with Armand, so in a way I was responsible for Will meeting her. And now she'd turned him into a vampire. I didn't know if Fiona had an ability or was simply perceptive, but her gaze caught mine. Her smile faltered, but she held it before looking away.

"I'll talk to Fiona," I said.

"Sure. I'll do a lap and talk to the other staff," Della said.

"I'll come with you," Ilian said, his eerie grey eyes locked on Della.

"Awesome," Della said flatly. She marched off with Ilian trailing after her.

Fiona was on her way over with a tray full of glasses, so I positioned myself at the end of the bar. "Oh hey!" she said, setting down the tray on the bar and slipping behind it. "How are y'all doin'?"

"Good, thanks," I said, as she started putting glasses into the washer with practised hands. "How are you?"

"Not too bad. Is this about Will?" She closed the machine and came to stand across the bar from me, toying nervously with the hem of her black T-shirt.

"What about him?" I asked, since she'd given me an opening.

"I'm sorry y'all don't approve of what I did," she said, making a visible effort to maintain eye contact. "He really wanted it, and he'd thought the decision through. I care about him a whole lot . . . and I helped him through the change."

"I appreciate that. And I know how stubborn Will can be."

Fiona looked grateful, and I wasn't sure how long that was going to last. I checked around us for eavesdroppers, then got to it. "I'm actually here on slayer business."

Fiona gripped the bar. "What business?"

After what we did to her friends, I understood her fear. "There've been attacks on customers at Armand's bars. Have you seen anything suspicious?"

Fiona looked up while she pondered. "I don't think so. I've had a couple days off to help Will adjust – I didn't know about it until Armand told me today."

I believed her, so there was no point in drawing it out. "I should go to find Della. Thanks for your help."

"Any time. Thanks for bein' nice . . . you know – about Will. He's around here somewhere if you wanna say hi." Her smile was genuine, crinkling her eyes. I could see how she and Will worked – her softness against his sharp edges.

I clocked Della and Ilian across the room when something hit my foot, followed by a tug on my jeans. My scowl was ready when I realised the culprit was a little boy . . . in the middle of a packed bar. I retrieved his car from under a stool and crouched down to speak to him. He had brown, wavy hair parted to one side and a serious little face.

Accepting the car, he looked up at me with the guileless, liquid-blue eyes of innocence. "I'm Tony. What's your name?" The music was loud, but his clear voice carried.

"Hi Tony, I'm Mina," I said. I wasn't a kid expert, but I guessed he was around six. "Are you by yourself?"

A tall, bleached-blonde man swept him up, and I stood too in case Tony needed help. "Sorry if he bothered you," the man said, his body language nervous as he glanced around the bar. "He's supposed to be in the office – I couldn't get a sitter."

The boy rested his head on the man's shoulder. "Sorry, Daddy. My car wanted to go for a drive."

I looked properly at the man then. He'd worked at the bar since John Carter owned it – not a great character recommendation. But from the adoring way his son gazed up at him, I had to give him some credit. "Next time, tell your car to stay in the office," he said, his sternness melting away the longer he stared at his little boy.

"Before you go, can I ask you something?"

The man's expression turned serious as he nodded at me.

"When you've dropped Tony off, can you come back to answer some questions?"

He looked relieved. "I already told Della everything I know."

"I'm bored," Tony said. "Bye, Mina."

"Bye Tony," I said, laughing.

"Thank you," Tony's dad said, weaving through the crowd in the direction of the office Armand hardly used.

Ilian appeared so silently that he startled me. "Who brings a child into a bar?" he asked disdainfully.

"His dad works here. I don't think he'd bring him if he had a choice," I said.

"Children should be protected," Ilian said, his voice softening. "I virtually raised my siblings – I understand that responsibility. Have you found anything useful?"

So the scary vampire had a kinder side. "Nothing yet. I'm going to keep looking around."

Ilian nodded and went to the bar.

Setting off towards my friends, I tried to check over the bar as Della would. The dancefloor was full of people singing along to 'All I Wanna Do' by Sheryl Crow. Nothing suspicious caught my eye.

One person looked out of place among those who were dancing, chatting and drinking. A figure in a long leather coat was leaning against the bare brick wall at the back of Empire, his dark hair flopping over his face: Will. The crowd shifted, revealing a grinning girl beside him that definitely wasn't Fiona. She was running her hands through her curly black hair, head tilted to one side.

Usually, I got no slayer impulses whatsoever. I hoped for the best and tried to help people. But today they were screaming at me to fix whatever this was.

I followed Will and the girl closely enough to catch the emergency door on my foot. The alleyway outside Empire was dark and smelled like alleyways generally do, a mixture of rubbish and other disgusting things. It was my second in one night – lucky me. I dragged a box of empty bottles against the door to keep it open, as the only handle was inside. The music from Empire was a comfort while every instinct jangled out a warning.

Will and the girl had vanished into the shadows between buildings. Then a car passed the end of the alleyway, illuminating the couple towards the darkest end. Away from the street and civilisation . . . great.

Since this was Will, I left my stake inside my jacket, but I was ready to grab it. He wasn't the only vampire on the streets of New Orleans, and at least one had lately developed a taste for murder.

"Well?" the girl was saying as I inched closer, my eyes finally adjusting. "Aren't you going to kiss me?"

"Not exactly," Will said.

Then he sank his fangs into her throat.

Chapter 22

With no hesitation, I grabbed my new stake that Saint Germain had given us and rushed towards them. From this close, I could see the girl's face, and there was no trace of fear. She looked blissed out, her eyes closed and lips parted as Will drank. He broke away moments later, wiping a thumb across his lower lip. With his fangs extended, he was beautiful and vicious. Neither of them seemed to have noticed that I was there.

"Look at me," Will murmured. He pulled the curtain of her long, curly hair down over the marked curve of her throat. "You need to *forget* what I did and all about me. All you know is that you had a great time with your friends, but you had a lot to drink and got hurt."

"I really did," she said, smiling up at him. "Aren't you coming inside?"

"I would," he said, running a hand down her face, "but you won't remember me."

The girl drifted inside with a happy look on her face, kicking the box as she went. The door clanged shut behind her, locking us out.

"Are you gonna use that, or shall we go inside?" Will asked, his grin dazzling and absolutely deadly.

"Don't tempt me," I said, pointing the tip of the stake at his chest. "Didn't you listen to what Della and Jared said? I don't know if the slayers would stake you for what you did, but do you want to test them? And did you just do some mind-melt thing on her?"

Will shrugged, raising an eyebrow at me. He pushed the tip of the stake away and I put it back into my jacket holster. "I make people forget – I can't control them or anything. I take the blood I need consensually and don't kill, so your precious code is intact. No big deal."

"I beg to differ. Wait – are you the one who's been picking off people connected to Armand's businesses?"

"Not me. First time trying that here – honest."

I had no idea if he was full of it, but I wasn't about to take him on alone. "Let's get back inside. Maybe Della or Jared can talk some sense into you." I reached for the door before remembering that Will's new friend had closed it behind her. Looked like we'd have to take a walk down the long, smelly alley. This night was getting better and better.

"Wait."

All of a sudden, Will's voice was the most interesting thing. I turned around to face him, and he was looking into me with those mesmerising grey eyes.

"*Forget*," he began, the word infused with power. "Forget what you saw and what we said. We came into the alley for some air and accidentally got shut out here."

"Are you OK?" Will's face went out of focus and came back in. He was holding onto both of my upper arms. "You zoned out there."

"Sorry," I said. "It's been a rough few days."

We set off slowly down the alley, kicking crushed leaves and scraps of rubbish out of our way. I tried not to inhale too deeply. "You never did tell me how it went with your Dad," he said.

"You kind of overshadowed it by getting turned into a vampire."

He smiled wickedly. "You say that like it's a bad thing."

"Depends on the kind of vampire you are." As we got to the street, the orange lighting turned his grin devilish.

We walked into Empire as the cover band took to the stage. They were meant to be doing all kinds of classic rock goodness.

Della joined me and Will as we were about to hit the dance floor. "Hey, new vamp," she said, and he gave her a toothy grin. "None of the staff noticed anything out of the ordinary these past few days, so Ilian took off. Maybe whoever it was will stop now Armand's back. How'd you do?"

"Same here. No one knows anything."

"Great!" Della said. "Let's go hang out then do another sweep later if needed."

The lead singer belted out the first line of 'Carry on Wayward Son', as he gripped the microphone, his long hair swaying like Axl Rose.

"That's my cue to go," Will said, pointing to the bar. He strode off, black leather jacket flapping.

Della led the way towards the front of the crowd where Libby was bouncing around and singing along. Jared and I rocked in time to the music, singing and laughing and letting go of the worries that had got their claws into us this week.

When the final chords of Kansas died out, the band plunged

straight into 'Cryin' by Aerosmith. Jared pulled me close, and everyone else fell away. He was singing quietly, and every now and then I caught snatches of his low, slightly husky voice. Even though the lyrics weren't the most romantic, our feelings were real. His thick, wavy hair had fallen over his forehead, and the roaming lights behind the band caught his eyes every once in a while, treating me to a flare of pale green rimmed with hazel. He had this smile that was just for me, lips slightly parted and eyes soft. He wasn't the same person as when we met, but we fit together better than ever. Then he kissed me and I forgot about everything else.

We danced and laughed, and it was exactly what we needed. The tiredness didn't register until the band strummed the last chord of 'Don't Fear the Reaper'.

"Good night, y'all!" the lead singer shouted into his microphone, one hand raised as everyone clapped and whooped.

The crowd dispersed, some people slipping out into the night and most heading into a crush around the bar.

Della eyed me and Jared critically, her arm around Libby. "You both look beat. I think we should call it a night."

"Me too," Libby said through a yawn as she rested her head on Della's shoulder.

There was no sign of Will. I felt like maybe I'd wanted to tell him something, but it was gone for now.

The four of us set off onto the dark, busy street, and the cold hit me. I'd only shivered once when Jared pulled me against him. I got as close as I could while not falling over our feet. He wasn't a source of warmth like he used to be, but his proximity helped.

We walked fast without talking much, the soothing bustle of

New Orleans carrying on around us despite the temperature. Voices and music all blended together, creating a sensory immersion where there was no room for anything else. A lot of places had got fall decorations in place, sheathes of dried corn and sunflowers in shop windows and cute straw scarecrows tucked behind balcony railings. Stands for the fall fair were ready to go, covers pinned over them so we wouldn't get a proper look until tomorrow.

Della followed my gaze to a balcony overhead with garlands of orange leaves spiralling down. "We see out the fall right until the end of November, but you'll get some Christmas stuff sneaking in soon."

The mansion looked especially sinister from across the street with the lights off, its charred walls and barred windows fitting for the horrors that had happened here. I loved living with my sister and friends, but the people who had died here constantly played on my mind. Current finances meant we couldn't move out, but it would be healthier to get some distance one day.

We hadn't caught up on all of the missed sleep from travelling to and from New Mexico, so we headed straight to bed. I barely had time to think about Jared, alone in the attic on the floor above, before I crashed.

The next thing I knew, I woke after nine. Usually, I'd be volunteering at the police station at this time. Even though I was missing it during my hiatus, I was grateful for the extra sleep today. Libby and Della still seemed to be asleep, and the attic was silent overhead. Jared needed all the rest he could get after using his new ability yesterday, and I wasn't complaining if he got back to sleeping at night and being around in the day.

Full of purpose, I dialled Cafferty's number. He didn't bother with a hello. "Usually I'd ignore a call at this hour on my day off."

"No, you wouldn't," I said. "Someone might have a grandma who needs help crossing the road or a kitten stuck up a tree."

"I think the kitten thing is firefighters, and I'm sure they love the stereotype," he said. "So you're wantin' to go to that location in the swamps?"

"Yeah," I said. "Are you free to come with me?"

"I guess my PlayStation can wait. I'll be right there."

I was waiting outside the mansion when Cafferty arrived, a coffee for him in my hand. Libby kept a stack of to-go cups in the kitchen.

"You don't need to butter me up, you know," he said, accepting the cup. "I know you'll use some absolutely compelling reason to convince me to let you come along, so I'm skippin' to the end."

"Good move. Before we go, I should tell you that Saint Germain turned up at the slayers' meeting. Like you thought, he wasn't impressed when you told him that you didn't find the cult's location."

"Thanks for the heads up – not that I didn't see it coming," Cafferty sighed. "And we're about to visit another group that I have to keep from him."

"Yeah . . . Sorry to pull you into this one." Cafferty shrugged affably, so I moved on. "I'm assuming you know how to get out there. I wasn't sure on the best footwear." I gestured at the chunky boots I'd borrowed from Della.

"I've got us covered. And those'll do it." Cafferty was wearing his leather jacket, jeans and a big pair of steel-toe-capped leather boots, perfect for ass kicking. I hoped he wouldn't need to do any.

Chapter 23

I'd not spent a lot of time on the water, and this airboat was a new experience. It was small and low, with a cage at the back that contained a massive propeller. When we got up to speed, the rotation sent a constant plume of spray out behind us. It was so loud at top speed that we had to wear ear defenders, reducing the incessant roar to a vibrating hum. It was familiar, and I wondered if that might have been the engine roar at the end of Dad's answerphone message. We'd already known he was likely to be out here with Clem, but it felt like confirmation.

The sound of falling water and the whir of the blades might have been comforting, but the murky brown water was undoing that. I had some idea of the deadly creatures that lurked in the depths. Around us, shrouds of Spanish moss trailed from enormous, straight trees growing right out of the water, their roots exposed like splayed fingers.

Captain Hebert reduced the speed. I tugged off my ear defenders, full of questions. "Are there alligators out here?" I asked, a shadow gliding under the surface. Was that a long, flicking tail?

"We got all kindsa critters," the captain said in his French-tinged Cajun accent. His laugh turned into a rattling cough.

"Otters, wild boar, turtles . . . Some funny folks too. You sure you don't just want the tour and then I'll take you back?"

"We're good thanks," Cafferty replied. "Like I said, we'll not be long. We need to see somebody and then we'll come right back."

"You want the stories, since y'all are payin' me?" the man said. He made a hacking sound and spat into the river.

"Go right ahead," Cafferty said, grinning at me. He knew I loved that stuff. I settled in, enjoying the gentle movement of the boat.

"In Cajun legend, we got our very own swamp monster," Captain Hebert said, his sun-leathered face cracking into a broad grin. "Beast called the Rougarou. It prowls the swamps round here, lookin' for children who misbehave. Stories go that he got the body of a man and the head of a wolf. You might call 'im a werewolf, though I wouldn't let 'im hear ya." He chuckled again. "He flies around on a giant bat, and if he spies children staying up too late, the bat drops 'im down your chimney. Not a bad way to get your kids to bed, you know?"

"It'd work for me," I said. "Are there any other stories?"

"Think we got time for one more. I'm sure y'all heard of dat pirate Jean Lafitte, right? He used to leave his booty all over the place. This one time, he killed somebody and buried 'em with treasure, binding the spirit to the box. That's how ya turn a ghost into a *fifolet* – kind of a floatin' light. So if y'all see a blue light, you wanna turn dat boat around, 'cause the light gonna lead y'all astray."

The captain fell silent as we glided through the brown water. The autumn colours were spectacular, and I was grateful to see them before winter took hold. I'd heard that would happen much later here than in England. Burnt oranges deepened to scarlet, fallen leaves mingling with green algae on the fringes of the water. As we drew closer to Dad, the peace around us lost its hold on me. I was voluntarily travelling towards him, after what he'd done to Jared, and this time he'd holed up with a potentially dangerous group armed with vampire-hunting weapons.

"Anythin' we need to discuss before we go in there?" Cafferty asked.

"I haven't exactly got an iron-clad plan," I admitted.

The captain let out a strangled cough that might have been a laugh, but Cafferty ignored him. "What do you want to get out of this?"

"I want to see what he's planning and if he knows anything about . . . you know," I said, glancing at the captain. "Also, I need to warn him about a few things."

"Sure. All right if I let you take the lead? He'll likely be more suspicious if it comes from me. Besides, I'm not exactly here in an official capacity, so it's best if we don't tell anyone what I do." Cafferty trailed a hand in the murky water – a lot braver than me.

"Makes sense," I said.

"'Scuse me," the captain said gruffly, "we're almost there." The last word sounded like 'dare' in his Cajun accent.

I'd got so used to the endless trees and water that the house on stilts was a jarring sight. Its surroundings were striking, with heavy branches of golden and brown leaves draped over the wooden structure. The building was unsettling, as if the motives of the occupants had shaped its appearance. Every window was boarded up, and it had been extended over the years to give the house a looming, misshapen appearance. No one had cleared away the brown leaves heaped around the stilts, and the atmosphere was one of gloom and abandonment. Small fishing boats moored along a lopsided pier were the main clue the house was inhabited at all.

"You sure this is the place?" Cafferty asked, deep lines forming across his forehead.

"Only one at the co-ordinates you gave me," the captain said.

With the noise our airboat was making, one thing was certain. If the occupants were home, then they'd know we were coming.

The captain moored the boat at the end of the makeshift pier of wooden planks and pillars. It sagged with every step.

My relief at hitting dry land was short-lived. Cafferty scooped up a long stick as we stepped onto the spongy earth. "Follow in my footsteps. I'll test the ground with this stick. Take it slowly and keep your eyes on your feet. There's mud around here that'll take you right down."

I followed his advice, my heart pounding fast in contrast with every agonising step. One misplaced foot could leave me sinking without a trace. Occasionally, the mud dragged at one of my boots with an ominous sucking sound.

It was hard to concentrate on the treacherous ground with that house on stilts ahead. It looked even more imposing from down here, the crooked angles creating countless hiding places. "Always assume people could be armed, especially with the back story you told me," Cafferty said, prodding the ground before each step. "Keep your hands on display so they can see we're not about to pull guns."

The scattered nerves I'd been feeling drew together into a hard ball of dread. I'd been fretting more about seeing my dad than the group he'd joined forces with, but I should've given them more thought.

We inched along the soggy, uneven ground, drawing nearer to the ladder.

"I don't like accessin' this place without the use of my hands, but we're kinda low on options." Cafferty set one hand on the mossy wood of the ladder and started to climb.

I waited until he was halfway up before following. The moss had rough and slippery patches, so I placed my hands carefully and climbed slowly, even though I would've preferred to scramble up.

The ladder wobbled when Cafferty climbed off at the top. I clung to it, taking time to breathe and reclaim my balance before I climbed on.

He was waiting on a wraparound porch, a wooden awning casting us in shadow. "Wanna do the honours?" Cafferty asked, gesturing at the door.

It was swollen and uneven from years out on the swamp. I knocked hard, the wood damp and weirdly flexible under my knuckles.

With a painful creak, the door opened. There was no light on inside, and the awning overhead made it hard to distinguish the man's features. The shotgun at his side was clear enough though.

Cafferty stepped in front of me, blocking my body with his. "I've come to see my dad . . . Jeffrey Shepherd," I said, looking around Cafferty. That was probably what he'd been trying to avoid when he made a human shield.

A light clicked on somewhere behind the man, illuminating his thin, deeply wrinkled face. His eyes were deep-set and suspicious, and the stench of tobacco and old sweat rolled off him. It didn't take long for me to put my twinge of recognition to rest. He was the man from the photograph that Dad had broken ties with for being too extreme. I wasn't thrilled about Dad's plan to expose vampires and have them registered, but it was a rare case where he was the lesser of two evils.

"You got no reason to worry," Cafferty said, hands raised and his tone level and authoritative. "Like my friend said, she wants to talk to her father and then we'll go."

The man's battered camo jacket and trousers hung off a lean, wiry build. He lifted the gun higher, pointing it at Cafferty. "And isn't that just what a spy would say?"

There was a horrible, drawn-out moment where the man looked down the barrel at Cafferty.

"You don't need to point that at me," Cafferty said in his most soothing voice. "I'm not armed. We told you why we're here."

The man gave a thin, sly smile. "Shepherd ain't inside right now. Not sure if he told you who I am. The name's Clem. Now we're acquainted, y'all can come on in."

"We're fine to wait out here," I said.

Pointing the gun upwards, Clem fired at his own awning. The boom left my ears ringing, and splinters of wood rained down over us. "That wasn't a request. Next bullet goes into flesh if y'all don't come inside. And before y'all try to play the hero," he said, pointing the gun at Cafferty again, "I want both of you." The roar of an airboat starting cut through the silence, and all three of us watched our boat leave. "Looks like y'all had better come in," Clem added.

Cafferty nodded, walking through the door first. I followed, nerves swirling in my stomach as I closed the door behind us. With the boat gone, we were stranded with Clem.

The cramped hallway smelled eye-wateringly bad – a combination of sewers, cigarette smoke and mould. Clem beckoned for us to follow him into a room that was like a hunting lodge from hell. Animal heads hung from the walls: a once majestic stag with glass eyes that looked right into me, a boar with its mouth hanging open and even a snarling bear. A fire roared in a rough-hewn wooden fireplace, making the room stuffy and lacing the air with woodsmoke.

Sofas lined the room and a table in the middle was full of overflowing ash trays, papers and casually strewn around stakes and crossbow bolts. The sounds of voices and feet stomping up and down stairs reverberated through the house, but we were alone in the room with Clem.

Cafferty was giving the room a onceover too, the muscles in his neck forming tense cords. "How long do you expect her father to take?"

Clem set the gun down by the door, standing with his arms folded in the doorway. The windows were boarded up, so there'd be no getting out of here. "I knew it was a bad idea lettin' Jeff stay with us. I left his spineless Community for a reason. Now, sit your asses down and answer a few questions."

I followed Cafferty's lead, sitting on the sofa beside him with foreboding rushing through me. Dust puffed up around us, clawing at the back of my throat.

The heat from the fire was almost unbearable. Sweat trickled down Clem's cheek, and he mopped it off with a sleeve. "Why should I believe you're Jeff's daughter?" he asked, before noisily running his tongue around his mouth.

Who would lie about that? I pushed down the nervous impulse

for attitude – Clem's gun was within reach. "I don't have any ID, but I've seen the picture of you and Dad. He said you joined the Community after being attacked by a hidebehind – that it nearly killed you. You were a member of his group, so you've probably got one of those raven tattoos."

Fear crossed his face before it went blank once more. "You think you know everythin', don't ya? Well, you got one thing wrong." Clem slid one shoulder out of his camo jacket. A puckered circular scar with a slash through it marred the skin of his upper arm. "In my group, we show our commitment with brands. The fire purifies and bonds us together."

I swallowed, acting tough even as my gaze found a metal poker sticking out of the fire. It didn't seem wise to look away from Clem for too long.

Sure enough, he was scrutinising me. "OK, so you're one of his girls. That don't explain what you're doing here."

"I found out he was here and wanted to see him." Surely that would be plausible for a lot of families.

Clem sneered, scooping up the gun. He strode across to stand over us, holding the weapon loosely at his side. "Now why don't I believe you?"

"It doesn't matter," Cafferty said. "Mina's father obviously isn't here, so she and I had better go outside to call another boat."

"Did y'all really think that would work, boy?" Clem asked, holding the gun up across his chest. He had his finger on the trigger, but it wasn't pointed in our direction. "I've coughed up phlegm globbers more intimidatin' than you. Where do you fit into this, anyhow? Ain't she a little young for you?"

Cafferty tensed beside me but didn't rise to Clem's needling.

"I'm a friend. You don't need to worry about me."

Heavy footsteps announced the teenage boy before he staggered up to the doorway, a wooden box weighing down long, skinny arms. "Hey, Clem? Where do you want the huntin' gear for the—"

"Keep your goddamn mouth shut, boy!" Clem snapped. "Put it in the back with the rest."

"Hunting gear?" I asked, unable to keep my mouth shut.

Clem grinned widely. "Hasn't your daddy told you that's why the two of us parted ways? He wants to educate humans, and we want to eliminate paranormals. Can't exactly live and work together with that kinda difference in ideology. We kill the creatures who hurt us – it's that simple. Your dad's TV broadcast got us thinkin' that we gotta focus on one type of beast – get organised. I for one want to make a difference before the end of days."

Clem had to know he was talking about killing innocents. I was so scared I almost couldn't keep it together, but anger gave me some strength. "And what about the *paranormals*, as you call them, who want to live their lives without hurting anyone? Do you kill them too?"

"Tell me, little lady . . . What do vampires eat?"

His question caught me off guard, and when I gave no answer, he went on with a knowing grin. "They don't eat at all, do they? The filthy bloodsuckers drain our bodies until we're dead. To them, we're nothin' but prey, and I can't have that. I put them down."

"That's murder!" I was so incensed that the unfiltered thought popped out.

Striding forwards, Clem bent down until the gun was rested on his knees. Both he and the weapon were way too close to me.

"You sound like one of them sympathisers, girly. Jeff must be so disappointed in you."

"That's enough," Cafferty said. "We've done everything you asked."

Clem sneered. "I'm nowhere near done with you yet." He strode over to the fire, putting his gun down to withdraw the poker from the flames. It had a circle on the end that matched his own arm, the metal glowing orange. "Perhaps I ought to leave you with a lasting reminder of my message."

"Put the poker down," Cafferty said. He surged to his feet and grabbed hold of the gun with impressive agility.

"I'd listen to him, if I were you," Dad said from the doorway.

Chapter 24

I'd never been so happy to see Dad. Clem straightened up, scowling. "I want you and that boy outta here, Jeff. You can't be bringin' strangers to our place."

"I've already secured somewhere else to live," Dad said smoothly. "I'll be taking my daughter and her friend home now. We can trust them not to share our location or what they've seen – you have my personal assurance."

"Like I said – I ain't finished with them yet." Clem was still gripping the branding iron.

Dad moved in closer, apparently unfazed by the scorching weapon in unpredictable hands. His green eyes were furious but steady. "You might have left my group, but you still owe everything you do here to *me*. You started your endeavour from the roots of my own. We're leaving *now*. I suggest you think real hard before doin' somethin' that gets you and your people killed. Violence will never yield genuine progress. Vampires are merely people who have been changed. It could happen to anyone, including you or me."

When Dad got like this, he was terrifying. Clem adjusted his grip on the poker, trying and failing to look tough. "I'd rather die,"

Clem said through a snarl. "Now, you might as well get them out of my sight. And leave my gun behind, while you're at it."

"With pleasure," Cafferty said. He removed the ammunition and kicked the weapon under the sofa.

I stood up, beginning to feel hopeful that we might get out of here without anyone getting burned or shot.

Dad stayed in the doorway as I filed past with Cafferty behind me. "You go down first," Cafferty said.

Climbing down took a lot more effort. I clung to the slimy ladder, aware of how much less strength and coordination I had on the way down. With my adrenaline spent, I felt shaky and worn out.

The ladder swayed as I got past the halfway point. Cafferty was already climbing down, as much in a hurry as I was to get out of here. Finally, my feet sank into the swampy ground. I grabbed a stick from a pile that had presumably been left for the purpose, adopting Cafferty's approach of prodding the earth before planting my feet.

Across the muddy patch of earth, Chase was waiting in an airboat at the end of the pier. Clem and his gun were definitely a worse option at our back, but I wasn't looking forward to a boat ride with Chase and Dad either.

I kept at my careful process, avoiding spots where the stick plunged too deep. Before long, I was navigating the wobbly pier.

I climbed into the boat across from Chase. I'd had enough of people scowling at me like I was the absolute worst today, so I gave back as good as I was getting.

"Don't know what you're frownin' at," Chase said. "You and your little friends are the ones who ruined everything."

"How – by saving my boyfriend from dying? He could've burned to death – you're lucky I don't shove you off this boat to take your chances with the alligators."

Chase let out a hard, surprised laugh. "You got more fire in you than I thought."

The boat swayed as Cafferty and Dad got in. I don't know where Dad found the confidence to smile at me after what he'd done to Jared. With his eyes still fixed on me, he addressed Chase. "I hope you're not givin' my daughter a hard time." Chase flinched, even though Dad hadn't been that harsh. "All she did was derail an ill-conceived plan. One I now know was wrong."

"Wrong," I said flatly, as Chase leaned over the side of the boat to untie it. I was only tempted for a moment to shove him in like I'd threatened. "You could've killed Jared. I'd say that's quite a long way past wrong."

Chase started the engine, ending the conversation. He wasn't going to get Dad out of it that easily. I scrambled to find the ear defenders from my bag, shoving them on to deaden the noise as the boat roared away from Clem's ramshackle pier.

I watched the house until it faded into the distance. Chase turned down the power, and I removed the ear defenders. It was time to let Dad have it. Cafferty's expression was grim, but he remained quiet. I knew he'd be ready to offer backup if I needed it. "If I didn't have to be here, I'd want nothing to do with you. I can't believe you tried to kill Jared. Do you really care that little about me?"

Dad looked at Cafferty. "I'd prefer to have this discussion later with family alone. I'm sure you understand, detective."

"I don't understand any of your actions," Cafferty said levelly.

"Cafferty is my mentor, and he's one of the few people I can trust," I said. "This is your opportunity to talk to me."

Something unreadable flickered over Dad's face before he relented. "Fine. I suppose it doesn't hurt for the detective to hear the truth – he'll need to know soon enough anyway. I love you, honey. But this is bigger than all of us. I'm deeply sorry for what I did to Jared. I swear to you that I had a blanket to cover him. But I needed the world to see him burn first – to prove what is hiding in their midst."

"You risked his life," I said. "For all you knew, he was going to die. You think you're so different from Clem, but you're just as bad." The peaceful greenery passed by in a blur, with all of my concentration focused on this little boat.

"I'm sorry you feel that way, honey. I went there hoping Clem and I could reconcile and that I could bring him to my way of thinking, but some people can't be helped. I'm in the process of securing a place in the city where your mom and the rest of us will be safe. And I know that taking Jared was a mistake," he said, his eyes so very green and full of conviction. "It was too strong a sign to ignore. First your mom arrived, living proof that vampires existed. And then Libby told me that Jared was coming with you, the boy Emma had already revealed to me was a vampire. It became clear that vampires were worthy of my focus as the gateway to revealing cryptids, aliens and everything else. That was all I needed to come to New Orleans, the home of vampires in the United States, as well as the chance to spend time with my daughters, of course."

"When the Shepherd gets a sign, the Community takes notice," Chase said as fervently as Dad but without that intangible charisma. "If he thinks vampires are gonna cause the end of days, then that's what's gonna happen."

"You're skippin' ahead a few steps," Dad said gently, but Chase visibly wilted. "My belief is that an informed public will start the right debate. The government will be forced to register and tag all paranormal beings, as well as developing a defence strategy and a body of laws should an uprising occur."

Cafferty spoke up quietly but full of feeling. "You want to expose members of paranormal communities to intense scrutiny. Like with humans, a small percentage don't play by the rules, and there are systems to deal with them."

Dad considered Cafferty gravely. "If my daughter trusts you, I'll lend you the same consideration. According to a prophecy that's been verified numerous times over, we got less than two years before paranormal beings end the world as we know it. I'm sorry for the impact my actions will have on those beings who follow the rules, but all of us will have to make sacrifices for the good of the many."

The apocalypse theory was too huge for me to fathom, and built on the shaky foundations of premonitions. I'd seen Armand's visions come true, but even they were unpredictable and subject to change. The prospect of Dad being right gave me a shiver of unease, but this wasn't the time.

"I don't think you and I will ever agree on that," I said, still struggling to keep my cool. "But there's something you can do if you want to start making it up to me." Like always, Dad had brought the focus onto him. Even if his apocalypse fear somehow ended up being valid, people were losing their lives to a killer right now.

"If you're going to ask me to veer from my mission, then that's somethin' I can never do – not even for you, honey." Emotion radiated off Dad so strongly that it seeped into me. Chase had been quiet since Dad's putdown, but I was aware of his sullen presence as he steered the boat.

"You can stop calling me that," I said evenly. "Things have changed in the last ten years."

Could it be that the great Shepherd looked ashamed? "I am sorry . . . Mina. I'll apologise as many times as I need to, if it'll bring you back to me. I have faith you'll do that one day when it becomes clear that I'm right. Now, what was it you came here to talk to me about?"

At least he knew I hadn't come to socialise, so he wasn't entirely delusional. "Have you seen the news the past two days?" I asked.

Dad's cheek shifted like he was chewing the skin inside it. Libby used to do the same thing when she was nervous. "I take it we're talkin' about the vampire ripper case."

"That's the one. I find it interesting that a supposed vampire kills someone and tells the newspaper about it right around the time you turned up. You know, trying to reveal vampires just after you failed to do it."

The sparkle of devious intelligence in Dad's eyes filled me with discomfort. "The idea has a certain flair, and it will get people talking about vampires. But you don't think it's me, do you?"

"Most vampires like Mum and Jared don't kill, so there's a small pool of suspects. If it's not you, it could be someone you know, either a vampire or someone pretending to be."

Cafferty was a silent, solid presence at my side. A sideways glance confirmed he was giving me a proud smile.

"My people would never resort to violence. They follow my lead absolutely in that." Conviction set Dad's features in a hard mask. "I give you my word that me and my Community aren't responsible. I simply took it as another sign that I arrived here looking to reveal vampires, right when a vampire with the same objective made themselves known. It couldn't be clearer. I need to find the murderer, stop them from killing and convince them to work with me to expose the truth. Once the uprising is averted and my mission is done, I can concentrate more on my family."

I couldn't control the longing that set in, even after what he'd done to Jared. I'd spent my whole life wanting exactly what he was offering. Luckily Cafferty cut in before I said something I'd regret. "I assume you're not plannin' to break any laws – like impeding a criminal investigation, for example."

"Of course not," Dad said, ice forming beneath his friendliness. "I'm merely a concerned citizen expressin' an interest in a local matter."

"So you're planning to investigate?" I asked.

"I'm entirely within my rights to follow the case," Dad said.

"And if you overstep those rights, the police will act accordingly," Cafferty said, his strength showing through the civility.

"I'm sure they will, detective." Cafferty and Dad's gazes locked in a battle of wills.

The swampy river had mostly looked the same up to now, but I spied a familiar skyline in the distance. We were running out of time with Dad, and he was likely to slip away as soon as we reached dry land. "There was another reason why I came. Your message made it sound like you weren't going to reach out, and I have to warn you about something. A powerful vampire has been sniffing around the New Mexico ranch, and he's looking into . . . groups . . . who are interested in vampires in the area." I caught myself before I called it a cult.

"A powerful vampire?" Dad said, his expression turning fanatical. "I'd love to meet him. If he could be convinced to share my message with the world . . ."

"You really wouldn't," I said. "He's dangerous. If he finds you and your people, he'd kill everyone to stop you from revealing vampires. He's accumulated so much wealth and power over the years that he has more to lose than anyone."

"We can take care of ourselves," Dad said, his gaze becoming dreamy and faraway. "We must be on the right track if influential vampires know who we are."

He really wasn't getting it, but I couldn't make it any clearer. He and Chase were both grinning like I'd handed them a prize instead of a warning.

The pier where we'd picked up our original airboat came into view, and I took a last look at Dad. He was still wrapped up in what I'd told him. I was so angry at what he'd done to Jared, but mostly I felt hollow. I'd done what I came here to do and, once again, Dad cared more about his next mission than his family.

"Thanks for the ride," I said when the boat bumped against the pier. Chase tied it up so we could get out.

Cafferty climbed out first, but an idea struck me. "Call me when you're in your new place. I've lived here a while. Maybe I can help with your investigation." If he bought it, what better way to keep an eye on him?

Dad's ego knew no bounds. After a flicker of surprise, a victorious grin stretched tight across his face. He thought he'd won me over. “I’d like that.”

“We’d better go,” Chase said gruffly. “Before someone asks what we’re doin’ here.”

“You’re right,” Dad said. “I’ll look forward to seein’ you.” He loaded so much feeling into the words that I couldn’t help but feel moved. Cafferty and I watched Chase untie the airboat and back it away, the engine loud in our ears as it churned up the water. Dad watched us too until we couldn’t see him anymore.

Chapter 25

After our ordeal, I treated Cafferty to shrimp po'boys from Deanie's – one of our favourite sandwich shops. In City Park, we sat on a bench under a tree with fronds of Spanish moss hanging down around us. We started eating, neither of us talking about when I'd last visited this park with him. I'd taken it upon myself to visit a crime scene on my first day doing work experience with the police. I'd seen a lot more bodies since then.

"You're doin' real good, you know," Cafferty said. "I know you don't like the sentimental stuff, but hear me out. Since you moved to this city, things have been . . . intense. And you've handled it all with a level head. Not just that – with bravery. You're more than ready for cadet school, and I'd love to get you volunteering again as soon as I can."

"Thanks," I said. "It's like I brought an endless string of disasters with me."

"Nah, you didn't do anything. This city needed help before you came. But there's a lot of good here too, and people like us are making things better."

"Then you have the people like my dad, who makes everything ten times worse."

"You said it. My gut's telling me he didn't do this – he seemed genuine. But I get the impression your dad is good at making people believe what he wants."

"He is," I said. "I don't think he did it either, but this is too important to get wrong."

"It is, which is why I'm gonna stop by the morgue," Cafferty said. "Armand's coming to see if we got a real vampire on our hands. If so, that will rule out your dad and any other human."

"Can I come too? Technically, I'd be keeping away from the police station like I promised Boudreaux."

Cafferty eyed me. "You know you're in the minority of people who'd ask that question. But I don't see why not. I'll pick you up outside the mansion at sunset, and we can meet Armand at the morgue. Assuming we do rule out your dad, we could do without him rummagin' around in the investigation. I'm not sure I put him off." Cafferty screwed up the wrapper of his sandwich and tossing it into the nearest bin.

"I don't think anything would – which is why I'm thinking of helping him. Hear me out," I said, grinning at Cafferty's exaggerated outrage. "He's going to investigate anyway. If he'll let me come along for the ride, chances are we won't find anything out, but I can keep an eye on him. And if we get anywhere, I'll feed it back to you."

Cafferty leaned his elbows on his legs, one fist pressed against his mouth while he thought. "I don't like it. But I understand. You'll keep me in the loop every step of the way?"

"Definitely. Thank you for trusting me."

Assuming I could convince Dad to let me tag along, I doubted I could change his behaviour much. But perhaps I could keep him from doing something the rest of us would have to live with.

"What do we do about Clem?" The thought of him hoarding weapons on the swamp made me queasy.

"I wasn't technically supposed to be there," Cafferty said, "but I could've pulled him up on charges for threatening me with a deadly weapon. I think instead I'll hand it off to our weapons and firearms division and say we had a tip off. We'll have a better chance of taking down the whole group that way."

"OK, that sounds good," I said. Clem deserved to be caught before he used those weapons.

Jared was up and about by the time I got back, and Libby put us to work in the new *Lost Boys* room. The contractors had finished remodelling, and now the painting and detail work began. Usually I found this kind of work soothing, but my head was already in the morgue. I wanted to be involved in the investigation, but I'd seen enough morgue scenes on TV to know what I was getting into.

"What's up?" Jared asked. We were painting a section of wall grey, attempting to make it look like fallen rubble where the contractors had mounded up fibreglass.

"How could you tell?" I shot back, grinning as I dipped my brush into the sludgy paint. Jared had a way of making me loosen up. I'd already updated him on what we'd found out, but he could obviously tell I hadn't let it go.

Concern made his eyebrows come down low. "Let me guess what's on your mind. I'm gonna go with Dad or morgue."

"Try all of the above," I said, tackling the lumpy fibreglass.

"I keep going over what Dad said and I'm pretty sure I believe him, but I'm going wild thinking about what he's planning. And yeah, the morgue visit might be a step too far, even for me."

"Wish I could come with you," Jared said.

"No, you take Will to the blood bar. He's still new, and he needs reliability more than ever. Now stop worrying about me. Don't make me paint you."

Jared laughed, prying my fingers off the paintbrush and letting it sink into the paint. "You've got no chance. Vampire strength, remember?" He demonstrated by pulling me in fast and close.

"Don't overdo it," I teased. "Remember you're dating a slayer." Granted, not one with Buffy's supernatural strength, but I was handy with a stake.

I loved being close enough to see that wicked glint in Jared's eyes and all the small details of his face – the thick lines of his eyebrows, the small mole on his upper lip. That drew my attention to his mouth, and I was a goner. I kissed him hard, and he made a soft sound of enjoyment against my lips.

"Hey! Less smooching, more painting!" In case her point hadn't landed, Libby clapped her hands loudly.

Arms still around Jared, I pulled back. "I should get ready anyway."

I was so nervous on the ride in Cafferty's car that I stayed quiet. The fall fair was starting up, but I was too busy thinking about seeing a body and finding out once and for all if my dad was involved.

The New Orleans Forensics Center didn't look like much.

It was a dull concrete structure only one floor high and set back from a cheerful purple T-shirt shop that definitely upstaged it.

Armand was waiting in the doorway. "You invite me on the best outings," he said dryly. He was dressed all in black, which suited the occasion.

"Sorry," Cafferty said cheerfully. "I assume it comes as no surprise that Mina is here."

"Not in the least," Armand said with a smile. "I'm sure she would also like to get this over with. Shall we?"

The coroner was a grey-haired, serious man who offered little conversation. His eyes were a pale, watery blue behind thick glasses, and he was a similar height to me. My breathing quickened as I took in the rows of metal drawers – I knew what they contained. The coroner pulled one out and left us to it.

There was no mistaking what was inside the long grey bag on its silver pallet, a tag dangling from the end. I steadied my breathing to prepare myself. If I was going to start training as a police officer next year, I needed to keep it together around sights like this. It was the only way to find out who killed the victim and give their families some peace.

"Before we do this, what do you want from me?" Armand asked, his tone cold and verging on bored. This usually meant he was shutting down emotionally. I could learn a thing or two from him.

"Would you like to start?" Cafferty asked me.

Gaze locked on the body bag, I thought through my options. "We need to know if the killer is a real vampire . . . Also, is there anything else you can tell about them from the bite?"

"Good," Cafferty said, nodding. "Also, can you . . . you know, touch the body and get a reading?"

"I can help with Mina's queries once I see the body, but not yours, detective. I can't read the dead, and even if it were possible, I wouldn't try. Messing with them would only pull parts of myself towards their darkness, or bring things into the light that never should be."

"A simple no would've sufficed," Cafferty grumbled, reaching for the zip.

I would've found their camaraderie cute if it wasn't for what we were about to see.

Chapter 26

Cafferty unzipped the body bag and pushed it open. My hand automatically flew up to cover my nose and mouth. I was less likely to hurl if I couldn't smell anything.

I noticed details one at a time, trying to tuck my emotions away so I could see the body objectively. Thick stitches cut across the greyish white skin of the man's chest and down the centre of his body in a Y shape. Autopsies had to be done to find out what happened to victims, but the evidence of them was hard to take.

The man's closed eyes were unpleasantly flat, his lips and skin too pale. He looked like he'd been in his late twenties or early thirties, which set me off imagining all the people he'd left behind. We were here for them, even though it was too late for our victim.

Armand crouched down to inspect his neck wound. Even though I didn't want to, I moved closer when Armand did.

The skin around the torn flesh was puckered and bloodless. To my untrained eye, it resembled a vampire bite, but I waited for Armand's assessment. "A young vampire did this," he said, straightening to his full height. My eyes lingered on the wound before I backed away too. "The bite is messy like a less experienced feeding, but those are certainly genuine fang marks."

Some relief broke through the sombre mood – finally we had confirmation that my dad didn't do this.

Cafferty checked out the wound, frowning. "OK. What else?"

"It's likely a male due to the spacing of the fangs. You're looking for a young vampire, Matt, which is not good news. As you've seen, the newer the vampire, the more impulsive and bloodthirsty. Coupled with the letter to the press and the Tarot calling card . . . I believe the vampire will kill again."

Cafferty let out a long breath, zipping up the bag. "Got it. So we need to act fast."

The worst thing about these cases was that it was too late to save the victim. But Armand had given Cafferty some clues, and we had to hold on to that.

Cafferty dropped me off at the mansion, politely refusing my invitation to join us. I was glad he was forming a tentative friendship with Armand. Both of them needed more to their lives than work.

Rushing around to get ready for the fair did me good. After visiting Dad and the morgue, I needed to stay busy.

"Finally! We were about to leave without you." Libby appeared in my bedroom door long enough to insult me before dashing off.

"We weren't," Della said as I joined her by the door. She was already in her coat, waiting for my whirlwind of a sister. "How'd it go?"

"Seeing bodies doesn't get any easier. Armand said the killer is a new male vampire, so that's something for Cafferty to go on."

"I'll let Paige know later," Della said, a glimmer of loathing crossing her face when she said Paige's name. "Now let's quit the slayer talk and get to the fair."

"Agreed," Jared said, appearing in the living room doorway. "Unless you wanna talk about it some more?"

"I'm fine, thanks," I said. "Guessing you overheard what I said to Della?"

"Yup," he grinned. He looked really good in a chunky green hoodie that said 'Honolulu Volcanoes' in yellow and white – an American football team from the city where he was born.

"How'd it go with Will?" I asked.

Jared opened his mouth, but no sounds came out. He frowned. "I feel like I had something to tell you, but it's gone."

"I'm sure it'll come back if it's important."

We collected Will and Fiona on the quiet street outside the mansion – no signs of the fall fair here.

Della, Libby and I were wrapped up in thick coats, gloves and chunky hats, while Fiona had gone for denim and Will wore the usual leather. Jared was just wearing his hoodie. That was a fashion choice on their part – vampires didn't need the insulation.

Jared and Will went off ahead, talking animatedly. Will was adjusting well to being a vampire, and he had Jared in his corner.

"Ooh, is there a secret vampire handshake?" Libby called ahead with no regard for our surroundings. She was lucky we hadn't hit the busy part of the fair.

"Like we'd tell you," Will called back.

"It's nice to have friends with common interests, I guess," Libby said.

Fiona hung back with us, smiling shyly. "So, things are good with Will?" I asked.

"Yeah – he's a great guy. We've seen each other every day since our first date. Thanks for letting me come along."

"Of course," Della said.

After that, we ambled through the French Quarter, soaking up the atmosphere. Someone had strung purple and orange ribbons between streetlamps and balconies, with silk fall leaves trailing down. Baskets of dried corn stalks, acorns, pine cones and colourful squashes separated stalls selling food and autumnal merchandise: leaf garlands, clothes in rich autumnal shades and paper bags of autumn snacks.

Fiona went to catch up with Jared and Will, which was probably for the best when we found a stall selling apple fritters on foil trays. We watched the vendor dip apples into a pale batter and fry them to crispy golden perfection. Finally, she spooned syrup over each tray.

We ate while we walked, the crunchy batter and sour apple paired with sweet syrup. Our fingers were sticky when we caught up with our vampire friends. They eyed the syrupy trays as we threw them away.

"So, we're about to hit the witchy part of the fair?" Libby asked.

"Yeah, that's the main event," Della said.

"Does New Orleans have a history of witchcraft?" I asked. "I know some people practise voodoo, but I'm guessing this is separate."

"That's right, and it's not only history," Della said. "There are practising witches in the city today, but a lot of them are discreet. Some do the tourist thing, but more keep it on the down low."

Finding out about vampires had been such a big deal that I hadn't given much thought to other dimensions of the supernatural. "So, is this fair run by proper witches or people wanting to make money?"

"Supposedly a mixture," Will said, with Fiona tucked under his arm. "It's a good time anyhow." I'd only seen Will talk that enthusiastically about Brad Pitt movies, so this had to be worth seeing.

We reached Fulton Square, a space lined with trees that was nestled between tall buildings. Garlands of yellow and orange flowers threaded with fairy lights looped from tree to tree. 'It's a Kind of Magic' by Queen was playing quietly.

Stalls were set up between the trees, and each one was sprinkled with tealights in jewel shades of pink, purple, red and teal. Some vendors sold candles or spell kits with different magical properties. Others sold herbs dispensed from glass jars or magic-themed treats. We joined the flow of the crowd.

The nearest stall was manned by a tall, curvaceous woman with a grey afro and an emerald-green coat. Several cauldrons surrounded by trays of ice were set up in front of her. "Welcome, friends. Can I interest y'all in a potion? Just for fun – no active ingredients here."

I went for a Boysenberry Bliss. She ladled the purple liquid into a short, round glass. Pink smoke curled up from it and the colour shimmered from pink to purple. She dropped a handful of purple sweets into the bottom that made the drink fizz.

"Enjoy," she said, handing it over before she served the others. "Y'all can return the glasses when you're done."

The drink tasted of sweet, potent berries, and I enjoyed sipping as we wandered past cauldron stalls and trays of spell ingredients. When the drinks were gone, we bought black cat cookies with warm, gooey chocolate in the centre.

The bucking broomstick in the corner drew Jared and Will in. We nibbled our cookies with Fiona looking on while they took it in turns. Jared did pretty well, clinging on with all of his vamp strength while the broom bucked and threw him around.

"You did good, kid," the ride operator said as Jared staggered off, his eyes bright with exhilaration.

Will didn't fare as well. The leather jacket immediately got tangled around the broom and he was flung over the front of it. I'd never seen him so dishevelled: the floppy hair wild around his face as he stood up all flustered. It was pretty awesome. Fiona straightened his jacket with a look of adoration, which he fired right back at her. They both had it bad.

After that, we opted for a quieter activity of making broomstick pencils from bunches of twigs tied to the pencil with string.

Jared constructed his tiny broom with the utmost concentration, whereas Will muttered and slammed the equipment around. "I don't think crafts are my thing," Will said, holding up a mostly bare broom. One of the twigs fell off. "I'm gonna get another drink."

"As long as it's not from a living source," Della murmured. She was grinning, but it was clear that she meant it. Something she'd said stirred up a memory, but I couldn't quite get hold of it.

"I'll keep an eye on him," Fiona said, abandoning her pencil too.

Will rolled his eyes, taking Fiona's hand before they strolled off, the crowd parting around them.

"That boy knows how to make an exit," Libby said.

"How's this for an *entrance*?" a familiar voice muttered. Two vampires were standing over us. One of them was Ilian, our grey-eyed friend that Paige had sent to trail us around Empire. He was with a tall blonde female with a buzz cut who was usually at Saint Germain's side.

"I take it you're not here to start trouble," Della said, patting her side so the shape of the stake was visible.

"We wouldn't dream of it," the female said through a sneer.

"Carmilla and I need Mina and Jared to come with us," Ilian said.

"Not gonna happen," Della said calmly. "Your boss and the slayers have a truce."

"She's right," Libby said, speaking up even though she looked terrified.

"This conversation will uphold your truce," Ilian said. "No harm will come to them tonight." I wasn't sure I believed that. Whatever it was, Saint Germain couldn't want anything good.

"I think we should go hear him out," Jared said, looking to me for my answer.

I wasn't as experienced a slayer as Della, but I had skills. I stood confidently, even as a tremor of dread ran through me. "Fine with me."

Chapter 27

The Hotel Demeter was a beacon in the darkness, its bright cream paint brilliantly illuminated. Ornate plaques with curling, detailed plasterwork and window arches told me exactly what kind of place this was, as did the cream-suited doorman who let us inside.

The foyer was lit by an enormous crystal chandelier, the gleaming tiled floor reflecting the light. Everything about the hotel screamed luxury, from the mahogany grandfather clock to the clusters of seating occupied by elegant people.

We followed the two vampires to the lift. Jared took my hand, offering a smile that didn't touch his eyes. I tried to smile back, but I doubt it was very convincing.

The mirrored lift was playing tinkly music that would've set me on edge on a good day. Ilian took a key from his pocket, which was connected to a chain that disappeared under his suit. He inserted it into a discreet hole at the top of the numbered floor buttons. When he turned it, the lift rose.

"Are we going to a hotel room?" I asked. Saint Germain had houses around the city, but being taken to a hotel room seemed especially sinister.

"Saint Germain owns the hotel. We're taking you to his private club," Carmilla said haughtily.

"If Saint Germain says he wants to talk, that's all. You'd know if he wanted you to disappear," Ilian said. If he was going for reassuring, he missed the mark by quite a long way.

The lift opened out into an immaculate cream room with a high ceiling and thick carpets the same colour as the walls. That was a bold design choice given the clientele's gory tastes. A white and chrome bar took up one corner with rows of bottles behind it. Circular tables were spread out around the room. Since this was Saint Germain's club, I assumed the faces staring at us were vampires. Even on different skin tones, the lack of sun exposure was obvious. There were other vampire tells, a certain coldness and ruthlessness, but I was too nervous to look for them.

I spotted Saint Germain, and he wasn't alone. Armand was sitting at his table, looking deeply unhappy. Saint Germain was sipping from a crystal glass of whiskey like he couldn't care less.

"Welcome, y'all," Saint Germain said as his henchmen led us over. "Thank you, Carmilla and Ilian. Y'all go on and get yourselves a drink." The two vampires left, and Saint Germain gestured at the two empty chairs. "Please take a seat. Can I offer y'all some refreshments?"

Jared and I did what Saint Germain said, but I wasn't about to drink anything he gave me. "I'm fine, thanks," I said at the same time that Jared declined.

"Suit yourselves," Saint Germain said. "So, what do y'all think of my place?"

"It's very nice," Jared said through a glower.

"Perhaps we can move this along," Armand said icily. "While

Mina is still young."

Last time we were with him and Saint Germain, Armand had played the bored, disinterested vampire, and it seemed like he was doing the same thing now. It was probably smart to act like he had little attachment to us. It wasn't worth giving Saint Germain any ammunition.

Saint Germain's glare could've melted through to bone, though he replaced it with a bright smile. "Of course. I'm sure you're *dyin'* to know what you're doing here."

Jared gripped my hand under the table. "Yes, *sir*," he said, insolence creeping in.

"I'll get right to it then," Saint Germain said, looking at Jared with glittering eyes. "I know what you can do, my boy. I saw you on the television. I haven't forgiven you, Carter, for failing to mention that fact. I'm starting to question what good you are to me. First you don't track down the meddling paranormal fanatics in New Mexico or have any useful visions *whatsoever*, and now this." Saint Germain insisted on referring to Armand by his real name, tying him to the murderous brother Armand had killed to save us.

"With all due respect," Armand said in a dry voice that suggested the opposite, "I've told you multiple times that my power doesn't work on command. And as for Jared's developing power, I hardly thought it relevant. He can last mere minutes in the sun without dying before being rendered exhausted and utterly useless."

"Don't sound like your friend values your ability very highly," Saint Germain said. "But I see all the potential in the world in it. A vampire who can walk in the day . . . The possibilities are endless. I have no doubt your power will only grow, boy. I saw something special in you when we first met."

"What is it you want with me?" Jared asked quietly.

"I want you to work for me," Saint Germain said, "in case you hadn't figured that out. I have big plans for you, my boy. I pay well, and there's a certain amount of security from being one of my people."

"What if Jared doesn't need to keep the slayers off his back?" I asked, regretting it as soon as the words popped out.

"That would be his choice, wouldn't it?" Saint Germain said. "Since you're drawin' attention to yourself, darlin', perhaps I can reframe my request in terms young Jared will understand. You *will* be joinin' my operation. When I call, you'll come. I'll do my best to be reasonable about it." I didn't believe that for a second. It was too late to play the benevolent businessman.

"I already have two jobs," Jared said levelly, even though his tours had dropped off lately.

"Doin' tours and workin' at your *lovely* mansion," Saint Germain said with obvious disdain. "I'm sure you can make time for me. Especially if it means keepin' your girl safe. There are some dangerous vampires around. I would hate for Mina to fall foul of one of them when she's out there keeping our fair city safe." I tried to look brave, but the threat was chilling. Coming from him, death wasn't an empty promise.

"I'll do it," Jared said. Saint Germain's eyes widened, as if he'd expected that to take longer. "We could keep going back and forth, but enough is enough. You'll win in the end, so there's no point." Full of outrage, I wanted to argue for Jared, but I stayed quiet. He was doing his best to keep us alive.

"That's rather a defeatist attitude, my boy," Saint Germain said. "But since it gets me the outcome I want, I'll not push the issue.

Before you rejoin your friends, I have a parting sentiment. I'm sure you hate me in this moment, which doesn't bother me in the slightest. But I do hope you'll come to see that this could be a good arrangement. How long has it been since you've felt like part of a commu-ni-ty?" He drew out the last word. Something he'd said seemed to have resonated with Jared, because his expression was troubled.

Saint Germain went on, full of smiles and charisma. "I remember that when I turned, I spent years attending glorious parties, telling stories of my life that no one quite believed. Then somebody would suspect what I was and I'd have to run again. It's a lonely life that leaves one feeling quite . . . adrift. But I'm sure having such good friends that you wouldn't know what that feels like, would you?"

Jared shifted around in his chair, and I realised Saint Germain was right. I'd felt bad for Jared all those times he couldn't eat or had to sleep while we were going about our lives, but I hadn't known that being a vampire had cut him off from us in ways we couldn't understand.

"Before you go," Saint Germain began, "there's somethin' I'd like to ask you. Where did your kidnappers take you? And could you make an identification when I capture them?"

Saint Germain was too astute. I'd not anticipated questions about that day. Jared sat up straighter, virtue and honesty radiating off him. "Sorry. They kidnapped me and took me to a field in the middle of nowhere. I was blindfolded most of the time, and whoever that man was, he wore a mask. You heard his voice on TV – you know as much as I do."

Saint Germain nodded thoughtfully. Unconsciously, my gaze

flitted to Armand. He was still looking bored and disinterested, though some discomfort was showing. "I assumed as much. There was one more thing I wanted to know. How did you escape?"

Jared must have thought ahead, because the story came out as naturally as any truth. "The camera got broken, and I ran and hid in the confusion. They didn't expect me to be mobile during the day."

"Of course . . ." Saint Germain drew out his reply. "I think that'll do for now. Carter, walk our friends out. Then come on back for a lil' tête-à-tête with me. Oh, and be sure to give the boy his pager."

Armand nodded, his lips downturned slightly. His only rebellion was that he marched us through the room without another word to Saint Germain. Jared had been drawn into Saint Germain's orbit as we'd feared, but somehow we'd kept our presence in New Mexico and at my dad's Community from him.

The eyes of the other vampires bored into us on the way out. No doubt their sensitive vampire ears had heard that Saint Germain had a new toy.

We rode the lift down in silence. Jared tried to speak, and Armand held up a hand to stop him. "Outside."

The doorman let us out onto the street. Then Armand set off at a fast walk until the hotel was a decent distance behind us.

"I was afraid this would happen," Armand said. "Your father has a lot to answer for."

"I know," I said, guilt drawing tight around me even though it wasn't my fault.

"So far, I've managed to hide the ranch's location from Saint Germain. I don't know how long it'll be before he figures it out or finds some way to get me to talk," Armand said.

"Let's hope Saint Germain loses interest and it never comes to that," I said.

"Saint Germain doesn't know I can heal others – just myself," Jared said. "At least we have that going for us."

"That we do," Armand said. "I have to go back in. I'd tell the two of you to stay out of trouble if you didn't seem to find that impossible."

"We'll do our best," I said.

Armand turned to go, and Jared called at his back, "What about the pager?"

"Right." Armand sighed, returning with a black device for Jared that fit in the palm of his hand. "So you can be at our illustrious leader's beck and call."

Armand flitted back towards the bright edifice of the hotel. Jared tucked the pager away and wrapped his arm around me as we hurried off in the opposite direction.

"We knew it was coming," Jared said, looking anxiously into my face.

He must have seen some of the tumult churning inside me. Dad had tried to expose vampires, and instead had only revealed Jared to Saint Germain. If his failed attempt had rippled into our lives, what would happen if he succeeded? We had no choice but to stop him again.

"We did," I said. "And we'll make it work. We've survived worse."

"I'm hoping we'll come to a point where we don't have to grade on such a low curve."

I nestled in to him, his body cutting off some of the night's chill. The fall fair was still going strong around us, people chatting over their purchases and sipping steaming drinks. The air smelled of pumpkin flesh, cinnamon and apples.

We walked fast, the events of the past few days cycling through my mind even though it was doing us no good. We had to make the best of the new path tonight had put us on.

Chapter 28

Libby, Della, Will and Fiona were huddled around a table when we got back to Fulton Square.

"Finally!" Will said as we sat down. "I was going to come after you, but Della threatened me with imminent death."

"I made implications," she said. "I told you Saint Germain is the last person you wanna meet. If you get a power, he'll want you to work for him."

Will looked annoyed, though I wasn't sure if that was directed at Della or his lack of a power. "And that would be a bad thing?"

"Unless you *want* to be under the control of an evil vampire dictator, then yes," Libby said, turning to Jared. "Did he see you on TV?"

Jared nodded. "He wants me to come work for him. Could be worse, I guess. He said he might call on me from time to time."

Wrongness swam around in my stomach, but I couldn't do anything about it.

"We'll keep an eye on the situation," Della said. "Now unfortunately, the two of us have to go on patrol. It's a routine sweep, so we should be home pretty fast."

"Sounds like tempting fate, but what do I know?" Will said, offering Fiona a hand. He pulled her up in one clean move that brought her close to his side. "See y'all soon."

They wandered through the crowd with their hands clasped, predators among the humans.

Jared's eyes were low, his finger tracing along the grain of the wooden table. I wanted to stay with him after the encounter with Saint Germain, but Della was right. Our position with the slayers was precarious enough with Paige watching and hating our every move. We had to behave and do our bit to protect the city.

"Can I come?" Jared asked. "I need to get out of my head . . . and Taz did say the slayers needed a vampire vampire hunter."

"OK with me," Della said. "What Paige doesn't know can't hurt her. We'll take you home first, Libs."

She pouted. "I hate being the one who always gets left behind. But I also don't want to poke danger with a pointy stick, so . . ."

We headed back to the mansion through the hubbub of the city, moving between people bundled up in sweatshirts and scarves. Libby and Della kissed at the doorway, and the three of us left Libby behind.

"We have an area to check, and we tend to do a few passes before calling it a night," Della explained to Jared as we set off. "I'm guessin' you don't need a stake."

Jared showed his human teeth in a broad grin, an effective reminder of his hidden fangs. "I'm good."

Slayer mode came down over all of us. Jared was less practiced in it, but he had natural instincts to work with. These days, I found the sense of focus more easily, observing the street closely and knowing which details to focus on and which to pass over. The fair made it more difficult, with people lingering in groups and extra live music dulling the ability to pick up sounds. Only a truly brazen vampire would attack in a crowded place, but the danger on nights like this was the ones who separated people from their friends.

Jared checked down every dark alley and scanned shadowy balconies, super-efficient with eyes much more attuned to the darkness.

At one point, his gaze jerked towards the midnight darkness alongside a bar. "I hear something." He darted into the space in a blur. Della palmed her stake and edged into the alleyway more cautiously.

The light from the street cut off abruptly as I followed, a terrifying lack of vision that left me open to all kinds of threats. Opportunistic humans could be as much of a danger, and the dark often hid vampires. I pulled out my stake as my eyes slowly began to adjust.

Jared was back before I had to face any creatures in the darkness. "Consensual," he said, fangs showing.

I put my stake away. It kindled a strange feeling when I saw him like that: fear mixed in with attraction towards this more frightening version of him. "Let's keep going," I said, even though there were other things I'd rather be doing.

We completed our route and repeated it again without incident. Luckily for the fall fair crowds, we couldn't spot any vampires misbehaving. On the third lap, Della said, "I'm gonna call it. Let's do a few more blocks, then I think we're done for the night."

A cool wind swirled the last of the dead leaves around our feet.

Winter was a breath away. Della had told me in the past that the residential streets on the outskirts of the French Quarter were favourite vampire haunts, being poorly lit and a few blocks beyond the nightlife. People split off from their friends or took a shortcut home, and bad things happened.

As the light and nightlife noise faded behind us, I withdrew my stake. I'd got more confident with patrolling, but I hadn't needed to stake many vampires.

Jared froze. "There's a dead body nearby . . . Maybe half a block over."

Della pulled a hand through her long braids. "You sure you don't have another power?"

"Thankfully not. Super smell in this city would be the worst. It's this way."

Della and I followed him further into the residential community. There was no one around, so we were likely to find the body.

"I smell spilled blood . . . couple hours past its best." Jared wrinkled his nose. He gripped my hand, and for once I was the one squeezing too hard. I saw the victim down the street. Another life had been reduced to a smudge of shadow on the pavement.

Chapter 29

"I'll call Cafferty. We just passed a phone." Della jogged back in the direction we'd come, and I went on with Jared.

Most people in my life would be trying to shield me or deciding what I could cope with. I valued how Jared let me make my own decisions, even if it was debatable whether they were good ones.

As we got closer, I valued being treated like an equal less and less. My eyes gradually adjusted, picking out a human shape. Then we were standing over a girl. She looked younger than me, her dark hair fanned out and arms crossed over her chest. Despite the peaceful pose, she hadn't died that way. Clotted blood clung to one side of her throat, and the corner of a tarot card showed under her fingers. She was another ripper victim.

I crouched down next to Jared. He leaned in to inspect the bloody mess of her throat, a dark crimson against the waxy white of her skin. His nostrils flared, and from the shape of his lips it seemed his fangs had made an appearance at the smell of blood. It was impossible to ignore even for me – a bitter mingling of rust and decay. I wanted to look away, but the girl deserved my attention. Someone had stolen her future and reduced her to another victim.

Jared frowned. "I don't get it . . . Looks like a female bite from the narrow fang spacing. In fact, I'm sure of it."

"Armand thought the vampire was male." I stated the obvious as I tried to figure out what it meant.

"Step away from the body, please." The voice was firm but familiar.

We did what Cafferty said, standing up and backing off. "So, I just had an anonymous call patched through."

"That'd be me," Della said, breathing hard as she ran up to us.

"You're lucky I was nearby. The ambulance and a patrol car are on the way. You three see who did this?"

"Unfortunately not," Jared said, Della and I shaking our heads.

"Looking at what someone did to her, maybe it's better that you weren't here," Cafferty said. "Anythin' else you can tell me?"

"My best guess is it happened two hours ago," Jared said, "and I'm certain from the shape of the wound that a female vampire is responsible."

Cafferty rubbed his eyes. He looked even more tired than usual. "Two different killers . . . that makes things more complicated. Wish we could thrash it out, but the three of you have to go. We don't need it on the record that you found another dead body."

"Thanks, detective," Jared said.

We jogged towards the hustle and bustle of the French Quarter, leaving Cafferty and the girl's body behind us as the wailing sirens drew nearer.

Jared's pocket buzzed. He grimaced, tugging out the chunky plastic pager. "Saint Germain wants me. Timing sucks, but I have to go. Do you mind . . .? I don't wanna leave you right after what we just saw."

The experience hadn't quite caught up with me yet. "I'm OK,"

I said automatically. "You should go." What choice did he have? Saint Germain wouldn't accept being ignored.

Jared gave me a swift kiss on the cheek before leaving us on the street. "I wish he didn't have to run around after him," Della said.

"Me too," I said. "Can we go back to the mansion? It's been another long day."

Libby was curled up on the sofa with a pile of mansion paperwork when we got back in, her eyes half-closed.

"Finally! Are you OK?" Libby asked, looking more alert as she sat up. She caught the papers as they started sliding off her lap.

"Depends on your definition. We found another person who'd been killed by the ripper . . . Well, Jared did." Della sat down next to Libby. "The body was posed the same way but Jared said a female vampire got her. So there might be more than one of them working together."

My sister trailed a hand through Della's braids, considering her for a drawn-out moment. Then she looked up at me. "That doesn't sound good . . . but I can deal as long as you both keep coming back in one piece."

"We will," I said, even though we couldn't guarantee it.

"Where's Jared?" Libby asked, leaning in to Della.

My stomach clenched, what we'd seen tonight and Jared's new obligation hitting me. "Saint Germain wanted him."

"Already?" Libby shook her head, waving a dismissive hand. "We can't help that right now. You're the one I'm worried about. Why don't you go to bed?"

As soon as she said it, tiredness pressed down on me. I got ready slowly, delaying the inevitable. I couldn't stop picturing the bodies I'd seen – the man in the morgue and the girl abandoned on the street. And we were dealing with two vampires, so we had one extra murderer on the loose.

Jared still wasn't home, so I crawled into bed. The thought of him being out there with Saint Germain left me feeling restless.

The next morning, it took me a while to get moving. The mansion reopening was coming up, so Libby would have plans for us to work on the new room. It was also nice to have the bonfire to look forward to tonight, and I tried to keep my inner gaze tuned on that. Not on victims in morgues or drained of their blood on deserted streets . . .

Della and Libby were bustling around the kitchen. I put the cereal on the table and then grabbed a cup of tea using someone's leftover hot water.

"Well?" Della asked. "Are you gonna tell her?"

Libby sighed, picking up her mug from the side. "I haven't had enough coffee for this. So . . . Dad called and invited us to breakfast."

"And you said no because he almost killed Jared," I said, with a warning in my voice.

"Not exactly . . ." Libby took a long gulp of coffee, wincing. "Damn, that's hot. You went to see him, so I thought it'd be OK."

"I went to question him about being a serial killer!" I said. "No way am I sitting down to breakfast with him."

"Have to say, I'm on your sister's side," Della said to Libby. "But I'll go with you if you want. I don't approve of what the guy did, but you shouldn't have to see him alone."

Libby grinned. "And you know I would totally do that. We have stubborn genes."

"That we do. Which is why I'm staying here."

"Mi-na!" Libby's voice came out in a long whine. "I told him we'd both be there! He said how sorry he is and he wants to tell you again himself."

"I bet he does, but I'm still not going." Dad couldn't just give commands and expect us to come running.

"He says he has some information that you need to hear. Something about that vampire you're both fascinated with?" Libby said, her desperation growing the longer she kept talking.

He had me there, and I was sure he knew that when he told Libby. At some point, I'd need to face him. "OK. He can tell me what he knows, but I'm not going to be civil."

Libby looked ready to start an argument, but instead said, "Whatever you want."

Probably trying to placate me, she went to get the newspaper, but it didn't have the intended effect. The ripper had killed last night, and there was their second letter.

After the reporter's article outlining the details of the second victim that I knew too well, the letter was there in print.

To the people of New Orleans,

Are there any more believers among you? Has a second victim with their throat all bloody convinced you?

There are those who would do anything to protect our secrecy. They should fear me. I promised more victims, and I have delivered. I believe it takes more murders to be classified as a serial killer, so perhaps you will take me more seriously then.

Until next time.

Yours,
A vampire of New Orleans

"The ripper's going to kill again," I said.

"Between the slayers and police, we'll get them," Della said.

"I hope so."

Jared hadn't stirred when we left, and I felt guilty that I was going to see Dad again. However hard I tried to avoid it, he kept pulling me back in.

Della led us to a residential street that even Libby hadn't visited. The trees were putting on a brilliant show of oranges, browns and yellows. The fallen leaves were crunchy underfoot, and it was a chilly day for New Orleans.

My determination grew the closer we got to Dad's house. He was pulling the wool over Libby's eyes, but mine were wide open. I could be around Dad without falling for his charm, and if he knew more than he'd told us, then I'd get it out of him.

Della slowed down outside the most depressing house on the

street. The pointed Gothic peaks on the roof had potential, but the mould-grey building appeared to be leaning forwards like its foundations were slipping. A crooked sign over the door read 'Quarter Hotel', though I doubted anyone had stayed here this decade.

"If I hadn't seen the ranch, I'd say we'd taken a wrong turn," Libby said.

"Yeah, this place has Dad written all over it," I said. Nerves were kicking in, so I pulled myself together and knocked on the door.

Chapter 30

Dad opened the door, his smile so warm and benevolent that I wanted to turn around and leave, even if he knew something about the ripper. "Good morning. Won't y'all come on in? Afraid we got us a fixer-upper here, but there ain't a whole lot of options when you need a place fast. It certainly has charm though, and we can make it our own." Typical of Dad to leave no space in the conversation for anyone else.

Libby practically skipped inside, while Della and I trudged behind. Everything in the hallway was grey, from the mouldering wallpaper to the loose, threadbare carpets. Mould fanned across the walls, and swollen damp patches marred the ceiling. A wide staircase led upstairs, and a reception desk ran along the back of the room. I drifted over there, examining the pigeonholes that once would've contained messages for guests and a board covered with hooks that still held a few keys.

Dad appeared beside me. "Did you ever get into those Stephen King books I left back in Whitby? You could always pretend like we're staying at The Overlook."

I got a twinge of nostalgia, even though I knew that was what Dad had been angling for. He couldn't know that I'd read those books way too young, clinging to one of the only things he'd left behind. I'd loved them too, inhaling stories of vengeful, bloody girls and possessed cars. "I don't know . . . Looks more like the Bates Motel to me."

Dad let out a bark of laughter. "I'm glad I passed on my interests to at least one of you girls."

"Yeah, Mina can have that one." Libby popped up on his other side. "I use all the movie stuff at the mansion though."

"I need to take a look around that place." The proprietary way he said that put me on alert. I didn't want him worming his way into our lives here.

"Libby said you had some news about the ripper investigation," I said coldly.

Dad's flash of surprise quickly gave way to easy confidence. "She did?" He turned to Libby with a faintly disapproving look. "I'm sorry, honey. You must have been mistaken."

Libby shrank before our eyes. "You're probably right."

"I don't think she'd get that wrong," I said. "It's almost like someone misled her to get both of us here."

Dad definitely wasn't used to being confronted by me, but from the look on his face I doubted he usually got it from anyone. "I'm sorry you feel that way. It wasn't my intention. Are y'all hungry?"

"Famished," Libby proclaimed, never a fan of the big confrontation.

"Let me show you the kitchen," Dad said, ushering her away with a hand on her back.

"I hope it's cleaner than the rest of this place," Della murmured.

"Hey!" The cheery voice gave me a jolt. It didn't belong in this murky place.

Ellie was carrying a box of cleaning products, Chase trailing behind her. "I didn't know you were comin'. I hope your dad didn't bring you here to clean. This place is a lost cause."

"We're here for breakfast," I said.

"Not sure you'll want somethin' cooked here," Chase murmured, still surly but at least making an attempt to play nice.

"The kitchen's pristine," Dad called. "Y'all make yourselves at home and I'll finish off breakfast with Libby here."

"I'll go for backup," Della said, marching off after them.

"We should get back to cleaning. Chase suggested burning the place down and starting again, but I think that's a tad extreme," Ellie said.

The chandelier over our heads was crusted with dirt and threaded with cobwebs. "I don't know. Maybe he has the right idea."

"Listen," Ellie began, hugging the box against her. "I'm so sorry for what these idiots did – I had no idea. It won't happen again."

I nodded, not sure I could trust myself to respond politely. I'd seen the adoration Ellie laid on Dad whenever she looked at him. Would she really have stopped the plan if she'd known? "Is Mum here?"

"Third door on the right upstairs," Ellie said. "She'll be happy to see you."

I wasn't convinced about that, but I thanked Ellie and set off. The sounds of conversations and reluctant cleaning faded as I climbed. The air was worse up here, claggy with dust and underlaid by mildew. Even though the stairs bowed down under my weight, I didn't dare to use the banister with its splintered supports scattered across my path.

The hotel might have once been a beautiful place to stay –

I could see the bones of it underneath the decay in the high, moulded ceilings and tall windows. But now it was one of those places that made my breathing shallow, and I doubted it was the mould. Some buildings just felt unpleasant.

I counted the doors carefully in the hallway. In this hotel, an error might mean falling through the floor. I knocked hard, and Mum's voice was croaky. "Come in."

Thick curtains blocked out the sun, and a lamp illuminated Mum in golden light. She was sitting cross-legged on an unmade bed, a lit cigarette in her hand. She stubbed it out at the sight of me.

"Hi, honey! How are you?" She tried to find some enthusiasm, but mostly sounded tired. Her hair fell in long tangles past her shoulders, and her black dress looked creased and slept in. Maybe being around Dad wasn't agreeing with her like I'd thought.

"Not great," I said. "Did you know what Dad was planning to do to Jared?"

She flinched. "I knew he had something up his sleeve, but not that – I swear."

I'd never understood Mum's thinking, and this was no exception. "And you're OK with him behaving like that and trying to reveal vampires? You must know that if he succeeds it'll completely wreck your life. Everyone would know what you are, and you'd have to get registered and who knows what else."

Mum gave a tight, unconvincing smile. "Your dad's acknowledged that he was wrong to take Jared. You know what he's like – he believes so strongly in things and, on this occasion, he got carried away. And as to revealing what we are . . ." Mum paused, toying with the cigarette stub as if she regretted putting it out. "Honestly? I hope he won't succeed."

"Have you told him that?" I asked, though I suspected I knew the answer.

Mum hesitated, her eyes getting that slightly wide, fearful look that Libby had inherited. "I did once. His conviction is one of the things I admire most about him, but it tends to mean he doesn't listen to reason."

"That doesn't sound very fun," I said, picturing a life where my opinions were ignored, even completely gone against, by the person who was supposed to love me most.

Mum made another Libby face, the one I'd rarely seen since my sister and I worked on our relationship. It was like a shutter came down. "It's my decision."

"Mina! Mum!" Libby's voice carried clearly even though she was on a different floor. "Breakfast!"

The thought of sitting down to eat with Dad made me want to throw something. Even though he'd been gone for most of my tantrums, I couldn't afford to have one now. If I was going to spend time with him, I planned to find out everything he knew.

Chapter 31

The kitchen wasn't in as sorry a state as the rest of the house. It once probably had an industrial look, with stainless steel counters and cupboards. The windows had been scrubbed in here, though grime lingered at the edges, and the counters were spotless.

Hayes, Ellie and Chase were sitting across from Della and Libby at a scarred wooden table that had seen better days. From the way it jarred with the kitchen's sterile decor, I guessed it'd been dragged in from elsewhere.

Several covered dishes were arranged on a long heating plate, and greasy smells emanated from them. Most of the places at the table were full when Mum sat at one end and Dad at the other. I slotted in between Libby and Mum.

"Breakfast is served," Dad said grandly, uncovering the dishes. "In your honour, I made a full English breakfast." The name sounded odd in his thick Southern accent. "Hope I remembered it right – it's been a while."

Everyone started serving themselves, and I filled my plate while I thought through the best plan of attack.

"Well, it smells really good," Libby said, taking an enormous bite of bacon. She closed her eyes, nodding as she chewed.

"Thank you," Dad said grandly, dipping his head.

One part of parenting Dad had always got right was feeding us well. He'd cooked heaps of crispy bacon, spicy sausages and beans, all served with thick slabs of toast and butter.

There wasn't a lot of conversation at first. Mum sat there quietly with her mug of black tea, looking unusually relaxed. I let them have some peace while they ate, tucking into my own breakfast.

"So, what do y'all do for entertainment round here?" Ellie asked chirpily.

Della smiled warmly. "What do you like doin'?"

Ellie's answer was tentative. "I love horses, and I read a lot. We're very busy with research on the ranch, so we don't get a whole lot of time for hobbies."

That sounded like she was missing out on a lot, but I tried not to judge. "Jared just took me to a beautiful library. Maybe we could go some time."

A massive smile brightened Ellie's face once more. "I'd love that!"

I noticed then that she was mostly pushing food around her plate, and so did Chase. "You didn't sleep well again last night," he said tenderly. He only showed that side to us around Ellie.

"Nightmare," she said, cutting her bacon into tiny pieces. "I went for a walk, and that helped."

"Next time, wake me," Chase said gently.

"Was there anything prophetic about your dream?" Dad asked, all intensity and zero compassion.

"I don't think so," Ellie said apologetically, her head low like she'd let him down.

That fired me up to start questioning Dad, but Della got in there first.

"Will the other members of the Community be coming to New Orleans?" Della asked. She didn't even stumble when she said 'Community'. One of these days, I was going to accidentally call them a cult to their faces, and there'd be no taking it back.

"Depends on what we find here," Dad said smoothly. "At the moment, I'm thinkin' this might be a good place for us long term. I mean . . . you girls are here. That's a big part of the decision."

Libby grinned, even though we were tagged on as an afterthought.

"It's a very different set up here from the ranch," I said, taking Della's opening to do some digging. "Will people be coming and going as they please?"

Dad fixed me with a hard stare, and Ellie squirmed across the table. "It's time for me to say somethin'. This may bring up some uncomfortable truths, but I think we need to air them."

Chase had been quiet and slouched down through most of the breakfast, but now he sat up straighter.

"If I'm gonna be in your life, as I want to be, I need you to understand what we do here. I get the impression y'all think I've been keepin' people with me and they don't get a say-so. I hope y'all have seen here today that we're a family, cast out by our blood relatives to make one of our own. Nobody would be here if they didn't want to be."

Libby's lips turned down and she looked like she might cry. I spoke up when she didn't, first reaching under the table for Libby's hand. "So, you left our family and made a new one of your own?"

"We know we've not been good parents," Mum said. Her eyes

gleamed with pinkish tears. "But we really are trying. We want you to be in our lives, and the Community is a big part of that."

Neither Libby or I spoke, and after an awkward moment Hayes did. "Y'all mind if I say somethin'?" Dad gestured for him to go ahead. "It's hard to know what it's like in the Community if y'all don't believe the end is near as we do. But when I came here, it was like I'd found my reason for being. We're gathering evidence to convince people of what's out there. This is home – wherever the people at this table are. This is what I'm meant to do." The fervour in his eyes was intimidating. I'd only ever felt that strongly about the closest people in my life, but he'd poured all of his love and protectiveness into Dad's cause.

"It's good that you've found a purpose," Della said carefully.

"We all have," Ellie said. "I know this might look strange if you're not in it, but your dad is onto something. I know he is."

"I'm trying to understand," I said. "So, what are your plans for while you're in the city, Dad?"

He looked pleased with himself that I, of all people, had singled him out. "Now, I'm concentratin' on trackin' down this vampire ripper. They're tryin' to do the same thing we are. Like I said on the boat, if I can convince them to stop killin' and achieve their goal another way, maybe they'll go public with me."

"Have you got any leads?" I asked, trying not to sound too keen.

"Not yet, but it's only a matter of time," Dad said with a confident grin. Ellie, Hayes and Chase were unified in their smiles and enthusiastic nods while he spoke.

So far, he'd shown me nothing to suggest he was up to the challenge. "You think you can catch a vampire murderer without getting killed?"

Dad leaned forwards. "If I can't convince him to stop, no one can. After reading those letters, I don't see why I can't. Together, he and I can achieve everything he wants. Peace is always the answer."

"You couldn't convince Clem to go along with your plan. He wants to kill anything he deems not human enough, doesn't he?" I asked. Della stiffened on Libby's other side. She cared as much about the slayer code as I did.

Dad bit inside his cheek, considering me. "Clem is a very troubled man. There are few people that don't come around to my way of thinkin', and he's one of them."

"We didn't need that energy in the group," Chase said. "You're judgin' what we do, but he's the one about to get people killed."

"How so?" Della asked.

"I . . ." Chase slouched down in his chair, eyes on Dad. Almost imperceptibly, Dad shook his head. "Ain't none of our business," Chase said.

"We don't know for certain what he has planned, if anything," Dad said. I'd thought he was shutting the conversation down, but instead was he trying to take the glory for himself? "All we saw at the swamp was a lot of flyers for local events. I asked him about it, but he wouldn't tell me."

"You think he's planning somethin' violent at a big event?" Della asked.

"If I were inclined to speculate, that's what I'd say."

That sent us into an uneasy silence for the duration of the meal. Dad would love to brag if he knew anything about the vampire ripper case, but we were a step ahead. He still believed we were dealing with one vampire and didn't have access to the slayers and police's knowledge as we did.

When everyone seemed to have finished, I made our excuses. "I think it's time for us to go, but thank you for breakfast." Dad had given us plenty to ponder.

"I *so* appreciate you girls comin'. You don't know how much it means," Dad said. He and Mum both stood up, and he went over to put an arm around her shoulder.

For most of my life, that sight was all I'd wanted. Even now, I felt reluctant satisfaction. My parents were happy, and Libby wanted us to be a family. But I couldn't let myself fall for it after what Dad had done.

"Thank you for having us," Della said.

That snapped Libby into motion. "It's been great, but I need to get to work on the mansion."

"And I'm *so proud* of you for that," Dad said, pulling Mum closer. Her smile wasn't as convincing as his.

"Hopefully we'll see y'all round here soon? You're welcome any time," Ellie said. Her gaze darted to Dad as if asking for permission.

My thoughts were racing as we got out onto the street, and I tried to get them in some kind of order. Dad's desire to track down a vampire killer was far from ideal, but Clem was the most imminent threat. "Dad seemed worried about whatever Clem's planning. I can't figure out what his game is. He wants to kill vampires, but he's planning to target events packed with humans?"

"I don't get it either," Della said. "All we can do is tell Cafferty and the slayers. I'll find a way of lettin' Paige know without tellin' her how we found out."

"Yeah, we don't need to bring Saint Germain any closer to Dad," I said. He was already looking into local cult activity. If Dad kept sniffing around for the ripper, he might attract the dangerous vampire we already knew about.

Libby shuddered. "Don't talk like that. At least the weather is cooperating for the bonfire." She turned her gaze up at the pale blue sky. "I remember my first one – you're gonna love it."

The sunny, breezy autumn day was good company on the way back to the mansion, though my head was pretty full. Della went off to Empire, promising to update Paige about the vigilante rumours if I called Cafferty.

Jared hadn't stirred when I got back. Libby headed to her office to do some paperwork, so I phoned our detective friend. He wasn't at his desk, but the dispatcher put me through. "Should I be worried?" he asked.

"Probably," I said, familiar with the dance of talking to him in code on the police radio. "Remember that super amenable friend of Dad's that we met out at the swamp?"

"Yeah, unfortunately I do," Cafferty said warily.

"He's collecting event flyers like he's planning something, but I don't know what."

"Shit. I'll put the word out that there's a potentially violent group looking to cause trouble," he said.

"Thanks . . . I'll let you go."

"One more thing – the weapons and firearms team went out there, but there was no sign of the gear."

"I kind of expected that," I said, still disappointed. Clem seemed paranoid enough to hide the weapons at the first whiff of trouble. We'd have to find another way to take him down.

"Same here. Thanks for the heads up."

I left the apartment as Jared came down the attic stairs in

baggy grey pyjamas. "You're up and about early," he said, planting a kiss on my forehead.

There was no way this would go down well, so I just said it. "I went to see my dad."

He raked a hand through his hair, making the bedhead even wilder. "Why would you do that?"

"Dad hoodwinked Libby into coming. I think he was trying to prove he's not a total creep, but it's going to take more than breakfast."

"Right . . ." Jared said, his brows coming down low in thought. "I'm trying to see why you'd go there after what he did, but man, it's not easy."

I took his hand, threading our fingers together. "I know, and I'm really sorry. We found out something potentially bad too."

Jared sighed. "OK, hit me with it."

"Clem has a collection of flyers, like he might be planning to do something at a big event. Cafferty's on it, and Della's going to tell the slayers."

Jared gave a tight smile. "One more reason it's fun to be a vampire, I guess. Don't worry – I'll be careful. No going near guys with big sharp sticks."

"Good," I said. "While we're on the subject of bad guys, how did it go with Saint Germain?"

"Not what I expected," Jared said. "He wanted me to sell a bunch of antiques to private buyers. He sent me to different houses, like he didn't want any one place to know how much stuff he's offloading."

"I wonder if he's strapped for cash," I said, feeling some small satisfaction that life wasn't all rosy for Saint Germain.

"I can guess why. I overheard him telling Ilian that Paige has an endless shopping list of equipment for the slayers. But he's completely obsessed with catching the ripper, so he's throwing funds at the situation. All of his money is tied up in property, so that's why he needed cash."

"I really wish you didn't have to work for him, but if all he's doing is using you to run errands then I suppose it's not too bad."

"I know that face you're making," he said. "You know I don't have a choice."

"I do," I said, leaning against him. "I don't have to be happy about it though."

"I'm not sure this next part will make you any happier. He's invited us to this party he's throwing in a few days, and I got the feeling it isn't exactly optional."

"Terrific," I sighed.

"Can we not talk about the horrible people we can do nothing about? How are you doin' after the past couple days?"

"I'm managing," I said, pushing away images of all the things I'd seen. "I'm not sure it gets any easier, but that's probably a good thing."

Jared nodded, pulling me into a hug with one hand behind my head and his fingers woven into my hair. His other hand drew me in close at the waist. Even though Jared and I weren't quite in agreement, we were here for each other, and that was what mattered.

A theory came with the quiet moment. "Could Clem and his people target the bonfire tonight?"

Jared frowned, his eyebrows scrunching into his thinking face. "Big crowd of humans and probably vampires . . . He might, but there are countless other events before Christmas. He could hit any of those."

"Maybe you should sit this one out, to be on the safe side," I said.

Jared let his arm fall from my shoulders. "I'm pretty sure I can take Clem, and I'm not going to live in fear. Everything will be fine." His hand curved around my jaw in a nicely distracting way.

"It had better be," I said.

After the darkness of the past week, we spent a rare quiet day helping Libby around the mansion. She was seriously excited about the bonfire, and I latched on to that feeling.

Della came back around twilight. Vampires all over the city would be waking up and getting ready to go on their merry way, including the pair of vampire rippers who might be picking out their next victim. There was also the spectre of Clem, ready to cause chaos. The slayers and police were due to have a presence at the bonfire, so they'd be ready if he tried anything.

Bundled up in coats and hats, we were soon ready to take on the night. "Bonfire time!" Libby said.

Chapter 32

The sun was a fiery line of orange at the bottom of a greying sky when the four of us got to the bank of the Mississippi for the bonfire. People were milling around, pausing to buy drinks or apples dipped in chocolate from vendors.

Three tall pyres were set up by the river, though they wouldn't be lit until later. We walked close enough to look up at one. The pyre was symmetrical, made up of thick logs closely packed together.

"The structure makes it burn slow and bright," Jared said, coming up behind me in a hug. He rested his chin on my shoulder, his cheek stubbly when he leaned it against mine. "It looks a bit *Wicker Man* for my liking, but what can you do?"

"We should stand back when they light this thing. You're more flammable this year."

"Good call," he said, chuckling against my ear. "I like seeing the sun again with you."

"Me too," I said, leaning back against him.

We chatted for a while, enjoying the atmosphere and the sight of the glossy black water beyond the pyres.

When the sky was truly dark, Will and Fiona arrived looking

cosy. Even though I wished Will hadn't rushed into becoming a vampire, she'd come along at the right time for him. He deserved this happiness.

"Hi, everyone!" Fiona said. "Looks like we arrived just in time." A flaming torch flared across the crowd, and the carrier slowly made their way towards the first pyre.

"Not a fan of fires," Will said. "I'm here for the party."

"And that's where the slayers come in," Della said. "People will be drinking in the dark. We need to make sure there aren't any vamps lookin' to take advantage."

"Jared and I would *never*," Will said, clapping a hand on Jared's shoulder.

"I couldn't be more proud," Jared said. "As long as you mean it."

"Cross my heart," Will said, drawing an X over his chest with one finger.

"Don't worry," Fiona said. "I'll keep him honest."

"Will you now?" Will asked, their faces so close I guessed a kiss was imminent. I pulled Jared away to give them space.

A drum beat thrummed through the crowd before the distinctive voice of Gerard McMahon came over the speakers with the opening of 'Cry Little Sister'. The torch bearer was cloaked in shadow as they touched the flame to the bottom of the pyre. It caught immediately, fire dancing over the wood in a dazzling display. Smoke infused the crisp air coming over the Mississippi, and Jared held me tight against him. He moved my hair and planted a gentle kiss on my neck as we watched the pyre burn.

A strong hand closed on my wrist and I yanked it free, spinning round. Mum held both hands up in surrender. "Sorry, honey."

"I didn't know you were coming," I shot back, the crowd jostling us and the fire crackling in the background.

Dad appeared at her side. "We wouldn't miss out on a New Orleans tradition."

"Let's go," Jared said, his gaze hard.

"Wait," Dad said in his commanding voice that demanded a response, but Jared was already pulling me away.

We'd got separated from the others, and we kept moving through the crowd until Mum and Dad disappeared behind us.

"Sorry," Jared said shortly. "Not ready to face him yet. Or possibly ever." Some humour crept in.

"Not a problem. Shall we watch the third fire?" The second one had already been lit, so we moved towards the third as the wood caught.

Jared stood beside me, his face grim and glowing orange.

"Hey! We lost you for a minute there." Libby sprang up, Della on her heels. The crowd noise and fire's crackle were loud, but Libby was louder.

"We saw Mum and Dad and made a hasty exit," I said.

"Right . . ." Libby said, eyeing Jared.

"Are you OK?" Della asked him, always ahead of Libby on the compassion front.

"I will be," Jared said.

The three pyres were blazing, and the atmosphere had shifted to a party. People were dancing between the fires with drinks in hands, and 'Alright' by Supergrass was playing. A few uniformed police officers were moving through the crowd, so hopefully it wouldn't get out of hand.

"Slayer time," Della said. "We have to meet Beau between pyre one and two to get our orders, but we shouldn't be too long."

"Come on, Jared," Libby said, hooking her arm through his. "I'll let you buy me a sour cream baked potato. Meet us near the food stand later?"

"Sure," I said, kissing Jared.

They disappeared into the crowd. I didn't like them being out of sight. There was a different energy now the party had started, with people pushing from every direction as we moved towards the meeting point. It'd been a while since we'd seen Will and Fiona. I hoped he was behaving.

Beau was staring at the nearest fire when we found him, his expression thoughtful. When he clocked us, he smiled. "Paige needs us to do passes of the crowd until the fireworks display, then another team will step in."

"You're coming with us?" I asked.

"Paige's orders." Beau looked a tad embarrassed. He should be – first a vampire babysitter and now him? This was the kind of night when I missed Rosario even more keenly. She'd have done her best to make sure everyone at a packed event like this one was safe and that every slayer adhered to the code. I wasn't sure Paige was up to the task.

"I have something for each of you." He palmed a small object and handed it off to me. Examining it in the firelight revealed straps and a mechanism with a space in the middle. "Is that . . .?"

"Quick release for stakes," he confirmed. I strapped it to my wrist as Beau handed one to Della.

Shielding what I was doing as best I could, I took the stake from my jacket and slipped it under my sleeve. One push of a button delivered it smoothly into my palm. "That's great!"

"These from Saint Germain's budget?" Della asked disdainfully.

"I don't care where the money comes from, as long as we get equipment like this," Beau said. "There's more on the way – body armour, compact crossbows – you name it."

"I'll look forward to it," Della said curtly.

We kept our stakes hidden as we patrolled through the crowd. Even though I resented having a tag-along, Beau was good at this, moving easily through the masses of people and making quick assessments. It became apparent that any vampires in attendance were only here for a good time so far. I glimpsed Mum and Dad from a distance once and passed by Will and Fiona with a wave. We spent a while weaving back and forth through the crowd, and everything remained as it should be.

"Almost time for the fireworks," Beau said. "You wanna come hear Mr Saint Germain's address?"

He was everywhere – at slayer meetings and presiding over festivities like they needed his blessing. If I didn't despise him so much, it would almost be funny that someone invited a highly flammable vampire to preside over a bonfire.

Della's scowl summed up how I felt as we made our way across to the stage by the river. Saint Germain was wearing one of his white suits, which was made even brighter by a spotlight. He was waving at the gathering crowd, who saw him as nothing more than a businessman with his fingers in a lot of pies. Ilian and Carmilla stood in front of the stage.

"Well, good evenin' y'all," Saint Germain said to a round of cheers and whoops. "It is my privilege to open the fireworks display. Our city is known for its celebrations, and the end of fall is certainly an occasion worth marking. I have big plans for our beautiful home, and I thank you for continuing to lend me your support. Now, without further ado . . . let us look to the skies."

The blackness overhead erupted in an explosion of white stars that fizzed as they fell.

Clem and his friends chose that moment to attack.

Chapter 33

Someone in the tightly packed mass of people screamed, but no one reacted. Most eyes stayed on the sky where fireworks exploded over and over again, sending cascades of colours bursting and falling. I'd heard screams of true terror before though, and Della and I pushed in that direction.

A vampire was holding her face and howling as a skinny white guy pulled a stake from his pocket. Beau grabbed the guy from behind, pinning his arms to his side. He thrashed and fought while Beau dragged him towards the stage. It was empty, so no doubt Saint Germain had been spirited away.

Della and I hurried after Beau, scanning the crowd for more trouble. Everyone else seemed to be admiring the sky. We arrived behind the stage as Beau kicked the man's legs out from under him. Then he held the man to the floor by his throat, sitting on his legs. I'd have to remember that move. Della had scooped up his stake in the scuffle, and she was still holding it as we crouched down with Beau.

"What did you do to her?" Beau asked.

"Like I'd tell you," the man spat, his face contorted with hatred. "You should be thankin' me, if y'all are one of them slayers."

"If you're one of those fools who kills indiscriminately, then you're nothing like us," Beau said. "How many of you are there?"

The man let out an unhinged laugh. "We're everywhere."

I jumped up, desperate to find Jared, but I paused to hear what the man had to say.

"What did you do to that vampire?" Beau pressed.

Della grabbed the torch from his hand. "I think I know. Is this UV?"

Della and I took off at a run. My vampire friends and family members could be anywhere. Some people had figured out something was up, leaving while fireworks still lit up the sky and the pyres burned. Others were still staring upwards, oblivious. I couldn't see any police officers or other slayers, but they had to be here somewhere.

Will lurched in front of us, fangs bared. Fiona clung on to his arm. "There are assholes shining UV torches in people's faces to see if they're vampires. I want to kill them, but I need to get her out of here," Will snarled.

"Don't worry about me – kill away," Fiona said, her face all twisted up.

"Don't kill away," I said. "Getting out of here sounds–"

A torch shone right in my face. I swiped the air with my hands, momentarily blinded. By the time I recovered, the woman who wielded the torch was on the floor.

Della was crouched beside her, two fingers pressed under her jawbone. "She's alive – no thanks to you," she said accusingly to Will. "Did you have to hit her so hard? You could've killed her – she's out cold."

"Ahh shit – still getting used to that vampire strength. We're out of here. Stay safe. Hey – both of you, *forget* that you saw us just now."

For some reason, Della was crouching by an unconscious woman. That light must have done a number on me, because I felt dizzy and disoriented. I remembered her shining it in my face but nothing else. "What happened to her?"

"I have no idea," Della said, checking the woman's pulse with two fingers to her throat. "Her pulse is weak, but she's alive."

The screaming started again. Someone wailed, "Oh my God, she's dead!" A crowd had formed around the woman Della had checked on, and we backed away. She was distinctly not dead, unless corpses groan and move around.

Panic was infecting pockets of the crowd, and I knew how that felt. The fireworks display had finally ended and people were either hurrying away or clustering in groups near the pyres, but there was no sign of Clem's friends. If he had more people here, they were being discreet.

"We have to find Jared and my mum!" I said, reaching that depth of desperation where my pulse and breathing were coming too fast.

"We will," Della said, right before we saw the worst. My mum was on the floor, holding her face at the opposite side of the nearest pyre. My dad was nowhere to be seen.

Clem came into view, leering down at my mum. He picked her up as we started running. He had one arm hooked under her knees and one under her arms as he started staggering towards the flames. We were too far away. I was going to have to watch my mum die. "No!" I screamed, pumping my arms as I skidded over the uneven earth, close enough to the fire to feel its heat.

Clem swung his arms back to build some momentum, sagging under the weight of her. Then my dad came from nowhere, tackling Clem and Mum to the ground.

Della moved in fast, helping me drag my mum away from the fire. She was groaning and trying to get up as my dad and Clem scrambled to their feet. "I shoulda known she was one of them filthy creatures," Clem snarled.

"She's my wife," Dad said. "Speak to her with more respect. Whatever you're trying to accomplish today, this is not the way. You have to see now that my peaceful methods are the answer."

"I dunno, violence seems to be workin' great to me," Clem said cheerfully. "We got at least four of 'em by my last count. Put the bodies on the pyres or in the river – nice and easy. Cleansing the world with fire and water. I'll be goin' now. We got most of the bloodsuckers anyhow."

I went numb, like my body didn't belong to me. Jared couldn't be dead . . . I'd know if he was hurt – wouldn't I?

Clem drew a gun out of his pocket, holding it low by his side. "What d'ya say, Jeff? You gonna try and stop me?" He hadn't been afraid to use that shotgun at the swamp.

Dad held his hands up, shaking his head slowly. "I hope you'll come around."

Sneering, Clem ran off.

"I need to find Jared," I said, in danger of losing it.

"I'm here."

Jared's voice was tired and quiet and the best sound in the world. I crashed into him, wrapping my arms around his waist.

"Hey, I'm OK," he said softly, brushing away my tears. "Are you?"

"I am now you're here." I buried my face against his chest, breathing him in. Drawing back, I said. "My mum's face got burned. Do you mind . . .?"

"Not at all."

Mum's skin looked shiny and blistered in the firelight. Libby had appeared at her side, full of concern. "I don't know if Mina told you that I can heal people," Jared said gently. "I just need to touch your skin. It's effective, but it might be uncomfortable."

"Go ahead – thank you." Mum closed her eyes as Jared rested his fingers on her face. She shuddered, tensing up when the healing began.

Dad looked on, scrutinising Jared with way too much interest. When he finished, Mum touched her face gingerly. "That's incredible – thanks again."

"Any time," Jared said.

"I should've gone after him," Dad said.

Mum shook her head, grabbing his arm as if she suspected he was a flight risk. "Not tonight. You and Clem both need time to cool off. And if I have any say, I'm not sure I want you going after him at all."

"I know I can talk him out of it. I'll go to see him tomorrow." Dad cupped Mum's cheek.

She glowered but didn't try to argue. Stubbornness was a strong trait in our family.

Jared threaded an arm around my back, and I leaned on him. Libby and Della were in a similar posture beside us. With all of the drama done, I was worn out. All I wanted was a hot shower to wash the smoky smell off and then a warm bed.

I called Cafferty when I got home to update him, and he promised me he'd look into it.

When I woke up, I got ready sluggishly, very glad school was closed for the run-up to Thanksgiving. What an absolute mess of a night. Clem and his cronies were lucky they'd got away. It made me uneasy to think of them out on that swamp, planning their next attack.

I listened to the local news on the radio while I got ready, and the bonfire attacks were barely a footnote in the discussion. According to the reporter, the crowd got out of hand, but there was no mention of murderous vigilantes or vampire bodies. As Clem said, they must have got rid of the dead vampires. Four sets of friends and families would be worrying about where their loved ones were, even if Clem only saw vampires as monsters.

I was brushing my teeth when the phone started ringing. I expected someone else to get it, but it rang and rang. The answerphone clicked and Dad's voice came out, more broken than I'd ever heard. "Girls, it's me. I can't say much on the phone, but I need to see you. Ellie's dead."

Chapter 34

Heart racing, I wrenched the phone off the hook, but Dad had hung up. We'd only seen Ellie yesterday, full of warmth and positivity, and today she was gone. I hit redial, but the phone rang and rang.

Libby and Della came out of the bedroom, and Libby's face fell. "What happened?"

Heat stung behind my eyes. "Dad left a message on the answerphone. Ellie's dead. I don't know how . . ."

Libby's face was awash with emotions, her tears threatening to spill over.

"Did you call back?" Della asked.

"He's not answering the phone."

"We can't do anything right now," Della said. "Let's have some breakfast and take a minute."

"OK," Libby said shakily. "I can't believe it – Ellie just got here . . ."

And now she was dead. We could've been friends, visiting libraries together and talking about books . . . Chase must be beside himself.

We hardly talked over tea and toast. I forced myself to swallow one bite after another. Soon, the doorbell rang, and I knew I'd see Dad before I opened the door.

Heavy rain fell behind him, a fitting backdrop to his sorrow. The damp chill crept into the hallway, and I rubbed my arms. Dad's roguish grin was missing, and his eyes were red against sallow skin. He held his arms open. "Please, honey."

Indecision froze me on the spot. If I let myself get close to him again, it'd be harder to keep my distance. But losing someone is the worst, and before I knew it, I was stepping into his arms.

All of my anger and hurt were there, hot and tightly woven, but my body was still comforted by our closeness. He smelled faintly of wood smoke from the bonfire and also like *him* – like he always did when I was a little girl with a skinned knee or a bruised heart.

Pulling back, I reminded myself of all those years he'd not been there. I had to keep him at arm's length for my own wellbeing. "I'm so sorry about Ellie," I said, knowing those words never stretched far enough. "Do you want to come in?"

"Thanks, honey," he said, his voice uneven.

I shut the door behind us and led him into the kitchen.

"Dad . . ." Libby stumbled out of her seat and threw herself at him, sobbing.

They stood like that until Dad peeled himself away. "You mind if I make coffee? I need to get my head straight."

"There's instant in the cupboard above the kettle," Della said. "I'm sorry for your loss."

He sniffed, nodding with glassy eyes as he quickly made a black coffee. We all sat at the table, our half-eaten breakfasts abandoned. Dad sipped his drink, his expression glazed over at first. Slowly, it cleared, and he set the mug down.

"What happened?" I asked.

His lips curled into a sneer. "That vampire we're all lookin' for . . . He got her first."

"We don't know it's a he," I said, remembering the female bite on one of the victims.

"That's true," he said sombrely. "You girls have always been smart. I need that more than ever. I need *you.* I'm guessin' she couldn't sleep last night and went out walking. They . . . She was found not far from our place."

"What did the police say?" Della asked.

"Your friend Cafferty came, and he was very kind. He asked a lot of questions and told us to stay put while they investigate. He might have reminded me not to get mixed up in the case, but that isn't possible. I want that vampire – not gonna lie about that. But I need to find out what happened to Ellie too. She was a good girl . . . Her death has to mean somethin' – I'm destined to find this vampire and use them to tell the world about their kind."

Once again, he was thinking in extremes, but he was right that these vampires needed to be stopped.

Dad rubbed his stubbly jaw, his eyes contemplative. "You got any ideas about what to do now? You know how much I welcome your input."

"I have plenty." Jared was standing behind me in the kitchen doorway, arms folded and stern faced.

Dad stood up, approaching Jared. "Son, I apologise for what I did. It was poorly thought out and desperate. I still believe the existence of vampires should be revealed, but I swear I won't bring you into it again. I misread what I was meant to do."

"Poorly thought out?" Jared's laugh was bitter. "You could've killed me."

"I could have," Dad said levelly, "but I didn't. And maybe that's something we should all ponder. Not only did you not die, but what I did revealed a power you wouldn't have discovered otherwise. Tell me any vampire you know who would voluntarily walk out into the daylight to test it."

Jared's lips parted, his eyebrows dipping low in thought, but he said nothing. I also couldn't find the words. Dad was right that Jared had been given a chance to live his life in the day again. What Dad did was wrong, but not all bad.

Finally, Jared spoke. "You have a point – I'll give you that. But I don't know why you think Mina should help you."

"Actually, I see it as keeping an eye on him. I want this ripper caught as much as anyone, but I'm not going to help you reveal vampires." I turned the last part on Dad.

"I can't promise you that," Dad said. "This is what I've been working towards. I love you girls, I really do, but I'm not prepared to give this up. It's too damn important – it's the fate of humanity we're talking about."

I still couldn't see why he believed so hard in an apocalypse based on a few people's premonitions, but an unpleasant feeling stirred. Armand also had visions from different places and times, so it wasn't beyond the realms of possibility. "Fine, then I'll come to keep you out of trouble."

"And so will I," Jared said. "Seems as good a time as any to push how long I spend out in the daylight."

Even through the grief, Dad gave a victorious smile. If he thought he'd won me and Jared over, he didn't know either of us very well.

"Are you sure?" I asked Jared.

"I'm not leavin' you alone with him," Jared said.

"I deserve that," Dad said, his smile faltering. "So where are we goin' first?"

"I'd love to help, but I need to get ready for work," Della said.

"I should make a move too," Libby said, putting a hand on Dad's shoulder. "Let us know if there's anything we can do."

He grasped her hand. "Thanks, honey. I'll settle for catching this creature."

When Della and Libby left, I got straight to it. "We're probably not going to find a vampire during the day, so what's the plan?"

"You might want to start with this," Libby said, coming back with the newspaper in her hands and Della close behind. "The Times Picayune got a third Dear Boss letter."

"You actually listened when I told you about Jack the Ripper's letters?" Jared asked.

"Now that's not fair," Libby said, gesturing at him with the paper. "I need to listen if I'm going to insult you properly."

Libby and Della scanned the letter first, their eyes growing more troubled as they read. "Here," Della said, handing the newspaper to me. "Looks like more of the same. I'm sorry y'all, but we're really gonna have to get goin'."

"Take care," Libby added.

"You too," I said.

Jared, my dad and I crowded around the newspaper to read. The article ran down the details of the murder, which matched the others precisely. It hurt to think of these cold, clinical descriptions of a victim and her final movements as being about Ellie. Once again, the journalist described a human posing as a vampire, so the ripper hadn't succeeding in exposing their kind yet. And then came the letter about our friend.

To the people of New Orleans,

Do you believe in me yet? The bodies are piling up: three of them drained of blood from torn throats. I know I've rattled the vampire elders by going about this so publicly, but the ends must serve the means.

I'm disappointed that no one has come close to catching me yet. I'd rather looked forward to the chase, but unfortunately the slayers and police of New Orleans aren't proving themselves to be up to the challenge.

Time is running out for another victim. I do hope it isn't someone you hold dear.

Yours,
A Vampire of New Orleans

Chapter 35

"Multiple vampire elders," Dad mused. "What a coup to track them down. You mentioned one powerful vampire, honey. There isn't a group I could meet that you're aware of, is there?" Dad asked, his eyes calculating.

"Sorry to disappoint you, but I don't know every vampire in the city," Jared said airily. That was technically true, but I wasn't sure if Dad would accept it.

"I'll add that to the list of things I want to know," Dad said. "But for now, my priority is catching that creature. Getting their letters printed in the newspaper is a great help to the mission, but I need to track them down too. Having a real vampire onside is crucial. I wouldn't bring your mother into the spotlight for this, or you, Jared."

Jared let out a surprised laugh. "Do you want to catch the killer or make a spectacle of them?"

"Can't I do both?" Dad threw back.

"Let's concentrate on what's important," I said, sensing that this could get heated. Today wasn't about our frayed relationship.

Jared nodded, his jaw muscles twitching. "Fine with me. So, what's the play?"

I had nothing. I was tempted to call Cafferty, but he'd likely still be tied up with investigating the latest victim . . . Ellie. I wondered if they'd moved her from the scene yet. We'd seen her only yesterday, her personality livening up Dad's dreary home. And now she was just . . . gone.

"I have an idea," Dad said. "We got a byline here. How about we go by the Times Picayune offices and find us the reporter?"

"Assuming they're not out covering a story, that's as good an idea as any. Are you going to be OK on the walk to the office?" I asked Jared.

"You don't gotta worry 'bout that," Dad said. "I brought my car."

I'd expected Jared to insist on walking even though it'd lose him the day recovering afterwards. "Thank you," he said begrudgingly.

"No way." Even though Jared had quirked up the collar of his denim jacket and pulled his hat low in preparation for a dash to the car, he stopped in front of it. It was still cloudy after the downpour, but it must have taken something big to divert him from sheltering in the car. "Is that a 1950s Plymouth Fury?"

"A '57," Dad said with his fingers in his belt loops. "Bought it off an old guy who said the previous owner died in it." He winked at Jared. Some of his swagger had returned, but he couldn't shift the sadness of losing Ellie from the lines around his eyes and mouth. "I know I can get kinda . . . fixated on things. And that goes for my favourite Stephen King books too. Movie's not bad either."

I squinted at the rusted black car, trying to imagine it painted red. "That's the car from *Christine*?"

"You got it, kiddo," Dad said, striding around to the driver's side to unlock it. "This here's a sedan, so it has four doors instead of two, but it's near enough."

Dad got in and slammed the door. Jared paused with one hand on the back door handle. "I'm doin' my best to hate him, but he really does have his moments."

"Tell me about it," I said, following him into the car.

'King of Wishful Thinking' by Go West was playing on the radio. The leather of the back seat was cracked and crunchy. I reached for the seat belt as Dad pulled out, but there wasn't one. I slid across the seat and Jared put an arm around me, pinning me against him.

Dad grinned at us in the rear-view mirror.

The Times Picayune newspaper office was a narrow, mint-green building on three levels. Straight, spindly balconies marked off each floor.

It was pretty cool in the newsroom – the kind of place I might have wanted to work had the police not grabbed my interest. Huge copies of news stories covered one wall – disasters pasted alongside sports and politics.

The room was divided into cubicles where reporters were working feverishly. Dad showed no concern for other people's concentration. He sidled up to a young, harassed-looking man with thinning hair and wire glasses. It took only moments for the man to go from stressed to begrudgingly helpful, pointing out a desk a few cubicles over.

Dad gestured for us to follow him. "He's really somethin', isn't he?" Jared said.

"That's one way of putting it," I said.

The woman at the desk appeared to be in her late twenties or early thirties. She had thick black locs twined into a messy bun and smooth, dark brown skin. "Can I help you?" she asked, very pointedly still typing.

"Sorry to interrupt your work," Dad said with a dazzling grin. "We read your article about the vampire ripper. Great piece." Jared glowered through Dad's posturing, but neither of us spoke.

The woman stopped typing, her harried look giving way to coy gratitude – not her too. "Thank you so much! It's an interesting case – I didn't need to do all that much."

"Don't be so modest," Dad said, leaning an elbow on the partition by her desk. I stepped in closer, the newsroom chatter almost obscuring their conversation. "It takes talent to draw out the details like that. I'm following the case myself. A friend of mine was one of the victims – the latest one, in fact." His eyes filled with tears, which could easily have been genuine. In the context of his speech, I wasn't sure.

The reporter, on the other hand, was grabbing tissues and pushing them into Dad's hands. "I am so sorry! It's bad enough that she was killed, but for someone to make such a performance of it, pretending to be a vampire . . ."

"It's been terribly difficult. The police are being very thorough, and they told me about the details they left out of the press, like posing the body with tarot cards. But hearing the full story of the paper receiving the notes would really help to give me some closure." With his usual magnetism and the tears gleaming in his green eyes, I think the reporter would have given him anything.

"Of course," she said. "As long as you keep it to yourself . . . The police are sure the notes are genuine because the killer attached a tarot card matching each victim's to their notes. As you said, they made us leave that out of the paper, so only the killer would know."

The ripper, or rippers, had gone to great lengths to prove they wrote the letters. I wanted to ask questions of my own, but I was afraid of breaking the spell Dad was casting. Though I didn't like relying on his manipulation, I'd keep my feelings to myself if it brought us answers.

"That is remarkable," Dad said. "I'd love to see one of the notes."

"I wish I still had them," the reporter said, looking very sorry, "but the police took them as evidence."

"Oh that *is* a shame," Dad said.

"I do have something else I can show you," the reporter said, sitting up straighter as she reached for her desk drawer. "We and the police have received other notes and calls."

She pulled a grey cardboard folder out of a tidy drawer and flipped it open on her desk. "The police have looked into each of them, but as far as I know they've not led anywhere. A lot of people want attention, but it doesn't seem like they're connected to the case."

"Fascinating," Dad said, still not breaking eye contact with the reporter. "Did any strike you as particularly interestin'?"

"There was this one call that stood out to me," she said, a smile playing across her lips. "Are you sure you're not trying to get your own scoop?"

Dad leaned in as if imparting a secret. "Just a concerned citizen who's lost someone. We really do need to go, but I'd love to see whatever has you smiling like that." Jared was shifting around uncomfortably, and I felt it too. Dad was applying the pressure now.

The reporter took a typed sheet out of the file and handed it to Dad. "How do you know it's this that has me smiling?"

He chuckled, accepting the paper. Was he flirting with her? We all wanted to find the vampire that killed Ellie, but that would be a step too far. I read from beside Dad and Jared stood behind us. "What are we lookin' at?" Dad asked.

"A 911 transcript that came through round midnight on the night of the first murder. This is the part that I thought was significant."

Caller: Oh my God, I think I killed him . . .

911 dispatcher: Please stay calm, sir, and state your name and location.

Caller: The name's Ray, but you're not listening to me! I didn't take that much blood, and he just collapsed. I'm new to this but I never killed nobody before – you have to believe me!

911 dispatcher: I understand, sir. Now if you could state your name and location we can be of assistance.

Caller: Actually, never mind. I have to go . . .

"Do you think this was the ripper?" I asked.

The reporter looked up at me in mild surprise, like she'd forgotten I was there. "I did wonder . . . The timeline of his call matches the first murder, and it sounded like the man had bitten someone, but as far as I know the police haven't managed to track him down to officially rule him out as a suspect."

My excitement at the lead dissolved. If the police hadn't found the caller, we had no chance.

Dad presumably reached the same conclusion. "We'll not take up any more of your time. Thank you so much for your help – it was a pleasure to meet you."

"I . . . You're so welcome." If the reporter had expected more from Dad, she'd be sorely disappointed.

Dad got out of there fast. Jared and I fell back as we left the hustle of the newspaper office. "I have to give your dad credit – he's seriously good at getting what he wants. Terrifying, but good."

"Shame we didn't get any information we can use," I said.

Jared gave a grim smile. "I don't know about that. I guess one good thing can come from being Saint Germain's lackey – I think I met the guy from the 911 call the other night."

Chapter 36

"Seriously?" I asked. "How do you know it was him?"

"Same first name and nervous manner. He works at one of Saint Germain's blood bars," Jared explained quietly. We were in the empty entrance of the newspaper office, but it was still worth being cautious.

"So how about we go tonight? See if he can tell us anything," I said.

"See if who can tell us anything?" Dad appeared in front of us.

Jared clammed up, conspicuously looking anywhere but at Dad. I understood why Jared didn't trust him. But Ellie had been his friend much longer than ours. It seemed unfair to cut him out of investigating her murderer. "Jared might know the vampire from the 911 transcript. Shall we go to question him? It's our friend's birthday party later, but we could go before then?" I wasn't in the party mood after Ellie's death, but that wasn't Fiona's fault.

"Sure thing," Dad said, his astute gaze passing from me to Jared.

Jared told him the address in a subdued voice, while Dad's eyes glittered like he'd won the lottery. When Jared finished, I said my piece. "Do you know what blood bars are?"

"I have some idea," Dad said.

"We'll have to get you in there, so you need to be on your best behaviour. Only talk to vampires if you're with us and only for the benefit of the investigation. Got it?" I asked.

"I wouldn't dream of betraying your trust," Dad said. "Thank you for sharing this with me."

"You'll need to bring Mina's mom along," Jared said. "You shouldn't get hassled if you're with a vampire."

"Not a problem," Dad said. The day had turned colder, and Dad rubbed his arms through his coat. "Can I give y'all a ride anywhere?"

"I'm not sure where we're going yet, but thanks," I said.

"Thank you for today," Dad said. "Honestly, the circumstances couldn't have been worse, but one good thing is that it's brought the two of us closer again."

I wasn't sure what to say to that, so I nodded. "We'll see you tonight."

We set off holding hands, and I could feel Dad watching us. I didn't turn around.

Jared puffed out a loud breath even though he didn't technically need oxygen.

"You did well, being civil around him," I said.

"Thanks," Jared said. "I gotta admit, I think he's growing on me."

I couldn't put my complicated feelings for Dad into words, so I stuck to what I knew. "Let's tell Cafferty about your blood bar friend."

"Not exactly my friend, but sure."

Jared dug out some change for the payphone and I called the station. "Oh, hey Mina!" I could hear Wendy's smile down the phone. "He's on lunch. Want me to patch you through?"

"Thanks."

I quickly explained to Cafferty that we had news we couldn't share over the phone, and he said we could come to meet him.

"He's at Empire," I said.

"At least he's close," Jared said. "Sooner I can get out of the daylight, the better."

Even though Jared was squinting against the watery autumn light, gripping my hand tighter than was technically comfortable, I felt the first touch of hope since we'd heard about Ellie. We were getting closer to the ripper, and I was doing it with Jared. There were things to be grateful for even amidst the sadness.

By the time we got to the Empire of the Dead bar, being out in the day was wearing on Jared. He took off his cap and sunglasses when we got inside, exposing bloodshot eyes and pallid skin. "Are you sure you don't want to go back to the mansion? I can take it from here."

"I can hang on a little longer," he said, giving me the ghost of a smile as he kissed my forehead. I leaned in to him, still worried but trying to let him forge his own path.

The dance floor was covered with tables, and a few people were tucking in to greasy food under the cages of animal skeletons.

Cafferty was already sitting in the corner where the ceilings were lower and no one else tended to venture during the day. 'Linger' by the Cranberries started playing as Jared and I made our way over.

"Hey, you two. I just ordered – you want anything?" Cafferty asked me.

I checked around for a waiter. There was no sign of Armand, but Tony's dad caught my eye and came to the table.

"Good to see you, Mina. What can I get y'all?" he asked, pulling a notebook out of his pocket.

"You too. Just a cheeseburger for me, please. How's Tony?" I asked as his dad noted my order down.

"He's doin' good," he said. "Thank you for showin' an interest in him."

"No problem."

"Don't think I ever introduced myself – name's Elijah." He looked apprehensive, so I gave my friendliest smile.

He hurried off to the kitchen and Cafferty sipped his coke. "I hear you knew the latest victim – I'm sorry."

"Thanks," I said. "Anything new to report?"

"Frustratingly little," Cafferty said. "Same sort of neck wound, same crossed arms and tarot card in one hand. We got a handwriting analyst on the notes, but they're struggling to pin down who this person is. Usually, they can pick up on personality traits from their wording or the shape of the letters, but the vampire ripper is all over the place. Even the tarot cards don't point to much. Armand said the last two seemed pretty random."

Cafferty paused when Elijah returned with his burger. "That was fast – thanks."

"Yours will be right along," Elijah told me.

I thanked him, refocusing on what Cafferty had told us. "I wonder if the notes and cards don't point to one person because there are two killers – the first two victims were bitten by different vampires. What were the marks like on . . . Ellie?" It hurt to say her name in this context, like she was just another piece of the vampire ripper puzzle.

Cafferty picked up his burger but didn't bite down yet. "Armand took a look at the crime scene photos for me. He said the marks are definitely male but much tidier – like the vampire is getting much more efficient. As you saw, the first victim's neck was a mess."

"That's scary," I said. Cafferty nodded as he took a big bite.

"And unusually fast. We all know I couldn't control myself when I turned." Jared looked sorry for biting me all over again.

"You didn't even know what was happening to you," I said to him, holding his hand under the table before continuing to update Cafferty. "And that's not all. We saw the letter in the paper this morning and went to see the reporter who wrote the article."

Cafferty rubbed his eyes. "Of course you did. And?"

"She said the paper and you guys at the police have had a bunch of letters and calls from people claiming to know something about the ripper, and one of them seemed promising." I recounted what we'd learned about the 911 call potentially confessing to killing the first victim and how Jared might know who the caller was.

Cafferty ate while he listened, swallowing when I finished. "I remember that one . . . Nobody could track him down. I'd go to the blood bar myself, but I'm steering clear of Saint Germain. He's putting pressure on about the ripper. He wants evidence and confidential documents that I can't hand over – mostly because we don't have much to go on."

"We're going tonight," Jared said. "I'll call Saint Germain to explain as much as he needs to know. He did say he wanted to help with the investigation."

The idea of involving Saint Germain appealed to me even less than trusting Dad, but we couldn't snoop around his place without letting him know.

Cafferty sighed. "I don't want you getting mixed up in this, but I trust the two of you. You'll find the guy, question him and get out, right?"

"Definitely," I said, though things were rarely that simple. "We'll let you know what we find out."

"Thanks. I should get goin'," Cafferty said, tossing some money on the table. "I'm still on shaky ground with the police, but I'm getting there. And I hope it won't be long 'til I can bring you back on board too. There's still plenty of time to get experience in before you join the cadets."

"Thank you," I said. "For that, and for helping us."

"Of course," Cafferty said. "Let me know if there's any news, and I'll do the same." Then he headed off.

"I don't know 'bout you, but I'm happy to hang here a while. I don't wanna face the daylight yet, and maybe we can have some us time while we wait for your burger?" Jared said, moving close enough to make everything inside me tighten in anticipation.

"What did you have in mind?" I asked, knowing full well what he meant.

He surged forwards to kiss me, his lips pressed hungrily against mine as he pulled me close. I melted against him, desperate to erase all of the space between us. He nipped my lower lip, and I shivered as he trailed kisses down my neck to my collarbone.

His mouth stopped moving, and I froze with his lips touching the vulnerable skin of my throat. If he was about to lose control, it was too late for me.

He tore his mouth away, looking all around us. The room was the same as always, people eating and talking quietly over background music – the end of 'Black Hole Sun'.

"I smell fresh blood," Jared said.

"It's not mine, is it?" I asked, touching my throat in case he'd nicked me with a fang.

"No, you're good. It's faint – coming from over there, I think."

He was pointing at the exit that led to the alleyway. It was the one where Will and I had accidentally got trapped outside, and I had the weirdest feeling about it.

Dismissing that for now, I patted my jacket, comforted by the presence of my stake. "It could be nothing – I'll go and check."

He caught my hand. "It's daytime – probably not a vampire. I'm coming with you."

"Fine," I said. There was no time to argue. If the blood was fresh, someone might need help.

We hurried across the room, Jared a few steps behind me. "Stay in the doorway," I said. "I don't want you to get hit by any more sunlight than you have to."

He started to object, but I opened the door, withdrawing my stake just in case. The alleyway was mostly in shadow, so I needn't have worried about Jared.

It wasn't dark enough to hide tiny, sweet Tony drinking from a woman's wrist.

Chapter 37

I fumbled my stake, bobbling it in my hands before I got a good grip. Tony's eyes had been vacant, the need for blood carrying him far away. Now they locked on me as he continued to drink.

The woman was leaning against a wall, smiling with her eyes half closed.

"Hold the door," I said to Jared as I marched over there.

Tony broke away, shrinking back further into the shadows and still watching me. The woman had done this before. There were scars inside her elbow and along her other wrist. She stuck a plaster over the wound and pulled down both sleeves.

"Wait," Tony said, his voice small and worried. The woman turned to him, so I could only see her back. "Don't tell anybody what I did, OK? Just . . . go back to your friends." Even though he was a scared little boy, the power in his command shivered over my skin.

The woman stood up, eyes glazed. She swept past us and went back into the bar.

Even if it hadn't been consensual, there would've been no slaying. I shoved the stake back into my holster with shaking hands. Shock was doing a number on me. Who would make a child into a vampire?

"I'm trying to be a good boy – I promise. Daddy says the slayers will get me if I'm bad," Tony said in a small voice, cowering away from me.

"I'm not going to get you, but we need to talk with your daddy. And don't even think about using that power on me."

Tony was so small and sad, and he'd be that way for ever. It wasn't fair. I held out my hand, feeling like the kind of fool who reaches out to stroke a lion. Tony came across slowly, his gaze darting to the patch of sunlight at the end of the alleyway. Then he took my hand in his cold, smooth little grip. I was familiar enough with vampire skin not to flinch as we walked inside together, Jared at our backs. His grave appearance told me he'd heard everything.

Elijah clocked us and his face dropped. He beckoned to one of the waitresses, a tall brunette that I didn't recognise, and she stepped behind the bar in his place.

"Is everyone OK?" Elijah asked breathlessly.

"We're fine, Daddy. I stayed in the shadows away from the sun, but Mina saw me."

Anger flashed across Elijah's face, but he squashed it quickly. "You were supposed to be in Armand's office. We promised him no more accidents, or the slayers will come."

"I was hungry, and that lady was nice. You let me have her blood before." Tony's voice turned petulant, and he gripped so hard that I had to wrench my fingers free.

He looked up at me, his hurt eyes brimming with blood-tinged tears. So I tried to pacify the small, deadly child. "Sorry, buddy. You've got quite a grip."

He grinned. “Daddy says I’m the strongest.”

“Can we talk in Armand’s office?” I asked.

“Please,” Elijah said. Jared came along, his expression pained.

Tony plopped himself on the floor. The room was tight for four of us. There was a desk and chair, a filing cabinet and a bookshelf crammed with everything from fortune-telling guides to Agatha Christie novels.

“Is he . . .?” Jared began, not seeming to know where to go with that.

“Whatever you were going to say, he’s still my son,” Elijah said fiercely. “He was changed earlier this year.”

“And Armand knows?” Jared asked quietly, so much pain locked behind his eyes as he watched the little boy brumming his cars around our feet, hopefully not listening to us.

“He does. He’s been great, actually. And everythin’ has been fine until the past couple weeks. But my boy’s power came in while Armand was in New Mexico, and I was juggling Armand’s businesses.” It wasn’t the first time we’d come across a mind-control power. I’d thought I was going to die when John Carter used his on me.

“I make people do what I want,” Tony said cheerfully. “I just learned how.” So he *was* listening.

“I’ve been homeschooling him since he was turned,” Elijah said.

Jared and I both went to speak at the same time, and he gestured for me to go. “Who did it?”

Elijah’s face crumpled. “It’s all my fault. It was supposed to be me.” He looked down at Tony. “I asked John Carter . . . you know. To do it, but to me. At the time, I trusted him. I didn’t find out what he was really like until it was too late. This was his idea of a joke. He didn't care that the older vampires of the city strictly prohibit turning children. Of course, he was dead before there were any consequences. Anyway, I learned my lesson and I wouldn't want to end up like John, but it was too late for Tony . . ."

"Jesus," Jared said, dragging one hand down over his mouth.

I'd had a parent ditch me to become a vampire too, and my anger towards Mum rose up all over again. "What were you planning to do if John had turned you?"

"I would've left it up to Tony when he was an adult . . . asked if he wanted to join me."

And instead, Tony would be a child for ever. I was too furious to think clearly, but there was one question I had to ask for Tony's benefit. "Does Saint Germain know?" John had seemingly passed on his mind-control ability to little Tony. When a vampire with powers turned someone, they usually ended up with their own unique ability. It was unusual for John to have passed on that same power, and Saint Germain would love to have a vampire in his circle who possessed it.

"No! You're not going to tell him, are you?" Elijah's eyes were wide in true terror.

"He won't hear it from us," I said, not wanting to be around Elijah for any longer. What he'd done felt too familiar. "See you soon, kiddo," I said, crouching down to Tony.

He was humming tunelessly to himself, so I hoped he'd missed a lot of the conversation. "Bye, Mina."

Angry tears slid out of my eyes as I stormed out. I was crying mostly for Tony, but also for myself. My mum was making small steps towards being there for us, but she could never undo the decision to run away and become a vampire.

Jared pressed a kiss into my hair.

"I'm fine," I said. "I just really want to go home."

"Me too," Jared said. He had to have been exhausted after being out for so long during the day, and all of my strength had gone too. I hugged him, and we clung to each other.

"We should go before one of us falls asleep standing up," Jared murmured.

"Sleep . . . That's definitely what I feel like doing," I said, grinning up at him.

"Rest is overrated," Jared said, his expression wicked. "Let's go."

We grabbed a to-go box for my burger before setting off. It was more of a stagger than a walk back to the mansion, our hands clasped and feet dragging. The day was still gloomy and overcast, but the cool air took the edge off my anger. Angsting about Mum becoming a vampire wasn't worth the head space, and what Elijah had done seemed to have made him miserable enough. It was Tony who'd have to suffer. "Will Tony ever mature, or will he keep thinking like a little boy forever?"

"Let's hope he'll mature as the years pass," Jared said. "Being stuck in a child's body will be bad enough, but he won't live long being impulsive and breaking the rules."

That made me feel worse, but it had to be said. It was up to Elijah to keep his son safe until the day he could do it for himself. Then, if Tony was anything like me, he might be better off keeping his distance from the parent who let him down.

"I'm guessing this explains the vampire attacks surrounding Armand's businesses," I said.

"Guess so. Armand will put a stop to it now he's back."

It took longer than usual to trudge up the stairs inside the mansion. I put my burger in the fridge, and then the two of us flopped back on my bed.

"I swear I'll only close my eyes for two minutes," Jared said, rolling onto his side and draping an arm across me.

I snuggled in closer, enjoying the weight of his arm. "I've heard that before."

A loud buzz jolted me out of the sleepy feeling.

Jared groaned and plucked the pager out of his pocket. "Urgh, Saint Germain needs me." Jared pushed himself off the bed, wobbling when he stood up. "Saves me calling him about the blood bar lead, I guess. I can tell him in person."

I propped myself up on one elbow, trying to squash the wave of self-pity. Jared had no choice about running around after Saint Germain, but that didn't stop me from wanting to tackle him down to the bed. "And you need to go out in the day *again*?"

"That's why he wanted me on board." Jared shrugged. I debated lying there and sulking, but I dragged myself to my feet and hugged him, probably tighter than necessary. "Good thing I don't have to breathe," he said, laughing. I slackened my grip. "I'll come back by nightfall so we can go to the blood bar. I assume we're still going to Fiona's party later? It feels kind of messed up to celebrate, after Ellie and Tony . . ."

My instinct was to stay at home curled up in bed, but that was no way to live. "I know what you mean, but I think we should go. Make the most of our moments and all that?"

"You're right," Jared said. "Will and Fiona will appreciate us putting in the effort."

With a kiss on my head, he was gone. My bed was calling to me, but the urge to power-nap had passed. I was due to meet up with Will soon anyway to help him pick a present for Fiona, so I made myself a cup of tea and carried it around while I got ready. I put on a T-shirt with a design I thought Will would get a kick out of and grabbed my leather jacket. The sky through our living room window was dark and swollen with rainclouds again, so I took an umbrella.

Will was waiting outside the mansion and stubbed out his cigarette when I came out of the door. "I know you don't like it when I smoke. But what's it gonna do – kill me?"

I rolled my eyes, not taking the bait. "Let's keep to the problem at hand. It's your girlfriend's birthday and you've bought her nothing."

"And that's why you're here – to help me in my hour of need." He noticed my *True Romance* T-shirt. "Nice shirt. I see myself as more of a Jason Dean, but Clarence is good too."

"Winona Ryder's character is the only aspirational one in *Heathers* and you know it," I said as we set off walking. "OK . . . tell me what Fiona likes."

"How am I 'sposed to know?" he said, grinning when I gave him my deadliest side eyes. "OK . . . She likes those cute little Goth outfits your sister wears. Skulls, bats . . . that kind of thing."

I sighed, seeing where this was going. "Have you heard of a shop called Fanged Friends?"

"No, but it sounds like my kind of place."

"If you show me your fangs, I'll set Della on you."

Will lifted his upper lip to show human teeth. "No fangs here."

We carried on tossing well-meaning insults back and forth, but my heart wasn't in it. I'd not spoken to Emmeline since Halloween, when she apologised for using Della to kill Veronica.

She'd convinced us that Veronica had killed Della's mum, but it wasn't true.

Not only was I missing Emmeline's shop, but her friendship too. It was probably time to mend this fence. The last twenty-four hours were a harsh reminder that life was too short to hold grudges.

We entered as 'Cruel Summer' by Bananarama was playing, and the shop was busy as usual. The Halloween decorations from last time I came in had been replaced with fall ones. Leaves in autumnal colours were attached to spirals all over the ceiling that slowly twirled. A group of teenagers were examining the spooky jewellery, and people were scattered around the shop perusing the racks of Gothic clothing.

Will was looking all around him, from the vampire teddies crammed around a shelf at the top of the room to a rack of vampire costumes. "This place is great," he said, in danger of showing some genuine enthusiasm.

"I'm glad you think so," Emmeline said. I'd been deliberately avoiding where she was standing behind the counter, but I couldn't postpone it any longer.

The green streak at the front of her grey afro had been replaced by an orange one, but otherwise she looked the same: her dark brown skin unlined although she was pushing fifty, and her expression unreadable. "You came back."

"I'm helping Will choose a present for his girlfriend. She's blonde and into cute Goth stuff, and I'm guessing she's about a size 12 . . . A US 8, I mean?"

Will's contribution was a shrug as he strolled across the shop, running his hand along the rails of clothes.

Emmeline came around the counter. "Let me see about that."

Being near her was filling me with so many complicated emotions that I was glad she was keeping it professional.

Will continued wandering aimlessly, but Emmeline moved through her shop with purpose. She smiled at customers and offered advice as she collected items from around the store, hanging dresses and tops over her arm.

"All right. Come on over and let's take a look," she said, and we followed her to the counter.

She spread out an array of clothes that were mostly black with accents of bright colours, ribbons and lace edges. "Do any of these look like your girlfriend would choose them?"

"Mina?" Will asked.

Considering the selection, I pulled out a black dress with a fitted bodice and lace edging. The skirt flared out with electric blue pleats. A ribbon in each thin strap matched the blue.

"She'd look good in that," Will said approvingly. He tugged the label towards him and grimaced. "I'm ten bucks short. Both of you, *forget* the price of this one. Twenty bucks will be fine."

Everything went hazy as Will held out a twenty-dollar bill. Why wasn't Emmeline taking it?

She crossed her arms as my head started aching dully. "Your powers don't work on me."

"Will doesn't have powers," I said. Was I the only one who had no idea what she was talking about?

He tugged his hands through his hair, leaving it wild. "What . . . How?"

The shop had cleared out in a rare moment of quiet. Emmeline swept across to the door and turned the 'Open' sign around to 'Closed'.

She came back to stand on the other side of the counter, arms folded and displeasure breaking through her usual composure. "Any witch worth her salt in this city has a shield up against vampire powers."

Chapter 38

Emmeline was a witch. That was enough to mess with my head, but I was still stuck on Will having powers.

"This isn't the first time you've pulled the wool over Mina's eyes, is it?" Emmeline asked, her eyes glinting with fury.

She grabbed a wooden box from under the counter, pulling a small glass bottle from a huge array with nimble fingers. She uncorked it and held it out to me. "Breathe in deep, *cher*."

I generally wouldn't sniff on command, but I inhaled deeply, smelling the astringent punch of rosemary among other things. Emmeline reached across and touched two fingers to my forehead. "Remember, Mina."

The words zinged with intention. Memories rushed back with such force that I clung to the counter, my vision going starry and black like I might pass out.

When I recovered, I got the urge to hit Will hard enough to knock him on his back. I couldn't believe he'd violated my trust like that. "You bit a girl in the Empire alley and made me forget it? And nearly killed one of Clem's friends at the bonfire. You're lucky I don't stake you and ask Emmeline to help me hide your body!"

"That's always an option," Emmeline said, leaning her elbows on the counter to watch the drama unfolding.

"I'm sorry," Will said bluntly. "I know that doesn't mean much, but I am. You've been so good to me . . ." He trailed off, pushing back his floppy hair. He did look sorry, but that wasn't good enough.

"You should've told me about your powers . . . and you definitely shouldn't have used them on me."

"Noted," Will said. "And just so you know, I can't make you my puppet or anything like that. I can only wipe memories."

"Well, if you do anything like this again and the slayers find out, then you're on your own."

"Can't argue with that," Will said, his hair falling over his face again. This time he left it there as a shield. "I owe you an apology too," he added to Emmeline. "I'll get Fiona somethin' else."

"I'll lend you ten dollars – not that you deserve it," I said, handing the note to him. Becoming a vampire was a massive adjustment, especially after having to deal with two of his siblings being killers, but it didn't excuse what he'd done.

"Thanks," Will said, his usual confidence and sarcasm missing. "I'll pay you back."

Emmeline took the money with an air of suspicion. "I'm not the first person to point out the corrupting influence of power. I'll give you the benefit of growing into yours, but take this as a warning. Today you showed me your power. Next time, you'll see the extent of mine."

"Message received," Will said, not meeting Emmeline's eyes as he picked up the dress bag. "I'm gonna duck outside. See you in a minute?"

"I'll be right there," I said, still processing his actions and what Emmeline had revealed.

When the door closed, I got right to it. "You're a witch . . . Witches are real." My friends had told me as much at the fall fair, but it was different from seeing it. Dad had also mentioned them back at the ranch. I wasn't sure how I felt about one of his claims being proven right.

"We are," Emmeline said. "I was gonna reach out to you, and here you are. I am truly sorry for what I pulled you and Della into over Halloween. I should never have said Veronica killed her mother."

"To be fair, we would've been mixed up in it anyway," I said, "but you shouldn't have lied."

"In the spirit of honesty . . . I regret it if I put you two in any more danger, but I'm happy you got Veronica. It feels like Thandie can rest now her murderer is gone."

My throat tightened. "Now, back to the you being a witch part."

"Your man is a vampire but you're finding witchcraft difficult to comprehend?" Her smile was guarded. "There'll be plenty of time to discuss that. You got another vampire on your hands that needs you."

Will was walking back and forth in front of the window, watching us with hollow, hungry eyes.

"He's still adjusting," I said, surprised that I wanted to defend him despite everything.

"He needs to do it fast. I can see darkness in that one. He might become more of a burden than you can bear."

"Is this a witch thing? Did you have a vision?" I asked.

"In a manner of speaking. I tend to see people as they truly are.

We'll talk soon, *cher*. I fear it might not be in the best circumstances. The witches have been talkin', and it appears something bad is brewing with the vamps. We don't know what it is yet, but we will soon."

I could've done without that extra worry, but what was one more? Emmeline reached out her hand and I took it. Her grip was warm and firm. My anger towards her was lessening, leaving behind the certainty that it was right to have her back in my life.

"Thanks for warning me about Will," I said. "See you soon."

"I hope so."

Will's grin was strained when I let myself out of Fanged Friends. "Are you hungry?" I asked.

"Depends if you're offering," he said, something harsh and primal lurking beneath the joke.

We set off towards the mansion, Emmeline's warning niggling at me. "I'm giving you one pass, but you can't afford to mess up like that again."

"I know," Will said quietly.

"I'm not sure you do. It's not just about losing your friends. There are no second chances with the slayers. If you hurt someone, they'll kill you."

Will looked serious for once, and slightly stunned. "I can keep a handle on this – I swear. I don't just use this ability for selfish reasons, you know. I made my stepmom forget that you were the one who . . . you know, did what you did to Sam."

That explained why she was civil around me, but it didn't make it right. "I get why you did it, but I don't think you should've decided that for her."

"You might be right," Will said, pushing his hair back. It

flopped right back down over his eyes.

"I know I am. Now go to a blood bar before I have to call the slayers."

Will looked down at me from under his floppy hair. "It makes sense now why Jared's such a boy scout, with you in his corner."

"Welcome to the club."

He saluted me and marched off down the street, the black Fanged Friends bag dangling from his fingers.

I followed the sound of whistling to the kitchen. Jared was wiping down the surfaces, and the pristine shape of the room suggested he was nearly done. "I think I'm doing something wrong here . . . I don't get to eat the food but I still clean up the mess."

"Nah, you're doing something right," I said, wrapping my arms around his waist. "Are you nearly done? I have something to tell you. Well, two things."

Jared hung the cloth over the tap and leaned against the counter, arms folded. "I don't know how much more I can take today, but go ahead."

"First, Emmeline's a witch."

Jared raised his eyebrows. "That figures . . . Only makes her more terrifying though. What's the other thing?"

"OK, that was easy. This one might pack more of a punch . . . Will got his power, and he already used it on me."

Jared's expression changed in a flash, his hazel eyes turning to hard flints. "What can he do?" he asked quietly. I'd never seen him look so dangerous.

"He can make people forget. I saw him feed on someone, and he used his power on me. But before you go and rip his head off, I've forgiven him. I'm mad as hell, but I told him that's his one mistake. You know how hard the change was for you."

"You're right," Jared said. "But I'll have a chat with him about the consequences of misusing his power again, especially against you."

"Go ahead. Do you mind telling the others about Will and Emmeline while I get dressed? We'll be cutting it close to fit in the blood bar before Fiona's party."

"Sure thing. I already told them Tony's a vampire – it's been a day for big reveals." Jared extended a hand towards me and I let him pull me into a hug. "And hanging out with your dad twice in one day – I think I deserve a medal."

"You do – an extra shiny one."

I heard Libby hitting the roof about Will while I made my cup of tea downstairs. Then it was time to get ready, so I went for comfy jeans and a cream cardigan with a beaded choker and red lips to dress it up. I was too nervous about visiting one of Saint Germain's blood bars to give fashion much thought.

Jared and I reconvened by the front door of the mansion. "Wow – you look great," he said.

"So do you," I said. He'd tackled his messy curls with a bit of gel and put on a green checked shirt. "How did they take it?"

"I assume you heard the shouting," Jared said dryly. "Thanks for leaving that one to me."

"I've had eighteen years of Libby reactions. We're not close to even yet." I lifted Jared's wrist to check his watch. "We need to motor if we're going to make it on time to meet my parents."

Jared frowned. "Are we making a mistake taking them to a club full of vampires?"

"Mum should be fine, and Dad said he'd behave. We can't cut him out of this – he wants to find Ellie's killer as much as we do."

"And use them to expose vampires to the world," Jared added as he unlocked the front door.

On the way, Jared updated me about Saint Germain. He'd promised us a free ride into the blood bar, without the usual rigorous screening active participants had to undergo. This would be my third blood-bar visit, which had to be a record for a human who wasn't going there to be bitten. The first time I'd seen Thandie feeding on someone, and last time Armand had helped me come to terms with Jared's fanged status. If this visit went the way I hoped, we'd be able to question the 911 caller whose story sounded a lot like the first murder. The more experienced I got, the more confident I was that working for the police was right for me. I was determined to see this through, for Ellie and the other victims.

"I forgot to ask . . . what did Saint Germain ask you to do this time?"

Jared paused to check both ways before we crossed the road. "He's fuming about what Clem and his guys pulled at the bonfire. He had me searching every hovel around the city where they might have holed up."

"And no one's looking at the swamp?"

"I didn't mention it." Jared grimaced. "I was afraid my next instruction would be to go there and kill them if I did."

That was what I'd been afraid of when Jared started working for Saint Germain – his boundaries being whittled away.

Mum and Dad were waiting across the road from the blood bar. Mum predictably looked like she didn't want to be there, but Dad's smile made my nerves spike. There was a calculating quality that vanished when he saw us. "It's good to see you both," Dad said, lingering on Jared.

"Thank you for trusting us to be here," Mum said. It was such a rarity having them show up for me that I wasn't sure how to behave.

Jared stepped in, ignoring the way Dad was looking at him. "Let me give you some advice about how these places work. I'm assuming you've been before, Mrs Shepherd, but bear with me. The etiquette is to keep your eyes on what you're doing and not on other people. They deserve privacy, and some of them are dangerous."

"Got it," Dad said. "I'm tryin' to earn your trust here, and I see this as my opportunity."

"That's good to hear," Jared said stiffly.

"Shall we?" Dad gestured like the whole scheme was his. Mum hung on to his hand, and I hoped she could keep him in check.

Jared's gait was tense as he set off for the doorman. Security was much tighter than at the original blood bar we'd talked our way into – the one Will's half-brother, Sam, had burned down.

Jared explained quietly that we had permission to be there. The bouncer eyed the four of us, giving a rattling cough before he spoke. "Y'all might be allowed to come inside, but I keep a clean house. Y'all start any trouble, and you'll be answerin' to me, got it?"

"We hear you loud and clear," Dad said, staring the man straight in the eyes even though the bouncer was a foot taller and wider.

"We understand," Mum echoed, shrinking against Dad's side.

It was the bodyguard who was left squirming as we passed. What would it be like to live with Dad's brand of magnetism? I saw how it could go to a person's head, giving them an inflated sense of self-importance.

The previous blood bar had been hidden beneath a nightclub, the patrons of which had looked used up by the life they'd led there. This blood bar had an entrance like a luxury spa. We signed in at a black marble reception desk with a beautiful female vampire behind it, her skin a dark, velvety brown and her eyes enormous and mesmerising. Knowing Saint Germain, that could've been a power she possessed, so I avoided eye contact.

After that, we were in.

Chapter 39

The windowless panelling inside the blood bar created a suffocating effect. We were in a large central atrium populated by several impressive vampire bodyguards. The quiet murmur of voices came from all around us, and I realised some of the panels were hinged to create private booths. Behind them, humans were playing at being vampires in some booths and real ones were getting fed in others. This proximity of vampires and unknowing humans was only able to exist because of the privacy.

"Saint Germain had someone book us in with Ray," Jared said in a low voice. "He's not expecting us, so he might be skittish. If he tries to bolt, I'll deal with him."

"Remember I'm here too," Mum said, with strength I wasn't used to from her.

Jared led the way to a panel in the middle of the room. Dad and I followed with Mum close behind. He looked positively delighted. A terrible sense of foreboding was growing in my gut, but it was too late to do anything about it.

Raising his fist, Jared knocked on the wood. "Come in!" a thick southern accent murmured, and the four of us entered a space done out with plush, red velvet seats and carpet in a deeper shade of maroon. A table to one side displayed plasters and bandages. Each panelled wall featured a painting of someone being fed on by a vampire, their eyes closed in pleasure as they offered their wrist or throat.

The vampire looked young, but that didn't give any indication of how long ago he'd been turned. He was very thin, his cheekbones sharp and his large eyes creating the illusion of innocence. That also wasn't worth relying on. He had stringy hair that fell to his shoulders, and he kept pushing it back from his face.

Jared closed the door and the vampire sprang to his feet. "I wasn't expectin' an audience. So, which of y'all are here to watch and . . .?"

"Sorry to disappoint, but none of us are here to feed you. Saint Germain told us we could ask you a few questions," Jared said. Dad stood back with Mum, true to his word so far.

Ray the vampire's eyes got even wider when Jared mentioned Saint Germain. "If y'all aren't gonna feed me, then I'll . . ."

He moved so fast, my eyes couldn't keep up. One moment, he was standing at the back of the booth, and the next he was at the doorway.

I thought we'd lost him, but Mum blocked his escape. Mum had always been distant and disconnected, but being in vamp mode suited her.

She grabbed the vampire by one shoulder, looking to Jared like she was awaiting orders. Dad shrank away until his back hit one of the panelled walls. It wouldn't hurt him to be a little afraid of Mum.

Jared came to stand by Mum, his expression disturbingly cold.

"Sit," he said to Ray, so commanding that I would've been afraid if I didn't know him so well. "We aren't here to hurt you. We want to ask you a few questions and then we'll go."

Ray backed into the nearest seat, hands raised as if Jared had turned a gun on him. "All right! All right. But I doubt I'll be able to help. I work here for Mr Saint Germain and I go home – that's about it."

Jared glanced at me, and I took my turn. "We know you called 911 the night of the first ripper killing. Can you tell us what happened?"

"Wasn't me," Ray said, glancing at the exit behind me. "Don't know why I'd call no cops – I didn't do nothin'."

I hesitated in the face of his denial, weighing what to say next. His nervous manner hadn't changed, and I couldn't tell if he was lying.

Mum spoke up, her tone hard. "I'm not sure I believe you, *Ray*. We read the transcript of your phone call. We know you killed someone the same night the ripper did." Mum was terrifying, and I couldn't have been prouder. "Does that mean *you* are the ripper?"

Ray eyed the exit again, swallowing hard, but he stayed put. "All right! I'll talk. That ripper ain't me – I swear. I fed on someone that night, and I didn't take all that much blood when he started dyin' on me. So I split. I know I shouldn't have done it, but I was scared."

"Did you leave anything on the body afterwards?" I asked, growing more confident. No one but the killer, the police and some of the press knew about the tarot cards.

"Why would I do that?" Ray asked, appearing genuinely

baffled. "I've not been a vamp all that long, but my sire taught me right and I never killed a human before." Ray yanked his hands through his long hair. "I shouldn't have gone out huntin' by myself."

"I think we've heard enough." Ilian slid between the gap in the panels, holding it open for a female vampire with warm, light brown skin and long black hair. "Saint Germain asked me to listen in, and I'm so glad I did. Miranda? Will you check Ray's story please so we can let our friends go about their night?"

Miranda had a quiet way about her, but Ray scuttled to the back of the booth like she was his worst nightmare. "Please don't . . ." he said. "I'm telling you the truth, I swear."

"I believe you." Her voice was kind and melodious. "This will only hurt for a moment, and if you're telling the truth, no other harm will befall you."

Jared spoke up. "What are you going to do to him?"

Ilian ran a hand over his smooth head. "Miranda simply makes contact with someone's temple to extract a memory. Depending on what she sees, we'll go from there."

I had no idea what to do, and part of me wanted to know what Miranda would see. Before I could decide whether or not to intervene on Ray's behalf, she touched his head. He gasped, his eyes rolling back in his head as his whole body stiffened.

Then she drew back her hand, flexing her fingers. "His description of the events was true. He fed from a man and ran. He's not the ripper."

"What happened to the body?" I asked.

Miranda shrugged. "That's not my area. Perhaps he wasn't dead and went home or to the hospital, or some other misfortune befell his body after death. It may not have been found at all or may have been considered to be an animal attack. All I can tell you for sure is that Ray is not the ripper."

"We'll take it from here," Ilian said. "I know your slayer code covers this situation, but I'm sure you'll let it slide on this occasion. As no one found a body to confirm the kill, I think we can let Ray live if he doesn't make the same error again."

I was torn. The code had become so engrained in me, but what was I supposed to do – stake this vampire while he sat there and sobbed? That wasn't right either, especially when I wasn't sure what happened to the victim. "We'll go," I said.

Jared and Mum moved towards the door, but Dad hung back. "I have one more question."

Ilian turned his attention on Dad properly. "And who might you be?"

"Sorry, but we really have to get going." I looped my hand through Dad's arm, gripping harder than necessary to hammer the point home.

"Another time, perhaps," Dad said, letting me pull him into the main atrium.

Unease prickled up and down my back as we left, like someone was going to stop us. We kept walking until we reached the corner of the street.

"So, I take it none of us think he's the ripper?" I asked quietly. "That vampire's vision confirmed as much."

"Which means the killer's still out there," Jared said.

"I wish you hadn't stopped me." Dad was brooding at full force. "That bald-headed vampire seemed like he could've been useful to know."

"Believe me when I say that Mina just saved your life," Jared said. “You wouldn’t want to bring yourself and your goals to Ilian’s attention.”

Dad chewed inside his cheek, considering Jared. “Then I guess I owe you some gratitude, honey. Now, I have to get goin’. I have an appointment with Clem.”

“Are you sure you need to talk to him?” I asked.

“I’m guessin’ you more than most people understand that it’s my duty. I have to do what’s right,” Dad said.

“I agree with our daughter,” Mum said, “but I know neither of us will change your mind. Thank you for bringing us along,” she added to me. “It means a lot that you asked. Good night, honey.” We said our goodbyes, and she offered a last smile over her shoulder.

“I never thought I’d say this after how she treated you,” Jared said, “but your mom was pretty cool tonight.”

“She was,” I said. “It’s a shame we hit a dead end with Ray though. I’d rather not come face to face with the ripper, but we’re back to square one now.”

“We’ll get there,” Jared said. “But now we have to go to a party.”

Chapter 40

It felt like we'd been at the blood bar for ages, but we set off on time for the restaurant. My head was a blur as we weaved through the night crowds. Today, we'd lost Ellie, learned about Will's power and met a child vampire. But our promising clue at the blood bar had led nowhere. Jared put his arm around me as we walked, and I was grateful that he'd been there for the wild ride of a day.

When we met Libby and Della outside Nine Steps to Hell, I tried to let everything go. Sometimes, letting a problem simmer was the best way to solve it.

Armand had inherited this restaurant from his brother, among other businesses. It did great food and had a Dante Alighieri exhibit. I wouldn't be going in there again, since Sam had stalked his victims wearing a replica of Dante's death mask. I would've asked Armand to get rid of the exhibit, but the restaurant was built around that idea.

I pushed that thought away, only to be confronted by the painting of the nine circles of hell down the stairway to the restaurant. It was as beautiful and disturbing as you could want it to be, the tormented faces in each circle painfully detailed.

Thinking about the painter had me twisted up inside more than the imagery. Our false friend, Lucas, had done it, right before betraying us to Armand's brother, John Carter.

Determined not to bring down the mood, I focused on the design inside Nine Steps. It had a castle theme, with electric lanterns attached to faux stone walls. '99 red balloons' by Nena was playing, which provided a much-needed pick me up.

The smell of barbecue food was thick in the air, and everyone was chatting, drinking or tucking into their meals. Feeling more grounded, I followed my friends to a table decorated with black and silver balloons. There were no numbers in sight, but that was possibly a vampire thing. Do they want to be reminded that they're not aging?

The four of us settled around the table, jostling for places and discussing the menu. Will and Fiona were crossing the restaurant, holding hands and gazing adoringly at each other.

Watching their affection from the outside, I resolved to give Fiona a shot. She hadn't taken Will away from us by changing him – he was right here. And if he got his wilder urges under control, he'd make a go of being a vampire. I was still mad at him for messing with my memory, but I decided to give him the benefit of the doubt.

"Hi, y'all," Fiona said, grinning nervously around the table. I felt for her – fitting into a tight-knit group was tough.

"Happy birthday!" I said, standing up to hug her. "The dress looks great."

"Thank you," she said. It had to be a good sign that she was wearing Will's present. "I hear you had a little somethin' to do with this."

"I might have. I'm glad you like it," I said.

We sat down around the table, and Elijah appeared to take our orders. "Hey. Y'all ready?"

"Twice in one day," I said. "Armand's got you running all over town, hasn't he?"

Elijah smiled. "He's a good boss. I like working across his businesses. Thanks, you know, for how you reacted to Tony. Not many people know about him, and he felt good about how it went today."

"No problem," I said. What Elijah had pulled his son into was despicable, but that wasn't Tony's fault.

Elijah looked down the length of the table, as if remembering everyone else was there. "Thanks . . . Anyhow, what can I get y'all?"

We all ordered from the fall drinks menu and the humans ordered food. Each couple gave Fiona a present while we waited for our drinks. She loved the black rose earrings from me and Jared, squealing when she realised that Libby and Della had brought her the matching bracelet. She put in the earrings and Will helped her to fasten the bracelet.

After that, Elijah brought the drinks. Mine was fizzy apple with a brown sugar leaf floating on the surface. A candle floated in Fiona's.

Her eyes were damp with pink tears as we sang to her, and she blew out the candle. She leaned in to kiss Will. I caught Armand's eye over at the bar, and he nodded at me. A lot of elements of vampires' lives ground to a halt when they were turned. Like Jared, Fiona hadn't been given a choice about it. Veronica had been building an army to stand against Saint Germain, and one of her minions had turned Fiona.

When the food came, Fiona and Will stood up as 'Chantilly Lace' by The Big Bopper started playing. "I think we're gonna go check out that Dante exhibit," Will said, nuzzling his mouth against Fiona's neck. She nudged into him with a warning glance. Even though his half-brother had killed his victims wearing a Dante mask like the one in the exhibit, either Will must not have made the connection or he wasn't letting it bother him.

"I notice you're not inviting the other vamp at the table to come with," Jared said with a grin.

"I'm not sure you'd be into it." Will winked, as Fiona dragged him away.

We tucked into our food while Jared sipped his drink. My spiced pulled pork sandwich and apple sauce tasted really good. I'd almost finished eating when my gaze strayed to the entrance of the restaurant.

Paige, Beau and a trio of particularly unpleasant slayers were standing at the bottom of the stairs, perusing the room with the intensity of predators. Paige had brought in some new people lately, and the only thing I knew about them was that they seemed to enjoy kicking the crap out of other slayers during training.

Della and I stood at the same time, the remains of our food abandoned. "We need to put a stop to whatever that is," she said.

"Agreed. Stay here and take care of Libby," I added to Jared. "I know you're on Saint Germain's safe list, but better not to risk bringing them over here."

Jared's jaw muscles twitched, but he nodded. "I'll sit tight for now, but if there's any trouble . . ."

"Be safe," Libby said, forcing a smile.

Paige waved Della and me over even though we were already

on the way. Her red hair was scraped back in a high ponytail that made her seem especially severe, and her lips were a glossy crimson. "The two of you didn't get anywhere, so we came to take a look around. Saint Germain is freaking at that ripper guy, and we need to be *way thorough* in places with a lot of vampire activity. I mean – if we find and kill him, we get the reward money. I've got my eye on a new Toyota pickup for the slayers – I'm sure you get it."

Della replied in her usual calm manner. "You didn't give us a whole lot of time, but it's good to see y'all."

"Sorry to turn up unannounced like this," Beau said. "Are you here on business or pleasure?"

"It's our friend's birthday," I said. "But we've not seen any signs of vampires breaking the code." I willed myself not to look towards the vampires I cared about: Jared with my sister, Armand behind the bar and Will and Fiona having some alone time in the Dante exhibit. As newer, less predictable vampires, they were the pair to worry about.

"I'm *so* sorry," Paige said, all fake sympathy. "Please . . . go hang with your friends. We'll do a quick pass of the room. Oh, and in case you were wondering, that's an order."

She turned her back on us with a flip of her ponytail. Beau shrugged as if to ask what any of us could do.

Della and I went back to Libby and Jared. "How 'bout you stay and catch up these guys? I'll go find Will and Fiona and get them back here," Della said.

I was glad Della had taken that job. If Paige came over, I wanted to be here for Jared. She was known for pushing the code, even if he was part of Saint Germain's fold like her.

So far, the slayers weren't causing trouble. On a quiet night, the five of them strafing between the tables would stick out. Tonight, there were clusters of people talking and staff moving around, so it wasn't too obvious.

Armand sidled over to clear our glasses. "I take it she's checking up on us?"

"Looks like it," I said, sitting down reluctantly, even though the thought of slayers roaming while Will was out there was making me twitchy. "Are any other vampires here?"

Armand scowled. "The child is safe. I know what you're thinking, and I implore you to see how this plays out before acting impulsively." He was right, but it was hard to sit back and watch everything unfold.

Across the room, Paige peered inside the Dante Alighieri exhibit. I pushed back my chair, ready to offer backup if Della needed it.

Della appeared from the dark space to address Paige. She had her back to me, but I could tell she had a problem with what Della was saying from the agitated bounce of her ponytail. Whatever Della said worked, because Paige stalked away.

Will and Fiona slid out of the exhibition, following the wall around the room towards us.

That was when all hell broke loose.

Chapter 41

Elijah was crossing the room with a tray of glasses in his hand. A female slayer grabbed his shoulder, and the tray crashed to the ground. The music carried on playing, but the crowd noise ceased while everyone got a good look. Some people clapped at the spillage, but most of them returned to their food and conversations. Will and Fiona were frozen at the edge of the room. She was tucked against his side, while he looked ready to kill someone.

Della rushed towards the slayer who was still holding Elijah. I did the same, Paige's orders be damned. She was on her way to the scene too, grinning like this was her idea of a good time. We reached the slayer as she was trying to drag Elijah up the stairs.

"Hold up!" Della said. "What'd he do?"

"Hey now, isn't that supposed to be my question?" Paige asked.

Beau came over as well. "We're not here to make a scene," he said quietly.

"This one looks shifty and he's sweating buckets," the slayer hissed, still holding Elijah's collar. "He's hiding something."

Not too surprising when his son was a vampire. We really needed the slayers to remain in the dark about that.

It would've been easier if Tony hadn't come pelting across the room, fangs bared. Armand's office door behind him looked ready to fall off broken hinges.

Armand was on his way over, horror dawning on his face as Tony sprang at the slayer holding his dad.

The fighting kicked off all at once in a dizzying frenzy. Tony bit the slayer's leg through her jeans. She screamed, trying to pry him off. Beau crouched down, talking to Tony without any effect. He still hung on, snarling.

Armand leaped in front of Paige when she went for Tony, and the two entered a verbal sparring match. Elijah prised his son's mouth off the slayer and spirited him away towards Armand's office.

Finally, the customers noticed something was up, tossing money on their tables and then rushing towards the stairs in a stampede. If they left with a story of a fanged child attacking people, Dad and the ripper's work of revealing vampires would be done for them.

Then Will arrived to save the day. He blocked the stairway and appeared to be inviting the fleeing customers to *forget* what they'd seen. Beau seemed to have cottoned on, steering stragglers towards Will. He and Beau led them upstairs.

While they were taking care of that, I tuned back in as Jared leaped in front of the broken door of Armand's office, blocking one of the slayers from getting to Tony.

I reached them as Jared was reasoning with the slayer. "He's a frightened little boy who got turned into a vampire against his will. We have it under control."

"Apparently, you don't. That little shit broke the code," the slayer spat, tugging at her blonde plait.

"No one else needs to get hurt," Jared said. "I work for Saint Germain. In fact, he has me on his protection list, as you should know. I'm happy to take it up with him, if you like."

In answer, the slayer swung her fist back and let it fly. Jared was out of the way before the punch could land.

"Leave her alone!" A furious yell cut through the fighting, and I spun around to see that the restaurant had emptied out apart from us.

Will was rushing down the stairs, horror etched into his features. Fiona and Paige were fighting in front of him, their hands moving in a blur of fists and Paige's stake. I had no idea what would make Fiona take Paige on.

I was halfway across the restaurant when Fiona lunged towards Paige's throat, fangs bared, and Paige's hand came up in a practised jab.

Her stake sank into Fiona's chest, blood blooming around it. She fell to the ground, and Will blurred to her side. When I reached them, Fiona was in the grip of terror, blood trickling from her mouth, but fading fast. "I'm sorry," Will whispered. "I wasn't there..."

Will had used his ability on the customers of the restaurant to erase what they'd seen tonight, keeping the existence of vampires secret at the worst personal cost. Fiona died in his lap with his arms around her.

Paige was standing over the two of them, her hands empty. She looked uncharacteristically shaken up. "She went for me first. You all saw that, right?"

Della's mouth made a firm line, her eyes pained. "I saw. She was trying to stop you from going upstairs after Will, but knowing Fiona I doubt she would've really hurt you."

"How was I supposed to know that?" Paige said. "I stuck to the code! The little kid gets a pass for tonight after what happened, but I did everything right. I was just going to talk to the guy about what he did to the customers – I wasn't going to hurt him!" Despite it all, I believed her. In fights, we all had to make hard decisions. Fiona would've done anything to protect Will.

"We're leaving," Paige snapped, stalking towards the stairs.

Grief had left Will blank, but it lifted when Paige spoke. Faster than should've been possible, he leaped towards Paige. Jared was there, wrapping him in a bear hug. "Get out of here," he said to Paige and her cronies, straining to keep hold of Will as he snarled and twisted.

"I'm sorry," Beau said. "I wish that could've been avoided." Then he fled with the rest of them.

Will wrenched free with a roar, tearing up the stairs. All of us gave chase, including Libby.

We hurried out onto the busy street, but there was no sign of the slayers . . . or Will.

"Is he going to kill them?" Libby asked.

"I'll see if I can track him," Jared said, giving me a parting glance before disappearing into the crowd.

I hated the thought of him going after slayers, especially with Fiona lying there downstairs, blood pooling around her in the dress Will had bought for her birthday. It didn't feel real that she was dead, after celebrating with us. Tony and any of our other friends could've joined her so easily.

"I'll deal with Fiona," Armand said softly. "She doesn't have anyone except Will . . . I'll take care of everything."

"You want our help?" Della asked.

"No, get yourselves home," Armand said. A vacant look came over his face, one I knew well. He was glimpsing some time from the past or future. He blinked hard, running a hand over his mouth. "The city only grows more dangerous – it doesn't take visions to see that."

"What did you see?" I asked.

"A hospital bed – hardly the best omen, but it must be important somehow," Armand said stiffly. "As I said, my recent visions have been rather fragmented."

"OK then. We'll hunker down at the mansion," I said, not fully able to concentrate while Jared was out pursuing Will. Was one of us going to end up in hospital before all of this was over?

The three of us walked back there, arms tightly linked with Libby in the middle. She made us hot chocolates when we got back and we huddled together on the sofa upstairs, too rattled to even watch TV.

My hot chocolate went cold after a while and I set it down on the table, but Jared still wasn't home. "He'll come," Della said. "Hopefully with Will."

I wanted so much for her to be right that I clung on to it until the apartment door opened. Jared slouched in, looking tired and very hungry, his eyes rimmed in red. "I couldn't find him."

"Let's hope he lost Paige and the slayers too," I said.

"Even by our standards, today has been a lot, and it's the big mansion reopening tomorrow. I vote bed." Libby untangled her legs and stood up, offering Della a hand.

"That sounds perfect," Della said, letting Libby pull her up. "Let's check on Will tomorrow. Before we go, you've been out all night. Do you need to feed?"

Jared's eyes latched on to Della's throat and he swallowed hard. "Yeah . . . please."

Della sat back down and extended her arm. Libby and I went to get ready for bed. Jared hated us seeing him feeding unless we needed to.

I felt shattered and upset as I brushed my teeth. Fiona was gone. As far as I could tell, Paige had acted within the code, but it was tough to accept.

When I finished getting ready, Jared was waiting outside the door. The jittery signs of hunger were gone, but he looked sad. Without a word, he enfolded me in his arms. Against Jared's chest with his arms tight around me, some peace settled in. "Can you sleep in my bed tonight?" I asked. "Since you've just fed and everything. I don't want to sleep alone." After seeing Will lose Fiona, I wanted Jared close.

He kissed the top of my head. "Neither do I. Don't worry – I'm not going anywhere."

Jared went to get changed and brush his teeth, so I was in bed with my back to the wall when he came in. I left the lamp on for him out of habit, not that he needed it with his vampy night vision.

He hesitated by the door. Even amidst the sadness, I felt warm anticipation as he slowly crossed the room, eyes never leaving me.

He slid into my bed. At first, he lay facing me, looking at my face and trailing his fingers through my hair. "I love you," he said, his voice uneven.

"Love you, too," I said, shuffling forwards until our faces were almost touching. He gave me a small, secretive smile, his hazel eyes soft, before we kissed. Even though I was wrapped up in grief and exhaustion, the kiss felt dreamy and sweet. I inched nearer to him, relishing in the feel of his body against mine. Before long, we gave in to tiredness and Jared turned off the light.

Settling under his arm, I felt the gentle pull of sleep. Before it dragged me down, I thought about Ellie and Fiona: one girl lost to a murderer and one to a slayer.

In the morning, I woke to Libby clattering around the apartment. The Mansion of the Macabre reopening had been overshadowed lately, but it'd be good for us to have a focus for today. Jared was still asleep, so I slipped out of bed quietly. I was still thinking about Ellie and Fiona. It was hard to believe they were both gone.

Before going to help Libby, I went to ring Will, dreading who might pick up. It was horrible facing Will's stepmum after what I'd done. I'd killed one of her children and got the other arrested. Even though neither had left me with any choice, I didn't expect her to forgive me. Will had made her forget that I did it for now, but I still had to face her.

The phone rang for ages and I was about to hang up when Will's stepmum answered. "Hello?"

"Hi, it's Mina. Can I speak to Will, please?"

"Hi, Mina," she said cheerfully. "He didn't come home last night, but I'm sure he's fine. I might have seen him, but I can't quite remember . . . That's been happening a lot lately. Anyway, I'll be sure to tell him you called. Bye, honey."

The line went dead, and I hung up. What she'd said felt seriously off, especially the part where she thought she'd seen Will but dismissed it. Libby came in as I dropped down on the sofa, stewing on the conversation.

"How's Will?" she asked, handing me a cup of tea.

I took a tentative sip, and it was the perfect temperature. "Thank you. He's not there. I think he went home and messed with his stepmum's memory before leaving again."

"Poor Will. I wish we could do something," Libby said, taking a long gulp of coffee.

"Me too," I said. Hopefully he'd come back when he was ready without causing any permanent damage, but until then there was nothing we could do. "Today's all about you and the mansion. What's the plan?"

Libby preened, but the phone rang before she could answer.

I grabbed it. "Will?"

"Sorry, it's Cafferty. Armand caught me up. Is Will still gone?"

"Yeah. We don't know where he is," I said.

"I have news too. A group of vampires went to Clem's house on the swamp last night and killed everyone."

Chapter 42

"My dad went out there last night," I said haltingly. Cafferty fell silent on the other end of the phone while I struggled to think through the shock. "He was going to have one last attempt to talk Clem around after what he did at the bonfire."

"Mina?" Libby said from beside me, fear trembling through her. I grabbed her hand, squeezing it while I tried to slow my breathing.

"Listen to me," Cafferty said, his tone soothing. "We don't know if he was there or not. He could've been in and out before the killers came. I haven't been out to the swamp yet, but they're gonna bring the victims back to the city when forensics release them. In the meantime, I'll call over there and see if anyone can tell me who they found, or describe them at least."

"OK," I said, so numb that I could barely take anything in. "Thank you."

"I'll call you the second I hear anything. How about you call your mom to check if he's home?"

"I . . . I'll do that. Thanks."

"Sit tight at the mansion – I'll be in touch soon."

"Wait – can I ask one more thing? Who . . . who would do something like that?" My brain wasn't working at full speed. All I could think was that my dad might be dead.

"Let's just say I'm going to visit our mutual friend Saint Germain to see if he's responsible, but I'll call the team over at the swamp first."

"OK . . . that makes sense. I'm going to the swamp . . . I want to see for myself . . ."

Cafferty intervened gently. "The police have cordoned off the area – you wouldn't get anywhere near. Talk soon – hopefully with good news."

I couldn't summon any hope from what Cafferty had said. "Thank you . . . I hope so."

It was only when we both hung up that I remembered Libby was standing next to me, a mask of anxiety drawn down tight over her features. "What is it?"

"That was Cafferty . . . Someone killed everyone at Clem's swamp house last night. And Dad might have been there."

"What?" The colour drained out of Libby's face, and she burst into wracking sobs.

Jared rushed in and held me tight against him. That was enough to set off my tears too. If Dad hadn't gone to see Clem, none of this would be happening. "I need to ring Mum and see if he's there," I said through juddering breaths, forcing myself to slow down and breathe.

"Good idea," Jared said. I was grateful for vampire hearing, because I couldn't keep repeating the story without completely falling apart.

Libby rushed away while I dialled Mum's number, and I heard

her explaining to Della through her tears as I listened to Mum's phone ringing. If Dad could just pick it up and reassure us that he was fine . . .

"Hello?" Mum croaked.

"Mum? Is Dad there?" I asked.

"No." Her fear came through already. I'd never been able to hide anything from her. "He said he might stay at Clem's if the discussion went on. Why – what happened?"

Panic clawed at my chest, almost shutting off my voice completely, but I managed to get it out. "Cafferty called. Someone killed everyone at the swamp last night. He doesn't know if Dad was there but . . ."

"He was," Mum said shortly. "Come over – all of you. We need to be together."

She hung up before I could reply, and for once I was glad that she wasn't into small talk. I couldn't think of anything else to say. Libby and Della came in with their hands clasped. Libby's eyes were red but the sobbing had stopped. "Mum hasn't heard from him. She wants us to go over."

The four of us got dressed in a haze, throwing on mismatched outfits before piling into Della's car. Cafferty had told us to stay put, but we had to see Mum.

It was clear and sunny weather, which seemed especially cruel. Della drove us to the rundown hotel, the only sound the rumble of her Jeep and Libby sobbing again. She'd curled up on the front seat beside Della while Jared kept hold of my hand in the back. It helped, but a hopeless feeling had opened up in my chest like Dad was gone. I had not a shred of Armand's talent, but every instinct told me Dad was dead. "We should call Armand after this . . . to see if he's had any visions. Actually, it doesn't matter," I said, as my thought process caught up. "He would've told us, wouldn't he?"

"You're right," Jared said. "Let's get to your mom's. Maybe she'll know more."

Libby found her voice and started rattling through the fears I was trying to bury deep. "He's probably dead, isn't he? If he was there, then he has to be. They wouldn't have let him go if they killed everybody else."

"He could be fine," Della said. "If he escaped into the swamp, he may not be able to call."

The swamp full of treacherous earth that could drag you down and alligators that attack humans who get too close.

Libby rested her head against the window, her face turned towards the streets scrolling past. "I should cancel the mansion thing tonight," she said dully.

"Don't worry about the mansion," Jared said. "I'll take care of it later."

Della parked outside the hotel, its funereal façade matching how I felt. Chase opened the door for us, and he looked awful. He'd lost Ellie, and now Dad was missing. "I'm so sorry about Ellie," I said, my voice wobbling. We should've reached out sooner.

He nodded, sniffing. "Sorry about The . . . your dad too."

Hayes appeared in the doorway of the kitchen, the only one of us smiling. "Take heart, girls. I believe all of us would know if somethin' had befallen The Shepherd. He's still alive – I know it."

"Thank you," Libby said. I knew Hayes meant well, but this wasn't the time for his Dad fixation.

Mum appeared behind Hayes in the kitchen doorway, a mug

in her hand. She slipped past him, cradling the mug against her. Her eyes looked hollow, but she spoke with ferocity. "I told him not to see Clem. He was so sure he could convince them to avoid more bloodshed. And now . . ."

"Cafferty's going to find out if Dad . . . if he's at the swamp," I said, beginning to feel steadier. "Hopefully he'll have news soon."

"I wanna say somethin'," Chase said awkwardly. "I know I've been shitty to y'all since the moment we met, and there's a reason for that. I agreed not to tell you yet, but things have changed . . ."

"You can tell us," I said when he stalled. "Whatever it is, we're in this together."

"Well, that's good then," he said, "because I'm your brother."

Chapter 43

Silence fell over us, only broken by Mum coming to stand beside Chase. "It was a surprise to me too, but I don't see why it can't be a good one. Your dad told me when I came to the ranch."

"What? How?" Libby sputtered. I couldn't come up with anything more eloquent.

Chase's smile was wary. "My mom met our dad around twenty-two years ago, and here I am. It didn't work out between them, and he moved to the UK not long after I was born."

My heart broke for Chase. I'd resented Dad for leaving us to run the Community, but he'd left Chase first to form our family. "How did you find him?"

"He and Mom kept in touch over the years. When he came back to the States, I tracked him down. That was when I learned about the Community." He took in a deep breath that came out ragged. "She ain't with us no more, so he's all . . ."

"I'm here for you," Mum said. "And I'm sure my girls will be too, once they have time to adjust."

"I'm getting there," I said. "Libby and I wrote the book on difficult sibling relationships. If she and I can get past that, we can too."

Libby narrowed her eyes at me, but she was smiling. "She's right. We'd like to get to know you."

"And this seems like a good time to start leaning on one another," I said. I'd spent long enough with the police to know that missing-person cases were often drawn out and riddled with uncertainty. The practical train of thought ran out, and my eyes started prickling again.

"Thank you both," Chase said gruffly. "And sorry . . . for bein' such a dick."

"You had a good reason," I said.

A heavy fist knocked on the door, and fear spread from face to face. "Your dad has a key," Mum said. "If that's the police . . . I don't think I can take it."

"I'll open it," I said, giving Jared and Mum time to retreat from the daylight.

The door stuck on my first try, but eventually I got it open. Dad was standing there. He looked filthy and exhausted, his face muddy and shadowed with thick stubble. I crushed him in a tight hug.

"Easy, honey," Dad laughed weakly. "I've had quite an ordeal."

"Sorry," I said breathlessly, my heart racing as I stood back to let him in.

Everyone crowded around Dad, and he looked pleased through the fatigue. "Let's take this show into the kitchen. I could sure use a coffee."

Jared and Della leaned against the kitchen counter while the rest of us sat around the table. Relief played out across every face. "What happened?" I asked.

"I went to try and reason with Clem. He was unwilling to listen, and it was late by the time we were through. I planned to spend the night there and return home this morning. I awoke to their screams in the middle of the night."

Dad's gaze darkened. I saw the scene unfolding as he described it, felt the terror of the people attacked while they slept. "I stumbled through the house, clouded by sleep. Vampires were everywhere, biting throats and tearing through flesh like human life meant nothin'. I didn't need any more signs that vampires will bring about the end, but here was another. I stumbled through all that death, and I was spared. I hid at a distance behind the trees, and when the vampires left, I walked alongside the river until I found an abandoned boat. I paddled all the way back to the city. And at some point, I dropped my keys."

"We're all very grateful that you're back," Mum said, reaching across the table to take Dad's hand. "What now?"

"I'm no closer to finding the ripper, and for once the path isn't clear in front of me." Dad looked deeply troubled.

"It'll come to you," Hayes said, with an eerie amount of conviction. "Give yourself time to recover, and the path will be revealed again."

"You're right," Dad said, his own expression becoming uncomfortably zealous. "I appreciate all of you coming here for me, but I need to rest."

So, we were dismissed. Was I glad Dad was alive? Absolutely. On board with all of his past beliefs and actions? Not even close.

"There's just one more thing. Chase told us you're his dad too," I said.

Dad's composure didn't falter. "I would've explained when the time was right. I've only just come back into your life – it was too soon."

"Just once, it'd be nice if you let us decide," Libby said. After everything Dad had done, the secret brother had pushed her over the edge.

"I'll always do my best for you girls," Dad said, leaning on the table to stand. "But, like I said, I should get some sleep."

"I'll walk y'all out," Hayes said, standing too.

After he let us out, we got straight into Della's Jeep. Libby slammed the front passenger door so hard that the whole vehicle shook. "Sorry," she said to Della. "I just can't believe him! Who does he think he is with his secret child, Darth Vader?"

Jared looked startled. "You made a pop-culture reference! It happened – I'm rubbing off on you!"

"Laugh it up," Libby said. "That means I'm rubbing off on you too."

Jared fastened his seatbelt, shaking his head with a despairing grin. "Now we know your dad's safe, I have to admit that the thought of him trudging through swamp sludge kept me going."

"I'll keep that one in my pocket for next time he's being infuriating," I said. "Hey, do you mind if we stop at Will's house to see if he's there?"

"Of course," Della said, hitting the indicator before changing lanes.

Libby slouched down in her seat, groaning. "Remind me why I didn't cancel the reopening tonight?"

Della slowed down at a set of traffic lights, her smile showing in the rear-view mirror. "Because you've worked hard and you deserve the success."

"Oh, that's right," Libby said. "And there's that pesky matter about needing to pay the bills."

A few minutes later, Della stopped the car outside the little blue shotgun house that Will shared with his stepmum.

The curtains were all drawn, and even before I knocked I guessed no one was home. It had been worth a try. I hoped that wherever he was, his emotional wounds were healing.

We spent the day scrubbing every inch of the mansion, even the parts the public wouldn't see. If I stopped for too long, I thought about the people we'd lost. We wouldn't get Ellie and Fiona back, but Will was still out there. For now, we had to concentrate on keeping the mansion afloat and hope he'd come back when he was ready.

Della made a delicious shrimp étoufée for dinner: a thick, spicy stew poured over white rice. Then it was time to get ready.

Jared appeared in my doorway as I was sorting through my clothes and make-up.

"So, are you excited about ditching Lestat for Michael tonight?" I asked. Usually, I enjoyed our roles as Lestat and Claudia in the *Interview with the Vampire* room, but I was looking forward to mixing it up.

"Only because you're playing Star," Jared said. "Libby was trying to convince me to get my ear pierced earlier."

I laughed. "She never changes. Do you want to shower first?"

He made a show of sniffing under his arm. "I'm pretty sure vampires don't sweat, but sure."

When it was my turn, I used Libby's Body Shop vanilla shower gel and took my time under the hot water. Usually, I rushed around getting ready for school or working with the police, so it was a luxury not to hurry.

I put on a fluffy blue dressing gown. Jared was kicking back in the living room wearing most of his Michael costume. "It's not fair that you look so good in jeans and a grey T-shirt," I said.

"I think it's the vampire thing," he said, uncharacteristically embarrassed. I liked that. "I'm looking forward to seeing you in the Star dress."

"OK, I'll go and put it on."

Libby resembled the actress who played Star more than I did, with her hair falling close to her waist and the dainty Hollywood actress thing going on. But I felt good when I put on that lacy white dress, adjusting the thin straps and heart-shaped neckline.

For a change, I needed to make my curls wilder. I smoothed some mousse through the lengths and then tipped my head upside down to scrunch.

Libby would handle the make-up, so I went out to show Jared the costume so far. His eyes widened. "You look . . . I don't know how to describe it. You look better than Star."

"I'll take that as a compliment," I said.

Jared grabbed a leather jacket from the back of the chair and shrugged it on. "What do you think?"

I thought he shouldn't dress like that all the time, because I wouldn't be able to function. "Pretty good," I said, slow, delicious warmth spreading through my body. "We need to do something about your hair though."

He followed me into my bedroom, so close behind me that I craved more. Instead, I grabbed the can of mousse from where I'd thrown it on the bed.

When I turned around, he'd moved right up to me without a sound. "That's cheating," I teased.

"Will said something about letting myself enjoy being a vampire," he said, twining one of my curls around his finger. "I listened."

"I'll need to thank him, you know . . . when he comes back." That made me feel sad again, so I got back on track. "Let's look at this hair."

I rubbed mousse between both hands, my heart quickening as I sank my fingers into Jared's hair. His eyes were soft as I ruffled up his thick waves, giving it more volume like Michael's. Being this close to him was still a rush. "That looks so much better," I said, wiping my hands on the towel hanging from the radiator.

When I turned back, Jared scooped me up with a hand under each leg, holding my dress in place. "Trying out the vampire strength now?" I asked, seeing him eye to eye for once.

"Might as well use what I've got."

With his hands supporting me, I took the initiative to go in for a kiss. I held both cheeks while we kissed, feeling his hands through the thick fabric of my skirt. I was more than ready to take the next step. I wanted all of him.

"Mina!" Libby yelled so loud that Jared fumbled me. Vamp reflexes kicked in, and he lowered me to the floor.

"Does she have some sister power that kicks in at the worst possible time?" Jared grumbled, his eyes twinkling.

"Definitely," I murmured, then yelled back, "Coming!"

Libby had her make-up spread out by the living room mirror, while 'Peace of Mind' by Boston blasted out. "Let's make you look like a star," she said in a terrible American accent. "Like a star, like Star – get it?"

I closed my eyes and left myself at Libby's mercy. She was used to doing quick make-up looks at the mansion, and we'd barely finished the song when she said, "You're done!"

When I opened my eyes, they were surrounded by eyeliner, and my lashes were thick with mascara. Dark red gloss stained my lips.

"No touching those lips – either of you," Libby warned. "We should get in our positions. Game faces on!"

Chapter 44

Libby had employed contractors and all of the staff's strengths to recreate David's hotel that had sunk into a cave in *The Lost Boys.*

Ragged pieces of white fabric trailed down from the ceiling, dividing the room into sections. Fibreglass moulding gave the appearance of craggy, crumbling cave walls, with dim lighting completing the effect. A Jim Morrison poster decorated one wall and the iconic gilded bottle of blood was set amongst a range of treasures horded by the vampires.

For a moment, the new space was overlaid with my memory of the old one. We'd once had metal steps and a raised platform, pumping in dry ice to represent a dream infiltrated by Freddy Krueger. At Halloween, I'd hidden under that platform, slicing open Sam's leg and giving myself the advantage I'd needed to survive.

Jared dispelled the memory by indicating the bed in the far corner. It was piled with blankets and shrouded in heavy white curtains. "We could always wait for the tour group in there?"

"Libby would kill us, and the others will be along soon."

"Spoil my fun." Jared grinned. He really did look like Michael with his leather jacket and big 80s hair. I'd be more than happy for him to keep it on after work.

One of our regular mansion staff, Connor, launched himself into the room, kitted out in biker leather and adjusting a blonde David mullet wig. "The lock to this room's busted. Libby said to tell you she's gonna call out a locksmith," Connor said. Between my memories and being distracted by Jared, I hadn't noticed.

Connor's bouncy presence energised me, and I started looking forward to tonight. What better way to shrug off my worries than to step into someone else's life? Star was under David's influence, but she knew who she wanted. I looked at my own version of Michael. Jared was pacing the room restlessly, sending the white curtains drifting back and forth like forlorn ghosts.

"What?" I murmured as the other members of the vampire gang burst in, laughing and catcalling like their characters.

"It stinks in here," Jared said, one hand cupped over his nose. "Well, it does to me anyway."

"It doesn't smell great to me either, but it must be worse for you," I said. Libby was experimenting with different scents in the mansion rooms. This one was meant to be old cave with a side of incense, but it smelled more like burned flowers and damp.

"I'll live, or you know – whatever you call this." He gestured at himself, grinning.

I pulled him close using the lapels of his leather jacket. "Whatever it is looks good from where I'm standing."

With her usual impeccable timing, Libby's penetrating voice carried through from the next room: our cue to take our places.

One of the biker vampires bounced across the room as the tour group entered, silenced by the finger to Libby's lips. Della was hovering at the back of the group, a huge smile on her face. "I brought take-out," the biker vamp said, casting his gaze over the tourists, "but I don't think there's enough."

"I'm sure they won't mind," Connor said loudly, approximating the arrogant voice Kiefer Sutherland used to play David. He grabbed one of the takeaway cartons and opened it, inhaling deeply. "You're our guest, Michael. I have to insist that you go first."

Jared accepted the box and a pair of chopsticks, pretending to scoop some rice into his mouth. He yelped, setting the carton down with shaking hands. "They're maggots!"

"Really?" Connor said. "Sorry about that. How about some noodles?"

"I'm not fallin' for that," Jared said.

"That's enough," I snapped, going over to stand with Jared.

"Suit yourself," Connor said, tossing the carton of rubber worms over the crowd.

Squeals rippled through them and Libby folded her arms in fake displeasure. "Can't you vampires ever be serious? Come on, everyone – if you'll follow me . . ."

While the crowd were distracted, the rest of our vampire gang had crept behind them. "Boo!" one of them howled and the others leaped into the crowd, whooping and shrieking.

Chaos erupted, with members of the tour group scrambling in all directions and fake biker vampires leaping out from behind the curtains along with my real one. I danced around through the group, and Libby had to disguise her grin as the two of us steered the guests towards the exit.

The door closed behind the tour group. "That was awesome,

guys," Connor said to another round of whooping. "Let's celebrate in the staff room!"

The other staff members bounced over to the door, and Connor paused. "You guys comin'?"

"Nah, you go ahead," Jared said. "We'd better reset the room."

"Make sure you get all the worms!" one of the biker vampires called as they left with Connor.

Jared's gaze roamed around the space. "I smell real blood . . . over all that incense and stuff."

"Did all of the tour guests leave?" I asked, scanning the space. Apart from a sprinkling of rubber worms, everything looked fine. Still, unease worked its way in. Jared's sense of smell wasn't usually wrong.

"Libby does a quick head count in case we get any hiders," Jared said, his gaze lingering on the curtained corner of the room. "Oh no . . ."

It took me longer to see what he had: blood along the hem of the white curtain.

We went over together, dread sinking deep barbs into me. I wasn't armed, since I was wearing a flimsy dress with no room for a weapon. But I had a horrible feeling I was walking towards a victim, not someone to be afraid of.

Jared pushed open the white curtain. Cafferty was sprawled on the bed, his throat caked in blood.

Chapter 45

We rushed to his side. Jared pressed his fingers to Cafferty's wrist at the same time that I checked the clean side of his throat, trying not to look at the congealing blood. Nothing.

"Please . . . You can't be dead," I said, tears blurring my vision. There was so much blood . . .

Jared clapped a hand over the bloody mess of Cafferty's throat, closing his eyes. "I can't feel anything," he said, anguished and desperate. "When I heal someone there has to be a spark of life . . . I'll try mouth to mouth."

Jared leaned over the body of my mentor, my friend and one of the last people I'd wanted to see dead. His eyes were closed and the clotted blood at his throat looked extra vibrant against the waxy white of his skin as Jared tilted his head into the right position.

"I'm going to kill whatever vampire did this to you," I said through my tears, because I had no idea what else to do.

Cafferty moved his head, and Jared sat back with a look of pure relief.

I put a hand on his cheek. "Matt? Come on – you can do this."

He groaned, his eyes opening to narrow slits. "What the hell . . . happened to me?" His voice was scratchy.

"I'll call an ambulance," Jared said. "The bleeding's stopped – you're gonna be fine." Then he jogged out of the door.

"A vampire must have attacked you, but you're OK now," I said, shaking from sheer gratitude.

Cafferty sat up slowly, holding on to his neck. "Everything's hazy . . . I remember going to see Saint Germain . . . I feel terrible." He supported his forehead in both hands, and I was worried about him all over again. He'd gone ghastly pale and looked like he was about to pass out.

"The ambulance will be here soon. They'll help you."

Cafferty inhaled deeply, and his gaze locked on me.

Horror registered as Cafferty grabbed me, too fast and strong for me to fight him off. He pulled my neck towards his mouth, snapping and snarling with red-rimmed eyes and fangs protruding. I pushed hard against his chest to keep him at arm's length. He was brand new, which made him strong, ravenous and absolutely devoid of reason, but I had to try. "Matt!" I said, struggling to keep him off me. He was forcing me further and further down onto the bed, his mouth inching towards my throat. I was tired, so sure that this was it. "Jared!" I screamed, common sense finally kicking in.

He was there in a blur, holding Cafferty in a bear hug as I scrambled off the bed. "I was about to call the ambulance, but I guess we don't need one," Jared said grimly. "You go. I'll get him calm."

I got to the top of the stairs as Libby was seeing the tour group out of the front door. Della was waiting on the ridiculously uncomfortable skeleton chair.

"That was so good!" Libby said when she saw me, her joy faltering. "What now? Do you not think it went well?"

"It's not that. Cafferty's in *The Lost Boys* room. He's a vampire."

"What?" Libby wrapped her arms around herself. "Shit! I'll cancel the rest of the tours, but what do we do for him?"

"Jared's taking care of him . . . I need to get back up there."

"Of course," Della said. "Be careful. He's new . . ."

"I know," I said, the bleak possibilities for Cafferty's future unfolding in front of me. "Thanks."

I ran back up and found Jared standing sentry next to Cafferty. He was sitting on the bed with his knees tucked up, a bloodstained cloth in his hand as he cleaned his throat. He looked miserable. "I'm so sorry."

"Don't worry," I said. "Jared actually bit me the day he was turned. You're doing great."

"Hey," Jared said good naturedly. "So, we should get to a blood bar."

Cafferty rubbed his eyes hard. "OK . . . Jesus, I can't believe this is my life now."

"You'll get used to it. Like Mina said, you have a handle on the blood lust – that's a good sign." Jared steered Cafferty out of the room, pushing harder when his longing eyes lingered on my neck.

The downstairs hallway was empty, so Jared and Cafferty had a clear shot to the front door.

I watched them from the top of the stairs, but I couldn't let Cafferty go without one more question. "Wait . . . What were you going to say about Saint Germain?" I called down.

Cafferty's face hardened. "You can probably guess. He was tired of me not getting results in the ripper case and wanted to lock me down."

Even though I wasn't surprised, having it confirmed was

another weight on me. "Get what you need and we'll see you soon."

I joined Della and Libby in the apartment. They were curled up on the sofa together, but I felt too restless to join them.

"I have a question," Libby said, biting the skin around her thumb. "How the hell did they get in?"

"The lock to *The Lost Boys* room is broken," I said.

"Oh right . . . The front door is fine though," Libby said. "I unlocked it to let the tour group out."

"Cafferty just told me who did it too – Saint Germain," I said.

"That means he's probably got a key to the mansion then," Della said. "Maybe from the contractors or some other place, but either way we need to get out of here. I'll call Armand. I'm sure he'll let us stay in one of his properties until we can get the locks changed."

She phoned him from the living room while Libby and I packed. Haste made me clumsy. Saint Germain's vampires had turned Cafferty and got into our home, the one place we were supposed to be safe.

Before long, Della called me in, holding out the phone. "Armand wants to talk to you."

"Sorry about our detective friend," he said. "Jared and I will help him. He'll adjust – he has the strength of will for it."

"Thank you," I said, clutching the phone tighter. Sympathy always pushed me too far.

"I was about to call you when Della beat me to it. I had a very intense vision of you going into an abandoned hospital in pursuit of a vampire. Does that sound familiar?"

"Nope. One day can you see me going into a spa maybe?"

"Sorry." He chuckled darkly. "Perhaps it makes sense of

the snippet I saw of a hospital bed as well. I believe it happens very soon. There were fall decorations outside and storm clouds overhead."

I checked through the living room curtains. "Like tonight? Della and I are going on patrol, so I'll see if she knows where it could be."

"I've been feeling uneasy about a lot of things. The vampire ripper for one thing, and then Saint Germain turning Matt . . . Please be careful."

"I will – you too." The ripper had been overshadowed for now, but it could only be a matter of time before they killed again.

He went on, bringing back my focus. "I've given Della the details of somewhere safe to stay. A friend of mine uses magical wards to protect their home. No one will find you there."

"I don't know what we'd do without you," I said.

"Let's hope you won't need to find out."

After I got off the phone, I finished packing and grabbed some things for Jared from the attic room. I couldn't stop thinking about Cafferty.

Jared came home as I finished packing. "How is he?" I asked.

"Not great," he said. "I left him with Armand. He's keeping a handle on the blood lust, but he's just had the life he knows ripped away from him. I know how that feels."

"You and Armand will help him," I said, grabbing Jared's hand. "We all will."

Libby and Della came into the living room with bags on their shoulders. "We should get out of here," Della said. "Jared – can you walk Libby to the address Armand gave me? He found us a place to stay until we get the locks changed."

"You can't patrol!" Libby said, her face blotchy and furious.

"Someone turned Cafferty and left him here for us to find. If that's not a message, I don't know what is."

"We have a responsibility," I said. "And we'll be careful."

"I don't know," Jared said. "I don't like the idea of you bein' out there either."

I had a bolt of inspiration. "So how about you come with me and Della stay with Libby?"

Jared looked like he'd got all revved up for an argument, and he hesitated. "Actually, that's not a bad idea."

Della sighed, but then she nodded. "That makes sense. I don't wanna leave you tonight," she said to Libby. "We'll meet you where we're staying after patrol. Here's the address." She handed me a slip of paper, and I tucked it in the back pocket of my jeans. "Don't stay out too long, and be alert to anyone tailin' you. Saint Germain leavin' Cafferty here could only be the start of things to come."

"Got it," Jared said. "Shall we get kitted out and go?"

"That works for me," I said. "Armand had a vision that might be a lead, so we can start there."

I grabbed weapons while the others hauled our bags downstairs. When we parted ways, Jared and I were immediately on the prowl. I hoped no one was hunting us in return.

Chapter 46

We considered the derelict hospital from across the street, my mental alarms screaming. "Do you think this is it?"

"It's the only one that fits Armand's description," Jared said. "Remember how Della took you to that flooded clown museum? This place is worse."

"Let's hope not. That building was about ready to collapse around us."

I used my quick-release mechanism to drop the fancy new stake from Saint Germain into my hand. I loathed him, but the weapon felt good in my palm. Jared eyed it with a mirthless grin. "How about you keep that point turned away from me?"

"I can do that," I said, as we crossed the road. The hospital could've been pulled straight from *The Night of the Living Dead*, minus the shambling zombies. It was made of red brick with cream stone edging around windows and decorating the tower at the front of the building. The stone entrance was divided into three archways that may have once looked welcoming. Now the windows gaped open, black spaces that anything could crawl out of. It was one of those buildings that felt evil down to its bones.

Jared pulled us back into the shadows. Ilian was coming down the street, wearing a sharp suit as usual. Why was one of Saint Germain's favourite minions heading into an abandoned hospital?

"Looks like he's the reason for Armand's vision," Jared said into my ear. "Saint Germain has him looking for the ripper – maybe he has a lead. Let's follow him."

As we crossed the road, I thought back to my early investigations with Jared. Things had changed so much since then. I'd changed. I could've done without a lot of our experiences, but I liked who I'd become.

Rather than walking straight through the front doors, we followed Ilian's path around the side of the building, those empty black windows looming over us. Weeds grew up past our knees, broken glass crunching underfoot.

Jared was absolutely focused, staying close to my side and constantly checking our environment. I couldn't find that inner peace, passing the stake back and forth and taking concentration even to breathe steadily.

There was no sign of Ilian, but eventually Jared stopped us by one of the windows. "This one should work."

I really didn't want to climb into the hospital building, touching down on who knew what on the other side. Luckily, Jared was driving us forwards, carefully raising one leg and putting it over the frame. He swung the other leg over, and the darkness swallowed him.

My turn. A lot more clumsily, I pulled myself up to sit on the frame, the glass long gone. Taking a deep breath, I dropped into the hospital.

Jared had already clicked on a small torch even though he didn't need it, keeping the beam low. It illuminated a bleak picture. The exposure to nature hadn't been kind. Fuzzy black mould had spread over most of the walls, and the rest sagged and bulged with damp. Fragments of glass and dead leaves littered the floor, which was covered in broken, dirty tiles.

There were four metal beds still in the room, and the sight turned my stomach. Decaying leather straps were attached to them. It was an unpleasant reminder of the Roswell museum that had scenes showing aliens being captured and experimented on. "What kind of hospital was this?"

"Not a good one, from the look of things," Jared said.

A trolley sat by one of the beds, and we approached it together. We could've headed straight into the hospital, but Jared and I seemed to have been clutched by the same need. Even though we were in patrol mode, our fingers brushed against each other as we reached the trolley.

The tools were corroded, but I wasn't convinced all of those reddish stains were rust. Pliers, a drill and saw were laid out neatly. Beside them, a wooden box trailed two frayed wires that connected to metal tubes. "Electroshock therapy? I've seen enough."

"Agreed," Jared said. "Let's look for Ilian."

The door was open, and the beam of Jared's torch illuminated a bolt on the outside. An unsettled feeling gnawed in my stomach.

"I'll keep the torch down and cut it off if we see any movement," Jared said.

I followed him into the corridor, holding on tightly to my stake and focusing in on what I could hear. Nothing yet. I wondered if Jared's vamp ears were getting anything.

The corridor extended out in either direction, an endless expanse of blackness. Already, the cold and damp had sunk down deep. Jared kept the beam low by our feet, and I could only make out the walls of the corridor and the occasional outlines of gurneys. He shone the torch into another empty ward. At this point, I preferred that. My sense of dread was simmering, like it knew something was coming.

We carried on like that until we came to an administrator's office. "Let's try in here," Jared said.

There was a shelf of mouldering books along one wall, the stench of damp clinging to the back of my throat. Quiet dripping came from somewhere – hopefully water.

The chair was pushed back from a desk in the middle of the room. Files and papers were strewn across it as if the person who worked here had expected to come back. Jared shone the torch across them. "Just a bunch of patients' notes."

"Let's check this place as quickly as we can."

Jared turned off the torch, plunging us into darkness. "We have company."

The reality of our situation hit me with the absence of light. If Ilian was here, was he alone?

Footsteps echoed through the hospital. Vampires could move silently when needed, assuming that was what we were dealing with. That meant they likely didn't know we were here . . . yet. Our scents and the sound of my heart would give us away soon enough. It started beating harder at the thought.

"What a shithole," a low voice said, further down the corridor but still audible. "Why the doc picked this hospital to work in, I'll never know."

"Because it's a shithole, you idiot," another voice said. They were getting closer. "No one would stumble here by accident."

"She's got a serious case of paranoia having us guard the place. Who would come here?"

"I think she had the right idea. There are intruders on the other side of this door."

This was it. My heart kicked up a gear until I was pumped up on adrenaline.

Jared pointed behind the door, finger on his lips. I obeyed, stake ready and wishing I knew the plan.

"Little pig, little pig – let me in," one of the vampires crooned as he pushed open the door, hiding Jared from view and leaving me wedged against the wall. "Hey, where's the human? I could use a snack."

"Nobody here but us vampires," Jared said evenly. "I have a message for the doctor."

"I might believe you . . . if I couldn't hear a heartbeat getting faster as we speak." The vampire's tone turned cruel, his footsteps moving further into the room. I wasn't sure where the other one was, but I decided that was my cue.

I crept forwards, catching my first glimpse of the two vampires. They both looked like they'd been turned when they were around Jared's age and were wearing smart suits that were out of place in the ruined hospital.

Not delaying any longer, I pulled back my staking arm and slammed the point into the nearest vampire's back. My aim had improved. The stake went in deep, and from the way he was clawing between his shoulder blades in sheer panic, I'd nicked the heart. If I could ram it in deeper, he'd fall.

His friend got to me first. He held my arms against my sides, his fangs snapping at my neck. I bent my knees and slipped out of the vampire's grip.

He leered at me while Jared and the other vampire fought fiercely. Jared was fast and strong, but his opponent was also a force to be reckoned with. My stake from Saint Germain was still jammed in his back, so as far as the vampire inching towards me knew, I was unarmed.

Luckily, my jacket contained a surprise as well. One tug of the Velcro and I freed a very thin, twisted stake.

"What you gonna do with that little thing?" the vampire sneered, trying to snatch it from me.

That left him wide open. "This," I said, thrusting the stake as hard as I could. He turned at the last moment, hissing when it drove through the flesh of one side, hitting bone.

I wasn't going to make the same mistake again, so I yanked the stake out before the vampire recovered. He roared, his arm shooting out too fast for me to dodge. His fist crashed into my cheek, hot pain flaring. I staggered, my vision flashing red for a second.

Jared grabbed the head of the vampire he was fighting and pulled so hard that his neck made a horrible snap. He whipped my stake out of the vampire's back and drove it deep into his chest. When the vampire dropped, it filled me with resolve. I wouldn't miss again.

The vampire lunged for my throat, and I jabbed the stake towards his chest. His own momentum worked against him, driving the wood in deep.

This time, there was no doubt that I'd hit the mark. The vampire's face was vacant before he hit the floor. I retrieved my stake as Jared appeared, offering me the other. I cleaned them both with a cloth from my pocket as best as I could. Then I stashed one in my jacket holster and the other in the quick-release in my sleeve.

"What happened to your cheek?" Jared cupped my jaw on the bruised side of my face. "Want me to heal you?"

"Later," I said. "We can't have you crashing out. There might be more of them."

Jared clicked the torch back on, illuminating the two rapidly decomposing bodies at our feet. "What should we do about them?"

"We need to get out of here," I said, ignoring the wave of guilt. They hadn't exactly given us a choice. "Can you hear any more of them?"

Jared shook his head. "Not right now. Wonder what a doctor's doing here."

"I don't know, but it sounds potentially terrible. Let's keep looking."

My cheek was throbbing and the rush I got from fighting had upped and left. We combed through ward after ward, a nurses' station and more offices until I was certain the doctor must have been absent tonight.

"We've only got a couple rooms left in this part of the hospital," Jared said. "And we shouldn't stay close to those bodies any longer than we have to. I reckon we should check the final rooms and call it a night."

"OK," I said, frustrated that I'd killed a vampire and got hit in the face but we might have nothing to show for it.

"Wait . . . I hear something," Jared said. "Machinery, and one human heartbeat."

"They're keeping a human here," I said, imagining all kinds of awful things a vampire doctor could be doing to them.

My instinct was to go storming in, but I went with Jared's more measured approach. He turned off the torch and pushed the door open a fraction so we could see inside. The bluish white light was dazzling and at first, I couldn't see anything. My sight came back in fragments. Shiny equipment and bright halos of lights. A white-coated female leaning over someone . . .

The former leader of the slayers – Rosario.

Chapter 47

I grabbed Jared's arm to steady myself. The last time I'd seen Rosario, two of Saint Germain's henchmen had been dragging her from St. Louis Cathedral on orders to kill her. She'd been gone for weeks . . . We'd mourned her. And here she was . . . alive, though not in a good position.

She was strapped to a chair with a drip attached to one arm and electrodes taped to both temples that connected to a machine. Another electrode snaked away from her other hand and she had compresses taped to various places, including one on her chest that showed over the top of her T-shirt. Her short dark hair was long overdue a wash, and her golden brown skin had a pallid tone.

The white-coated figure had her back turned to us, and I couldn't bear to leave Rosario in there for any longer. Had she been held captive all this time? "Now?" I mouthed at Jared.

He nodded and pushed the door further open. I freed a stake and stormed in with more confidence than I felt. "Release her, and I won't need to use this."

Rosario grinned. She looked thinner than before and completely exhausted. "Took you long enough." It was so good to hear her soft Mexican accent again, her fire not extinguished by whatever she'd been through.

White coat's surprise gave way to a harsh laugh. "The doctor is due back at any moment, and she'll have you killed for this. If you're lucky, it'll be a quick death."

"Not if she doesn't find out. What are you and the doctor doing here?" Jared asked, his eyes flicking around the brightly lit, sterile space. The walls were white and the fixtures were chrome, a dazzling contrast to the rest of the hospital.

"And have them kill me instead? I don't think so."

I pointed the tip of the stake at the assistant, or whoever she was. Jared came to stand beside me, his body tense and ready. He didn't need a weapon.

The assistant looked afraid, glancing from me to Jared. She removed the needle from Rosario's hand and pulled off one electrode at a time. Rosario winced as the sticky pads came away from her skin, flexing her fingers and pulling against the straps at her wrists. Soon, she was free from everything except those restraints, and there the assistant hesitated. "Do you give me your word that you won't hurt me?"

Rosario's eyes blazed with fury, even as tired as she was. "No way."

"I'm out of here. Your friends can free you." The assistant ran out of the room, skidding on her heels on the slick floor.

"Let's get you out," I said, unbuckling the cracked leather restraints from Rosario's wrists. They were the only part of the room that wasn't modern.

Jared frowned, looking between Rosario and the open door. Before he had time to explain why, Rosario took off. We raced after her, but she'd always been faster than me. The time in captivity hadn't slowed her down.

Jared turned on the torch and the light bounced as we ran into the corridor, catching on the assistant's white coat ahead of us. The heels were slowing her down, and Rosario was gaining ground.

We caught up as Rosario leaped in front of the woman's path. "You think I'd let you go after what you did?"

"I'm sorry! I was only doing what I was ordered. They would've killed me if I'd refused." The assistant flinched away from Rosario.

"Don't do anything you'll regret," I said to Rosario. "Think about the code." Rosario would've died to abide by that once, only killing vampires who attacked humans. But she'd obviously suffered through unspeakable things since we'd seen her.

"Oh, I won't regret this," Rosario said. "The code only applies to vamps, and she's human. Unlike me."

Jared sprang as Rosario raised her hands, blue sparks flickering between her fingers against the darkness.

"Don't touch her!" I shouted, hoping Jared had seen what I had. "Please don't do this, Rosario."

"I can't let her live and do to others what they've done to me." Rosario placed her fingertips on either side of the woman's head.

There was a flash of blue. A shudder went through the woman, her face contorting in agony before she crumpled.

"It's too late to heal her – she's dead," Jared said.

"And so am I," Rosario added.

I wondered if she'd chosen this, like Will, or it'd been thrust upon her like Jared. Either way, it was time to go. "We need to get out of here."

Going back into the musty darkness of the hospital made my

heart sink. I wanted to be far away from here so we could make sure Rosario was OK. First we found Cafferty had been turned and now her.

Jared kept the torch at his side as we moved fast down the corridor. I followed them into the next open ward, and Rosario swept the broken glass from the window frame with one hand. She was wearing worn jogging bottoms and a T-shirt, but the cold wouldn't affect her any more.

She and Jared climbed out with the easy elegance of predators. I landed heavily, one ankle twisting to go with the throb in my cheek. The three of us set off down the quiet street, and Jared noticed my limp. "Did one of the vamps do that?"

"I landed wrong – it's not that bad." It ached with every step, but I'd done worse.

Rosario had her arms wrapped around herself as her gaze darted up and down the street. "We've got somewhere safe to go," I said, pulling the address that Della had given me out of my pocket. "We can talk there. Have you fed? We could stop by a blood bar."

Rosario nodded. "They brought people for me . . . I'm good." Her lips turned down, and I guessed the revulsion was aimed at herself. "Thank you for helping me. I know I'm a mess – I wouldn't want me around."

Jared was also scanning the street constantly, and he kept at it while he spoke. "Do you have a handle on the electricity thing?"

Rosario scowled. "I control the electricity. It doesn't control me." She raised one hand and a glimmer of blue sparked.

Jared raised his eyebrows. "Impressive." I doubted that was the word he meant.

The busier the streets got, the more agitated Rosario became.

The happy hustle and bustle of the French Quarter had her crowding in closer to us. "How far is it?"

"We're here," Jared said.

The house was in the shotgun style like Libby and Jared's original place when I'd first arrived. I felt a tug of melancholy for that time before vampires and working with the police, but I wouldn't go back to it. I preferred knowing there were monsters in the darkness.

The house was painted lilac with dark purple pillars and lit brightly by a light on the wall. The window frames and door were bright red. A gold wind chime turned slowly in front of the window, a star inside a circle.

The door opened before we knocked, and Emmeline beckoned with one hand. "Please, come in."

She closed the door, sealing us into a warm space with a wooden floor, white walls and several colourful abstract paintings. An oil burner by the door dispersed a citrus scent into the room.

"You're friends with Armand?" I asked.

She nodded gravely. "That's a story for another time. Who's your friend? I should warn you that the wards in this house protect all humans who enter. There'll be deadly consequences for any who even try to go against them."

"This is Rosario – the former leader of the slayers," I said. "She headed up the team that took out Veronica."

"Then you're a friend of mine," Emmeline said.

"Thank you for havin' me." Rosario had become wilder and less contained than last time we saw her, though I wasn't sure if her experiences or being a vampire had caused it. "I hope y'all don't mind, but I'm beat."

"I'll show you to your room," Emmeline said, not seeming phased to have an extra fanged guest. "I'm sure Jared and Mina won't mind sharing a room." As long as Jared could handle the proximity to my blood, we definitely wouldn't.

Libby and Della came through the nearest door, their shock blurring into delight. "I can't believe it," Della said, a smile lighting up her eyes.

Rosario's smile was weaker. "Dead, but still walkin' around. I'd love to catch up, but I can't keep my eyes open. Do you mind . . .?"

"Take whatever time you need," Della said, her eyes about to brim over with emotion.

Emmeline pointed Rosario to the nearest room. "Bathroom is across the hall. Night."

"Let's talk in the kitchen," she added, once Rosario's door had closed.

Della and Libby sank down at the comfortably marked table, but Jared and I stayed standing. My ankle and cheek were giving me hell, and I needed to crawl into bed. "What happened to her?" Libby whispered.

"She was strapped down in a lab," Jared said. "A doctor was doing experiments on her. We'll find out more tomorrow, but I think Mina and I need to hit the sack."

Libby let out a surprised snort. Jared would've blushed if vampires did that. "Not what I meant. It's been a long day."

"It's been a long week," I said. "Let's catch up in the morning. Maybe Rosario will have more energy to talk then."

I visited the bathroom and then joined Jared in the guest bedroom at the end of the corridor. The walls were a cool green and all the fabrics were vibrant blue florals.

Jared had already changed into a vest top and shorts for pyjamas, but he was sitting up on the bed instead of relaxing back. "Do you want me to take care of your cheek and ankle?"

"If you're sure you don't mind. I know it drains you."

"I'm going to sleep anyway," Jared said. "I might as well knock myself out."

I sat down beside him, and it sank in that there was one bed in the room. I'd wanted to share a bed with him again, though I'd not got my wish in the way I'd hoped.

"Can I feel around the bone? I'm afraid it's gonna hurt." I nodded, and Jared gently felt along my cheekbone.

"There," I said, wincing at the spot under my eye.

"It's hard to be certain without an X-ray but based on this swelling, I'd say you have a hairline fracture. I can heal it for you."

"Thank you."

Jared ran his fingers along the swollen area until he landed on the most painful point. Then he pressed down. I swallowed a scream, squeezing my eyes shut. Burning pain was slowly replaced by a different kind of heat. It was the dreamy summer sensation of closing your eyes and feeling the sun on your face, the light glowing through your eyelids and warmth spreading over your skin. The wounded area tightened and ached under his fingers, until the pain was gone.

Before I could open my eyes, his lips brushed against the sensitive place he'd healed. A shiver of pleasure radiated where there had so recently been agony.

"How about that ankle?" he said in a low voice very close to my ear.

I nodded, keeping my eyes closed. His hand skimmed my calf

under my jeans, the fleeting enjoyment morphing into sharp pain as his hand closed around my ankle. I felt that heat again, then relief.

I'd expected Jared to fall back on the bed in an exhausted sleep after healing me twice. Instead, lips grazed the hollow of my throat, the brush of his tongue trailing upwards until it skimmed my earlobe. Then he was kissing my mouth, sweetness giving way to urgency as he pulled me onto his lap, his hands sliding up my back under the hem of my T-shirt. He'd touched me like that before and I'd been satisfied, but now I wanted more.

I put a hand on his chest, opening my eyes. "You wanna go to sleep?" he asked, his hair dishevelled and lips so full and inviting.

"Not what I had in mind," I said. "Did you bring . . . you know . . . protection?"

The sleepy look on Jared's face vanished. "Are you sure?" he asked, cupping my cheeks in his hands.

We'd been reminded time and time again how difficult and short life could be, and I knew that I wanted this. "Absolutely sure. Are you?"

Jared grinned. "No arguments from me."

We inched up the bed until we were lying side by side, kissing and exploring tentatively with our hands. Slowly, we became surer of ourselves and each other, moving in time until there was nothing between us.

The heated pleasure was like nothing I'd ever felt before, exploring each other's bodies with no restraint until we lay back, exhausted and happy.

"That was . . . everything," Jared said dreamily, pulling me close. "You're everything."

His cool skin felt so soothing that I moved closer, my head against his chest and his arms enclosing me. I was sleepy and so happy when I murmured, "I love you."

I heard him say it back as I fell asleep.

I was tangled up with Jared when I woke in the morning, my head under his arm and our legs entwined. For a few minutes, I was riding such a wave of contentment that our recent sadness felt a long way away. Even as I nestled in closer, enjoying him stirring and tightening his arms around me, the losses we'd suffered and outstanding worries crept back in. Rosario was back after suffering untold anguish. Cafferty had been turned yesterday. Will was still gone. My Dad could've died. And although the ripper had gone quiet, they were still out there. Was I missing anything?

Jared propped up his head on one hand. "Morning," he said, with a sleepy grin. "I know a lot of things are terrible, but that was one good night."

"It really was," I said. "And as much as I'd like a repeat performance, we need to get up. Life, responsibilities and all that."

"I wish we could hit the pause button sometimes," Jared said. "How are the cheek and ankle?"

I poked the places where I'd been injured. "Good as new."

We were the last ones down to the kitchen, and from Libby's smirk I suspected that she knew everything. She could think what she wanted – today wasn't about me and Jared.

The six of us filled every seat around Emmeline's circular table: two vampires, two slayers, a human and a witch. Someone had put a plate of thick slices of white toast dripping with butter in the middle of the table. I added honey and ate quietly while we waited for Rosario to tell her story.

"So, I have the floor, huh? I guess I used to like the slayers lookin' at me when I talked. Where do I even start?"

"What happened outside the church at Halloween?" I asked, wiping one buttery hand on my pyjama bottoms.

"I expected them to kill me, so I guess I got off lightly. One of them bit me and it hurt like hell. I passed out, and when I woke up I was strapped down in that hospital. And I wasn't human. I didn't know that right away. When the pain kicked in, I thought I was dying, and *Doctor Azalea* was there . . ." Her mouth snarled around the name. "She watched while her assistant took notes and I thrashed around, slicing wounds into my own wrists with the straps. It was when the cuts healed that I figured it out. And I was so damn *hungry*."

Her gaze flicked to Jared. "You know what that's like. Once I'd fully turned, they started experimenting. Taking blood from me, seeing how fast I healed, stuff like that."

"When did your electricity power manifest?" Jared asked.

Rosario frowned. "I didn't come by it naturally. They did it to me."

Chapter 48

"The doctor gave it to you? I don't understand," Della said. Her and me both. Libby looked stunned too.

"It wasn't her idea," Rosario said. "I don't think it'll surprise you to find out who's behind it: Saint Germain."

"No, it doesn't," Della said through clenched teeth. It made a dark kind of sense – he had the money and influence, and he'd proven himself capable of horrors.

"He's been trying and failing for years," Rosario said. "He doesn't have an ability, right? So he collects vampires with powers and does experiments on them. He keeps his favourites around as employees, but ultimately if it's a power he wants, his goal is to take it. My electricity thing only took a day or so to fully manifest after they transferred it. I'm his first success story – lucky me."

Jared's expression was pained, and he rubbed a hand over his face. "I'm guessing he'd like the power to go outside during the day."

"That one yours?" Rosario asked, grimacing at Jared's nod. "Yeah, I imagine that would be the ultimate. Sorry."

"You say he's tried and failed . . . What about the other vampires?" I asked.

"They all died – the ones giving up the powers and those receiving them," Rosario said flatly. "He hasn't tried the procedure on himself yet. He couldn't risk his life when it kept failing. When I was given mine, only the vampire who gave up the power died, but he isn't concerned about that."

"So now he can go ahead and take whatever powers he wants?" Jared asked, fear carving deep grooves into his skin.

"We can't allow it to pass," Emmeline said. "He'd become unstoppable – the most powerful vampire on Earth. We have to move now."

That echoed what Dad had said about his predicted apocalypse – that vampires were going to bring about the end of the world. Could he actually have been right? If Saint Germain became all powerful . . .

"I want in on that," Della said, and Libby's face scrunched up like she was holding something back. She never stopped Della from fighting for her beliefs, but it had to be hard to let her go.

"Me too," Rosario said.

Emmeline's expression turned grave. "I been around a lot longer than y'all, so let me give you some advice. There's a fine line between foolish and brave. Taking on Saint Germain could be deadly. Are y'all ready for that?"

We'd come across some terrible vampires, including the vampire ripper still stalking the city. But Saint Germain had the potential to do the most damage, not only to the people I loved but to the human race. I was definitely starting to think like Dad. "He'll become too dangerous. I'll do whatever it takes."

Jared reached for my hand. "I'm in too."

"All right. There are some people y'all should meet. I've already called a meeting at Toil and Trouble at eleven. I'm sorry we have to meet during the day. It's easier to avoid vampires on Saint Germain's payroll . . . present company excluded. So, if y'all can get there without burnin' up, you'll be very welcome. I can offer thick blankets and my shop van, Rosario, if you need it."

"Thank you," she said.

Emmeline's smile was grim. "Now, I only got one bathroom, so I suggest we start gettin' ready."

Jared and I lost the scramble to the shower. While we waited, I did plenty of fretting, barely able to comprehend what taking on Saint Germain would look like, with all of his influence. But if he was gone, everyone would be safer.

"Are you OK?" Jared asked, sitting beside me on the bed. "You zoned out for a minute there."

"Yeah. This week has been a lot – even for us."

"It has," Jared said, pushing my hair back from my face. "But there have been good parts too."

"There have. And the second this is over, I want lots of those good parts, please."

"You got it," Jared said, leaning in to kiss me.

"Shower's free!" Libby bellowed.

I jumped up, grabbing my towel. "Sorry. All's fair in love and hot water."

"Go ahead," Jared said. "I've seen you with a stake."

I could've done with a long shower to wash away some of the accumulating tension, but I decided to leave some hot water for Jared.

While it was his turn, I picked up the phone. After a moment of second-guessing myself, I dialled my parent's number at the hotel. It rang for a long time without anyone picking up so I ended up leaving a message. "Dad . . . It's me. I think you might have been right. One of those powerful . . . creatures is about to get a whole lot more powerful. Ring me back if you want to help." I left Emmeline's number before hanging up. I wasn't sure what telling Dad would achieve, but it seemed right.

Soon, Jared, Libby, Della and I were waiting by the door. "So this is what it feels like to be included," Libby said. "I expected it to be more glamorous and less terrifying."

"I prefer you far away from danger," Della said. "But you've always supported my slaying, so I can hardly stop you."

"And that's why you're my girl," Libby said, standing on her tiptoes to kiss Della.

I liked seeing my sister happy. With our upbringing, there hadn't been many physical expressions of affection, except between me and her.

Emmeline and Rosario joined us. "Rosario, you should try to avoid notice," Emmeline said. "Even though it's daytime, Saint Germain could have humans out looking for you."

"My Jeep's parked down the street," Della said. "It has tinted windows, and I can bring it right up to the door if Emmeline has blankets to cover you – daylight protection and identity concealment."

"Sounds like a plan," Emmeline said.

The four of them left in the Jeep after carefully protecting Rosario from the sun. After Jared refused a spot in the car, he and I set off on foot. The streets were quiet, and grey clouds drifted across a pale sky.

Jared held my hand tightly and set a fast pace, but he didn't seem as frantic as last time. "So how come I've never heard of Toil and Trouble?" I asked.

"It's members only," Jared said. "Oh, and locals say it's a magical speakeasy."

The confusion must have shown on my face. "I'm guessin' you didn't learn about Prohibition when you lived in England?" he asked. When I shook my head, he went on. "I'll give you the short version. In 1920, the powers that be made it illegal to sell alcohol, and that's always been a big industry here. So people set up secret bars called speakeasies all over the place – in barber shops, pharmacies and back rooms. It lasted about thirteen years, I think."

"OK, I'm with you so far. What makes it a *magical* speakeasy?" I asked.

"See for yourself. We're here."

Chapter 49

Swirling orange lettering spelled out 'Toil and Trouble' on the teal building. Burnt-orange velvet curtains covered the windows, and a 'Closed' sign was stuck to the one nearest the door.

Jared let me walk inside first. On the ceiling, colourful potion bottles were spread out over a silver background, from the brightest magenta to a deep emerald green. Each bottle was lit from within and streams of light poured from their open mouths, twisting and crossing paths.

The place was crammed with cauldron tables that contained bright swirling colours under sheets of glass. Behind the bar, bottles in all kinds of vibrant colours and strange shapes were displayed in rows. Our friends were already seated around a couple of cauldrons, including some unexpected faces.

"Pretty amazing, isn't it?" Jared said into my ear.

"That's one word for it," I said, as we walked over to the unlikely group hoping to take down a vampire kingpin.

Cafferty was leaning on the bar behind the others, so I approached him while they were still chatting.

"I'm so sorry for what I did to you," he said.

"Almost did," I corrected. "It's not your fault – you can stop apologising. Are you sure you're OK to be here . . . you know, around humans?"

He grimaced. "Not really, but I can hold it together. I'm not up to working yet. Boudreaux is covering for me, but I'm not sure how long that'll last."

"You're doing amazing. Most vamps would still be a mess by now."

He smiled weakly. "Maybe that will be my superpower – sheer stubbornness."

Reassured that he was handling things, I joined Emmeline, Jared, Rosario, Libby, Della, Armand and Elijah. Cafferty stayed at a distance.

Armand considered the group gravely. "So, this is the team who would take down Saint Germain. I presume you all understand the pressing nature. Emmeline and I have been watching his growing influence for a while, myself as the representative for a certain dissatisfied faction of vampires . . ."

"And me for the witches," Emmeline finished. "We felt somethin' brewing, but only now do we know what that is."

They acted so comfortable around one another: two separate parts of my life that unexpectedly fit together.

Emmeline continued. "If our suspicions are correct, then Saint Germain is planning to make himself the most powerful vampire there ever was. We need to figure out how to stop him, not forgetting the influence he already has and the vampires at his disposal."

"It won't be easy," Jared began. "As Emmeline said, he surrounds himself with vampires that have powers I couldn't have even imagined, and he's guarded wherever he goes."

Armand nodded. "If you could write a current list of those he has around him, and their powers, that would be very helpful. I spend most of my time trying to avoid him, so there could be players I've missed."

"There are more problems," Elijah said quietly, not as confident as the others. "As far as anyone in the city is concerned, Saint Germain is Claude Sejour, entrepreneur and philanthropist. We can't get caught with his blood on our hands."

"Remind me who you are?" Rosario asked. "I see vampires, slayers and a witch. Plus Libby. I'm wonderin' what you bring to the table."

"Thanks," Libby muttered.

Elijah looked nervous but stood his ground. "Armand's been good to me after my boy got turned. Helping out is the least I can do."

Rosario ran her tongue over her teeth, which made me twitchy. She was a new vampire in close quarters with humans, which rarely ended well. "All right. So we have a lot of problems. What's the solution?"

This was usually where Cafferty would be full of ideas and purpose. Instead, he stayed apart from us, grim where he would normally be positive and determined.

"Saint Germain's party tonight," Armand said. "Jared, Mina and I are going."

"Unfortunately." I'd been trying not to think about it.

"I could try to swing an invitation," Cafferty said.

Armand shook his head. "Sorry, Matt. You really are doing extraordinarily well, but we can't have you around humans at the party."

Cafferty nodded, helplessness taking up residence behind his eyes.

"It's kind of a public forum to take him down," Della said, and Libby leaned her head against her with a proud smile. "We wanna keep a low profile, not tell the whole town we killed their most celebrated entrepreneur."

"So we do it after the party," Rosario said, and I could practically hear her mind whirring. "The guests see him do his public thing. Apparently Saint Germain always takes the back way out – you know, so he doesn't have to mix with his guests. Those who are invited can follow him out of the party, and the rest wait outside with as many weapons as we can carry. He can just disappear."

"He'll probably only have a couple of guards on him then," Jared said thoughtfully. "That's how he tends to move from place to place."

"OK, so we're getting there, but do we bring the slayers in on this? They have weapons and all kinds of equipment," I said.

Della frowned. "I don't know if we can trust them. They're on Saint Germain's payroll, after all."

"I know this is nothing to do with me really, but I second the not trusting Paige and the slayers part," Libby said.

"OK, no other slayers," Rosario said. "But what do we think?" She looked around the table victoriously like she'd figured it all out. The rest of us were quiet, and I assumed that, like me, they were picking over her plan. It sounded feasible, but could we pull it off with so many unknowns?

"It may work," Armand said slowly, rubbing his forehead. "My visions have been non-existent about tonight – they never seem to come when I need them. Let's walk through it."

We spent the next hour talking through every eventuality. By the end, my brain was overloaded, but I had some hope that soon we could be rid of Saint Germain, and I wouldn't have to be afraid of him ripping Jared away.

"The only problem I can see is that someone worse could spring up in Saint Germain's place. And it don't solve the problem of all the powerful vampires he has behind him. They might not disband when he's gone." Della made an excellent point, and the rest of us looked at Armand, our leader appointed by unspoken agreement.

"Assuming that we succeed, we'll cross that bridge when we come to it. The vampires of this town know me. If needed, I'll put myself forwards," Armand said in a sombre tone. "Regardless of our chances, we need to act tonight. His doctor has perfected her procedure, and it's only a matter of time before he starts acquiring vampires to steal their powers. We don't need a trail of dead vampires and an unstoppable Saint Germain."

There wasn't much left to say after that. Emmeline bundled Rosario and Cafferty up in the van, and the four of us followed on foot.

We took off fast. It felt like the planned rebellion would be visible to anyone – a giant, bloody target painted on our backs.

"Can I just say that being included wasn't the fun and games I thought it would be? Feel free to leave me out whenever you like," Libby said.

"Like tonight," Della said, snaking an arm around Libby's waist. "You don't have an invite, and there's no way you're waiting in the dark with us."

Libby deflated. "You're right. You need to focus on keeping

yourselves alive. I don't want one of you getting killed trying to defend me."

"If this goes smoothly, no one is dying tonight," Della said.

I hoped with everything I had that she was right. "We should give Boudreaux a heads up. There might be a police presence at the party, and we don't want them to think we're the bad guys."

"Good plan. I don't mind callin' her. Then we should get some rest. It feels like we're goin' into battle," Della said.

That was a conversation killer, and we walked all the way to Emmeline's place in silence.

Emmeline let us in, lighting the oil burner after we entered. It released a sweet, herbal scent.

"You'd better gather your strength for tonight. In the meantime, I'll rustle up a protection spell for the mansion to keep Libby safe."

"Thanks," Libby said. "Do I cancel today's tours? The locksmith has changed all the locks and fixed the broken door, but I don't know if I'll be able to concentrate. And won't everyone be at the party anyway?"

"Not tourists," Della said. "Unless they want to cough up for a ticket to the dinner."

"It'll be good to have something to do while we're there," I said, guessing that was where Della had been heading. She smiled at me, confirming it.

"OK. Capitalism for the win," Libby said. "I should do a walkthrough to check everything is ready."

"I'll come. Want me to grab a dress for you? I should probably get a suit for Jared too," Della said.

"Thanks. We should probably play the part," I said. I'd rather be kitted out in my leather jacket with weapons, but there was no way I'd get into this party armed.

"Then it's all settled. How about some lunch first?" Emmeline asked.

We passed Rosario's room on the way to the kitchen. She and Cafferty were sitting close together on the bed, talking softly. Both of them had turned so recently. If they could find some solace in each other, I'd leave them to it.

We all had an ordeal ahead.

Chapter 50

I ate automatically, the party looming ahead of us. After lunch, Della and Libby got ready to leave. "I'll come back with weapons and clothes," Della said.

I hugged my sister tight, comforted by her vanilla scent and the familiar feel of her. "It'll all be over soon," she said. "You guys can do this – I know it." She looked shaken, but she was putting on a good front. At least she'd be protected by Emmeline's spell while we were fighting for our lives.

"I hope so," I said.

"I'll come with you to cast the protection wards on the mansion," Emmeline said. "Here – in case you need it." She handed me a key attached to a silver bird's skull.

Rosario and Cafferty were still holed up in her room, so Jared and I were as good as alone in Emmeline's little shotgun house.

We curled up on my bed, looking each other in the eye. "Can we really beat Saint Germain?"

"We have to," Jared said. "As soon as he starts getting powers, it's all over. No one would be safe from his influence." There we were – thinking like Dad again.

"So, Emmeline told us to rest. Any ideas how we're supposed to do that?" I asked.

In the end, we watched *Karate Kid* and *Rocky* back-to-back in Emmeline's cosy living room, since neither of us could concentrate on much, and Jared figured they might get us in the zone. I mostly watched the clock, dread growing as the evening drew closer.

Della came back with a dress for me and a suit for Jared. "I got one with a loose skirt so you'll be able to move."

"Thank you," I said. She'd picked a black knee-length dress with a high neckline. A bunch of bad guys would probably see my underwear if a fight broke out, but that would be the least of my concerns.

We got ready without our usual sense of fun. Della pulled my hair into a bun to keep it out of the way. The pins dug in as she positioned them, and every small pain grounded me.

Cafferty and Rosario surfaced, and he looked adorably sheepish. I decided against teasing him and almost went in for a hug, remembering that he was a new vampire before I did.

"We'll see you outside the party," Cafferty said, taking a noticeable step back from me.

"Saint Germain will never see it coming," Rosario said.

"Let's hope you're right," Della said.

All day, the party had crept up on us, and now it was time for me and Jared to leave. It felt strange being dressed up – Jared in a sleek navy suit and me in my black dress. I couldn't risk taking a weapon in case someone searched me, but our friends outside would have plenty.

Jared had booked a cab, and we held hands across the back seat all the way to the Garden District. The street was lined with trees, their leaves tumbling onto the road. Elegant mansions were set back behind ornate metal fences. Last time I'd been here was with Cafferty. We'd interviewed a woman whose son had been murdered by Sam, though we didn't know that at the time. I wondered how long it'd be before Cafferty could go back to being a detective, if ever.

Saint Germain had borrowed a mansion for the event – a dinner that sounded like an opportunity for the rich and bored of New Orleans to congratulate each other. The building was a beautiful white structure on two floors with pillars along the front.

We walked down a lantern-lit path across the manicured lawn, light spilling out of the huge windows. A thick garland of autumn leaves ran along each windowsill, fairy lights twinkling among them.

A well-dressed older couple were standing on the porch ahead of us. A few seconds of scrutiny determined they were human. The door opened, and a butler in a black tuxedo invited us in. We passed a sweeping marble staircase before entering a ballroom. Cream pillars supported the ceiling, and sombre portraits glared down from every wall.

Jared kept a tight grip on my hand, and for a second I let myself imagine we were only here for an elegant dinner. One night of risk could earn us countless evenings with our little group and days attending school or building up experience with the police, without worrying about Saint Germain. There'd be other threats, like the ripper who was still lurking, but we'd deal with them one at a time.

People in beautiful evening wear mingled around tables decorated with bouquets of flowers in autumnal shades. Quiet conversations blurred together over live piano music. I scanned the room for familiar faces, spotting Ilian and a couple of Saint Germain's other vampires but no sign of him. Armand hadn't arrived yet either.

After the cocktails and chat portion of the evening, we sat down to dinner with a group of strangers who pointedly talked around us. Most attendees were humans, because they were tucking into tiny portions of delicious, intricately decorated foods. They were sprinkled with tiny petals and drizzled with sauces, but the end of the night was drawing too close to savour the meal.

Paige wandered in when the desserts arrived, wearing a red satin strapless dress with a heart-shaped neckline. Beau looked happy and handsome in a black suit, and from the way Paige was gazing at him, she agreed with me. Neither of them seemed ready for a fight, which offered some reassurance. Perhaps Saint Germain wasn't expecting trouble.

He happened to enter as I thought about him. Ilian moved to his side, scanning the room with his cool grey gaze. A flood of vampires followed, fanning out around the walls. My nerves spiked once more. Why did he need so much backup?

"Thank you so much for comin'," Saint Germain said, his arms spread wide in greeting. He was wearing a silvery grey suit and holding a thin silver cane. "Between the end of fall and the onset of winter, it's a good time to reflect on what we have. I ask you to join me to raise a glass of champagne, and then you can go on out to enjoy our beautiful city."

Waiters swept through the room with trays of champagne flutes, and everyone left their tables to claim one. Jared and I stood alone in the increasingly animated crowd, our shared dread growing.

After the toast, the room slowly emptied around us. "As soon as Saint Germain leaves, we follow. The others will be waiting outside," Jared whispered. There were no vampires nearby to overhear, but it was worth being careful with Saint Germain's super-powered employees.

As we hovered, a shift was taking place. The humans were leaving, but the room was still full of vampires. "This doesn't feel right," Jared whispered.

Paige was standing off to one side, not brimming with her usual smugness. She and Beau looked nervous, and that made me even more afraid.

Saint Germain approached us with Ilian to one side of him and Carmilla to the other. "We're a little short on guests, I reckon," he said. "Let's bring in some more."

The glass doors opened, and Della, Emmeline, Rosario and Cafferty filed in, all dressed in black exercise gear and conspicuously lacking weapons. Saint Germain's vampires herded them until they were standing in a line beside me and Jared.

Saint Germain straightened up, tapping his cane on the ground. Someone grabbed me from behind, holding me in a vice-like grip. A quick glance confirmed my friends were similarly restrained.

"Here's my little escapee," he said, strolling across to Rosario. She put up a renewed struggle, and he chuckled. "We've been lookin' for you. How convenient that you came back to me."

Saint Germain's smile was chilling as he addressed the rest of us. "I find it a little insultin' that you thought this ragtag group could best me. Let me tell y'all how the night's gonna go instead."

Chapter 51

Della was on one side of me and Jared was on the other while Saint Germain's vampires held us in place. I struggled at first, but it was like fighting against a cage of stone. I needed to conserve some energy for whatever was to come. Beau and Paige were standing among Saint Germain's vampires, though they shared looks of uncertainty. Beau was fidgeting, but he wasn't leaping to our defence. In these circumstances, I didn't blame him.

"Is everyone here?" Saint Germain asked, squinting at us. "You know, it feels like we're missin' someone. Where's Armand?"

"Not here," Jared said, his voice clear and sure. Even though I was terrified, Armand's absence gave me some hope that we could still beat Saint Germain. He could be trying to save us in his absence.

"No, it wasn't him I was thinkin' of. There's someone else I needed." Saint Germain tapped his jaw with one finger. "Oh . . . that's right. Elijah, could you come on out here, please?"

Elijah came in and stood by Saint Germain. Ilian moved back, looking put out. Saint Germain clapped a hand on Elijah's shoulder, turning me cold inside. "I have this great individual to thank for learning about your plan. Of course, now I'll be able to see threats comin' for myself."

"What do you mean?" Cafferty asked sharply. I wasn't following either, too caught up in Elijah's betrayal.

"It's a tad early, but I can't wait to see what my first vision will be."

The realisation crashed down, and my legs almost went out from under me. "No . . . You can't have."

Saint Germain unfastened the top button of his shirt, revealing a bandage like the one Rosario had worn after her procedure. "My first successful transfer, but certainly not the last."

"Where's Armand?" Jared asked, his fear showing. I prayed desperately that I was mistaken.

"Oh, I do apologise – I should've made it clearer. The procedure was successful for *me*. The outcome isn't so favourable for the person who donates their power. Their life is the cost, you see, and one I'm more than willing to pay. Armand always undersold his clairvoyance, but I see endless potential in it. I'll simply work out the kinks, and then I have a whole pool of other powers to choose from."

Armand was dead. I pressed my lips together, barely containing the swell of emotion. Grieving would have to wait. We had to survive this first.

Jared had tensed beside me, renewing his fight against the hulking male vampire who was holding him.

Although sorrow threatened to pull me under, I held on to the reason Armand had been murdered. "Armand protected you, Elijah. How could you betray him?"

Elijah's expression turned sullen, but he kept quiet.

"She has a point," Saint Germain said. "How could you double-cross a friend like that? I think the girl deserves your answer."

"Saint Germain promised to keep me and my boy safe," Elijah said. "He offered me a salary, a vampire nanny . . . Hell – maybe he'll even turn me one day so I can be like Tony. That's all I ever wanted John to do. Surely you can understand that."

"I wouldn't trade someone else's life for anything," I said, vaguely aware of Ilian slipping out through the open doors. My arms felt numb from being held in place, and I shifted on the spot. Even if I somehow slipped free, there were countless vampires eyeing me hungrily.

"She's right," Della said.

"An admirable quality in you both," Saint Germain said. "I'm not sure the same can be said for you, E-Lie-Jah. The name seems appropriate. Ilian?" he called towards the door. "Bring our little guest in."

Just when I thought Saint Germain couldn't get any more despicable, Tony came into the room in front of Ilian. The little boy's hands were tied behind his back and his mouth was taped shut. His eyes looked terrified above the masking tape. He was wearing ear defenders, so at least he couldn't hear us.

"You swore you wouldn't hurt him!" Elijah said, stepping towards Saint Germain. Carmilla moved faster than I could comprehend, grabbing Elijah's arms from behind. Now he was being held exactly like us.

"And I'm sure it won't hurt a bit once the anaesthesia kicks in and I take his power," Saint Germain said. "Ilian, take the boy away." Little Tony struggled and kicked, but Ilian simply picked him up, cradling him against his chest with surprising care as he carried him away.

I made one more attempt to twist free, but the vampire clung on tighter. My arms throbbed, and my fingers began to tingle.

"See, I'm not a complete monster. I wouldn't have wanted him to watch what I'm about to do to his father."

Elijah barely had chance to show fear before Saint Germain sank his mouth into his throat and drank deep. Cafferty was pulling and thrashing down the line, but none of us could save Elijah.

He fought at first, as Saint Germain drained the life from him, but soon his body went slack. Two male vampires swooped in to claim his corpse before it fell. They carried him from the room without a drop spilled on the cream carpet. Saint Germain ran his hand across his mouth, licking a trace of blood off his fingers. "Now you see what I do to traitors who betrayed someone else. What to do with those who betray me?"

My gaze caught on Paige standing off to the side with Beau, and she looked even paler than usual. She was leading the slayers for Saint Germain, but she didn't seem to be in on this plan.

"You're talking about little more than children, with their whole lives ahead of them," Emmeline said. "It's obvious that we can't beat you. Let's you and I discuss it further, and release the others. I can assure you that I speak for them, and they will not try this again. I'm sure it would be valuable to have a witch on your staff." Emmeline's spine was straight and she looked fierce despite the vampire holding her arms behind her back.

Saint Germain leaned on his cane. "A witch in my employ – that *is* tempting."

He let a long silence fall, and in it I heard Emmeline take a long, shaky breath. "All right. Let me take a look at you."

The vampire at her back freed Emmeline, and she marched towards Saint Germain. "Well? Do I measure up to your requirements?"

They were about the same height, and Saint Germain stared straight into her eyes. He raised a hand to skim her chin. I couldn't see Emmeline's face, but the way she jerked her head away spoke volumes.

She slid one hand into her back pocket, withdrawing a handful of something. Saint Germain caught hold of her wrist, squeezing until she screamed. Black powder fell onto the white carpet. In a flash, Saint Germain took hold of her jaw. Then he yanked it to the side. I heard the crack, watching her body fall with a fresh burst of grief. First Armand and now Emmeline . . .

Beau stepped forwards. Paige grabbed his wrist, wearing an unfamiliar look of desperation, but he shook her off. "The deaths have to stop," he said calmly. "Your deal with the slayers only stands because you swore that humans would be safe around you."

"Well, technically she's a witch," Saint Germain said. "Or, she was. You got stones, boy. I don't like my employees to have a backbone – Detective Cafferty learned that lesson. I think I'm better off bein' rid of you along with the traitors."

"No!" Paige cried, clamping a hand over her red lips as soon as the plea escaped.

"What was that?" Saint Germain said. "Don't tell me you want to die along with your lieutenant. You *have* been more troublesome than I anticipated, complaining and squeezing me for funding. If you couldn't even catch that ripper, what are you good for?"

Paige hesitated, looking at Beau with more longing than I'd

expected. "I want to run the slayers for you. With all of our new gear, I'm closin' in on the ripper."

"So that's how it is," Beau said, true hurt playing out.

Paige's composure was cracking, but she held on to it. The drama had drawn my gaze away from Emmeline's body, but I looked at her again. I sagged in the vampire's grip, thinking about Armand as well. Where had Saint Germain left his body after he ripped out his power?

"I'm growing tired of these human trivialities. Carmilla and Ilian – escort our friends to the courtyard."

Fear resurged through the thick layer of grief. We'd run out of time. My arms were aching in the vampire's grip, and trying to wrench free did nothing.

"What? You can't do that!" Paige's heel clacked down hard on the marble floor, but Saint Germain simply adjusted his cufflinks, ignoring her. It was too late for her to plead our case.

Saint Germain's vampires jostled and murmured around the room, and Della took the opportunity to whisper, "Get ready."

I wasn't sure what for, but the order filled me with drive that I'd been lacking. I started scanning for exits as Carmilla and Ilian strode towards us.

"Oh, and when you're done here, Carmilla, track down the sister. Libby, isn't it? Revenge plots are so tiresome – I'd rather tie up every loose end." He couldn't go after Libby too . . .

Della dropped to the ground, pulling herself out of her vampire's arms at the same time that Jared wrenched himself free and barrelled towards Saint Germain. Cafferty and Rosario started fighting to get free again, but I was fixated on Jared. If he got Saint Germain, this would all be over.

One of the vampires let out a sound so loud and high pitched that it felt like my eardrums might explode. I clamped my hands over my ears, pain ripping through my head and making my whole body shudder. The vampire holding me let go, and I fell to the ground. Around me, my friends had all hit the floor too, clutching their heads while Saint Germain's vampires laughed and leered. Only certain people were affected by the noise still drilling into my ears.

Through streaming eyes, I saw one of Saint Germain's people grabbing Jared. His hands were also covering his ears as the vampire dragged him towards the door. I tried to stand, and the sound only intensified. The shrieking cut out right as Jared was gone. Vampires pressed in around us, leaving no room for escape. I pushed and yelled for them to release Jared, getting nowhere.

Saint Germain tapped his watch. "Ilian and Carmilla, if you please. My time is expensive."

Carmilla ran a hand over her buzzed blonde hair, grinning. Then she took that same hand and wiggled her fingers, jerking upwards. It felt like invisible ropes yanked me forwards, my legs walking jerkily like a broken doll. The doors that held my death sentence behind them moved closer and closer, my own legs carrying me to my death even as I fought.

Beau and Della walked in that same awkward manner on either side of me, both of their bodies writhing as they tried to free themselves from Carmilla's power. Rosario and Cafferty were snarling and grunting behind us. Paige hurried out of the room, not staying to watch the deaths she'd avoided for herself.

Carmilla puppeteered us through the doorway of the courtyard. Ilian closed the frosted glass doors the moment I felt her power sever.

Before I could use my freedom, Ilian froze the five of us on the spot. I wasn't sure which was worse – my body being dragged forwards against my will or straining to run and save Jared without anything happening.

Around us, the patio was ridiculously beautiful, a walled space with trellises covered in yellow flowers shaped like tiny trumpets. Sprinklers misted them with water – also handy for washing away our blood. I was going to die surrounded by flowers without the ability to move and save myself.

Carmilla grinned at us, a ruthless predator weighing up which prey she'd like to eat first. She was going to pick us off one by one while Ilian held us in place.

"The girl who caused Saint Germain so many headaches," Carmilla mused, drifting over to me like she had all the time in the world. "I think I'll start with you."

Fangs slipped over her teeth. "I'm going to enjoy this."

I couldn't even turn my head to look away. Panic raged through me as Carmilla leaned towards my throat, drawing out the moment.

Then she gasped. Bloody fingers thrust through her chest, followed by a palm holding a bloody, slippery-looking heart.

Chapter 52

The hand holding the bloody heart withdrew as I regained control over my body. Through the shock, I noticed a fine spray of Carmilla's blood had coated my face and arms. I wiped frantically over my mouth, pretty sure I hadn't swallowed any. We'd been through hours of stressful waiting when Della accidentally swallowed vampire blood over Halloween.

Carmilla's body fell, and Ilian was still holding her heart. He let it fall with a wet plop. He sighed, drawing a handkerchief from his pocket to wipe his bloody hand. "I was hoping it wouldn't come to that. She used to make excellent cocktails – little bit of blood in them and everything."

"Why would you . . .?" Della asked.

"Help you? I don't want to die in the near future at the hands of Saint Germain's doctor. Nor do I think it wise to let Saint Germain become the all-powerful possessor of countless abilities. Even I know how that would end."

"And you'd help us to stop him?" Rosario asked. "How do we know you're not going to report back to Saint Germain?"

"I'd have thought the proof is bleeding all over the patio." Ilian glanced at the frosted door leading back into the party room.

"That being said, we ought to move this along. At midnight, Saint Germain will receive the next power of many at the abandoned hospital I assume you're familiar with." He directed that part at Rosario. "It'll be done in the west wing, which is considerably nicer than the rest of that hell hole. He won't be too heavily protected tonight, since he thinks you're all dead. You won't get a better opportunity – day walking is the next power he has his eye on."

Visceral fear ripped me apart. I'd known that on some level when he'd taken Jared. Armand and Emmeline were gone . . . and Jared would join them if we didn't move fast.

"Thank you for saving us," Cafferty said, still looking shaken.

"I didn't do it for you. I want him gone – it's as simple as that. Unfortunately, I won't be there tonight . . . Jared is under lock and key, but I can get Tony out. I'm going to run with him – someone should keep that little boy safe. His power is strong, but I can guide him. I've always wanted a son . . . When I was turned, I thought I'd lost that chance." From the compassion on his face, I believed him. Tony's father was dead, and being in Ilian's care had to be better than being next on Saint Germain's list. And Jared was first . . . Ilian would've been handy in the fight with his ability to freeze people in place, but I understood him wanting to get Tony to safety. Saving Jared was our battle, not his.

"What are you going to do about her?" Cafferty asked. I'd been avoiding looking at Carmilla's body with its hollowed-out chest. She and her heart were already decomposing, flattening and breaking down as a counterbalance to her long life.

"Saint Germain will expect me to get rid of your bodies for him. I'll get rid of hers instead and tell Saint Germain we killed you, but one of you took her down in the struggle." Ilian explained his colleague's death without any emotion.

Della looked frantic. "Then he'll send someone else after Libby. Emmeline's protection spells won't work, now she's . . . gone."

"Then I suggest you get Libby out fast," Ilian said. "Move her to a secure location and guard her until this is over."

"We need to go," Rosario said. "We can save Jared and Libby – Saint Germain won't see us coming if he thinks we're dead."

Cafferty rubbed his eyes, their telltale red rims suggesting he was close to losing it if he didn't feed soon. "I hate to bring this up, but won't Saint Germain be able to do just that? You know – with Armand's power."

That brought a fresh tug of grief. "The doctor believes received powers take a day or so to come into full force," Ilian said. "If we're lucky, he won't see you coming or my betrayal until it's too late. Now get the hell out of here before I really do have to kill you."

Ilian unlocked a heavy iron gate that led out onto the dark street. The five of us hurried away. I resisted the impulse to run, because that usually led to being chased. How had today gone so badly wrong? Emmeline and Armand were dead . . . Elijah had betrayed us and been killed for it. And Saint Germain was preparing to kill Jared for his powers. If I thought about that for too long, I'd crumple on the pavement and be no use to anyone.

We stopped on the corner, all of us checking constantly for pursuers. "I'll go get Libby," Della said. "But where do I take her?"

"How about your parents' place?" Cafferty asked. "I don't think Saint Germain's people know about it." He reached for Rosario's hand, and she smiled up at him. "We need to feed, but we'll meet you at their hotel."

"You should stay with Libby," I said as we set off walking, even though I knew it would tear Della up to be left out of the fight. Her face confirmed as much. "She needs protection in case Saint Germain sends someone else after her."

Della nodded. "I don't like leaving you . . . but I have to keep her safe."

"I know," I said.

"I'll go get weapons from the slayer cave and see if I can wrangle up any trusted slayers to help," Beau said. "I'll tell Paige if she's there."

"No way!" Della said. "She would've let us die just now."

"She hates Saint Germain more than anyone for being constantly on her case," Beau said, "and you know how good she is in a fight."

"She is," Rosario said. "But you'd better be right. That's twice now that she's let me go off to my death to save her own ass."

"I know I'm right about her – she's deeper than you think. See you at the hospital." Beau jogged away.

The rest of us hurried onwards. Rosario and Cafferty went off to a blood bar, promising to be at the hotel soon. Then Della and I rushed together through the streets of New Orleans, the usual party going on around us while the time ticked down towards midnight. I could hardly believe I was walking away from Jared, but I'd be no good to him if I stormed back in and got killed. Regrouping for an armed attack at the hospital was our best shot.

At the mansion, Libby wrapped us both in a tight hug. "What happened?"

"We didn't get Saint Germain," I said, too choked up for the next part.

"Armand and Emmeline didn't make it – I'm sorry," Della said. Libby's face crumpled, and Della wrapped her up in a tight hug.

"I can't believe they're gone," she said against Della, her voice all broken up. "Where's Jared?"

I jogged up to the apartment, leaving Della to explain. I couldn't talk about Jared being gone, especially after losing Emmeline and Armand. I had to keep moving, so I wiped off the blood and assembled as many stakes and knives as I could find.

With my body strapped up with weapons, I made a call. The phone rang until Will's stepmum's recording invited me to leave a message. "Jared's been taken by . . . the big bad. We're asking everyone to come and help, so if you hear this, please come . . . We need you. He's found out how to steal powers, so no one's safe. I hope you're OK." I ended with the hospital address.

Once I got downstairs, Libby's eyes were red but she'd stopped crying. "I don't know how much more we can take. Della told me you're going after Jared . . ."

"Cafferty and Rosario will have my back," I said, my confidence sounding believable enough. "We're meeting them at the hotel."

"I called your mom and dad to let them know what's happenin'," Della said.

"Thank you," I said.

Della grabbed some weapons and we all headed out into the night. It had turned cold, and my senses were painfully bright and alert. I wanted to be at the hospital with Jared, and all of the diversions in between were slowly filling me with frustration.

When we got to Mum and Dad's place, they were waiting with Chase and Hayes in the entrance hall of the hotel. It looked cleaner and more hospitable inside, but Ellie was a noticeable absence.

"Della told us everything, and we're coming with you." Mum surprised me with a fierce hug.

"Are you sure? Saint Germain's vampires will be standing between us and Jared."

"Of course, honey," Dad said. "We haven't always been here for you, but we are now."

My emotions were so close to the surface that Dad almost tipped me into tears. "Thank you."

"I'm comin' too for tech support," Hayes said.

"Great. If you're all sure, can we go?" I asked, the midnight deadline piling on the pressure.

"I'll stay with Libby and Della," Chase said gruffly. "I hear they might have trouble of their own here. You go get Jared."

Libby, Chase and Della watched us go from the doorway. "You all need to come back in one piece and bring Jared with you. Got it?" Libby said.

"We will," I said, wishing I could be so sure.

Rosario and Cafferty were coming down the street hand in hand. Even though things were terrible, seeing them together made me smile. "You two worked fast."

"What happened to me put things in perspective," Rosario said. "I don't stay quiet about the things I want anymore."

She was right. Now we had to go and rescue the vampire I wanted.

The hospital looked even more forbidding this time, because I knew of the nightmares it contained. Somewhere inside, Saint

Germain was planning to steal Jared's power and take him away from us forever. But countless vampires with powers were blocking our path to him.

There was no sign of Beau and his slayer reinforcements, which I hoped didn't mean Paige had tipped off Saint Germain.

Dad was the only one of us who looked pleased to be there. "All of my work has led us to this moment. We'll save Jared, and I'll personally take down Saint Germain. I got a secret weapon – one good thing to come from Clem. Tonight is the night we stop the apoc—"

"The apocalypse – we get it," Cafferty said. "Instead of making speeches, how about we get inside?"

Taking advantage of Dad's surprise, Rosario cut in. "Saint Germain had me and Cafferty turned and tried to have us killed just now, so you can get in line to take him down."

"Can we fight over who gets to kill him after we've saved Jared?" I asked.

"Mina's right," Hayes said, his voice low and calm. "If some of y'all can get me to the generator room, I can try to cut the power to the building. If there's no power, then there's no machine to take Jared's ability."

"I probably shouldn't go anywhere near a generator," Rosario said, sparks rippling along her fingers.

Dad was watching, and I saw an eerie similarity to Saint Germain's fascination. "Cafferty and I will go with Hayes."

"So that leaves the three of us," I said, looking to my mum and Rosario. I'd never expected to be fighting alongside my parents. "Are you all sure you want to be here? I don't want you to get hurt."

"Don't worry about us," Dad said. "There's no way we'd leave you to do this alone." For the first time, it felt like he wanted to protect me, instead of having some agenda. "Besides, we came prepared." He opened his rucksack, showing an array of knives and stakes. "Clem had hidden his stash in case the police came, but I took the liberty of depriving him of it when I fled the swamp the other day."

"If we're decided, then we need to go!" I said, releasing the stake from my wrist holster into my hand.

"Y'all might want this to stay in touch," Hayes said, handing a walkie-talkie to Rosario. She nodded, slipping it into her pocket.

Everyone followed me around the side of the building, traipsing through weeds and broken glass as Jared and I had done only yesterday. I'd been in more than my share of dire situations, but I'd never wanted anything more than this. We needed to save Jared – there was no other option.

Rosario came up beside me. "Don't let the code enter your mind tonight. We've seen Saint Germain's vampires in action, so you take them down before they return the favour."

"Got it," I said. There'd be no hesitation when it came to protecting Jared.

"We should enter here," Rosario said, grabbing the lapel of Cafferty's coat to give him a quick, passionate kiss.

He smiled. "We'll cut the power and be right with you."

After hasty goodbyes, I pulled myself up onto the nearest windowsill, extracting the torch from my pocket.

Sweeping the light over the darkness revealed an empty room ravaged by exposure to the elements. I swung my leg over and landed in a crouch. We were in a ward full of beds still covered in moth-eaten bedding. Rosario and Mum followed as a vampire strode through the door.

Chapter 53

The vampire was small and curvy, her black hair cut into a thick bob and her sweet smile showing fangs. "Can I help you?" she asked.

Before we could answer, her hands came together as if she was holding an invisible ball. Fire bloomed in the empty space.

I grabbed a thin knife from the sheath between my shoulder blades, throwing it hard. The vampire batted it away, the ball of fire still cradled in her other palm. I couldn't tear my eyes from it. The thought of those flames eating into my flesh was all consuming. "That was rude," she said, taking aim at me.

Mum flung her body against the vampire, smacking into her shoulder. The ball of flame hit the wall in a whoosh of fire. Greedy flames licked across the wooden frame, and I feared that we'd lost already. Jared would die along with Saint Germain before we could get to him. Grabbing a ragged quilt from one of the beds, I smothered the flames. Heat came through the bedding, smoke rising up as the fire went out.

I returned to the fight as Rosario and the other vampire took aim at one another, Rosario's fingertips sparking blue and a fireball in her opponent's hand. They let their powers fly at the same time, and the fireball and bolt of electricity connected with a flare of blue light. The fireball spun off towards my mum.

There was no time to protect her, and she screamed as the fire came rushing towards her face. I was watching in such intent despair that I caught the moment she vanished. The fireball sailed through the space where she'd stood. It hit the tiled floor, sputtering out.

I was so sure I'd lost Mum when she reappeared, patting herself as if she wanted to make sure she was still here.

The vampire was gawping too, and Rosario took her opportunity. She clamped the vampire's temples between both hands, blue sparks sizzling. The vampire's body shuddered and contorted at Rosario's touch. When she let go, the vampire was dead.

"I have no idea what you just did," Rosario said to Mum. "But it was freaking awesome!"

"I didn't know I had a power," Mum said shakily, looking down at her hands. "I went into this dark emptiness for a few seconds . . . I thought I'd died. And then I came back." Vampires often got a power that showed some aspect of their personality. Though Mum's had taken its time to manifest, it reflected her penchant for disappearing on us.

"That could come in handy," Rosario said. "We should move."

I clicked off my torch as we stepped into the hallway because the lights were on in this part of the building. We consulted the overhead signs and set off towards the west wing.

We reached the end of the corridor when we were plunged into darkness again. I fumbled for my torch, panicking, until I realised what it meant. Hayes had cut the power, so Saint Germain's doctor wouldn't be able to do the procedure.

Relief coursed through me as the walkie-talkie crackled to life. Rosario handed it to me. "We did it," Hayes said. "It should be pretty dark where you are. Unfortunately, we won't know if they got a backup generator until we get to the west wing. We'll come find you."

"Thank you so much," I said, putting my torch back on as I followed Rosario and Mum down the dark corridor.

Hayes screamed so loud down the walkie-talkie that I almost dropped it. "Hayes?" I said, and there was no answer. Dad yelled before his voice was replaced by static.

"We have to go to them!" Mum said.

"We don't know where the generator is, and Jared's running out of time," Rosario said as we crept onwards through the darkness, only my torch lighting our path. "Cafferty's tough – he'll keep them safe."

Rosario was right. I blocked out the worry for the three of them. We had to keep on going.

"Someone's here," Rosario said, and I cut off the torch. We edged towards the side of the corridor, the mouldy stench of the wall enveloping us. I gripped my stake, listening out. More than one assailant was coming, and they weren't being quiet about it. I'd known we'd need to fight our way through tonight and wished I felt more ready.

"We kinda need that light to see where the hell you are!" Paige called out. So much for being stealthy.

"You gonna keep it down?" Rosario whispered sharply as Paige and Beau appeared in the doorway.

I switched the torch back on, and Paige covered her eyes. The two of them were wearing arm guards and lightweight chest armour, and both were armed to the hilt. They were using the gear they'd bought with Saint Germain's money against him.

"I didn't expect you to come," I said as we started off down the corridor again, the torch low at my side.

"I know I've been kind of a bitch," she said, arms folded and defensive. "Well, a lot of a bitch, OK? But he can't go ripping out people's powers – even I have standards. And if I have to sit through one more meeting where he tells us what to do . . ."

Even if her reasons for coming were questionable, I was glad of the backup. "Thank you for being here."

"Any time. Now let's get moving," Paige said. "The last thing we want is that creep reading our minds."

She strode ahead down the dark corridor, and Beau flashed us a grin before following.

A tall, lean figure came running straight at us, letting out a delighted whoop. I wondered how many more vampires that noise would attract.

Paige rushed towards the vampire with her stake raised, Beau at her side with a torch and his own stake. They reached the vampire as another figure materialised from the shadows. Before I could warn Paige, the new vampire extended a leg and sent her sprawling. In the darkness, I couldn't make out the vampire's features, but something seemed off about them. Their outline was rippling and swirling like a shadow trying to stay in human form.

The two vampires converged on Paige, the mass of shadow and the tall sinewy one. Mum, Rosario and I raced over there, my torchlight bouncing, as Beau started fighting the tall vampire. Paige was pushing herself off the floor as the shadowy vampire surged towards me, grabbing my neck.

My throat burned as I fought. Mum dragged hard at the vampire's fingers, trying to prise it off me. It hung on tight, and my vision went spotty as I gasped for breath. A fanged face appeared through the shadows, the vampire taking shape.

"Enough!" Dad appeared, his face bloody and furious as his hand shot out towards the vampire. I clocked the gleaming syringe right before the needle disappeared into the vampire's neck and Dad pushed down the plunger. It released me with a howl, convulsing and screaming as it dropped. Cafferty appeared, launching himself at the vampire Beau was fighting. That provided Beau with enough distraction to finish him off.

Rosario brushed off her hands against her trousers. "What the hell was in that needle?"

"Suspension of silver," Dad said. "One of Clem's inventions."

"Where's Hayes?" Mum asked, her sorrow already plain.

"He's gone – I'm sorry." Dad pulled Mum into a hug. "Are you OK?" he asked me.

My throat was throbbing, but it was nothing I couldn't handle. "I'm fine. Let's get to Jared."

"It shouldn't be far now," Rosario said. The loss of Hayes was awful, but with the rest of us together, it felt like we could do this.

"What's the hurry?" Another vampire sidled into view. She was leanly muscular, with thick black cornrows and dark brown skin. She stamped a foot, and a crack rippled across the floor towards us.

A handful of other vampires spilled out of the same doorway, forming a barrier across the corridor.

I could've screamed in frustration. Five more super-powered vampires were blocking the stairs that would lead us to Jared.

I risked a glance at my watch, and it was already quarter to twelve. Jared's time was slipping away.

Beau and Paige moved forwards to face the vampires with Cafferty and Rosario close behind. I advanced between my parents. My throat ached and the stake felt unsteady in my hand, but I'd kill every one of Saint Germain's vampires if it meant getting to Jared.

"I think I'll take you," the female vampire said, extending a hand to me. "Come here."

Cafferty blurred in front of us and grabbed the vampire, flinging her at the wall. Crumbling bricks fell around her, and she didn't get up again.

"Still getting used to that strength, Cafferty?" Rosario teased.

"Who the hell are you?" one of the vampires spat. "You know what? It doesn't matter. Let's kill them."

I couldn't see Rosario's face, but I imagined her smiling. Blue sparks glowed in her hands moments before she grabbed hold of the vampire who spoke. She screamed and juddered as Rosario hung on. The others ran for us in an angry blur of fangs. Dad's torch bounced around as he fought, showing skills with a stake. My eyes were adjusting, but between the fast-moving vampires and near darkness, I was battling on instinct. It was a horrifying thought that the vampires could see me and I couldn't see them. I kept slashing with my stakes, gripping both of them tight and keeping the points away from my friends.

Cafferty, Rosario and my parents were fighting hard around me, occasional blue sparks coming off Rosario. Paige and Beau were a terrifying team, fighting back-to-back as I slashed and stabbed alone, occasionally getting a stake to land.

Soon I lost track of everyone else as I tried to stay alive, slowly inching towards the stairs ahead. Just as I thought we might be winning, Paige let out an anguished scream.

She dropped to the floor at Beau's side as my parents and vampire friends finished off the last three vampires.

Beau was lying on his back, his throat ripped out.

Chapter 54

Even if Jared had been here, there would've been no healing Beau. His eyes were unseeing and his face was slack. His neck was all torn up, gore coating the front of his gear.

"This isn't happening," Paige said, her head lowered over Beau. Her voice was shaking. When she looked up, her eyes were dry and furious. "Saint Germain is going to pay for this."

With that, she took off up the stairs. I didn't need any more encouragement to find Jared. Even though I was exhausted and blood-spattered, I ran upstairs after her, with the others close behind. Jared was almost out of time.

It was obvious where the operating room was. A line of white light showed under only one of a dozen doors in the wing. That meant the back-up generator was operating, so we needed to move. Our torches were off, so I inched down the corridor with the others towards that band of light. I had one bloodstained stake in each hand but I pushed one back into the quick release in my sleeve. It was me, Cafferty, Rosario, Mum, Dad and Paige against whatever was waiting behind that door.

I got there first and took a deep breath, letting it out slowly.

I couldn't delay too long, since any vampires in the room would be able to hear my heartbeat.

I pushed the door open a fraction to see what we were getting into. The scene was both better and worse than I thought. The tiled white room was empty, and the wall across from us had a glass viewing window with a door beside it.

Behind the thick glass, Jared was propped up in a hospital bed, cracked leather straps holding his arms and legs down. The restraints weren't necessary, because he was unconscious. Needles and wiring were connected to his chest, and a white-coated doctor was fussing around him, repeatedly pushing her hand through short black hair.

My heart sank at the sight of Tony and Ilian, also unconscious on two beds at the back of the operating room. Ilian hadn't got Tony to safety.

Saint Germain was sitting up on a hospital bed, rolling up the cuffs of a pale pink shirt like he was about to preside over a board meeting instead of committing murder.

The doctor flinched when she noticed us, but Saint Germain looked more amused than anything else. When he spoke, his voice came through a speaker in the ceiling. "I thought y'all were supposed to be dead, but never mind. I got my first vision, and it was a doozy in any case. It didn't reveal all of y'all, but I got a glimpse of Ilian stealin' the child. That was useful enough to begin with.

"You're just in time for the show. Doctor Azalea was quite a find, with her power to anaesthetise with a touch. Jared is up first, then as you can see I have quite the busy night ahead." He gestured at Ilian and Tony.

Spurred into motion, Rosario started rattling the door by the viewing window and Cafferty punched the glass, flexing his fingers. The only other entrance to the operating theatre was on the opposite wall, meaning a trip through the hospital to find it.

"As entertaining as this is, the room is reinforced against vampire entry. But you're welcome to stay and watch your boy die."

Planting my hands on the glass, I stared at Jared through angry tears.

"Have to say, I'm disappointed to see you out there, Paige," Saint Germain said.

"Not for long! Lucky I came prepared – courtesy of my daddy's demolition company," Paige sang out. She took off her backpack and started unpacking blocks of C4 and wires.

"I'll go look for that other door," Dad said.

"I'm comin' with you," Rosario said. "I don't feel like getting blown up."

The two of them ran back out the way we came, leaving me with Cafferty, Mum and Paige. "We've killed your vampires and have you surrounded," I said in a loud, clear voice, hoping Saint Germain could hear me. My only shot was to buy more time for Paige or my dad and Rosario. Paige was merrily attaching C4 to the hinges of the locked door, but I wasn't sure how long she needed.

"Shall I start the procedure?" Doctor Azalea asked brightly.

"Please go right ahead," Saint Germain said.

"Wait!" I cried, scrambling for anything that might keep him talking.

"I'm the one who calls the shots in here," Saint Germain said. "But the girl is right. Hold on a second, doctor. I'm getting my second vision, and this one is much clearer." His gaze went vacant like Armand's had always done, before Saint Germain killed him for his power. "I see a tarot card in a dead hand . . . Well, this is interestin'. Looks like I no longer need any of you to find out who the ripper is – I'm about to see for myself." Horror passed over his cold, aloof features and he stared right at us.

"Paige . . .? You're the ripper?"

Chapter 55

Paige was a vampire? The one that'd been killing people?

She abandoned her explosives, coming to stand with me to stare Saint Germain down through the glass. "Dammit – I was *this close* to killing you before your power came in."

"But . . . you're not a vampire. You have a pulse," Saint Germain sputtered. I would've enjoyed seeing him so undone if I hadn't been lost too.

"I'm not a vampire," Paige said, "and I didn't kill anybody. I just posed the bodies and wrote the stupid letters so you'd think you had a vampire ready to spill about what you are."

"You found dead bodies and posed them?" I asked, wanting to understand as well as having another agenda. If we were talking, then Jared was still alive. Dad and Rosario could still get to him in time.

Paige sighed. "Are you really all going to make me tell this story? It was easy. All I did was wait for an overeager vamp on patrol and I let them do their thing. Then once they'd run off, I posed the bodies so it looked like a serial killer. I would've done more, but I had to wait for a vampire to kill."

Paige seemed so pleased with her cleverness, but she was

missing one crucial thing. Cafferty said it for all of us. "It really was multiple killers – that was why all of the bites looked different. You let innocent people die to annoy Saint Germain?"

"They'd have died anyway if I'd not been there," Paige said, sharing her scowl out around the group. "Saint Germain was always hassling me and getting in my business, so I wanted to give him a taste of his own medicine. Anyway, I saw how worried he got when that TV stunt could've exposed vampires, and that gave me a great idea. I could get the funding the slayers needed and stress the crap out of him at the same time. I was hoping he'd do something reckless enough to get himself killed too, but in the meantime, I was happy having him off my back while he ran around chasing the killer who didn't exist." She grinned brightly. "With the new gear and Saint Germain distracted, I was working on a way to take him down. I would've stopped right after that and found some vampire to frame. That's why I did the tarot thing – I was thinking of pinning it on Armand. Guess he's off the table now."

"You could've saved the victims . . . like Ellie," I said, feeling hollow.

"She was already dead when I got to her," Paige said. "Look, I know we all want Saint Germain to die. I did this for us! So we don't have to be under his thumb anymore. Now, let's get the door opened so we can finish this." She went back to her wiring.

Dad and Rosario appeared at the doorway on the other side of the operating room. Rosario was pounding on the door, but it was locked too.

"Once the procedures are done, I'll enjoy killing you for this." Saint Germain was glaring at Paige.

"No, she'll go to jail for tampering with crime scenes and

obstruction of justice," Cafferty said calmly.

Paige clutched a coil of wires against her chest. Then she dropped it and bolted. Cafferty took off after her, leaving me on this side of the glass with Mum.

"I'm growin' tired of these infernal distractions," Saint Germain said. "Start the machine."

"Please don't," I said, my hope all used up.

Mum banged her hands on the window, letting them rest there. A determined look settled on her face, and she closed her eyes. Then she vanished.

The panic that she might be gone for good this time was searing. Then she reappeared on the other side of the glass, inside the operating room. "It worked!" she said.

But it was too late for Jared. The doctor checked the wires attached to Saint Germain and then pressed a button on the machine. Saint Germain smiled broadly, shuddering as the transfer began to work.

Jared still wasn't moving, and I pushed away the tears as I took a last look at him. We'd come so close to succeeding, only to watch him die.

Saint Germain's expression changed, and a curl of smoke twined up from the machine. "What's happening?" he roared, his face turning red and the veins on his neck bulging. He rocked forwards and backwards, a convulsion tearing through him. Then he let out a scream of anguish and sagged back onto the bed.

Saint Germain had been a vampire for so long that the decay set in as we watched. Slowly, his body started flattening and breaking down.

Mum carefully disconnected the wires from Jared's chest before unstrapping his arms. I watched all the time, praying for any sign of life or movement.

I was dimly aware of the doctor prising the front off her machine. "This is impossible . . . It should've worked. No . . . The wires have been reconfigured. No one knows how to do that but me!"

With Jared freed, Mum ran over to the door by the viewing window and let me in.

I was by Jared's side in seconds, checking him over. He was still unconscious, but his eyelids fluttered, and he let out a quiet groan. I sank against his side, sobbing with relief.

Mum let Rosario and Dad in through the other door. Cafferty had returned with Paige, her arms cuffed behind her back. Her ponytail had come loose and tear tracks ran down her cheeks. The operating room was getting crowded, and they stayed outside it.

While I clung to Jared, Rosario slipped an arm around the doctor's neck, holding her in a headlock.

Dad took another syringe out of his pocket. "This here is a suspension of silver," Dad said. "If I inject it into your throat, I hear the resulting death will be very slow and painful." The doctor's eyes never left the needle. "So you need to bring my three friends around before I decide to use it. I assume if you can put them to sleep, then you can wake them."

The doctor nodded, and Rosario released her with a thunderous expression. It couldn't have been easy to let go of the vampire who'd done experiments on her.

Doctor Azalea laid a hand on Jared's forehead, and he jolted awake. Then she went across and did the same for Ilian and Tony.

The little boy looked disorientated, but Ilian wrapped him in a fierce hug. "You're safe now. It's all over."

Once I knew they were all right, I only had eyes for Jared. He looked exhausted and hungry, his eyes rimmed in red, but he was alive. "I thought I was going to lose you."

"I wasn't sure I'd make it either," he said shakily. "I should've known you'd save me."

"I still don't understand," Doctor Azalea said. She was raking her hands through her hair in front of the machine that had killed Saint Germain. "The vampire elders will destroy me for this . . . One of you must have tampered with it."

"Nope," Tony said cheerfully, sliding off the gurney. "You did it."

"I would never!" Doctor Azalea said.

"The boy is telling the truth," Ilian said. "I asked him to use his mind-control abilities on you before Saint Germain had his vision and you put us to sleep."

Doctor Azalea took off across the room. Rosario raced after her, hands glowing. She planted them on either side of the doctor's head with a sizzle of blue, and she dropped like a stone. "That was definitely in line with the code," Rosario said.

"No arguments from me," I agreed. "Tony, you just saved the day."

"I did, didn't I?" he said, his little face lighting up. "Ilian, does that mean I'm a good boy?"

"You sure are," Ilian said, his arm still around the little boy.

"I thought you two were going to run after the party," I said.

"I was, until I realised how Tony could help us take Saint Germain down for good," Ilian replied with a grin. "I didn't plan on ending up unconscious, but the rest played out as I hoped."

"It was very clever," Dad said, his arms around Mum. "We all just averted an apocalypse, folks – the one I've foreseen for so many years. The signs pointed to a vampire more powerful than any other, and we took him down before he truly began."

"If you say so," Ilian said.

Cafferty called through the door, "We should get out of here in case any more of Saint Germain's people come. I'll send a medical team in . . . to remove those we've lost." We'd rescued Jared, but Beau and Hayes had lost their lives. And perhaps Armand's body was here somewhere.

Jared's brows came down low in confusion, his gaze lingering on Paige in cuffs. "Did I miss something?" he asked.

"Yeah, Paige is the ripper – sort of. I'll explain later," I said, gently hooking my arms around his neck. "Can you walk?"

Light feet sounded on the stairs, and every pair of eyes in the room turned to the door. "Sorry I'm late," Will said. "Looks like I missed the big fight. Any civilians in need of a memory wipe?"

"We're fine," I said, scrutinising him. Apart from dark circles under his eyes, he didn't look too bad. "How are you doing?"

"Better now I've found her," Will said, focusing on Paige. "I just need to do one thing."

He used Paige's upper arm to yank her towards him. Her hands were still cuffed behind her, and she yelped. Cafferty took a step towards him as Will held Paige's throat. "I wouldn't do that, detective. My hand might just slip and crush her windpipe." He squeezed Paige's neck, chuckling when she sobbed.

"She'll do time for her part in this," Cafferty said. "Let go of her."

Will's grin was scarily devoid of morality. "Lucky for me I can make you all forget when I deliver my own brand of justice for Fiona."

"Will," I said. "I know you're hurting, and Paige deserves to be punished. She lost someone tonight – we've all lost people. Don't make us lose you too."

Will glared down at Paige, readjusting his fingers on her throat. Then he shoved her at Cafferty. "Let's get out of here before I change my mind."

Cafferty pulled Paige out of the room and Tony went over to Will. He looked up at him. "You can be a good boy like me, if you want."

Will cracked a smile. "Thanks, kid. I'll keep that in mind."

Chapter 56

"Let's get back to your brother and sister," Dad said.

Even after all of the heartbreak, I liked the sound of that.

We walked through the dark hospital together in a daze: me tucked under Jared's arm, Cafferty tailing Paige, Ilian holding Tony and my parents holding hands. Will and Rosario went on ahead. I hoped she was talking some sense into him.

I'd expected beating Saint Germain to be more satisfying, but I was too drained to feel much of anything.

When we got outside the hospital, Mum cleared her throat. She'd never liked attention, but she didn't falter when everyone looked at her.

"I know tonight's been a lot to process," Mum said, "but we'd love to hold Thanksgiving at our place tomorrow – at the old Quarter Hotel. I know not all of you eat, but you're more than welcome to join our family."

There was a time when I would've said no out of stubbornness, keeping the walls up that I'd built around myself in our parents' absence. "Right . . . Thanksgiving is tomorrow. That would be great – thanks."

Murmured assents went around the group, and Mum smiled.

"Good. We'll hold it in the evening, for obvious reasons. Come around when the sun sets."

"We've got a lot to celebrate," Dad said. "Not least my retirement. Think I need some quality time with my family. Maybe I'll even write a book about cryptids."

"As long as you leave vampires out of it," Jared said with a tired grin.

"I can do that," Dad replied, hugging Mum closer to him.

"I'm tired of running," she said. "I'm looking forward to staying right here."

Mum, Dad, Jared and I parted ways with our other friends and went to the hotel. I got some small satisfaction from the thought of Rosario and Cafferty escorting Paige to the police station. She wouldn't be letting anyone else die at vampires' hands.

As soon as we got inside the hotel, Libby almost knocked me over with a hug. "Is it over?"

"Saint Germain's dead," I confirmed, thinking about everyone else we'd lost in recent days. I told them about the loss of Hayes and Beau, and the two of them held on to each other.

"Wish I'd been there for the fight," Della said, "but I don't regret stickin' around for my girl. Y'all did a great thing. The whole city will be different."

"You're more than welcome to stay the night," Mum said. "I've given the whole place a good clean – you're no longer in danger of catching anything."

"Thank you," I said.

We all staggered upstairs in a daze. I borrowed a cloth from Mum to scrub the battle blood off my skin. Then Jared and I were asleep as soon as our heads hit the pillows.

Jared and I slept through most of the city's Thanksgiving festivities the next day, only getting so far as watching the New Orleans parade on television with Libby and Della. The colourful floats, live music and dancing looked like an amazing spectacle, but I was happy to wait until next year for the in-person experience.

Mum and Dad were busy in the kitchen all afternoon, but the four of us barely moved from in front of the television. I stayed glued to Jared's side, and it helped while I worked through the losses and victories we'd experienced.

"Even I feel wiped out, and I didn't slay anybody," Libby said.

"Fearing for everyone's life and your own is pretty draining," I said. The food smelled amazing, and I was surprised at how hungry I felt.

Chase came out of the kitchen, hovering over us. "Room for one more?"

"On this sofa?" Libby said sleepily. "I'd go for no, unless you want to sit on Jared's lap. I'd recommend the armchair."

Blushing, Chase sat down. Now we knew the reason for his animosity, it had lifted completely. We'd lost so much lately, but gained a brother.

Cafferty and Rosario arrived first when night fell, his arm around her shoulders. "You'll never guess what happened to us last night," she said. "There was this group of vampire elders waiting outside Cafferty's place when we got back from taking Paige to the police."

"I have no idea how they found us, but they had an interesting proposition," Cafferty said, picking up the story. "At first, I thought they'd come to kill us for taking down Saint Germain, but they were there to make us an offer. Ilian told them what happened, and they want some young blood – their words – to help run things in New Orleans now Saint Germain's gone. They decided that a slayer and a cop might be a good fit."

"Wait," Libby said. "Does that mean you two are the new vampire king and queen of the city? That is so cool!"

"I wouldn't get too carried away. My duties will include being back in charge of the slayers, so that's a good start," Rosario said. "But you can refer to me as 'your majesty' if you like."

"I'll be there with you to get the slayers back on track," Della said.

"Also, Boudreaux said I'm welcome on the night shift as soon as I'm ready," Cafferty added.

"That's great," I said. Boudreaux really was a great boss. If everything worked out and I became a cop, maybe she'd be mine too.

Will appeared in the open doorway behind them. The others said their hellos and carried on chatting to Rosario and Cafferty, so I went to Will.

"Don't ask how I am," he warned with a grin. "I'm fine . . . you're fine – everybody's fine."

"OK," I said, pulling him in for a tight squeeze. He hugged me back, and I felt some of the tension go out of him.

We all sat down around the table together, the delicious smells of gravy, meat and vegetables drifting up from covered pots. Ilian and Tony were a no show, but I understood that. Losing his father was a massive upheaval, and it would take time for Tony to get used to his new circumstances. I never thought I'd see Ilian as being right for that job, but I did.

"Before we start, it's traditional to give thanks," Dad said. "I hope y'all don't mind if I break from that slightly. I've made a lot of mistakes in my life, but the biggest one is leaving you girls. All three of you," he added, looking at Mum. She smiled cautiously at him. "I can't promise to let go of my research completely, but I'm no longer on the same path. Saint Germain was the unknown threat I'd feared all along, and he's gone now. I'll go back to the Community at some point to let them know, so they can decide on their own futures. And Jared – I hope you know you're safe around me. Once again, I truly am sorry, son."

"I want to believe you," I said, holding Jared's hand under the table as he nodded to Dad.

"We're both here," Mum said quietly, "and we're going to stay. It'll take time to earn your trust, but we're prepared to be patient."

"We appreciate that," Libby said. My sister and I had come such a long way, that we could be sure of being on the same side without even asking.

"That'll do for now," Dad said gruffly, his eyes shining. "Now, let's take a moment to give thanks."

I looked around the table, grateful for the people in my life and thinking about the ones who were no longer with us. Saint Germain was gone and Paige would have to answer for tampering with the crime scenes. We'd made the city safer, and my future had opened out in front of me. I'd finish school here and then join the cadets with my family and friends at my side.

Dad had lowered his gaze in prayer, and now looked up with a grin. "Let's eat."

Everyone tucked in, passing dishes back and forth. There were all kinds of new delicacies to try, like candied yams, turducken and sweet potatoes covered with marshmallows.

I started eating, content that after so much heartache, I'd found a place for myself.

The meal was full of brilliant food and conversation. Once we'd helped to clear up, I yearned for the quiet of the mansion. After conferring with the others, I spoke up. "It's been so lovely, but I think it's time for us to go."

We said our goodbyes. I'd almost expected Will to come along, but he fell back into conversation with Rosario and Cafferty. They'd be a good support system for him.

Then I set off with Jared, Libby and Della.

"So, what are we going to do tomorrow?" Libby asked chirpily.

"I'm too full to plan anything," Della said, taking Libby's hand with a grin. Music and chatter drifted across from the French Quarter, but the street we were on was blissfully quiet.

"If I don't get kidnapped again, it'll be an improvement," Jared said, swinging my hand back and forth between us.

"What is that – three or four times now?" Libby teased.

"Laugh it up," he said. "Since I'm good with the daylight now, how about we make another cemetery visit like on Mina's first day here?"

"I like that idea," I said. "As long as you tell me some spooky stories."

"Sure thing," Jared said. "I'll make sure none of them are true this time."

"Didn't I eat beignets and sunbathe last time you did that?" Libby asked.

"I'm not sure sunbathing will be on the cards in November," Della said, "but I'm on board for a trip to Café du Monde."

My life here was never going to be straightforward, but that wasn't what I needed. I had my friends, my family and a future I was excited about. That was enough.

Acknowledgements

When I first met my agent, I told her about Mina's story that I wanted to tell over three books. I'm so grateful for being able to finish that journey, and I have a lot of people to thank that have enabled me to get to this point.

First, I wanted to thank all of the readers, booksellers and people who talk about my books on social media. Without you, I wouldn't be able to keep doing this, and I really appreciate it.

To the brilliant UCLan staff for all of your support and enthusiasm. Special thanks to Hazel Holmes, Charlotte Rothwell, Graeme Williams, Jasmine Dove and Kathy Webb.

To Fred Gambino and Becky Chilcott for such a gorgeous design and cover. I feel very lucky, and I'm so proud of how these books look.

To my agent, Sandra Sawicka, for continuing to champion my writing and making me a better writer.

To Lauren James for editing this final book with me. I'm so glad we were able to finish the trilogy together, and I've really enjoyed working with you!

To my lovely friends who live in the United States and Canada for helping me to get so many details right: Hannah Kates, Erin

Talamantes, Katrina Brown, Kelsi Schreiber and Elizabeth Sagewood.

To Sharron Elwell for being such a support to me and for checking my wheelchair representation.

To Chelley Toy and Mia Kuzniar for being great friends and supporting me with the joys and challenges of publishing!

To Team Mina, for being fantastic friends and supporters of me and my books. I've so appreciated everything you've done and I've enjoyed working behind the scenes with you.

To the Good Ship, Swaggers and Fem 2.0 groups. You've made my publishing journey so much more fun and shared all of the highs and lows.

To my parents, my brothers and partners for your constant support. Thank you Mum and Dad for always being there and for being nothing like Mina's parents!

Finally, to my two boys, Kev and Nathan. I wouldn't have been able to do this without you, and I feel very lucky.

ALSO AVAILABLE

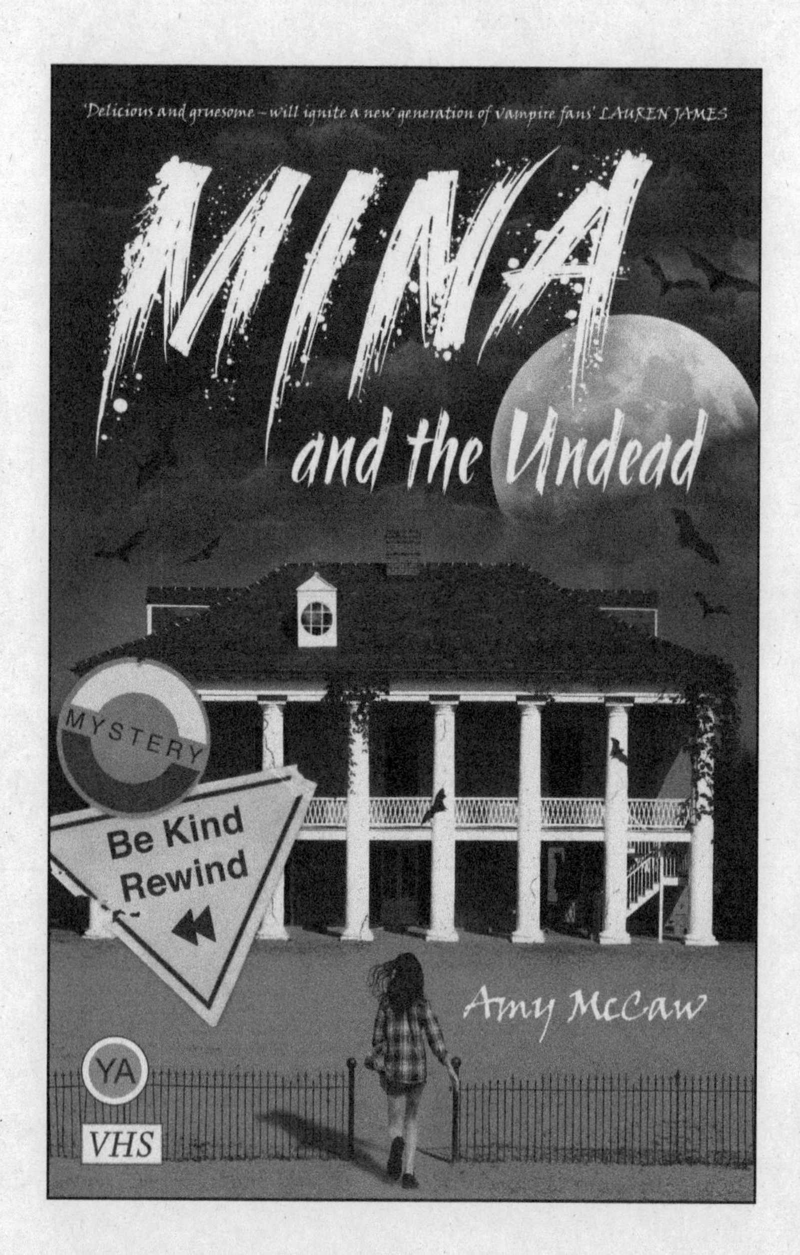

'Delicious and gruesome – will ignite a new generation of vampire fans' LAUREN JAMES

MINA and the Slayers

Amy McCaw

VHS

IF YOU LIKED THIS, YOU'LL LOVE...

JUSTIN SOMPER
VAMPIRATES
DEMONS OF THE OCEAN
"A swaggering tale of excitement and adventure that thrills from the very first sentence..."
CRESSIDA COWELL

HAVE YOU EVER WONDERED HOW BOOKS ARE MADE?

UCLan Publishing is an award winning independent publisher specialising in Children's and Young Adult books. Based at The University of Central Lancashire, this Preston-based publisher teaches MA Publishing students how to become industry professionals using the content and resources from its business; students are included at every stage of the publishing process and credited for the work that they contribute.

The business doesn't just help publishing students though. UCLan Publishing has supported the employability and real-life work skills for the University's Illustration, Acting, Translation, Animation, Photography, Film & TV students and many more. This is the beauty of books and stories; they fuel many other creative industries! The MA Publishing students are able to get involved from day one with the business and they acquire a behind the scenes experience of what it is like to work for a such a reputable independent.

The MA course was awarded a Times Higher Award (2018) for Innovation in the Arts and the business, UCLan Publishing, was awarded Best Newcomer at the Independent Publishing Guild (2019) for the ethos of teaching publishing using a commercial publishing house. As the business continues to grow, so too does the student experience upon entering this dynamic Masters course.

www.uclanpublishing.com
www.uclanpublishing.com/courses/
uclanpublishing@uclan.ac.uk